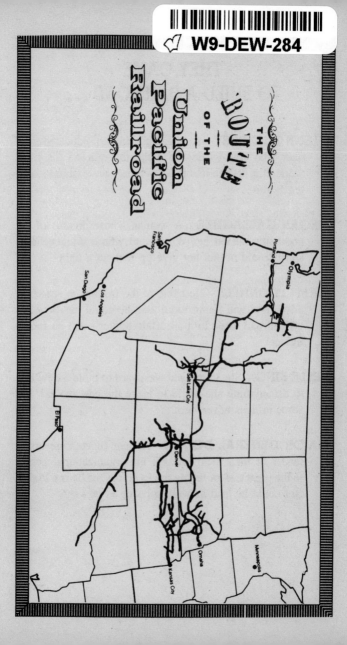

THE

ROUTE

OF THE

**Union
Pacific
Railroad**

THEY CAME
TO BUILD A RAILROAD . . .

GLENN GILCHRIST—An idealistic Harvard-educated engineer who was willing to make the railroad his life's work. But first he had to learn things no textbook could teach him . . .

MEGAN GALLAGHER—A woman whose dreams of the good life carried her West—and whose unquenchable spirit would not let her give up without a fight.

LIAM O'CONNELL—He came to the frontier in search of adventure, and found more than he could handle when the railroad made him a buffalo hunter—and an Indian fighter!

BELLE KING—She journeyed westward to build a new life, to do anything she could to leave the past behind. But some bridges never burn . . .

MAJOR GENERAL DODGE—A man of courage and a leader of men, who brought his organizational genius to the great task of laying tracks across the barren Plains. But could he lead as well in peace as in war?

AILEEN FOX—Her drunken husband abandoned her with two children to feed. Only her sister Megan kept her from returning East and giving up all hope . . .

THE CASEMENT BROTHERS—Two little men with big ambitions, they drove their crews to impossible feats of engineering. For them, the railroad was their way to fortune.

JOSHUA HOOD—Chief hunter and scout for the Union Pacific. He knew the Plains and the Sioux as well as any white man alive—but could he single-handedly protect the armies of railroad builders?

DOCTOR DURANT—The enigmatic power broker, with connections to the highest offices in Washington, D.C. Schemer or charlatan, he was a man whom it was never safe to cross.

BILL DONOVAN—A powerful, hot-tempered man with a grudge against the boss who fired him from the railroad—and the die-hard determination to use his fists to settle it.

RAILS WEST!

Franklin Carter

JOVE BOOKS, NEW YORK

RAILS WEST!

A Jove Book / published by arrangement with
the author

PRINTING HISTORY
Jove edition / May 1993

ISBN: 0-515-11099-X

Jove Books are published by The Berkley Publishing Group,
200 Madison Avenue, New York, New York 10016.
The name "JOVE" and the "J" logo
are trademarks belonging to Jove Publications, Inc.

PRINTED IN THE UNITED STATES OF AMERICA

10 9 8 7 6 5 4 3 2

FOR FRANK RODERUS
GREAT FRIEND AND FELLOW WRITER
WHO HAS ALSO LISTENED TO HEAR
THAT LONESOME WHISTLE BLOW

CHAPTER

1

Omaha, Nebraska, Early Spring, 1866

Construction Engineer Glenn Gilchrist stood on the melting surface of the frozen Missouri River with his heart hammering his rib cage. Poised before him on the eastern bank of the river was the last Union Pacific supply train asked to make this dangerous river crossing before the ice broke to flood south. The temperatures had soared as an early chinook had swept across the Northern Plains and now the river's ice was sweating like a fat man in July. A lake of melted ice was growing deeper by the hour and there was still this last critical supply train to bring across.

"This is madness!" Glenn whispered even as the waiting locomotive puffed and banged with impatience while huge crowds from Omaha and Council Bluffs stomped their slushy shorelines to keep their feet warm. Fresh out of the Harvard School of Engineering, Glenn had measured and remeasured the depth and stress-carrying load of the rapidly melting river yet still could not be certain if it would support the tremendous weight of this last supply train. But Union Pacific's vice president, Thomas Durant, had given the bold order that it was to cross, and there were enough fools to be found willing to man the train and its supply cars, so here Glenn was, standing in the middle of the Missouri and about half sure he was about to enter a watery grave.

Suddenly, the locomotive engineer blasted his steam whistle and leaned out his window. "We got a full head of steam and the temperature is risin', Mr. Gilchrist!"

Glenn did not hear the man because he was imagining what would happen the moment the ice broke through. Good Lord, they could all plunge to the bottom of Big Muddy and be swept along under the ice for hundreds of miles to a frozen death. A

1

vision flashed before Glenn's eyes of an immense ragged hole in the ice fed by two sets of rails feeding into the cold darkness of the Missouri River.

The steam whistle blasted again. Glenn took a deep breath, raised his hand, and then chopped it down as if he were swinging an ax. Cheers erupted from both riverbanks and the locomotive jerked tons of rails, wooden ties, and track-laying hardware into motion.

Glenn swore he could feel the weakening ice heave and buckle the exact instant the Manchester locomotive's thirty tons crunched its terrible weight onto the river's surface. Glenn drew in a sharp breath. His eyes squinted into the blinding glare of ice and water as the railroad tracks swam toward the advancing locomotive through melting water. The sun bathed the rippling surface of the Missouri River in a shimmering brilliance. The engineer began to blast his steam whistle and the crowds roared at each other across the frozen expanse. Glenn finally expelled a deep breath, then started to backpedal as he motioned the locomotive forward into railroading history.

Engineer Bill Donovan was grinning like a fool and kept yanking on the whistle cord, egging on the cheering crowds.

"Slow down!" Glenn shouted at the engineer, barely able to hear his own voice as the steam whistle continued its infernal shriek.

But Donovan wasn't about to slow down. His unholy grin was as hard as the screeching iron horse he rode and Glenn could hear Donovan shouting to his fireman to shovel faster. Donovan was pushing him, driving the locomotive ahead as if he were intent on forcing Glenn aside and charging across the river to the other side.

"Slow down!" Glenn shouted, backpedaling furiously.

But Donovan wouldn't throttle down, which left Glenn with just two poor choices. He could either leap aside and let the supply train rush past, or he could try to swing on board and wrestle its control from Donovan. It might be the only thing that would keep the ice from swallowing them alive.

Glenn chose the latter. He stepped from between the shivering rails, and when Donovan and his damned locomotive charged past drenching him in a bone-chilling sheet of ice water, Glenn lunged for the platform railing between the cab and the coal tender. The locomotive's momentum catapulted him upward to sprawl between the locomotive and tender.

"Dammit!" he shouted, clambering to his feet. "The ice isn't thick enough to take both the weight and a pounding! You were supposed to . . ."

Glenn's words died in his throat an instant later when the ice cracked like rifle fire and thin, ragged schisms fanned out from both sides of the tracks. At the same time, the rails and the ties they rested upon rolled as if supported by the storm-tossed North Atlantic.

"Jesus Christ!" Donovan shouted, his face draining of color and leaving him ashen. "We're going under!"

"Throttle down!" Glenn yelled as he jumped for the brake.

The locomotive's sudden deceleration threw them both hard against the firebox, searing flesh. The fireman's shovel clattered on the deck as his face corroded with terror and the ice splintered outward from them with dark tentacles.

"Steady!" Glenn ordered, grabbing the young man's arm because he was sure the kid was about to jump from the coal tender. "Steady now!"

The next few minutes were an eternity but the ice held as they crossed the center of the Missouri and rolled slowly toward the Nebraska shore.

"Come on!" a man shouted from Omaha. "Come on!"

Other watchers echoed the cry as the spectators began to take heart.

"We're going to make it, sir!" Donovan breathed, banging Glenn on the shoulder. "Mr. Gilchrist, we're by Gawd goin' to make it!"

"Maybe. But if the ice breaks behind us, the supply cars will drag us into the river. If that happens, we jump and take our chances."

"Yes, sir!" the big Irishman shouted, his square jaw bumping rapidly up and down.

Donovan reeked of whiskey and his eyes were bright and glassy. Glenn turned to look at the young fireman. "Mr. Chandlis, have you been drinking too?"

"Not a drop, sir." Young Sean Chandlis pointed to shore and cried, "Look, Mr. Gilchrist, we've made it!"

Glenn felt the locomotive bump onto the tracks resting on the solid Nebraska riverbank. Engineer Donovan blasted his steam whistle and nudged the locomotive's throttle causing the big drivers to spin a little as they surged up the riverbank. Those same sixty-inch driving wheels propelled the supply cars into Omaha where they were enfolded by the jubilant crowd.

The scene was one of pandemonium as Donovan kept yanking on his steam whistle and inciting the crowd. Photographers crowded around the locomotive taking pictures.

"Come on and smile!" Donovan shouted in Glenn's ear. "We're heroes!"

Glenn didn't feel like smiling. His knees wanted to buckle from the sheer relief of having this craziness behind him. He wanted to smash Donovan's grinning face for starting across the river too fast and for drinking on duty. But the photographers kept taking pictures and all that Glenn did was to bat Donovan's hand away from the infernal steam whistle before it drove him mad.

God, the warm, fresh chinook winds felt fine on his cheeks and it was good to be still alive. Glenn waved to the crowd and his eyes lifted back to the river that he knew would soon be breaking up if this warm weather held. He turned back to gaze westward and up to the city of Omaha. Omaha—when he'd arrived last fall, it had still been little more than a tiny riverfront settlement. Today, it could boast a population of more than six thousand, all anxiously waiting to follow the Union Pacific rails west.

"We did it!" Donovan shouted at the crowd as he raised his fists in victory. "We did it!"

Glenn saw a tall beauty with reddish hair pushing forward through the crowd, struggling mightily to reach the supply train. "Who is that?"

Donovan followed his eyes. "Why, that's Mrs. Megan Gallagher. Ain't she and her sister somethin', though!"

Glenn had not even noticed the smaller woman with two freckled children in tow who was also waving to the train and trying to follow her sister to its side. Glenn's brow furrowed. "Are their husbands on this supply train?"

Donovan's wide grin dissolved. "Well, Mr. Gilchrist, I know you told everyone that only single men could take this last one across, but . . ."

Glenn clenched his fists in surprise and anger. "Donovan, don't you understand that the Union Pacific made it clear that there was to be no drinking and no married men on this last run! Dammit, you broke both rules! I've got no choice but to fire all three of you."

"But, sir!"

Glenn felt sick at heart but also betrayed. Bill "Wild Man" Donovan was probably the best engineer on the payroll but he'd proved he was also an irresponsible fool, one who played to the crowd and was more than willing to take chances with other men's lives and the Union Pacific's rolling stock and precious construction supplies.

"I'm sorry, Donovan. Collect your pay from the paymaster before quitting time," Glenn said, swinging down from the cab into the pressing crowd. Standing six feet three inches, Glenn was tall enough to look over the sea of humanity and note that Megan Gallagher and her sister were embracing their triumphant husbands. It made Glenn feel even worse to think that those two men would be without jobs before this day was ended.

Men pounded Glenn on the back in congratulations but he paid them no mind as he pushed through the crowd, moving off toward the levee where these last few vital tons of rails, ties, and other hardware were being stored until the real work of building a railroad finally started.

"Hey!" Donovan shouted, overtaking Glenn and pulling him up short. "You can't fire me! I'm the best damned engineer you've got!"

"*Were* the best," Glenn said, tearing his arm free, "now step aside."

But Donovan didn't budge. The crowd pushed around the two large men, clearly puzzled as to the matter of this dispute in the wake of such a bold and daring success only moments earlier.

"What'd he do wrong?" a man dressed in a tailored suit asked in a belligerent voice. "By God, Bill Donovan brought that train across the river and that makes him a hero in my book!"

This assessment was loudly applauded by others. Glenn could feel resentment building against him as the news of his decision to fire three of the crew swept through the crowd. "This is a company matter. I don't make the rules, I just make sure that they are followed."

Donovan chose to appeal to the crowd. "Now you hear that, folks. Mr. Gilchrist is going to fire three good men without so much as a word of thanks. And that's what the working man gets from this railroad for risking his life!"

"Drop it," Glenn told the big Irishman. "There's nothing left to be gained from this."

"Isn't there?"

"No."

"You're making a mistake," Donovan said, playing to the crowd. The confident Irishman thrust his hand out with a grin. "So why don't we let bygones be bygones and go have a couple of drinks to celebrate? Gallagher and Fox are two of the best men on the payroll. They deserve a second chance. Think about the fact they got wives and children."

Glenn shifted uneasily. "I'll talk to Fox and Gallagher but you were in charge and I hold you responsible."

"Hell, we made it in grand style, didn't we!"

"Barely," Glenn said, "and you needlessly jeopardized the crew and the company's assets, that's why you're still fired."

Donovan flushed with anger. "You're a hard, unforgiving man, Gilchrist."

"And you are a fool when you drink whiskey. Later, I'll hear Fox's and Gallagher's excuses."

"They drew lots for a cash bonus ride across that damned melting river!" Donovan swore, his voice hardening. "Gallagher and Fox needed the money!"

"The Union Pacific didn't offer any bonus! It was your job to ask for volunteers and choose the best to step forward."

Donovan shrugged. He had a lantern jaw, and heavy, fist-scarred brows overhanging a pair of now very angry and blood-shot eyes. "The boys each pitched in a couple dollars into a pot. I'll admit it was my idea. But the winners stood to earn fifty dollars each when we crossed."

"To leave wives and children without support?" Glenn snapped. "That's a damned slim legacy."

"These are damned slim times," Donovan said. "The idea was, if we drowned, the money would be used for the biggest funeral and wake Omaha will ever see. And if we made it . . . well, you saw the crowd."

"Yeah," Glenn said. "If you won, you'd flood the saloons and drink it up so either way all the money would go for whiskey."

"Some to the wives and children," Donovan said quietly.

"Like hell."

Glenn started to turn and leave the man but Donovan's voice

stopped him cold. "If you turn away, I'll drop you," the Irishman warned in a soft, all the more threatening voice.

"That would be a real mistake," Glenn said.

Although several inches taller than the engineer, Glenn had no illusions as to matching the Irishman's strength or fighting ability. Donovan was built like a tree stump and was reputed to be one of the most vicious brawlers in Omaha. If Glenn had any advantage, it was that he had been on Harvard's collegiate boxing club and gained some recognition for quickness and a devastating left hook that had surprised and then floored many an opponent.

"Come on, sir," Donovan said with a friendly wink as he reached into his coat pocket and dragged out a pint of whiskey. The engineer uncorked and extended it toward Glenn. "So I got a little carried away out there. No harm, was there?"

"I'm sorry," Glenn said, pivoting around on his heel and starting off toward the levee to oversee the stockpiling and handling of this last vital shipment.

This time when Donovan's powerful fingers dug into Glenn's shoulder to spin him around, Glenn dropped into a slight crouch, whirled, and drove his left hook upward with every ounce of power he could muster. The punch caught Donovan in the gut. The big Irishman's cheeks blew out and his eyes bugged. Glenn pounded him again in the solar plexus and Donovan staggered, his face turning fish-belly white. Glenn rocked back and threw a textbook combination of punches to the bigger man's face that split Donovan's cheek to the bone and dropped him to his knees.

"You'd better finish me!" Donovan gasped. " 'Cause I swear to settle this score!"

Glenn did not take the man's threat lightly. He cocked back his fist but he couldn't deliver the knockout blow, not while the engineer was gasping in agony. "Stay away from me," Glenn warned before he hurried away.

"Mr. Gilchrist, sir!"

Glenn stopped and turned to see Megan Gallagher hurrying after him with her husband, sister, and brother-in-law in tow. "Damn!" he muttered.

Megan was out of breath and her cheeks were flushed either from exertion or anger or both. Her beauty was as raw and natural as the prairie and despite the unpleasantness that he expected, her appearance made Glenn's heart quicken with anticipation. Glenn yanked off his hat thinking that this Irish girl was so beautiful that it would almost be a pleasure to take her tongue lashing.

"You're not going to fire our husbands, are you, Mr. Gilchrist?" she said in a voice without a hint of a brogue.

"They disobeyed my orders, Mrs. Gallagher. Mr. Donovan is finished with the Union Pacific, but I told him that I'd be willing to take the matter of your husband and brother-in-law up at my office. Perhaps if . . ."

"To hell with it," Keith Gallagher said angrily. "He's made up his mind to fire us! Megan, I won't have you beggin'."

"I'm *not* begging," Megan Gallagher said. "But firing you and Hugh just isn't fair!"

"We can find other jobs."

"Where!" Megan demanded. "We all spent every dollar we could beg or borrow to come out to this terrible place in the dead of winter. We haven't even enough money to go home again!"

Gallagher swallowed and looked very uncomfortable. "We can find something," he said lamely.

"Listen," Glenn said, "let me think about this and hear your stories."

"We needed the money," Gallagher said hotly. "What 'story' business is there to talk about. If you don't want us, say so plain out and I'll find other work."

"Mr. Gallagher!" Megan cried. "The man just said he'd—"

"I heard him same as you. He's made up his mind to fire us, Megan. We don't need his damned work."

Glenn could see that this was shaping up to become a real battle between the hotheaded Irishman and his equally furious wife. "Listen, please, I . . ."

"Where can you find work!" Megan demanded.

"In Council Bluffs or . . . or down the river in St. Joe!"

"Ha! Doing what?"

"I can't say until we go there, Megan!"

"Perhaps," Glenn said, "it would be a good idea to find other work. This is going to be a hard, dangerous job and it's certainly no place for a married man with a wife and children to drag along behind the rails."

"You keep out of this, Mr. Gilchrist!" Megan stormed. "And

since when do we need an outsider to tell us how to run our lives?"

Several of those gathered about chuckled and Glenn could feel his cheeks warm. "I'm just trying to do my job," he said, "and a big part of that is making sure that people working for the Union Pacific Railroad don't act foolishly."

"Your job," Megan said, "is to build a railroad. My job is to take care of my husband. And he *needs* to help build this railroad, sir."

Before Glenn could think of anything to say, Megan Gallagher hurried away arguing with her husband who would no doubt seek sanctuary in one of Omaha's exclusively male saloons.

Hugh Fox tore off his cap. "I meant no disobedience, sir. We just needed the money. Neither of us knowed your rule about being married."

"Is that right?"

"Oh, yes, sir!"

Glenn noted that Fox wouldn't meet his eye and he felt the man was almost assuredly lying. "A man with a wife and children, you ought to have known better than to take such a risk, orders or no orders."

Hugh Fox was a short, handsome fellow. "This is Mrs. Fox— Aileen," he said, introducing his wife. "And my two children, David and Jenny."

Glenn could see how upset Mrs. Fox was at the prospect of her husband losing his job. "I think we can work this out," he said, knowing he wouldn't be able to face himself in the mirror tomorrow morning if he fired the two married men.

"Oh, thank you, sir!" Aileen exclaimed, grabbing his hand and pumping it with gratitude.

When tears began to roll down the young woman's cheeks, Glenn excused himself and hurried off toward the levee.

He felt physically and emotionally drained by the perilous river crossing and his fight with Donovan. He had been extremely fortunate to survive both confrontations. This affair with Gallagher and Fox had reinforced the idea in his mind that he was not seasoned enough to be making such critical decisions. It wasn't that he didn't welcome responsibility, for he did. But not so much and not so soon.

The trouble was that the fledgling Union Pacific itself was in over its head. No one knew from one day to the next whether it would still be in operation or who was actually in charge. From inception, Vice President Thomas Durant, a medical doctor turned railroad entrepreneur, was the driving force behind getting the United States Congress to pass two Pacific Railway Acts through Congress. With the Civil War just ending and the nation still numb from the shock of losing President Abraham Lincoln, the long discussed hope of constructing a transcontinental railroad was facing tough sledding. Durant himself was sort of an enigma, a schemer and dreamer who some claimed was a charlatan while others thought he possessed a brilliant organizational mind.

Glenn didn't know what to think of Durant. It had been through him that he'd landed this job fresh out of engineering school as his reward for being his class valedictorian. So far, Glenn's Omaha experience had been nothing short of chaotic. Lacking sufficient funds and with the mercurial Durant dashing back and forth to Washington, there had been a clear lack of order and leadership. It had been almost three years since Congress had agreed to pay both the Union Pacific and the Central Pacific Railroads the sums of $16,000 per mile for track laid over the plains, $32,000 a mile through the arid wastes of the Great Basin, and a whopping $48,000 per mile for track laid over the Rocky and the Sierra Nevada mountain ranges.

Now, with the approach of spring, the stage had been set to finally begin the transcontinental race. One hundred miles of roadbed had been graded westward from Omaha and almost forty miles of temporary track had been laid. For two years, big paddlewheel steamboats had been carrying mountains of supplies up the Missouri River. There were three entire locomotives still packed in shipping crates resting on the levee while two more stood assembled beside the Union Pacific's massive new brick roundhouse with its ten locomotive repair pits. Dozens of hastily constructed shops and offices surrounded the new freight and switching yards.

There was still more work than men and that was a blessing for veterans in the aftermath of the Civil War joblessness and destruction. Every day, dozens more ex-soldiers and fortune seekers crossed the Missouri River into Omaha and signed on with the Union Pacific Railroad. Half a nation away, the Central Pacific Railroad was already attacking the Sierra Nevada Mountains but Glenn had heard that they were not so fortunate in hiring men because of the stiff competition from the rich gold and silver mines on the Comstock Lode.

"Mr. Gilchrist!"

Glenn turned to see one of his foremen hurrying to catch up with him. "Yes?"

"Just got word from the telegraph office that Mr. Durant has hired General Jack Casement and his brother Dan to ramrod things once spring thaw is over. Jack is supposed to be the front man and his brother Dan will be handling all the logistics and paperwork."

"I've heard of them both," Glenn said. "They're supposed to be good men. We need them."

"I hear that they're a couple of bearded midgets," the man said with a chuckle, "but that's someone else's description, not mine."

"You'd be wise to keep it to yourself," Glenn said as he walked on.

The news of the Casement brothers' impending arrival cheered Glenn. As construction foreman, he'd been responsible for overseeing some of the road grading westward before the winter blizzards made that work impossible. And this winter, Durant had assigned him the task of inventorying the incredible mountains of supplies and hardware that were being stockpiled on the levees. Stores that should have already been moved to the safety of higher ground along Omaha's western boundaries.

It was astounding how much was needed just to begin construction of a railroad, the procurement of which had become a herculean task. Glenn had calculated that every mile of track they laid would require 2,500 railroad ties and Durant had ordered 50,000 that were now stored in forests like great barns laid down. Railroad ties had been a thorn in the Union Pacific's side from the beginning. The only timber on these plains was cottonwood, which grew in abundance along the rivers but which was soft and would rot out and have to be replaced in only a few years. So they'd come up with a process called "burnetizing" the ties, which impregnated them with chemicals that preserved them against rot for many more years. Hardwood ties would have to be imported from Michigan and the northern states and their cost was almost prohibitive.

Along with the mountains of railroad ties were the iron rails forged in the eastern foundries along with all the hardware that was required to build and hold together a sound railroad track. There were piles of fishplates, spikes, and bolts, stacks of shop equipment and tools, and carloads of repair and replacement supplies for the locomotives and rolling stock. The levees were packed solid over twenty feet high in places, and even though work crews had been transferring everything during this sudden change in the weather, the work and constant inventorying was complex and very slow.

What everyone was really waiting for was the long overdue arrival of Major General Grenville Dodge. Dodge was one of the Union Army's most celebrated officers and despite some reservations about working with Durant, the general had finally agreed to become the Union Pacific's chief engineer. As such, he would be responsible only to Durant himself, the United States President, and Congress. Glenn had never met General Dodge, but he was excited about working for such a famous man. Dodge had been wounded in the Civil War and had served the Union Army so gallantly that he had soon captured the admiration of President Lincoln as well as Generals Grant, Sherman, and Sheridan. His greatest contribution was in the bridge construction and the rapid repair and design of railroad lines crucial to major Union victories both in the North and the South. An engineer of no small acclaim, everyone said that Grenville Dodge alone could solve the Union Pacific puzzle. Durant must have thought so too because he'd offered Dodge the unheard of salary of $10,000 per year, complete and uncontested control of construction, and the accompanying title of chief engineer of the Union Pacific Railroad. Dodge was due to arrive in Omaha as soon as he resigned his commission from the Union Army and that was to be no later than May. Glenn could hardly wait for Generals Dodge and Casement to arrive because Durant was about to drive him crazy; the mercurial financier and entrepreneur had no engineering sense at all and refused to engage himself in the myriad of details and logistics upon which Glenn thought the successful completion of this entire effort depended.

Glenn threw himself into his work. The afternoon passed very quickly as the last supply train's cargo was unloaded and transported by wagon to be stockpiled along the immense levee. It was nearly dusk and the sunset was flaming the western sky over Nebraska when Glenn saw Megan and her sister Aileen approach him. Megan was wearing a clean dress. Her auburn-colored hair was brushed to a shine and her stride was long and purposeful. Her sister followed close behind.

"Good evening," Glenn said, wiping his dirty hands on his pants and resigning himself to another tough session.

"Good evening, Mr. Gilchrist," Megan said, forcing a smile that carried little in the way of warmth. "I see that you and the men have almost got the supplies stacked."

"That's right."

"So much!" Megan said, craning her head back. "My goodness but it looks as if you could build an entire city the size of New York!"

"Not hardly," Glenn said. He tipped his hat to the quiet, shy sister. "Good evening, Mrs. Fox."

"Good evening," she said. "We thought it best we came instead of our husbands."

"Why?"

Aileen swallowed. She looked to her sister for help. Megan said, "They're a wee bit upset, Mr. Gilchrist. And I think they're settlin' down a little in the saloons."

Glenn was not surprised. "Maybe it would be better if I talked to them in a few days when they've cooled down."

"Without any pay?" Megan asked, raising her eyebrows. "Now, Mr. Gilchrist, that doesn't seem quite fair, does it?"

"All right," he said. "They can keep working."

"And Mr. Donovan?"

"No."

Megan frowned. "Now that doesn't seem quite fair either, does it? To excuse two for breakin' your rules and punish the one?"

"Donovan was the man in charge," Glenn explained. "He's the one that I trusted to show responsibility and follow my orders."

Megan sighed. "Mr. Donovan is very unhappy."

"So am I," Glenn said, getting annoyed.

Megan seemed to understand that Glenn's mind was made up and that he could be pushed no further. She turned her face to the sunset and closed her eyes for a moment, basking in its glow. "I think this terrible winter is finished, Mr. Gilchrist. Thanks be to God. It's much harder and colder than it was in Boston. It's the winds, you know."

"Is that where you come from?"

"It's where we all come from," Megan said. "And it's a softer, gentler winter there than out here."

"Yes," he said, "but everyone tells me that this was the worst winter in many years. It was hard on everyone but it froze the river to eighteen inches and allowed us to lay track and finish bringing across these mountains of supplies. These Great Plains can be cruel and unforgiving."

"Like the Indians?" Aileen asked suddenly.

Glenn turned to address the woman. "Yes, Mrs. Fox, like the Indians. But remember, most of our employees are Civil War veterans. Men who know how to bear arms and fight. Besides, your husbands will be laying track, not surveying or even on the grading crews that stretch far in advance of the line."

"And you won't let Mr. Fox or Mr. Gallagher volunteer to work out there where they might get scalped, will you?" Megan asked pointedly.

"No," Glenn promised. "I'll keep them laying rails."

The two sisters exchanged relieved glances before thanking Glenn and hurrying off toward the sorry collection of shanties along the riverbank where they were wintering.

Glenn watched them until they reached their shanties and disappeared inside. He would never understand why men would introduce their wives and children to such deprivation as these must surely face following the rails westward. This railroad race west was no life for respectable women. The whores who had recently flocked into Omaha would mine gold from the pockets of the construction workers but the decent, honorable women like Mrs. Gallagher and Mrs. Fox would reap only hardship. Their men would work like mules and drink like demons. Unless Glenn judged Gallagher and Fox unfairly, those men would not bring their paychecks home to their families but instead would squander it in the tent saloons that would spring up along the U.P. tracks like mushrooms in springtime.

Glenn sighed and remembered how Megan Gallagher had chided him for trying to run someone else's life. She had been right. Glenn knew that what happened to such women and their children during this great railroad adventure was none of his business. His business was to help Dodge, Durant, and the Casement brothers build a transcontinental railroad linking east to west.

Glenn lingered on the levee beside the Missouri River whose surface was now coated with liquid gold. He tipped his hat to the shanty where Megan Gallagher had disappeared and then he headed off through the mud for town. He would have a few drinks along with some of the other officers of the railroad, then retire early. He was dog-tired and the strain of these last few days of worrying about the stress-carrying capacity of the melting ice had enervated him to the point of bone weariness.

Glenn realized he would be more than glad when the generals finally arrived to take command of the Union Pacific. He would be even happier when the race west finally began in dead earnest.

CHAPTER
2

Megan Gallagher had already formed a deep and abiding dislike for Nebraska. True, she had not taken a step north, south, or west beyond Omaha, but she was sure that this raw, windy country had nothing to offer a civilized human being., As near as Megan could reasonably tell, Nebraska was populated by fierce Indians, immense herds of shaggy buffalo, and enough rolling grasslands to drive the sanest person completely mad. Nor did Megan have much higher an opinion of the Wyoming Territory. Like Nebraska, it was simply land that had to be spanned by the Union Pacific Railroad in order to reach the West Coast. And somewhere between Wyoming and California, there was Utah and Nevada, one the home of the fanatical followers of Brigham Young and his Church of Jesus Christ of Latter-day Saints, and the other the wicked Comstock Lode.

Megan dreamed only of California. Now there was a place worth suffering to reach! In her mind, California was a place where the sun was always warm and the soil was always rich. You could be perpetually happy in California. California was heaven and all the country between heaven and this hellish and muddy Omaha was purgatory. Megan had read everything she could about California in her Boston libraries and knew that it was the sweetest and sunniest place on earth. Some people were proud to be called Nebraskans, but Megan Gallagher was not one of them. As far as she was concerned, this territory ought to remain the home of the Indians and buffalo.

But tonight she *was* alone in Nebraska huddled against the chill of evening. A candle flickered weakly in her miserable shanty and it was fed by the wind seeping through the wallboard cracks. The floor of the shanty was dirt or, actually, mud as the Nebraska earth thawed under the chinook. Megan had finally gotten her husband to scrounge up some pieces of tin that he'd spread on the floor, but the mud still oozed up between the brittle tin sheets to bake under their cast-iron stove like slices of gingerbread.

Where was Mr. Gallagher, Megan asked herself as hour after hour passed in cold solitude. How could his money have lasted this long the way he bought drinks for everyone? Megan stood, but not to her full height for the shanty was just a shade over five feet tall as that was the height of the boards that Keith had scrounged up for its construction.

Megan went to her front door. She opened it and stared out at a village of shacks not much better than her own. Less than forty feet away, shafts of lamplight lanced through Aileen's shanty walls and Megan knew that her sister was also waiting for her drunken husband. Lonesome and upset, Megan dragged a sheet of tin across her doorway and trudged over to visit her sister. Aileen's shanty was constructed exactly like her own except that in deference to the children and Hugh's insistence on a closed-off room, it had a tiny bedroom.

Megan knocked on the door and her sister instantly appeared. Aileen tried to conceal her disappointment. "I—I thought it was Mr. Fox," she said, forcing a strained smile.

"Can I come in?"

"Of course." Aileen was cradling her sleeping four-year-old daughter, Jenny. "We might as well wait together."

"I told Liam to let Keith and Hugh know that they weren't fired after all. That Mr. Gilchrist had changed his mind."

"Then they'll drink over Bill Donovan getting fired instead," Aileen said, her voice tinged with bitterness. "If it isn't one excuse, it's another."

Megan closed the door behind her. Aileen's shanty seemed even more depressing than her own and all she had to keep down the mud were some gunny sacks spread across the floor.

"I would offer you some tea," Aileen said, glancing at the broken stovepipe to her stove, "but . . ."

"I'm fine," Megan said, reaching for the little girl. "I'll hold Jenny, you rest."

"David is in our bed," Aileen explained as she handed her daughter to Megan. She sat down heavily, leaned her elbows on the table, and regarded her younger sister. "Megan, do you realize how wrong it was for us to interfere in our husbands' affairs today?"

"Wrong? What do you mean? If we hadn't 'interfered' as you put it, our husbands would be out of a job tomorrow!"

"Exactly! And we'd all return to Boston."

"To do what?" Megan asked, feeling herself tense up inside because this had been a point of contention all winter. "Return to the same factories and miseries that killed our dear parents? That got a brother shot to death for no reason save he had a new pair of shoes?"

Aileen wrung her hands. "But at least our husbands had jobs. We lived in tenement houses that had *real* floors."

"And rats. And consumption and the drink."

Aileen's voice took on a shrill edge. "The drink is here too!"

"Yes," Megan conceded, "it is. But there is a future for us in California."

Aileen slumped. Her hand absently brushed back her hair and she said, "There is if we can really believe Uncle Patrick's old gold rush letters. Don't forget that I've read them almost as many times as you, Megan."

"You've read them more," Megan told her. "I remember you reading them when I was still just a small girl. We were all so sure that Uncle Patrick would return from the forty-niner gold rush as rich as King Solomon."

Megan closed her eyes and rocked back in her chair. "Oh, the stories he used to send us from California!"

"I remember them well," Aileen said wistfully. "There was a place called Fiddletown. I recall it because we used to talk about how everyone there played a fiddle. We imagined that their music and dancing never ended while their friends plucked gold nuggets the size of chicken's eggs from the Sierra mountain streams for everyone to share."

"Yes," Megan said. "And there were other wonderful names like Chili Gulch where we supposed everyone ate nothing but chili and Chinese Camp, Dutch Flat, and Diamond Springs. We made games out of all those names."

"But then came news that Uncle Patrick was dead."

Megan grew somber. "It broke Mother's heart because Patrick had been her favorite brother. He'd promised to help."

"And he would have," Aileen said. "He was a fine man. I still say he must have struck it rich and someone killed him for his money."

This had been the great O'Connell theory that Megan had grown up hearing since early childhood. Until her parents' death, both had stubbornly believed that a miraculous golden legacy might yet appear, compliments of the ghost of Uncle Patrick.

Megan was through dealing in ghosts and dreams. "Now, Aileen," she said, "who could have killed our uncle?"

"Maybe when we get to California, we'll make it a point to find out. It's one of the things I mean to do."

Megan scoffed at the notion. "The past is behind us and if dear Uncle Patrick ever made a strike, his gold was spent long ago. If we are to prosper, it will have to be by our own devices."

"But the gold is played out, Megan!"

"I know. But remember that Uncle Patrick said the soil was the *real* treasure of California. That and its climate."

Aileen drew a deep breath and expelled it slowly. "Our men are not cut out to be farmers."

"Men can change," Megan reminded her sister. "Everything will change when we finally arrive in California."

Aileen seemed to take heart. She really smiled before she said, "You've always been the dreamer and I pray that your beautiful dreams will finally come true for us."

"A dreamer? I think not," Megan said, disagreeing with that unflattering label. "I'm a doer. Dreamers just sit and wait and hope for things to happen. I intend to make them happen."

"I'm sorry," Aileen said, "I meant that you were an optimist."

Megan thought about that. "Maybe," she conceded, "though God knows I've little reason to be."

"Are you talking about . . ."

"Never mind about Keith," Megan said. "I just believe that we can make a better life in California, and since we can all work our way across the country, Omaha's where we ought to be right now even though I hate all this mud and the dampness of this river bottom."

"It's almost springtime, Megan, and this winter has been awful. Sometimes, when the wind blows down here along this river of ice and my children are shivering and . . ."

Aileen couldn't finish as a wave of hopelessness and emotion robbed her voice. Her eyes grew misty and she looked away.

Megan put Jenny to bed and moved over to comfort her sister. "Aileen, there's no reason to cry. Our men both have steady jobs."

"Yes, but they're drunk and broke!" Aileen whispered. "Mr. Fox is . . ."

"Things will get better *very* soon," Megan promised. "I *know* that they will! The weather is turning and in a week or two we'll be leaving this awful riverbank. We'll cross these wide prairies as free and fresh as the wind and the mighty Union Pacific Railroad will deliver us to California."

Aileen reached out and squeezed her sister's hand. She sniffled and said, "You should have been a preacher."

Megan's green eyes crinkled with humor. "Impossible. I don't shave and you know I sometimes cuss."

"Yes, but you have the gift of words."

Megan was flattered. "Aw," she said, "you're just sayin' that."

"No, I'm not! Why, you even had Mr. Gilchrist right in the very palm of your hand this afternoon."

Megan laughed. "He's so young to be doing such big things. A boy wonder fresh out of some fancy college. I don't think he completely believes in himself yet, do you?"

"Not at all. The mystery to me is how he ever whipped Mr. Donovan."

"He got in the first lucky punch," Megan said. She raised her finger. "But next time they cross paths, Bill Donovan will tear his head off. It will be a bad and bloody thing."

"If Donovan doesn't drink himself to death or get killed first," Aileen said.

"Like Liam?"

At the mention of their youngest brother's name, Megan's brow furrowed with concern. Liam was seventeen, two years her junior, but he seemed even younger. Megan felt compelled to defend their brother. "Liam has a good heart and means well."

"Of course he does. Liam has always meant well," Aileen agreed. "But I'm half sick with worry over him. He's got a lot of growing up to do and this isn't the place for it. Mistakes out on this frontier will kill a man."

"Liam is smart," Megan said, not really wanting to talk about their only surviving brother. "He's smarter than he acts. He won't get killed."

"He will if he figures out a way to become a scout and a buffalo hunter," Aileen pronounced with certainty. "And that's what he intends to do."

"Wanting and getting are two separate things. Liam can't ride a horse or accurately shoot a gun. He'd never get hired as a hunter or scout."

"Don't tell him that," Aileen said. "Because—"

She was interrupted in midsentence when the shanty door slammed open and Hugh Fox stood swaying in the doorway. "Better get to your own home, Mrs. Gallagher. Keith is waiting."

Megan came to her feet and her eyes hardened for she had never liked her sister's husband. He was a slacker and wastrel and a very bad influence on both Keith and Liam.

"Good night," Megan said to her sister.

"What have the pair of you been brewing up now?" Fox demanded, eyes shifting back and forth between them. "Some kind of trouble for your men, that's for sure."

Aileen bit her lip but Megan flushed with anger. Ignoring the insult, she said, "Did you and Mr. Gallagher have a regular good time spending what little money we have left for milk, meat, and potatoes?"

Fox's leer dissolved and his handsome face turned ugly. "We should have refused to take back our jobs unless Donovan got back his position as engineer. If we'd done that, likely Gilchrist would have backed down rather than to lose three good men."

It was all that Megan could do not to laugh out loud. "I guess you don't watch the Missouri River every day like the women, Mr. Fox. There's dozens of men every day come leggin' it across the river hoping for a job with the Union Pacific as soon as the weather turns fair. Now why would Mr. Gilchrist worry so much about three rounders who disobeyed his orders?"

Fox blustered. He snapped his suspenders and crowed, " 'Cause he knows that we're the kind he needs to build a railroad!"

"Ha! You can't even fix a table and chairs for my sister!"

Fox turned purple with anger. He doubled up his fists and might even have attacked Megan except that Aileen threw herself in between them. "Please, haven't we all been through enough for one day? I won't have you both at each other's throats in my house."

Megan could see that her sister was really upset. She also realized that it was a waste of time to argue with Mr. Fox, drunk or sober. "Good night," she said to her sister as she passed by her brother-in-law who swayed in a cloud of whiskey fumes.

Megan only walked a few yards before she realized that her husband was standing outside their shanty relieving himself in the cold starlight. Megan sighed and went inside without a word of greeting.

"Hey," he called in a slurred voice, "ain't you even going to say hello?"

"Hello, Mr. Gallagher," Megan snapped, "and have you any money left to feed us until payday? Or will I have to stay up mending all night in order to buy a few potatoes for our pot tomorrow?"

Gallagher muttered a curse and barged through the doorway. "You're upset again, aren't you, Megan."

"Upset?" Megan shook her head and grabbed a frying pan. She brandished it and said, "Make a move toward me this night and I'll brain you, you drunken sot!"

Gallagher blinked owlishly. He scrubbed his jaw and finished buttoning his trousers. "What's wrong now, Megan?"

She lowered the frying pan. "I'm dirty, disgusted, and discouraged," Megan said. "We have no money and you almost got yourself fired today. That's what's wrong."

He took a step toward her but stopped when she raised the frying pan higher and warned, "I'm not in the mood, Mr. Gallagher!"

"You're never in the 'mood' anymore, are you? What happened to the girl I married!"

Megan could feel her eyes sting with salty tears. "The girl you married grew up and became a woman and not a very happy one. But she's stronger than she expected herself to ever be."

"I don't want a 'strong' woman," he said, fumbling for tobacco so that he could roll himself a cigarette. "Women ain't supposed to be strong. They're supposed to be pretty and soft and . . . and, well, good mothers!"

Megan swallowed painfully. "They become mothers all right, I just don't want to be a father too."

The tobacco sack slipped through Gallagher's splayed fingers. He balled his fists and took an advancing step but Megan stood her ground with the frying pan. "You've disgraced yourself enough already," she said, "don't make it worse than it is."

"Damn you!" he shouted, punching the air between them. "You dare to threaten me!"

Megan squeezed her eyes shut and felt a rush of tears cascade down her cheeks. "Go away! Don't come back until you're sober and with a day's wages, Mr. Gallagher."

"That's all you ever wanted from me," he screamed. "Isn't it! Just money!"

The charge was so ludicrous that despite herself, Megan began to laugh as if she had suddenly gone insane. She could not stop and it seemed to unnerve her husband.

"I think you *are* crazy!" he shouted, gaping at her as if she were a stranger. He bent down and grabbed for his sack of tobacco and almost lost his balance. With a struggle, he righted and steadied himself in their doorway, gulped and said, "Maybe I'll come back with wages."

"I'll be here," she said woodenly.

He wheeled around and staggered out the door. When she was sure that her husband was gone, the frying pan slipped from Megan's fingers and banged against her tin floor, and despite her best intentions, Megan covered her face and began to cry.

Later that night, as she sat mending the clothes that had brought them their only steady and reliable income for the past eight months, Megan tried to tell herself that this latest confrontation with her husband was just a phase that had to be endured until they reached California and he could find himself a job with some future.

There would be no real future building this railroad. Not for men like Liam, Hugh, and her husband. They would just grade roadbed, construct bridges, and lay track until the Union and the Central Pacific Railroads finally connected somewhere out in the West. After that, they'd be without jobs but at least they'd be in California. And maybe, if she had any chance at all of keeping her husband from squandering every last cent of his paycheck, she could even save a few dollars for California.

Megan sewed and darned stockings of bachelor railroad men into the early hours of the night. She wondered where her husband had found a place to sleep and she felt guilty for turning him out, but he needed to learn that a married man took on responsibilities. Keith wanted to make love every night and have lots of babies. Megan would not allow either to happen for she knew that if she were with child, she would be just as helpless as Aileen was with two children and a weak husband.

Physical union between a man and a woman ought to be a result of love and respect, shouldn't it? But if it were just everyman's God-given marital right—as the Bible said—then what could a woman do to make her husband treat her with dignity and respect?

Megan was not a churchgoer. Neither was Aileen. The Catholic Church had told her mother to always honor and obey her husband. Megan couldn't do that. She hated the fact that she was stronger than Keith and didn't want to be. It was just the way it was right now. Girls physically matured before boys. Megan was quite sure that young women emotionally matured before young men and perhaps that explained their husbands' irresponsible behaviors. It even made her more sympathetic and understanding, but not enough to allow herself to be used and impregnated so that she was in the same awful fix as her poor sister.

Wife or no wife. Church or no church. Bible or no Bible, Megan could not bend to the will of a man she did not respect. So she prayed that time and California would cure the sickness in her marriage and satisfy the dreams that kept her from feeling as old and as helpless as poor Aileen.

CHAPTER
▐▐▐▐▐▐▐▐▐▐▐▐ **3** ▐▐▐▐▐▐▐▐▐▐▐▐

The warm days continued, one after the next. Workmen accustomed to the sub-zero temperatures suddenly found that they were sweating profusely in the sixty-plus-degree temperatures. The sky remained a pale blue lid over the thawing earth and because of the chinook winds, the hated mud finally began to dry and crack. Each day, Glenn had the surface of the Missouri drilled and measured as the ice shrank steadily. The rails and their ties had already been removed after the crossing and a decision was made to prohibit all wagon, horse, and even foot traffic from crossing the river between Omaha and Council Bluffs. Many, however, ignored the order and took their chances just beyond the next nearest bend in the river.

The transfer of the huge stockpiles of rails and supplies did not progress as rapidly as Glenn had hoped but at least it was finally under way. They had two Danforth, Cooke and Company locomotives in assembly and five in operation working the levee as well as hauling ties, rails, and other hardware up the line to Papillion, twelve miles to the west. Glenn loved the powerful new locomotives. He'd spent a great deal of time in the new Union Pacific roundhouse that winter watching as each new locomotive had been uncrated and then reassembled and put into service. They were all 4-4-0's, and those built at the Manchester Locomotive Works in New Hampshire were considered by the chief locomotive engineers to be the best locomotives that money could buy. Glenn had realized that men could love women, money, horses, and power, but until Omaha, he had never realized that there was a breed of men who loved powerful machines. Glenn's favorite locomotive was named the Major General Sherman #1 and it had been one of the first to arrive by steamboat the previous summer.

The rolling stock of cars was also being assembled in the roundhouse. There were supply cars, triple-decked sleeping cars, an office, a mail car, and several cars specially outfitted to cook and serve large numbers of meals. Glenn was appalled to learn that the Union Pacific intended to feed its workers in shifts on tin plates nailed to fixed wooden tables.

"Nailed?" he asked one of the head cooks.

"That's right. The men rotate through in shifts, coming and leaving on a bell system. Once they leave, we toss buckets of boilin' water across the plates to wash off the leftover food so that we can slop more for the next meal shift."

Glenn shook his head. He resolved that he would not want to be around the dining car very often, especially at mealtime.

One afternoon when dark clouds rolled over the land and they were caught in a sudden rain squall, Liam O'Connell rushed up to introduce himself. "Mr. Gilchrist," he said, extending his hand, "as long as we can't work for a few minutes until this rain passes, can I have a moment of your time?"

Glenn had seen Liam before and knew that he was on the crew that was moving iron rails onto flatcars for transport over to Papillion. Liam was quite young-looking, sandy-haired with brown eyes tinged green and a cockiness about himself. He was slightly taller than average, and well muscled. He wore a handlebar mustache and a red silk bandanna around his neck. His smile was quick and wide.

"Sure. What can I do for you?"

"Well, sir, to begin with I want to thank you for not firing my sisters' husbands."

"What?"

"Megan and Aileen. You know. Their husbands were on that last supply train across the Missouri."

"Oh, yes. Well, fine," Glenn said, watching the rain blister the streets and turn it into gutters of mud. He hoped that this squall passed quickly even as he watched a canvas tarpaulin sail off a huge stack of coal and kite across the ice-covered Missouri.

"Ben, Jim! Chase after that or it's on its way to Lincoln."

The two workmen dashed out from under a shelter and went slipping and sliding after the tarp. Glenn cupped his hands to his mouth and yelled, "And be careful of the ice! It's pretty thin in some places!"

"Damned thin," Liam said, pressing back farther under the shelter and watching the pair chase the tarp. "But anyway, I was wondering if you might recommend me for a better job."

Glenn saw Jim and Ben hit the ice and take nasty tumbles. The wind was sheeting ice water across the surface and the tarp was airborne again and gathering altitude. Glenn knew that it was lost and he began to motion the pair back. They were far away and the wind was blowing too hard for shouting. Finally, they saw him and gratefully headed back off the thin river ice.

"We're going to have to get all those things cinched down tight or we'll lose them too."

"I'll be happy to help," Liam offered, "I've about moved all the rails and ties that I can stand."

"Fine," Glenn said. "Just tell your foreman that you're helping me the rest of the day."

"Actually," Liam said, clearing his throat and stretching to his full height, "I'd be more suited to work as a Union Pacific scout and hunter."

Glenn raised his eyebrows. "Have you any buffalo-hunting experience?"

"No, but . . ."

"Have you ever dealt with the Indians?"

"I can kill 'em as fast as the next man."

"We're hoping to make peace, not war with the Indians," Glenn said. "We've enough to do without dodging Sioux arrows."

"They're goin' to make a fight of it, Mr. Gilchrist. I heard that's what General Dodge believes."

"I heard that too," Glenn said. "But we're still trying to make a peace with them and we're not going to attack the Sioux without provocation."

Liam thrust his jaw out. "They've been provoking white people for twenty years, sir. I don't see how you figure any of that is going to change. Especially now that we're plannin' on slicin' a pair of iron rails smack through the middle of their hunting grounds."

"We'll see," Glenn replied. "But the truth of the matter is that I don't have a thing to do with hiring men as scouts and hunters."

"Joshua Hood has been named chief hunter and scout for the Union Pacific."

"I haven't met the man," Glenn admitted. "But I do recall hearing that name."

"He's none too friendly," Liam complained. "I already talked to him twice and he won't help me."

Glenn shrugged. "I'm afraid that I can't either. Each supervisor and foreman hires his own crews. If Mr. Hood doesn't need men, then . . ."

"Oh, but he does!" Liam objected. "He's looking for both scouts and hunters."

Glenn thought he knew Liam O'Connell's problem. The kid was pushy and aggressive in addition to being green and vastly overconfident. "Perhaps he's looking for men who have experience hunting buffalo or dealing with the Sioux."

"Well, how in hell is a fella supposed to *get* experience less'n someone gives him a chance?"

Glenn understood the young man's dilemma but it was the same faced by any man who wanted to try a new line of work. "I don't know," he admitted. "Maybe if you keep after Mr. Hood, he'll change his mind."

"Could you speak to him?"

"No."

Liam blinked and his eyes tightened at the corners. "Just speakin' with him isn't much to ask, Mr. Gilchrist. Maybe just tell him that we talked. That I volunteered to help tie down your tarps."

"I'm sorry. It's not my place to talk to others about who they should hire." Glenn also wanted to say that he did not know one blessed thing about Liam except that he had one very spunky and beautiful sister and another with children who always looked a bit unsettled and frightened.

"Well, then," Liam said, "I'd better get back to my own work."

"What about the tarps?"

"Some other time," Liam said, his mouth turned down at the corner as he stepped out into the rain.

Glenn frowned as he watched the kid saunter off through the driving rain. He found it difficult to imagine that Liam O'Connell was any relationship to his tall, auburn-haired sister. Except that they were both taller than average and very direct, they were opposites. Megan knew how to get what she wanted, but this kid lacked both subtlety and perception. Liam O'Connell was missing something in his personality. The kid had left Glenn with a sour taste in his mouth. There was something slightly out of balance with Liam that was unsettling.

When Liam left Glenn Gilchrist, he tromped through the mud and wound his way up the street toward the Union Pacific's immense stockyards where he'd last seen Joshua Hood with several of his new scouts.

Liam wished that he could ride a fine horse up the main street of Omaha with a buffalo rifle cradled across his saddle horn and maybe even a raccoon cap with its ringed tail dangling behind. Some of the old-timers wore fur caps and they looked as wild as Indians. Joshua Hood, however, was a curious mix of cowboy, vaquero, and mountain man. He wore leather pants and a buckskin jacket with Indian beads and tassels on the sleeves like an old-time trapper, but his hat was wide-brimmed, almost Mexican, and there were big-rowled silver Spanish spurs strapped to his high-heeled riding boots. Instead of the grass ropes favored by local cowboys, Joshua Hood used a sixty-foot braided leather reata, although Liam had overheard the man claim he was no cowboy. Hood's Colt revolver was a pretty thing with a yellow-boned handle and it rested in a beautifully carved holster and cartridge belt. There was an unmistakable touch of Texas and even Old Mexico in Joshua Hood's dress, but it was complemented by the hat and saddle of a northern plains cowboy and a breed of mountain man that was all but gone. The man didn't fit any mold and that made him impossible for Liam to gauge.

By the time that Liam reached the Union Pacific stockyards where the mules and horses were kept to pull the supply wagons to the tracks, he was covered with mud slung up from the churning wheels of freight wagons. He spotted Hood and several of his friends squatting under a low shed just as the rain suddenly died. Hood and his scouts paid Liam no attention as his boots made loud sucking sounds in the mud, but Liam knew that he had caught their interest.

"Mr. Hood," Liam announced, striding right up to the man. "I need a word with you."

"Talk."

Liam looked down at the squatting figure, then at his rough friends. "I'd like to speak to you in private."

Hood thumbed back his hat and gazed upward. "We've already

talked twice. Nothing has changed since then. I have no work for you."

"You're still looking for scouts and hunters, aren't you?"

"*Experienced* scouts and hunters."

"I learn fast."

"I'm sure you do, but fast isn't good enough. Sorry."

Hood tipped his head down and with that wide-brimmed hat, Liam couldn't see his lean, tanned face so he retreated in the mud. When he could see Hood's face, Liam was annoyed because the man's eyes were shut as if he were napping.

"Mr. Hood," Liam said, "I'm afraid that you *have* to hire me."

The eyes snapped open. "What the hell is that supposed to mean?"

Liam had gone too far to back down now. He played his hole card. "It means that the Union Pacific's construction engineer, Mr. Gilchrist, orders you to hire me," Liam told the frontiersman. "He said that he'd vouch that I'd earn my pay."

"He did, did he?"

"That's right. He said I would be fine."

Hood glanced sideways at his friends. There were four of them, like himself, all big, rough, bearded men in their twenties. One of them was missing an ear, another had an angry red sheet of scar tissue stretched across his left cheek dotted with tufts of black curly hair. He was one of the ugliest men that Liam had ever seen and his eyes were as cold and cunning as those of a Boston harbor rat.

Liam swallowed uneasily as the silence tightened down on his throat like a noose. He forced a smile. "I guess I'm going to need to requisition a company horse, saddle, and rifle, huh, Mr. Hood?"

"You ever shoot anything before?" the scar-faced man asked.

Liam knew the feel of thin ice. "A little."

Hood uncoiled. In his high-heeled boots, he was a solid six-footer but appeared taller, maybe because of his broad shoulders and wide-brimmed Mexican hat. He gazed around the stockyard with its pens and animals, shrugged, and drawled, "Come along out of town a ways."

"In this mud?"

"Sure." Hood led off with his four friends in tow.

"Mr. Hood," Liam said, hurrying after the man. "I never shot much. But I catch on real quick."

They walked down to the Missouri River where Hood found a rusting bean can. He threw it far out on the ice, drew his six-gun, and extended it to Liam. "Hit the can."

Liam swallowed. "I doubt I can without a little practice."

"All right, you got four practice shots. Hit it by the fifth."

"I'll try."

Liam took the weapon. He'd shot a six-gun a few times since coming to Omaha, but on each occasion he'd been drinking with Keith and Hugh while raisin' hell. Drunk, you didn't care if you hit what you aimed for. The idea was to make a show and some noise. Maybe watch dirt, mud, or ice spit up under the impact of the slugs. This was a whole different matter.

"Shoot, boy," one of the men rumbled.

Liam's cheeks colored at the use of the term "boy" and his fist closed hard on the bone handle of the Colt. He raised the weapon, thumbed back the hammer, and took aim. When he squeezed the trigger, he saw smoke and then a flume of ice jump about six feet from the can. He also heard one of Hood's ugly friends snort with derision. Liam fired twice more and closed the distance to three feet. His fourth shot was so close it kicked up ice and moved the can a bit.

"Number five," Hood said, not sounding impressed.

Liam realized he was sweating. He took a deep breath, held it, and fired. His shot sailed high. In anger, he thumbed back the trigger and fired again but the last cylinder was empty and Hood tore the Colt from his hand.

"If I had another five shots, I could hit it," Liam said angrily. "Give me another chance, Mr. Hood."

"Not with my gun and ammunition," Hood said. "What about a rifle? You any better with one of those?"

Liam saw one of the scouts was carrying a rifle cradled in his arms. It was a big-bored thing and appeared to be a single shot weapon. Liam jammed his hands in his pockets. "I've never shot one before."

"That's what I thought," Hood said. He reloaded his Colt, jammed it into his holster, and said, "You tell Mr. Glenn Gilchrist that Joshua Hood wouldn't hire you to grain and brush his horses."

Liam's jaw dropped. "Damn you, Hood!" he shouted as the man walked away. "I wouldn't work for you anyway!"

Two of the fierce-looking men stopped and started to come back but Hood said, "Let it go, boys," and the men followed after him like a pack of obedient mongrels.

"I hope the Sioux scalp all of you!" Liam yelled.

Hood chuckled out loud and then his men began to roar with laughter. That made Liam even angrier. So angry that if he'd had Hood's six-shooter still in his fist, he'd have put a hole in the other side of the scout's hairy face and made him laugh out the back of his skull as he marched into hell.

Liam sat down beside the river and listened to the storm rumble and he saw jagged bolts of lightning stab the eastern skies. The wind picked up, the can began to skate across the ice, and then it began to rain in torrents.

Through it all, Liam sat wrapped in his own dark thoughts. As long as Joshua Hood was chief scout and buffalo hunter, there would never be any hope of riding a company horse and fighting wild Indians. Or of killing buffalo and doing something besides the back-breaking work of a Southern slave.

"I hope they do scalp them all," Liam muttered as he pulled his hat down close over his brow and scowled at the tin can that was skittering this way and that in the whirling wind.

CHAPTER
4

The arrival of General John "Jack" Casement and his younger brother Daniel was the talk of Omaha. An executive meeting was called in Durant's personal railroad car, outfitted with all the amenities of a lush hotel suite with crystal lamps, polished brass fittings, and expensive oil paintings. Glenn was actually surprised to be invited and the night before the meeting he took a bath and had his suit sponged and pressed. He arrived at the meeting at one o'clock in the afternoon and was rewarded with a brandy and a quick welcome from the Union Pacific's vice president himself.

Dr. Thomas Durant was not the least bit physically imposing. He was angular, wore a goatee and mustache, and was in his mid-forties. Glenn found the man to be impersonal and very demanding. He had not met anyone who liked "The Doctor" as Durant liked to be addressed, but everyone feared and respected him. Furthermore, no one would deny that the former medical doctor had been instrumental in getting a penny-pinching Congress to approve the crucial Pacific Railroad Acts of 1862 and 1864 that provided the vital foundation grants necessary to begin a transcontinental railroad. That Durant was already rich and extremely influential was accepted. That he was committed to building a railroad at the least cost and in the most efficient manner was debatable.

"Mr. Gilchrist," Durant said, "you know most of those gathered here today, but it's my pleasure to introduce General Casement and his brother, Daniel, who will be in charge of construction and procurement."

Glenn turned to greet the brothers. Jack Casement was, as advertised, short and barrel-chested. When Glenn looked into the man's eyes he immediately sensed the same strength and determination he felt in Casement's firm handshake.

"General," Glenn said, "we've been waiting for you and your brother with more than a little anticipation. I stand ready to serve you both."

Jack nodded and his even shorter and younger brother smiled and shook Glenn's hand. "It will be a challenge."

"That it will, sir."

"Dan. I prefer you call me Dan."

"As you wish," Glenn said with a smile because the Casement brothers were so open, direct, and friendly that Glenn was sure that they were going to be a pleasure to know and work for. And there they exuded an air of immense competence that gave them an immediate presence.

Glenn knew their presence stemmed from an extensive knowledge of railroad building that he was sure would become apparent as everyone sat down and began to discuss the Union Pacific's great challenge. But to Glenn's annoyance, The Doctor felt compelled to dominate the discussion even though he knew little about engineering. In eloquent and long-winded passages better suited to fund-raising, Durant gave his view of the progress that his railroad had made to date and the most pressing obstacles that they faced.

Perhaps sensing the impatience his monologue was receiving from real engineers, Durant said, "Actually, gentlemen, money is my forte. My greatest talent lies in generating money— the lifeblood of this fledgling railroad. Without a swift and immediate infusion of funds, this effort will fail."

Glenn heartily agreed. More often than not, their Union Pacific payroll was late and that caused a great deal of unhappiness among the crews.

Durant continued. "I will be spending more and more time in Washington, arm-twisting Congress to support our work here. As you may already be aware, I am also courting capitalists in every major city and we are issuing Union Pacific stock in the form of our new Credit Mobilier. Mr. Oakes Ames will be one of our principle benefactors and you all know that his fortune probably exceeds that of the United States Treasury."

Several people laughed because The Doctor was only half joking. Oakes Ames was a congressman from Massachusetts who had built his family's small tool and shovel works into one of the country's largest industrial firms and was respectfully known as The King of Spades. His shovels were so common and highly regarded in the West that they were even bartered in lieu of money wherever currency was in short supply.

Durant cleared his throat. "Gentlemen, it is *my* job to see to it that the Union Pacific Railroad construction marches continually forward and that you are given all the men and materials necessary to build this line. It is *your* job to do the job."

Durant measured each man. "I have, through no small effort, secured a promise from Congress that this railroad will, in addition to the funds for building the line, also be given land grants of twenty square miles in alternating sections all the way to California. Furthermore, we don't even have to actually lay the track in order to receive congressional funds for each twenty-mile section. As soon as the roadbed is prepared, Congress will pay us."

"Highly generous," Jack Casement said, looking impressed and pleased because the Casement brothers were to receive $750 for every mile of track whose construction they oversaw.

"An absolutely essential concession if we are to do the job," Durant said.

Dan Casement cleared his throat. "I've heard that General Dodge has had a very busy winter."

Durant nodded. "As you are probably aware, after the war he was granted an assignment on our western frontier. Last fall and this winter, in response to the Sioux, Cheyenne, and the Arapaho attacks on isolated settlements and numerous acts of vandalism against the telegraph lines, General Dodge swept the entire Platte Valley of Indians."

"Does that mean that my construction crews will not be in danger of attack?" General Casement asked.

"I'm afraid it does not," Durant replied. "But you can be sure that we have sent a strong message to the Indians that this railroad will be built at any cost."

"Any word exactly when General Dodge will arrive?" Glenn asked.

"Soon," Durant said. "Certainly by May. In the meantime, General Casement will be in charge of driving the rails down past Papillion and we have set ourselves a goal of laying two hundred miles of railroad track by year's end."

Everyone looked to Casement who nodded sternly. "We can do it if we have the supplies and men."

"And you shall have them," Durant vowed. He looked to Dan Casement. "As I understand it, sir, you shall be in charge of procurement and logistics?"

Dan Casement, only a hair over five feet tall but with the same penetrating gaze and strong features as his brother, nodded. "I have already met with the supply supervisors and will be meeting at great length with Mr. Gilchrist to arrive at an accurate inventory."

"I'm at your disposal," Glenn said.

"Any immediate shortages, Glenn?"

"No. Luckily, we managed to get our last supply train across the ice."

"I heard about that," Jack Casement said. "Daring piece of work. Perhaps a bit too daring."

Glenn wanted to tell the little general that crossing the river that last time had not been his idea, but Durant's. And it *had* been far too risky.

"They made it," Durant said with a grin. "There is nothing in this work that doesn't demand great personal risk of life and property."

"Agreed," the general said, "but it is foolish to take unnecessary risks."

Durant's eyes sparked. "General," he said, "the ice held. Until it breaks up and flows south, there is no hope of getting supplies into Omaha by steamboat. We simply could not afford to stop supply operations for two or three months waiting for ice to melt in its own good time."

Glenn saw the color rise in Casement's cheeks but the little general held his anger and said, "What about the Central Pacific?"

Durant reached up and twirled the tip of his luxurious mustache. His dark eyes sparkled with amusement. "The Central Pacific is having even worse monetary difficulties that we are. My counterpart as vice president and general manager is a man named Collis Huntington who got lucky with a hardware store and made a few dollars. Huntington is rough and ill-mannered, but shrewd. I've already used him in the halls of Congress to our best advantage. But God Himself would be hard tried to get the Central Pacific over the Sierra Nevada Mountains within the next three years."

"Then," Casement said, "they are still in the Sierra foot-hills?"

"Exactly. The grades they are facing in order to get over the Sierras are an engineering nightmare."

"But I heard they had found a pass," Glenn said.

"Donner Pass," Durant answered in a solemn tone of voice. "I'm sure that infamous name is more than familiar to everyone present."

Glenn nodded. The grisly story of frozen death and canni-balism endured by the Donner Party exactly ten years earlier was still fresh in everyone's mind. Glenn could not imagine how, given what he had heard of that high, snow-bound Sierra pass, any competent engineer could expect to span it with a railroad.

Durant leaned forward, elbows on the table. "In addition, our determined but ill-fated California rivals have another monu-mental problem that we do not share."

Durant paused dramatically, then said with obvious delight, "They can't find enough labor. You see, the Comstock Lode is less than a hundred miles distance away and the lure of gold and silver is siphoning off the Central Pacific's most capable workers. So, in desperation, they have resorted to hiring Celes-tials."

"Chinese?" Dan Casement asked with amazement.

"That's right." Durant chuckled. "It's not something that had been publicized because if it were, investors would stampede in their haste to divest themselves of any connection with the Central Pacific."

Glenn had actually heard that Durant brought up the Chinese issue at every opportunity. It seemed wise, however, not to mention this fact.

"And so," Durant grandly proclaimed, "we have, in my esti-mation, at least three years head start on the Central Pacific Railroad and that means we cannot help but gobble up the lion's share of the government's generous western land and cash subsidies. If you gentlemen all work hard and well, I can guarantee you stock in our railroad and great personal wealth when we meet the Central Pacific at the eastern base of the Sierras."

"Then you don't foresee us trying to scale the eastern slope of those mountains?" General Casement asked.

"No," Durant said, "the forty-eight thousand dollars per mile in the mountains we receive from Congress is entirely inadequate. Our real profit is going to be in racing across these Great Plains. And before we are finished, I fully expect to average a mile of new track every single day we are on the generally flat plains of Nebraska and Wyoming."

Glenn's jaw must have dropped. However, the Casement brothers didn't bat an eye so Glenn closed his mouth and remained silent. He could not imagine slamming down rails at such an incredible pace over any extended length of time. Why, during the entire previous year they had not laid more than forty honest miles of track!

"I think a mile a day is reasonable and so does General Dodge whom I have been in constant contact with," Durant was saying. "Everyone agrees that it is possible except in winter."

"*If* we have the supplies and men," Jack Casement reminded everyone.

"Yes," Durant said. "And, to a large extent, that will be dependent upon you, Dan. Are you up to the task?"

Dan Casement nodded. "With Glenn's help."

Everyone looked to Glenn and he said, "We have enough railroad ties, rails, and hardware to push westward. But I am worried about the Indians. I expect that they will attack us at every point along the line."

"The Unites States Army will have something to say about that," Durant assured everyone. "And also, if you haven't met our chief scout and buffalo hunter, Mr. Joshua Hood, then you must certainly do so at the first opportunity."

"What are his credentials?" Jack Casement asked.

"He has lived with the Sioux and the Cheyenne," Durant said. "His father was a mountain man and a friend of Jim Bridger's. Hood knows the Indians' sign language and I have personally seem him use his weapons. He is a marksman and an expert with a rope and a six-gun."

Dan Casement smiled. "Excuse me, Mr. Vice President, but a 'rope' isn't going to be of much use out here unless he's planning to lasso a buffalo!"

Everyone but The Doctor laughed. And when his icy stare aborted their laughter, Durant snapped, "Hood is of the stuff of Jim Bowie and Sam Houston. He's a fighter but he's also smart enough to avoid a fight. He has already chosen his hunters and scouts and I have every confidence in him as does General Dodge. In fact, it was General Dodge who first recommended Hood as an extraordinary scout and hunter."

Everyone in the plush car nodded. Samuel Reed, another one of Durant's most trusted engineers and supervisors, said, "If General Dodge recommended him, then Hood must be pretty special."

"He is," Durant said. "But he is a gentleman not educated in the social graces—as you might expect from a man who has lived with savages. That is why I declined to invite him to this meeting."

The corners of Durant's mouth lifted in what might have been a smile. "In truth, I was afraid that if Joshua Hood saw and could read the guest list to this meeting, he would most likely have refused to attend."

It was a Durant joke and they all chuckled. Glenn had never seen Durant so engaging. He supposed it was because with the Casement brothers finally arriving to take charge of the actual construction and logistics, The Doctor felt a great burden lift from his thin, stooped shoulders.

"Are there any other questions?" Durant asked, looking at each of them in turn.

"Just one," Glenn said.

"Go on."

"We need more men to load the freight cars with rails and ties in order to get the levee cleared."

"You shall have them," Durant said, relaxing. "But not until I receive additional funds from Congress. Until then, you will have to do with what you have. I understand that there is a shortage of men but I can't very well imagine that Jack will want to shift them from the road-grading crews."

"I'm afraid not," Jack Casement said. "At least not for a week or two. In a few more days, Glenn, Dan and I will have a better feel for how we can best use the labor we already have on the payroll. As soon as we can, we'll transfer those supplies off the levee. Believe me, we'll be needing those rails and ties in a big hurry once we start to roll."

"How many ties do we have stockpiled?" Dan Casement asked.

"About ten thousand."

"Of those, how many are impregnated with zinc chloride to keep them from rotting?"

"Roughly a quarter." Glenn looked to the general. "The Doctor recommends we alternate the burnetized ties with the regular cottonwood, cedar, and oak at a ration of six to one."

"Four to one burnetized," Jack said quickly. "Any less than that and we'll be replacing them before we finish the railroad."

Durant opened his mouth to object, but then changed his mind. Glenn could see that the vice president was not pleased by this far more expensive ratio, but it made sense to Glenn. The idea was to lay track as fast as possible in order to gobble up land grants and government cash. However, you couldn't do that if you were constantly tearing up old roadbed because the ties were rotting out faster than you could build.

"Gentlemen," Durant said, "why don't we all have some refreshments and then get back to work."

Glenn discovered that "refreshments" were a glass of very excellent brandy and a cigar. Since Glenn did not smoke, he gave his to the little general. He stayed as long as was expected, then he left to go back to work.

He was on his way to the levee when a handsome muscular man on a fine sorrel gelding galloped up to his side and reined his horse to an abrupt standstill, spattering Glenn's pants with fresh mud.

"Are you Gilchrist?" the rider demanded without preamble.

Glenn studied the man on horseback. He was four or five years Glenn's senior, about six feet tall with very broad shoulders and a shaggy mane of thick brown hair. Like Durant, he wore a luxurious handlebar mustache but no beard or goatee. His face was deeply tanned and there were crow's-feet at the corners of his pale blue eyes. He had a square jaw and large, battered hands with dirt crusted under his fingenails.

His buckskins, Colt, and Spanish spurs left no doubt in Glenn's mind as to his identity. "You must be Joshua Hood, the Union Pacific's new chief scout and buffalo hunter."

"That's right," Hood said. "Are you Gilchrist?"

Glenn looked down at the spatterings of mud on his pants. "I am."

Hood studied Glenn closely and said, "I don't much appreciate you ordering me to hire a damned fool greenhorn."

"What are you talking about?"

"Liam O'Connell. He said that you said he had a job with me on your orders."

Glenn scoffed. "Liam is a liar. I told him that I have no authority or interest whatsoever in interfering with who you hire as a scout or a buffalo hunter."

"Glad to hear that," Hood said, his shoulders dipping a little as he relaxed. "And you can be sure I'll have a word or two with Liam the next time I see him."

"He's just a kid," Glenn said. "He's probably been reading dime novels of the Old West and has dreams of being an Indian fighter. I wouldn't judge Liam too harshly if I were you."

"Well, you aren't me, Mr. Gilchrist." Then Hood dug his Spanish spurs into the sorrel's flanks and galloped away, splattering Glenn with even more mud.

Glenn curbed his anger. He recalled that Durant had said that Joshua Hood was competent but entirely lacking in the social graces. The Doctor certainly had pegged his chief scout correctly. Glenn's impression was that Hood had a very short fuse and a streak of violence just beneath his rough exterior. He looked and acted like a man who would brook no interference and expected others to yield to his strong personality. He was the kind that would clash with those who opposed him rather than try to mediate differences. Glenn questioned Joshua Hood's ability to help forge a peaceful coexistence with the fierce Plains Indians.

"Mr. Gilchrist!"

He turned to see Megan Gallagher striding toward him wearing a very worried expression. Glenn removed his hat and went to greet the Irish beauty. "Good afternoon, Mrs. Gallagher."

"It's not so good," Megan said. "Have you seen my husband?"

"Not today. But I'm sure that he's on the job, maybe just west of town with Mr. Reed."

"I don't think so," Megan said. "Weren't the men paid yesterday?"

"Yes."

Megan sighed. "Then he must be drunk, probably lyin' in some muddy ditch dead broke."

Glenn shifted uneasily. "I wouldn't know about that, Mrs. Gallagher. I'll keep my eye out for him. If he's not on the job today, that won't set well with the company."

"He'll be fine once we leave Omaha," Megan said bitterly. "Sober, he's a hard worker. Right now, well, he's a bit unsettled."

Megan looked into Glenn's eyes. He found himself lost in them and barely heard her when she said, "He's still runnin' with Bill Donovan. Donovan is working for one of the freight wagon contractors. Have you crossed him yet?"

"No."

"Be careful of the man," Megan warned. "Do you carry a hideout gun, Mr. Gilchrist?"

"Of course not," Glenn responded, caught off balance by the suggestion.

"You should," Megan said, nodding her pretty head up and down. "A derringer would be a blessing if Bill Donovan jumps you."

"I'm not afraid of Mr. Donovan. I handled him before and . . ."

"And you were lucky. The Lord helps those who help themselves, Mr. Gilchrist. You didn't fire Aileen's husband nor my own. For that I'm grateful and so I'm telling you to get yourself a derringer. And just remember, two shots are better than one."

"I'll give it some thought," Glenn said. "Can I walk you back to your place?"

"No, sir. That would be a bad idea, now wouldn't it? All the other wives would think I'm nosin' up for favors from the boss and they'd not speak civil to me."

"I hadn't thought of that."

"Why should you?"

Glenn replaced his hat on his head. "I'd better get back to work."

Megan looked past him so intently that Glenn turned. She was watching Joshua Hood who had ridden just a short ways and was sitting his horse talking to a man on foot.

"Who *is* that man?" Megan asked.

"His name is Mr. Joshua Hood. He's our new chief scout and hunter. He's not very sociable, Mrs. Gallagher."

"Ah, but he has lovely manners," she said without elaborating.

Glenn frowned. He had taken an immediate dislike for Hood and it annoyed him to hear that this pretty woman did not share that same unfavorable opinion.

"Is your sister's husband also missing?"

"He came home," Megan said. "Drunk and almost broke. But at least he came home."

"Your brother, Liam, got me off to a bad start with Mr. Hood," Glenn said.

"Oh?"

"Yes, he told the man I'd said he should be hired as a scout and hunter."

Megan giggled. "That lyin' rascal! That's just like Liam to do such a thing."

"Well," Glenn said, "he's going to have to answer to Hood and me both."

"Liam is willful," Megan admitted. "But he has a good heart."

Glenn thought that was a charitable assessment but not a surprising one, being as how Liam was this young woman's brother.

"I'll watch for your husband," he promised.

At the mention of Keith Gallagher, Megan's eyes clouded with worry. "If you find him before I do, tell him that he should come home."

"I will," Glenn said, looking to the heavens as a bolt of lightning flashed brilliantly to the north somewhere up in the northwest corner of Iowa, then was followed a few seconds later by a tremendous clash and roll of thunder.

"Like the cannons of war, eh, Mr. Gilchrist?"

"Yes. I'm afraid we're in for another bad storm," Glenn said as the wind freshened and an ominous column of dark thunderheads marched toward them.

"It's going to be a hard spring," Megan said grimly as she studied the approaching storm. Her eyes grew distant. "I'm afraid of the Indians, Mr. Gilchrist, but more afraid of the weather."

"Things will get better," he said. "Everyone agrees that this winter was especially hard, even for Nebraska. And as we get organized and start to lay track, I'm sure that life will be a lot more comfortable."

"Do you still think we're foolish to follow our husbands to the West with your Union Pacific Railroad?"

"What I think," Glenn said honestly, "is that you were right when you told me your lives are not my concern."

Megan smiled. "I did say that, didn't I. It wasn't very nice and I apologize. You see, I was pretty damned angry at my husband at the time."

"And you're not now?"

"I'm more worried than angry," Megan admitted. "Much more worried."

Glenn didn't know what to say about that so he kept his mouth shut and tipped his hat before Megan turned and walked away. Something made Glenn glance back over his shoulder and he saw Joshua Hood. The Indian scout wasn't talking to anyone anymore. He was just staring at Megan Gallagher as she headed back toward her shanty down by the river.

Glenn felt an unreasonable pang of resentment and even jealousy even though he knew it was foolish and that he could not blame Hood. Staring at Megan Gallagher just seemed the natural thing for a healthy man to do.

CHAPTER
5

"Liam!"

Liam was sweating and cursing in the cold rain as he and four other men doggedly transferred five-hundred-pound rails from a huge iron stack over to a waiting flatcar. Three other flatcars were already loaded and there were six more to be loaded before his shift was over. Liam's back ached and his arms felt dead as he struggled to hold up his share of each rail's dead weight.

The rails were being transferred to Papillion and there were thousands yet to be moved. It was brutal but Liam favored working with rails over wooden ties, because cold iron didn't splinter into your hands—it just nipped off your fingers if you grew careless.

"Liam!" the voice called again.

He twisted around in the driving rain to see Megan Gallagher sloshing through the mud. Liam cussed. "Relief man!" he shouted hoarsely.

"No relief," the foreman bellowed. "Talk to your woman on your own damned time!"

"She's my sister," Liam grunted as he and the other four men heaved another rain-slick rail up from the stack and then struggled with it over to the waiting flatcar. They tossed the rail in place, blowing clouds of steam into the heavy rain.

"Give us a minute," Hugh Fox cried. "You've been driving us like mules since daybreak!"

Their foreman, a short but stocky man named John James, took a second glance at Megan and decided he liked the scenery enough to take a quick breather. "All right, boys, five minutes."

The men were so tired that they just dropped to their knees and climbed underneath the flatcar out of the rain. Liam hurried off to meet his sister hearing Fox call, "She's looking for her husband!"

Liam took his sister's arm and led her toward a supply shed. He knew that he was going to be late getting back to work, but he and the crew were exhausted and could use a few extra minutes.

"What are you doing out in this rain!" he scolded, shocked at his sister's wan appearance. "Megan, you shouldn't be running around in this cold, wet weather!"

They ducked inside the supply shed, rain slamming down on its tin roof. Megan shook herself like a cat, looked up at her younger brother, and said, "Do you know where Mr. Gallagher is?"

"For a couple of days, he slept in the same flea-trap hotel that I rent," Liam said. "Slept on the floor. I loaned him money to eat. Why'd you kick him out this time, Megan?"

"He got drunk and spent all his money again." Megan wiped rain from her eyes. Exhaustion showed in her every movement. "He didn't keep even a cent for food."

"That's no reason to throw a man out of his own house," Liam argued.

Megan stared at her younger brother. "It *is* a reason," she said. "Keith *has* to grow up! He's a married man who wants to have children. I can't have children wondering if he'll treat them and me the same way that Mr. Fox treats Aileen!"

Liam expelled a deep breath. He liked Hugh Fox, but not when he thought about how the man treated his family.

"Yeah," he said, putting his hands on his sister's shoulders. "I know Aileen is always half sick with worry. You and her are both working night and day with mending trying to keep food on your tables. I should have been helping you all along but I'm not much better at holding on to my paycheck than Hugh or Keith."

"We're not your responsibility, Liam. You don't have a wife or children. You've just yourself. But I want you to find my husband and tell him that he needs to come home. Mr. Gallagher and I have to talk."

"Even if he spent this last paycheck?"

"Yes," Megan said.

"What are you going to say to him?"

When Megan didn't answer, Liam scowled and said, "Are you finally going to leave him once and for all this time?"

"I don't know," she said quietly. "I want to get to California. This railroad can help us all do that."

"But it will take years! Megan, if the only reason you're here is to reach California, then maybe you should go back home and . . ."

"We don't have a home anymore," Megan said, looking up at her brother. "Don't you see that? It's just you, Aileen, her dear children, and me. We're all that's left. There's nothing to go back to in Boston. No jobs, no family, no future."

"Keith doesn't believe that," Liam said, needing to tell her the truth.

Megan clenched her fists at her sides. "Mr. Gallagher was the one that first talked about this railroad. About how he hated Boston and needed change. It was *his* idea to come here, not mine."

"I know," Liam said, "but he's talking different now. Maybe you should listen."

"And maybe *he* should listen!" Megan railed. "Dammit to hell, Liam! I didn't want to come out here in the first place but I could see that Mr. Gallagher's mind was made up so I agreed. Now, we've sold everything to last until steady work and we don't even have the money to return to Boston."

Liam knew this was true. Still, some perversity made him say, "Megan, a man has a right to change his mind once in a while."

"No!" Megan rested her forehead on her forearm that was pressed against the wall. "He's *got* to stick to something, Liam. A man who quits every time things get hard is never going to be successful."

"I'm about to quit this job myself," Liam confessed.

Megan looked up suddenly. "Quit? Why, we're just getting started. When this storm passes, and General Dodge finally arrives, this railroad is on its way to California. Every day we'll see new things, Liam. It'll be exciting building this great railroad—or just being a part of it all is a thing we'll always remember with pride. You can't give up now. Not just when it's all about to happen. Not when we're about to become a part of America's history!"

Liam hadn't thought about it that way. He felt a little ashamed of himself. He leaned back against the doorjamb feeling the rain spattering against the wall and spraying his face. "I don't know about any of this anymore," Liam confessed.

She touched his face. "What don't you know?"

He couldn't meet her eyes and his voice dropped to a whisper. "It's just that sometimes I don't think that I can stand up to lifting iron rails day after day. I don't know if I can work as hard as they're askin' us to work. I get pains in my back and shoulders so bad I can't straighten up in the mornings. Right now my hands feel like raw meat and a pain is cutting through my shoulders that makes me want to scream."

"Why don't you tell your foreman that and then see if he can give you easier work?" Megan asked, hands going to his shoulders and fingers massaging muscle.

Liam groaned with relief. Megan's hands had always been able to work miracles, but they couldn't get him an easier job. "Everyone asks for easier work. Nobody gets it unless they're special. And I ain't special. None of us Irish are. We're treated like slaves! The Civil War is over and they freed the Negroes so now the Irish are takin' their places as white slaves."

Megan's sympathy died as quickly as it had been spawned. She spun her seventeen-year-old brother fully around and said angrily, "Don't be ridiculous! You're free to quit."

"And starve?"

Megan bit her lip. She took her brother's swollen, chilled hands. "Liam," she said, "you're still real young so you can't exactly see the whole picture yet. But I promise you that things are going to get better for all of us. You won't be lifting rails or ties all the way to California. Neither will Keith or Mr. Fox. An easier way will show itself for all of us soon."

Liam wasn't listening. "I tried everything I could think of to get friendly with the hunters and scouts," he whispered brokenly. "I even told the chief scout that Mr. Gilchrist ordered me to work as a scout."

"I heard about that. It was a big mistake. Why'd you go and tell such a lie? It got you nothing."

"I hurt all over," Liam moaned. "I'm afraid my back is going to break and each day seems like forever."

"It'll get better. You'll get stronger and tougher," Megan promised, desperately wanting to give her brother hope. "And if you work hard, sooner or later, something good will happen. I just know it!"

"O'Connell!" The foreman's voice punched through the driving rain to find them. "O'Connell, get out here!"

"I got to go back to the gang," Liam said, closing his eyes and opening and closing his hands. "I'll get fired if I don't get back now."

Megan grabbed her brother. "Would you *please* tell Mr. Gallagher to come home."

"I will if you don't throw him out again," Liam said. "He moved out last night after payday so I don't know where he is now, but I'll find him as soon as work is done and send him back to you."

"Thank you," Megan said. "You're a good brother."

Liam took heart. Megan had always been able to give him hope. "And you're a strong sister. And we're both going to have to help Aileen and the children if they're to make it all the way to California."

"I know." Megan looked up into her brother's face. "You're getting stronger, Liam. I can feel you are and not just physically. You're going to be a fine man."

"Thanks," he said, squaring his shoulders. "Now go back to the shanty and get dry before you catch your death of pneumonia."

"Goddammit, O'Connell!" the foreman yelled. "Get your ass out here right now!"

"Go!" Megan urged.

Liam had an almost uncontrollable urge just to quit. His legs felt like rubber and he was not sure that he could last out the rest of the shift in this cold rain. He had seen lots of "rust eaters" suddenly drop to their knees screaming with the agony of back pain. Some of them had to be carried off to the doctor. Few ever returned to hard labor. Liam did not know what they did to survive after injuring their spines and he did not want to find out. The idea of being bent or permanently crippled at his age was terrifying.

"Go on!" Megan pleaded. "We can't let them beat us, Liam!"

"Right," he muttered, realizing that he'd been giving in to Megan's indomitable will all of his life.

"Send Mr. Gallagher home tonight!" Megan shouted into the deluge as thunder rolled down the Missouri River.

Somehow, Liam finished his shift but it left him staggering with cold and fatigue. Hugh Fox looked at him when they were finally alone and said, "Are you all right?"

"I'll live."

"You don't look good," Fox said. "What's the matter?"

Liam coughed. "Let's go into town and find Keith," Liam said. "My sister is half sick fretting about him."

Fox barked a laugh of derision. "Hell, Megan is just worried about how she's going to get to California. She's just usin' Gallagher to—"

Fox did not finish his sentence because Liam spun, grabbed him by the throat, and slammed him up against the shed they'd been standing under. "God damn you!" Liam swore, cocking back his fist and shaking with fury. "Don't you *ever* speak about my sister like that again! Either one of them!"

Fox struggled but Liam's fist held him as solid as the iron they'd been lifting all day. "Let go of me! Have you gone crazy!"

Liam shook himself, then he released his brother-in-law.

"What the hell is the matter with you!" Fox choked.

"It's just that I want you to treat Aileen better," Liam said. "I don't want you to spend all your money in the saloons after payday anymore."

Fox bristled. "You stay the hell out of my marriage, Liam! Don't try to tell me how to treat my own wife."

"I *am* telling you," Liam said, challenging Fox with his eyes. "I'm telling you to take care of your wife and children. My sister and my niece and nephew."

Fox shoved Liam aside. "I say to hell with you!" he bellowed, marching off toward town.

Liam caught up with Fox and fell in step with him. They walked in angry silence to the Railhead Saloon. The other men coming off shift were two deep in front of the bar and while Fox angrily rifled his pockets for change, Liam squeezed his way to the bar and bought them two double whiskeys.

"Here," he said to his sullen brother-in-law. "I meant no offense a while ago. I just want you to treat Aileen and the children better. She's a good woman, but not so strong as Megan. You know that she needs a little more help."

"You stay the hell out of my marriage," Fox repeated in a sullen voice as he took the whiskey Liam offered.

"Just take care of 'em," Liam said, staring into his companion's eyes. "When I see Gallagher, I'm going to give him the same advice."

"And he'll tell you to go to hell same as me!"

Liam tossed his drink down. The whiskey burned like the muscles in his back and shoulders. The whiskey-heat fanned through him right to his swollen fingers. It put timbre in his voice and made him say, "If you break my sister's heart or her health, I'll kill you, Hugh. I just think you ought to understand that right now. I won't warn you again."

Hugh Fox dropped his forgotten shot glass. He started to say something mean and contemptuous but with Liam staring at him so hard, he picked up his empty glass and gave it back to Liam.

"Neither me nor Keith is likely to change much, so let's have a few more drinks, huh?"

"Sure," Liam said, realizing that Hugh was dead right. He took the glasses and squeezed his way back up to the bar thinking of how badly his sisters had both married. Of how much heartache they faced unless something dramatic and final occurred to keep their husbands from ruining their entire lives.

Liam and Fox drank in a strained silence for an hour and then, at Liam's insistence, they began moving from one saloon to another, searching for Gallagher and asking everyone who knew the man if he'd been around. It was almost ten o'clock when they found Bill Donovan drinking with some of his new freighting companions.

Liam didn't care for them much but he wanted to speak to Donovan so he bought the man a drink and said, "Have you seen Keith Gallagher tonight?"

"Yeah," Donovan said. "He was just in here an hour or so ago. Left with one of the girls. Ugly thing with red hair."

The muscles in Liam's cheeks tightened like drying rawhide. "He took a whore!"

"That's right," Donovan said with a smirk. "Way I hear it, your sister isn't giving it to him so he's looking for a new woman. Who can blame any man when his wife turns him out in the cold?"

It took everything Liam had not to start swinging on Donovan. It took the sure knowledge that the big brawler would beat him senseless even if Liam managed to get in a couple of early, solid punches. "What's the whore's name!"

Donovan shrugged. "Why don't you ask the bartender when you buy me another drink?"

Liam pushed away from the man. He went and asked the bartender who said, "Yeah, her name is Dora. She works here."

Liam snatched up a full bottle of whiskey, then slammed five whole dollars down on the bartop. Enough for the bottle and a generous tip for the bartender provided he had the next right answer. "Where else does she work?"

"Got a room two doors down at the Embassy Hotel. Upstairs. She'll be back in a while. Just wait and . . ."

But Liam didn't need to hear another word. He pivoted away and headed for the door.

"Hey," Fox shouted, snatching the bottle from Liam as he knocked men aside rushing outside, "what the hell is the hurry!"

Liam didn't bother to answer. He had a pocketknife in his jacket and he clenched it tight in his hand. He stomped through the rain and mud to the Embassy, then charged up the stairs yelling, "Which room is Dora's!"

"Second on the right!" the desk clerk shouted. "But you two can't just barge into her room when she's with a man!"

"Liam!" Fox shouted, hurrying to keep up. "Keith is gonna kill us for this!"

"If I don't kill him first," Liam whispered as he grabbed the door handle and twisted.

The door opened a half inch and then a latch chain rattled. "Come out of there, you sonofabitch!" Liam screamed.

"Go away!"

Liam threw his 185 pounds at the door twice before the latch broke, tearing nails from wood. The door crashed open and Liam spilled inside. A kerosene flame flickered in a cold, dirty room smelling of whiskey, vomit, sweat, and raw sex.

Keith Gallagher was in bed with the whore riding on top. There wasn't much left to the imagination. The woman cursed at Liam but he ignored her.

"Keith, goddamn you to hell!" Liam shouted, yanking the pocketknife from his jacket and fumbling to pull the blade out of its handle. "I'll kill you for doing this to my sister!"

Liam lunged at the bed but Gallagher must have hit him with something harder than his fist because Liam felt his legs buckle. He struck the floor with his chin and momentarily lost consciousness. When Liam awoke, Gallagher was dressed, the sun was up, and the whore was gone. Liam groaned and tried to push himself to his hands and his knees.

"What the hell was the matter with you last night!" Gallagher demanded, his words slurred and his eyes horribly bloodshot.

Liam shook his head. "What happened to my pocketknife?"

Gallagher's eyes narrowed. "You said you were going to kill me. You mean that?"

"No," Liam said.

"You shouldn't have gone crazy like that," Fox smirked, "Dora thought you was cute."

"Yeah, but we told her you was just a kid and we showed her we was real men, didn't we, Hugh?"

Hugh chuckled. "We could have showed you how to pleasure a woman, kid. But maybe next time. Thanks for the bottle."

Liam knew that he could not kill both these men, even if they were drunk. And if he could, this was not the time, or the place. "You're welcome," he said quietly, not knowing how or where these men would die, only that they would die and soon.

Liam managed to push himself up to his haunches. He felt as if his head were about to explode. When he reached back and touched his scalp he felt blood.

"You got any money left?" Gallagher pressed, licking his lips. "Hugh and I are busted."

"I got a few dollars."

"You look like you could use a drink," Fox said. "I think we all could."

"My sister wants you to come home," Liam forced himself to say as he climbed unsteadily to his feet.

Gallagher chuckled. "I don't need her no more. Dora says I can come back for free."

Liam took a deep breath and released it slowly. He shook his head and muttered, "If she ever found out you were sleeping with whores she'd be finished with you in a minute."

"She'll always love me," he said, giggling. "Some women are that way."

"Yeah," Liam hissed.

"You going to be the one to tell her about Dora?" Gallagher asked, struggling to look serious and not giggle.

Liam thought about that for a minute. "No," he said finally.

"I got myself fired from the Union Pacific today."

Liam no longer cared because Gallagher no longer mattered. "What for?"

"They were treating a couple of us like dogs." Gallagher belched. "We all quit."

"What the hell are you going to—"

A tremendous noise drowned out Liam's question and it expanded until it engulfed the room. Liam's head twisted toward the window. "It's the Missouri. It's finally cracking up!"

"About damned time," Fox said, just before he hiccuped.

Liam staggered over to the window and yanked it open. He stuck his head out into the rain and its cold pellets felt good on his cheeks and cleared his mind. Then he stared east toward the Missouri and the street leading down to the levee. He saw men piling out of the saloons and racing for the river. For a moment or two, Liam couldn't begin to imagine what would be important enough to tear men out of a saloon. But then, in addition to the cracking and breaking up of the river's ice, he heard another sound. It was coming from the north like a runaway train. The sound grew louder and louder as if the train were going to explode through the Embassy Hotel.

Liam spun around, ghost white. "It's flooding!" he cried. "The Missouri is taking out the levee and our shantytown!"

Gallagher and Fox didn't give a damn.

"Get up!" Liam screamed, grabbing them. "It's your wife and children down there!"

Liam shoved them out the door and followed them down the stairs, whipping them with curses. They staggered out into the rain and the quagmire of mud to join the throng rushing wildly to save their friends and families down along the low ground.

But with the river's roar building and the rain gusting in torrents, Liam had a sick feeling in his belly that they would all be too late. That nothing on earth could save his sisters from being swept away in an icy flood tide of deadly destruction.

CHAPTER

6

Glenn was swept up in the crowd's panic as he raced toward the Missouri River. When the land began to drop off steeply, Glenn skidded to a halt. He could see in a glance that the ice-swollen Missouri had already broken through a hundred-yard stretch of earthen embankment and was breaching the levee. The roiling brown water was gushing across the supply depot's tracks. An immense stack of railroad ties had collapsed under the force of the surging current and was being swept downriver. The power of the water was so great that it had toppled three supply cars laden with rails. The rails were bent like hairpins and their flatcars would have been torn and swept away if they had not been attached to a locomotive trying to drag them to higher ground.

The engineer was shouting at the firemen and giving his locomotive full throttle. The locomotive's big driving wheels were spinning in the rising water but gradually it pulled forward to safe ground while a crew of men shouted encouragement and stood ready to try to uncouple the overturned cars if the river came up too quickly.

Glenn had never seen or even imagined such destruction. Everywhere he looked, people were pulling one another from the torrent. Glenn saw thousands of precious railroad ties being washed downriver and there wasn't a thing in the world anyone could do to save them. Most would be carried all the way down to St. Louis and the Mississippi River.

It was the sight of the low-lying shantytown that really chilled Glenn's blood. The muddy, ice-gorged Missouri River had surged through the poor settlement and carried away at least half of the shanties. Glenn saw men, women, and children hanging on to flotsam of every description. Fortunately, most of the shantytown was swept along behind the breached embankment and spared from entering the mighty main current. Some people were able to scramble to higher ground, but others were already being spun past the levee and sucked into the main current. Some bodies floated facedown in the current, many victims clutched debris or even ice floes and yelled for help as they were borne south to an almost certain watery grave.

Glenn plunged into the predominantly Irish shantytown, tearing off his hat and jacket. He was not alone. Hundreds of men were risking their lives to reach those caught up in the flood waters. Glenn saw a mother and child just twenty yards out in the river, screaming for help and being borne away by the rampaging Missouri. He dove headlong into the icy current, swimming for all his might. The ice-clotted water numbed his body and robbed him of breath. Glenn slashed and pounded through the water to grab the woman by the hair.

She was wild with panic and crawled at him. "Hang on to your child!" Glenn shouted.

He began to pull the woman by the hair but it didn't seem that he was making any progress. His arms felt lifeless. He was sinking when two men tied to ropes reached out and grabbed him. It took a half-dozen more men to pull them from the river's deadly grip.

When he was hauled to safety, Glenn lay choking and spitting up water. He was shaking so violently he could not clench his teeth. He rolled over and saw that the woman was in even worse shape but that her child was already being wrapped in blankets and hustled toward town.

Glenn pushed himself to his feet just in time to see Joshua Hood and four of his scouts come galloping out of Omaha on their horses. People scrambled in the mud to get out of the way and Hood drove his sorrel into the river, his reata whirring overhead as he made a perfect cast out to save a woman who was hanging on to a floating washbasin.

The reata settled neatly over the woman's head and Glenn heard the scout yell, "Hang on, Mrs. Gallagher!"

Glenn held his breath as Megan released the tin washtub and latched on to the braided leather reata with both hands. Hood dallied his reata around his saddle horn, reined the sorrel around in belly-deep water, and spurred the animal back toward dry land with Megan sledding out of the dark, churning Missouri. The instant that Megan reached the shallows, she was plucked out of the river by eager hands.

Hood yelled, "Turn my reata loose!"

The reata was torn free and Hood coiled it with amazing quickness, then reined his horse around and went charging down the breached levee only to spur his horse into the water again and make another cast toward a drowning figure. Hood's four other horsemen were doing the same thing and the most distant was already a half mile downriver pulling victims from its clutches.

"Would you just look at them!" a man shouted, his voice filled with awe. "Look at them rough sonsabitches rope and ride!"

Dozens of men cheered and began to slog and buck through the mud and water following the horsemen south as they kept spurring their horses into the river and dragging people to the shore. Glenn tried to run after them but he was so chilled that his legs wouldn't work and he kept falling down. He was covered with mud and had no strength. He was almost run over by a team of galloping horses pulling a freight wagon loaded with men and ropes.

"Ya!" the driver shouted as his wagon slewed through the mud an instant before Glenn crawled out of its path. "Ya!"

After the wagon shot past, Glenn realized that the driver was none other than Bill Donovan. The big Irishman chased the horsemen south and whenever a victim was dragged out of the river, he was hauled into the wagon. At the bend in the river, the wagon pulled up at the water's edge and Glenn saw Donovan grab a rope, tie it to his belt, and then dive into the current to rescue a man who was apparently going down for the last time.

"Come on, Mr. Gilchrist!" a man shouted, helping Glenn to his feet. "The river is still coming up! We got to get you and everyone else up on high ground!"

Glenn didn't argue the point. He wished that he could help more people but he was shaking so violently from the cold that it was all he could do to be helped through the mud and rising water back up to the high ground. All around him, people were dragging and carrying people to safety. It was a nightmare and Glenn found himself looking for Megan Gallagher and wondering if her sister and the two children had been spared from this tragedy. The rain was coming down in sheets and a huge bolt of lightning struck a big cottonwood tree just north of the levee and it exploded in flame like a pitch torch. Burning branches sizzled and smoked. Two bloated mules with death grins and protruding long white tongues bobbed and spun downriver racing neck and neck faster than they'd ever been able to run.

Liam O'Connell had sprinted out of town determined to save his sisters. He made certain that Fox and Gallagher remained close at his side and did not try to sneak off in the confusion and cage free drinks from some unattended Omaha saloon. Together, all three had left the town's higher ground and waded into the icy water. There were so many people both in and out of the river and the rain was so heavy that it was impossible to find or recognize anyone.

"Megan!" Liam shouted.

Gallagher and Fox also began to shout for their wives and families.

"Help!"

The three of them saw a woman-child clutching a railroad tie and an infant as they churned past. "Let's get them!" Liam shouted.

"But we can barely swim!" Gallagher protested.

Liam propelled his brother-in-law into the swift current. "I'm not much of a swimmer either, but we've *got* to try! We'll be heroes! Maybe even be given better jobs. Now come on!"

"But what about *my* wife and children!" Fox cried, wading out to his chest and then yelping in fear as the current threatened to lift him off his feet.

"They're either gone or probably safe up on high ground!" Liam tore off his coat and kicked off his boots. "Now come on! I can't save that woman and child alone!"

Gallagher and Fox looked at each other and then followed Liam into the river, wading out as deep as they could before the current bowled them over.

Liam had lied. Actually, he was a very strong swimmer and he was sure that he could reach the woman and her child, then hold them up until either the horsemen or the freighters downriver could figure a way to reach them. Even if that failed, he was certain that if he could endure the numbing cold long enough, an opportunity would present itself to reach the riverbank. As for Fox and Gallagher, well, luck or the Lord had shown Liam a way to save his poor sisters because even as he watched, the Missouri plucked his brothers-in-law up and sent them spinning downriver. The river was incredibly powerful. Dark and swirling, clogged with trees and limbs and ice all churning up a hellish stew.

"Liam, help!" Gallagher shouted as the current spun him south.

Liam dog-paddled and twisted around to see both men begin to beat the water in terror. They had panicked and tried to reverse direction and return to the shore but the current already had them much too firmly in its grasp. Now they were thrashing like wild things, eyes bugging with horror.

"Liam!" Fox screamed as he went under. With a detached fascination, Liam watched his brother-in-law's hand disappear twice before it didn't reappear. Gallagher was a stronger swimmer and he might actually have escaped except that one of the heavy burnetized railroad ties slammed into the back of his skull and drove over his body. If Gallagher had seen it coming, it might have been his salvation but it pounded him down in a cloud of swirling bubbles.

They were gone. One moment screaming and thrashing, calling Liam's name, and then . . . then nothing but muddy ice, boiling, treacherous water, and an undercurrent that threatened to swallow Liam up as well.

A noose of fear choked Liam and he very nearly lost his rational mind. And maybe he would have except that the woman clinging to her baby and the railroad tie was shrieking for help. Liam stopped dog-paddling, resisted an almost overpowering urge to swim for shore, and began to stroke hard toward the woman. He jammed and perhaps even broke his fingers against the tie before he realized he had reached her, and then he grabbed the railroad tie and hauled himself over it, shivering so violently that his teeth rattled like dice in a cup. When he looked up at the woman, he saw that she was more girl than woman, possibly only fourteen or fifteen years old and deathly afraid. She had an upper arm hooked over the tie and held her baby tight in her other arm. Her face was less than a foot from his own and the baby she clutched and tried to keep above water was obviously dead. Its mouth hung open fishlike and its flesh was bluish-gray.

"Are we going to die?" she shouted.

Liam clenched his teeth together to stop them from rattling. "No!" he choked. "We're not going to die."

The woman sobbed. She floated her thin body up against Liam's and laid her cheek on his arm. "I couldn't make it without you being here, mister! But I still think we're going to die!"

Liam stared ahead toward the first big bend in the Missouri. Every passing second carried them farther out into the middle of the river where the current was far more powerful. Once in the main current, there was no escape. Liam forced himself to think. He wondered if they could force their heavy railroad tie over to water shallow enough to get within range of the horsemen who were swimming their mounts out into the river and casting their ropes.

Maybe. Maybe if they really tried. In a few words, Liam told the woman what they had to do if they were to have any chance at all.

"But my baby! I can't . . ."

"It's dead!" Liam shouted over the roar of the river. "The baby is already dead! We got to save ourselves now! Let go of it!"

The woman's face went slack with shock. "No!"

Liam cursed and kicked at the water with all of his might, trying to drive the tie in toward shore or at least keep it from drifting deeper into the Missouri. The railroad tie floated only a few sluggish feet in the water. Liam saw Joshua Hood spurring his horse into the current and trying to intercept them before they could be swept around the bend and beyond any hope of rescue. Suddenly, Hood's sorrel was knocked over by a huge limb. Hood grabbed his horse's tail. The sorrel rolled completely over and for a moment, all that could be seen of the animal was its four legs waving like reeds. But a moment later, the sorrel righted itself and Hood somehow pulled himself back to the saddle. His reata, however, was hopelessly tangled around the sorrel. Two other scouts cast their ropes to Hood and he looped their nooses around his saddlehorn. A moment later, Hood and his struggling mount were dragged to shore. By then, Liam, the woman, and her dead baby were shooting around the bend and heading downriver with no rescuers in sight.

Liam could feel his strength bleeding into the icy torrent. He could barely think. "Hang on!" he shouted. "There's got to be another bend where we might be able to reach the shore!"

The woman nodded but there was neither hope nor under-standing in her eyes. Liam kept kicking at the water, trying to drive their railroad tie in closer to the Nebraska shoreline. It seemed like an eternity before the next large bend in the river suddenly loomed up just ahead. But when it did, Liam felt a surge of fresh inspiration because he saw a half-dozen other people who'd managed to rescue themselves.

"Kick and paddle!" Liam shouted as they were propelled down the river toward the bend. "Come on! Help me!"

When the young woman did nothing except clutch her dead baby and make feeble kicking motions, Liam yelled, "If you don't help, we're both going to drown!"

The woman either didn't understand or didn't care. In a rage, Liam thrust himself away from her and the railroad tie. If the foolish girl didn't want to live, that was her decision, he was going to take this last chance to save his own life.

Her cry was a lance that pierced Liam's heart. Over and over, with each stroke, he heard her terrible cry and after ten strokes, Liam gave up and allowed the current to reel him back out to her.

"Can you swim?" he bellowed in a voice loud enough to be heard over the river.

She just stared with incomprehension. Liam reached for her baby and she went crazy and tried to bite his arm. Liam drew back his fist and punched her in the side of the head with all his flagging strength. She slumped and began to slide off the railroad tie. The dead baby floated from her grasp and went bobbing away on the current. Liam grabbed the woman around the neck and twisted her onto her back. Then, with one arm, he began a side-crawl toward the bend in the river. He could sense rather than see or hear people shouting encouragement. Closing his eyes, he pulled with all his might, his feet kicking both the water and the unconscious woman. His breath came in tearing gasps and he felt the fiery touch of Satan. An ice floe struck and rolled him and the woman underwater. He screamed in silent terror and kicked the mud of the river bottom. Shooting back upward, he clawed his way back to the surface with the woman hanging on to his back like a leech.

He kept reaching out, pulling the icy water toward and under him, kicking and gasping and cursing until a hand clamped onto his wrist and he was dragged out of the Missouri with the woman still hooked in his left arm.

The next few minutes were lost to memory. It was only when Joshua Hood forced a pint bottle of whiskey between his teeth that Liam began to choke and then retch, bringing up muddy water.

"The woman," Liam chattered.

"She's alive," Hood said. "Try another gulp, O'Connell."

He did and this one stayed down. He heard Hood say, "I got my reata on your youngest sister and she's all right. The older one made it to high ground with her children."

Liam choked at the sudden vision of both of his brothers-in-law going down for the last time, their horror-stricken and accusing expressions branding his soul.

"I killed 'em," he gasped.

"No you didn't," Joshua Hood said, "you saved the woman and the baby was already dead. As soon as it came out of her arms, it floated facedown."

"But . . ."

Hood's voice gentled. "O'Connell, I tell you, the baby was already dead."

Liam wanted to explain that he was talking about Keith Gallagher and Hugh Fox. But the explanation wouldn't come. Maybe it would someday—a babbling deathbed confession to shock a weary old priest, perhaps—but not now.

Bill Donovan knelt beside Liam and instead of a pint bottle of whiskey, he had a quart bottle and he pinched Liam's cheeks and poured it down his gullet.

"You're a goddamn hero, Liam!" Donovan shouted. "We're all a bunch of goddamn heroes!"

Liam swallowed the cheap whiskey as fast as he could until he began to choke. He stared at Donovan and then at Joshua Hood and he was sure he heard the latter say, "I'll give you a try, Liam. I can always use a greenhorn with guts."

Liam stared up at the pelting rain with gratitude, overwhelmed with gratitude that Donovan and Hood could not tell that he was crying.

CHAPTER
7

The storm rumbled and grumbled south leaving in its wake eight hundred miles of flooding and destruction along the Missouri River. Glenn spent the next week working from sunup to midnight trying to collect and transfer to high ground all the railroad ties, rails, and supplies that could be salvaged.

It was a tough job. The force of the Missouri had been so great that it had swept most of the quarter-ton rails away like metal matchsticks. And as the river began to recede from its high point, you could begin to see them poking out of the water bent and tangled as fish hooks. What could be saved was saved at great risk to men who were ordered onto the water on flatboats.

Bill Donovan and other freighters were sent rushing south to collect whatever ties the river had tossed along its litter-strewn shore. In some places, ties meshed into giant, beaverlike dams as they were interwoven with driftwood, tents, and other debris washed out of shantytown. In other instances, the ties were pitched high up on the riverbanks or buried deep in muck. It was slow going to retrieve those rails but each was precious, especially those burnetized or imported from distant hardwood forests up by the Great Lakes or in the South.

Glenn's main concern was that of the workers and their suffering families. In the first hours after the flood had washed out the shantytown, anyone who had survived had just been thankful for life. But later gratitude turned to resentment. How could the Union Pacific management *not* have foreseen this disaster? Why weren't provisions made for the army of workers and the families so that they were spared this tragedy?

Durant had just left for Washington a few days before the flood and was unaccountable to the devastated families. General

Grenville Dodge, with his mind still fixed on eliminating the
Indian problems, had not yet resigned his Army commission and
so it was left to the Casement brothers and Glenn to appease the
Union Pacific's tragic survivors.

"You take their complaints," General Jack Casement said,
"and write them down and apologize like hell."

"Apologies won't put food on their tables or bring back their
lost ones," Glenn said.

"Of course it won't!" Casement snapped in one of his rare
bursts of anger and frustration. "But what else can we do?"

"They want money. They want to be paid for their losses."

"We're out of money," Dan Casement reminded them both.
"If we'd had enough money in the first place, we would have
moved all our supplies to higher ground much earlier and perhaps even had this line under way. If that had been the case, I
doubt anyone would have lost their lives or possessions."

"I know," Glenn said. "And I've reminded people that they
were warned on several occasions not to build that shantytown
along the river. There was plenty of land west of Omaha."

"Up on top and out in the wind?" Dan asked. "And I suppose
that The Doctor absolves himself of all responsibility?"

"Of course," Glenn said. "His orders are that we should
give preference to hiring men who lost their families. We're
also to offer widows and their children free transportation back
home."

"And feed them in the meantime," Casement said.

"I wasn't ordered to do that," Glenn admitted, "but we are."

"And we shall continue to do so," Jack said. "This is not
only a human tragedy but also an unmitigated public relations
disaster. I can hardly wait until the newspaper reporters find a
way to cross the Missouri and besiege us with their accusing
questions."

"That might be weeks yet," Glenn said. "The river is still at
flood stage all the way down to St. Louis."

"That won't stop them," Dan said. "Bad news attracts pub-
licity like crumbs attract cockroaches."

Jack nodded. "You're right, Dan. The best thing we can do
now is to try and get this railroad rolling west so that when
the trouble-mongers surge across the river, we can attempt to
divert their attention from this disaster and focus it instead on
the building of the railroad. Unfortunately, we have to wait until

the damned roadbed dries out. Otherwise, the ties will sink as if placed on a bed of quicksand."

"How is the roadbed to Papillion holding up?" Glenn asked.

"We've got some washouts," Jack admitted. "I'd say there's two weeks' worth of fix and repair. Some of the lower sections of roadbed were washed out underneath and they collapsed. The Union Pacific couldn't even deliver a hand-pump car to Papillion right now."

Glenn nodded. "I'd enjoy getting away from here and . . ."

"Oh, no!" Casement exclaimed. "I'm the one who's going to be getting out of here. I have no intentions of facing these people for mistakes that were made before me or my brother signed on."

"They were made against my recommendations," Glenn said tightly. "I was . . ."

Casement held up his hand. "Easy, Glenn. No one is pointing fingers at anyone else—at least not until the reporters descend on Omaha. When they do, we'll just try to steer them toward reporting on the progress we intend to make this spring. And if they aren't satisfied with that, then we refer them to Dr. Durant. Eh?"

Glenn relaxed. "Excellent idea."

"So just do your best." The general pulled out his wallet and extracted a thick sheaf of bills that he laid on the table before Glenn.

"What's this for?"

"Widows and children."

"I want to contribute too," Glenn said, extracting his own wallet and adding to the pile.

"Me too," Dan said, dropping at least a hundred dollars on the stack of greenbacks. "And I'll see if I can pass the hat around among some of our single men who have the good sense to save a little money."

Glenn took the money, but not without serious reservations. "I'm really unqualified to determine who should receive what and how much."

"Nonsense!" Casement exclaimed, clapping Glenn on the shoulder. "Someone has to do it. Why not you?"

Glenn did not have a ready answer. Besides, he was grateful that the Casement brothers understood that the displaced people of the shantytown needed immediate help in the form of food, shelter, and blankets. They needed to be told that they would be compensated for their suffering as best as possible by the Union Pacific.

Dan winked. "You're doing a fine job, Glenn, but I'll take over the duties of transferring whatever else can be salvaged. You set up a tent and distribute this money and take names of families that request transportation back to the East. You'll also need to keep track of whatever bodies are found—if recognizable."

"Sure," Glenn said.

Jack turned to leave. "This will all be behind us by the time General Dodge arrives in May. At that point, I'm sure that he will be wanting to transfer you to the front of the line. Maybe even out with the surveyors."

Glenn blinked. The surveying parties were preparing to leave very soon. They'd be foraging many miles ahead of the railroad itself. It would be very dangerous but also critically important work.

"What about it?" Jack asked. "Would the job of chief survey engineer suit you, or would you feel more comfortable remaining with the track-laying operation once we start to roll?"

"I need to think about that," Glenn said, knowing full well that his former title of construction engineer was superfluous now that the Casement brothers were in charge. "I'd like the excitement of going out in front, but . . ."

"What is it, the Sioux and the Cheyenne?"

"Partly," Glenn admitted. "Like everyone else, I've heard the stories of what they do to white men before they kill them. But I'm more than willing to take my chances up front."

"Then why the hesitation?" Dan asked.

Glenn felt a little uncomfortable with his next statement. "I've gotten attached to a lot of the crew and I feel as if I have a good deal to contribute here before I lead a survey party."

"Well said," Jack responded. "Why don't we just wait until General Dodge arrives and then see what transpires? He might banish us *all*."

Glenn smiled because he knew that General Dodge had specifically requested that the Casement brothers be in charge of track laying and construction procurement.

"You're doing fine work," Jack said as he and his brother left.

"Thanks," Glenn said after they were gone, "but handing out cash and sympathy hasn't a damn thing to do with being an engineer."

Glenn managed to acquire a tent, rug, table, and three chairs by the following morning. Acting on word of mouth alone, the survivors of the shantytown began to line up in front of the tent by nine o'clock that morning. Glenn's first meeting was with a man, his wife, and a child. They were ragged and dirty and the man had one arm in a filthy sling.

"Your names?"

"Peter Ryan," the man replied sullenly. "My wife Lucy and that there boy is named Bill."

"What can I do for you folks?"

"You can help us!" The man lowered his voice and leaned over the table. "I've a broken arm, Mr. Gilchrist. A broken arm from trying to pluck railroad ties from the river. And now, me foreman tells me I have to lift rails or lose me job?"

The Irishman arched his eyebrows and the flesh around his eyes grew pale with anger. "And me with a wife and child to support?"

"Now we be askin' ya, Mr. Gilchrist," the man's heavyset wife said, clutching her frightened-looking boy, "how kin me man lift rails with a broken arm? And him in severe pain day and night?"

Glenn came out of his chair and moved around to stand beside Ryan. "Let me see the arm."

Ryan groaned as he slipped it out of the sling. Glenn had been warned to be on guard against liars and cheats, but Ryan wasn't faking. Pain was deeply etched into every line of his face and when Glenn saw the hugely swollen arm, he felt a rush of guilt for harboring any suspicions.

"Here," he said, "there's twenty dollars for you and your family."

The man stared at the money as if he could not believe his good fortune. Lucy Ryan snatched it from Glenn's hand. "Twenty dollars," she whispered.

"No whiskey or strong spirits now," Glenn warned the injured man. "If you spend it on drink, I'll hear of it and you'll never work for this railroad. The money is for food and necessities."

"Whiskey is a necessity," Ryan said with a soft smile playing at the corners of his mouth. "As a fellow Mick, Mr. Gilchrist, I guess you can appreciate that fact."

"I can," Glenn said. "But this money is for food and a doctor. There's two good ones in town, I'll expect you to see one and then return tomorrow with a written doctor's report."

"And if the doctor says it'll be months before me man kin lift railroad ties?" the wife asked.

"Then we'll find you an easier job," Glenn promised.

"Then it'll be months," Ryan predicted.

"Come back tomorrow with that doctor's report," Glenn ordered.

"Can I tell the others how much money we got?" Lucy Ryan asked.

Glenn knew that whatever he said, the woman would tell anyway. "Sure," he said. "But unless they've broken bones, they won't come close to getting the same."

"There's some that have lost children," the woman said. "They can still work, but they lost children."

"We're very sorry about that," Glenn told her. "But you were all warned not to live down on the low river bottom."

"Aye," the man said. "But down low is where you must be to keep out of the hard, blowin' wind. And you know how bitter cold it was this winter, Mr. Gilchrist. Or maybe you wouldn't know, you bein' a gentleman and staying in a hotel."

"Keep me informed as to how soon you can go back to work," Glenn said. He looked past this family to the growing line that already stretched out from his tent. "Next!"

"Sir," a strapping young man said as he removed his cap.

Glenn eyed the man closely. He was about Glenn's own age, tough-looking with bold brown eyes. Glenn remembered his name was Brian Dunleavy. "What can I do for you?"

"Well, sir," the man said, "I'm the fireman that was on that engine that pulled the flatcars out of the risin' river."

Glenn waited for Dunleavy to continue. When he did not, Glenn said, "And?"

Dunleavy pushed out his chest. "Well, sir, the others that helped save your flatcars have asked me to speak in their behalf seeing as how I can read and write."

"Then speak out plainly," Glenn demanded.

Dunleavy strangled his cap. "Well, we think that since we risked our lives, we ought to be compensated by the Union Pacific. We ought to be paid right handsomely, Mr. Gilchrist."

Glenn blinked with surprise, then he popped to his feet and extended his hand and grinned broadly. "Your reward is the Union Pacific's thanks for doing your job."

It was Dunleavy's turn to blink. He looked down with surprise when Glenn snatched his hand and pumped it saying, "Congratulations! Tell your friends that the Union Pacific is very, very proud of all its brave employees who loyally served them during that recent emergency."

"But . . ."

"And because of your collective heroism, you'll all still have jobs and this railroad will have the money to meet the next payroll." Glenn smiled broadly. "So you see, Mr. Dunleavy, you've done a great service for everyone."

Glenn extracted his hand and used it to turn Dunleavy around and gently shove him out of the tent. "Next!"

The next few hours were hectic and filled with tragic stories. More than once, Glenn was called upon to comfort a grieving widow. One poor woman had lost both her husband and child in the flood and Glenn promised her free transportation from Omaha to New York the minute the Missouri River was passable.

Near the end of the day, a very heavy woman with one droopy eyelid and the most unappealing mole on the tip of her nose arrived with a dark-haired, pixielike girl of about fourteen or fifteen. The woman announced, "My husband and I want to do what's right by this orphan girl. She's got no home to go back to. No family to see to her needs. She hails from West Virginia."

The girl would not lift her head to meet Glenn's eyes. "What's her name?"

"Miss Isabelle King," the fat woman said, shifting her great bulk uneasily in the chair. "Her mother called her Belle."

"Miss King," Glenn said, bending over, "isn't there anyone that you could contact back in West Virginia?"

The girl met Glenn's questioning gaze. She had the largest brown eyes he'd ever seen and was very pretty with a heart-shaped face. Belle's dress was dirty and too small. It could not hide the fact that she was a fully developed young woman.

"I have no one," the girl said quietly.

Glenn turned to the obese woman. He had to force himself not to stare at her nose and wonder if doctors couldn't excise such an unsightly blemish. "Can she live with you until we can make permanent arrangements?"

The woman wagged her chins. "Oh, no! My husband says this railroad life is cursed and we're leaving for Memphis in the morning. I'm afraid to leave her with just anybody. Belle is almost a woman and there are some terrible men in this town that'd take advantage."

"I understand," Glenn said, unsure what to do about Miss Belle King.

"My man says that the Union Pacific got us all into this mess and it's your responsibility to make things right. He's sorry he ever heard of the Union Pacific or this miserable Nebraska town."

Glenn could see that the woman wasn't going to change her mind and that the girl was now his responsibility. He hadn't a clue as to what to do with Belle King, but he'd figure out something before evening.

"Thanks for bringing her to us. And good luck on the way to Memphis."

"We lost everything," the woman said bitterly. "We've nothing except the clothes on our backs and I think you ought to help us too."

"Here," Glenn said, digging money out of his pants. "Twenty dollars is the best that we can do for now. If you were staying, then maybe we could . . ."

"We're leaving at sunrise," the woman flatly declared. "My man said we can follow the river however far it takes to catch a ferry across. Might be we'll also find a few of our belongings and those of others something worth selling. I'm afraid we'll just find bodies."

Glenn said, "Belle, just sit here and rest. And don't worry, you'll be well taken care of."

Glenn escorted the woman outside. "I'm sorry your husband is so set on leaving. I think the worst is behind us now."

"Ha! The Sioux Indians will scalp half of you and the other half will freeze to death. I say the Lord sent this flood as a warning for us to quit the Union Pacific because it's cursed."

"You're wrong," Glenn said with exasperation. "But I wish you and your husband well."

The woman started to say something and it would not have been nice. But something made her change her mind and she wheeled around and waddled away. Glenn dismissed the rest of the people waiting to see him with a promise that he'd be back early tomorrow morning. He heard them grumbling as he went back inside the tent.

"I don't think the railroad is hexed," Belle said. "Maybe we are, but not the railroad."

Glenn sighed. "We're not cursed or even jinxed, Belle. And I wish that I could tell you how sorry I am about your parents. The Union Pacific can never hope to make things right. But I promise that we're not going to abandon you."

"What am I going to do now? I don't know a soul here. We only arrived the day before the flood. My poor mother and father! I loved them so."

"I'll find you a safe place and you'll be well taken care of until we can sort things out. Once things settle down, we'll talk about what you want and what can be done."

"I don't have any money, no family, nothing."

"The Union Pacific will help you," Glenn promised. "We'll do everything in our power to make amends for the loss of your dear mother and father."

The girl squeezed her eyes shut and tears ran down her pretty face. It wrenched Glenn's heart to see her grief. "I'm so sorry," he heard himself whisper.

"It's not your fault. We should never have come west. I was born in West Virginia but we most recently lived in Chattanooga, Tennessee. The Yankees ruined everything. That's why we left to come here. We thought that it was a chance for a fresh start."

"It should have been," Glenn told her. "But sometimes, misfortunes dog us. If we can just last through them, though, things usually get better."

"Are they better for you now?"

"I didn't say they were bad before."

"You didn't have to. I read a sadness in your eyes. You dress nice and you must be important, but you're not all that happy inside, are you?"

"Everyone has sorrows," Glenn admitted. "I lost two brothers in the war. My father, a highly successful industrialist and a pillar of his community, drank himself to death over them and my mother lost her mind. I finally had her committed to a sanitorium. She doesn't even know me anymore. The doctors assure me that she will never recognize me again."

Glenn swallowed painfully. "But we're not here to talk about my problems, are we?"

"No," Belle said. "You are tall and strong and handsome. You did fine, no matter what happened to your family."

"And you'll do fine too," Glenn promised.

The girl took his hands. "I believe you want to help, but does the Union Pacific?"

"Yes, of course. We'll give you a little time to think," Glenn said, choosing his words with care. "Maybe in a few days, or weeks, you'll have a better idea of what you want."

"Will you be here when I do?"

"I don't know," Glenn confessed. "The weather is turning warm and the railroad will be getting under way soon. I guess a big part of what happens to me will depend on General Dodge."

"I hope that he asks you to stay in Omaha," Belle said, brushing back her matted hair. "Mister?"

"Yes?"

"Any chance I can get a new dress and a bath?"

Glenn relaxed. This he *could* handle. "You bet. I'll just have to try to think of someone that I can put you up with."

Megan Gallagher pushed the canvas tarp aside and entered the tent. "Belle!" she exclaimed, hurrying over to comfort her. "I heard about your parents. I'm sorry."

Belle hugged Megan tightly. "Everyone said that you and your sister were saved. But when I didn't see you . . ."

"We found a room in town," Megan explained. "It's small, cramped, and drafty, but it's high and dry. Do you want to stay with us?"

"Are you sure? I heard you lost your husbands and everything!"

"We all need time for healing, Belle."

Megan looked up at Glenn. "With no small amount of persuasion, I convinced our hotel that the Union Pacific would pay everything—including meals, Mr. Gilchrist."

"Good."

Megan stood up. Her face was thinner than Glenn had remembered. There were dark circles around her eyes and she looked tired, troubled, but extremely resolute. "We'll need to talk, Mr. Gilchrist. The Union Pacific must be generous in its amends."

"We'll pay all your expenses until you return to Boston."

"Oh, will you now?'" Megan said, ice thickening in her voice. "Let me remind you that I have nothing and even worse, Aileen is a widow with two fatherless children! And if you think we'll settle for a few meals and a one-way ticket back to Boston, you're badly mistaken."

"Then we'll try to do more," Glenn said. "I can't promise anything, but we'll try."

"You'll have to do much more than try, Mr. Gilchrist. Much, much more."

Before Glenn could say anything, Megan took Belle's hand and led her to the front of the tent, then turned to look at Glenn. "Do you have any *real* authority, Mr. Gilchrist?"

"Some." He was offended even as he realized the question was painful but fair.

"Then we need to talk first thing tomorrow morning about Aileen, her children, and Belle."

"Of course," Glenn said in agreement as the Irish beauty led Belle outside and up the muddy street toward the center of Omaha.

Glenn went back to his chair and slumped down heavily. He'd already given all but a few dollars of the pooled money away and there had been dozens more people waiting in line when he'd told them to return in the morning.

What would he do then? What could he promise these poor families when the Union Pacific could not even meet its next payroll? What would become of the widows and the fatherless children?

Glenn closed his eyes and massaged his temples with his thumbs. And what did any of this have to do with engineering? The answer was nothing. He was a man completely unqualified to deal with this tragedy.

How had Belle plumbed the dark secrets of his own sad past? Glenn had always prided himself in being able to put up a good front. Never before had that front shown a crack wide enough for anyone to glimpse into his painful past.

Glenn sighed. This day had been the most difficult of his life. Far, far worse than dealing with the physical destruction

of the flood. He pushed himself to his feet absently thinking of
a saloon with a dark, quiet corner. But then he recalled that he
had given all of his money to the flood's survivors. And who
the hell knew when another Union Pacific payday would arrive
again? Glenn batted the canvas tent flap aside and stalked away
toward the Missouri River. Maybe a long twilight walk would
help to soothe his troubled soul.

CHAPTER
8

Megan sat on the floor below her sister. Through their grimy second-story hotel window, she could see that the sun was going to come up warm and bright and that this would be another lovely day. Aileen's children were asleep and Belle was staring up at the fly-specked ceiling.

Megan took her sister's hand. "Aileen, are you sure that you won't come with me this morning? I'm sure it would help with Mr. Gilchrist."

"I can't," she said, covers pulled up to her chin and eyes squeezed shut. "I've the kids to watch."

"Belle said she'd watch over them while we're gone."

"And I've no clean dress to wear."

Megan curbed her growing impatience. "You can borrow a clean dress just like I have."

"I wouldn't know what to say to the man."

"Then *I'll* do all the talking."

"I'd just cry," Aileen said, lost in her own dark despair. "And I look so terrible he'd be embarrassed and take pity on us both."

"Pity would be good," Megan said. "As long as it's backed up with hard cash."

When Aileen said nothing, Megan sighed. She *had* to make her sister understand. "Aileen, this is not a game we're going to play with the Union Pacific. They've only been offering a pittance to widows like us. A pittance and a ticket back home. We must do better than that for your children, if not ourselves."

Aileen's eyes snapped open at her sister. "There's nothing that will bring Hugh back to me. Nothing that can replace his love and devotion."

Megan ground her teeth in silence. A gossipy "friend" had been only too happy to tell her about the prostitute that their husbands had used in the Embassy Hotel the night before they drowned. Megan had made the person swear that Aileen was never to learn of that sad and painful infidelity. She needed to think that Mr. Fox had been faithful and in love with her to the very end. Aileen had never been able to admit to her husband's weakness for whiskey and other women, and there was no reason to change her mind after his death.

"Aileen, if Mr. Gilchrist doesn't think that it's worth your time to come to petition his railroad for justice, then it will hurt our chances of getting any real money. And we *need* money! For a new start. For the children's sake."

Taking her hand, Aileen said, "You tell Mr. Gilchrist that my poor Hugh was a fine man. That he died trying to save a woman and her baby, just like your husband. They died heroes, Megan. No matter what else our men done, they were heroes."

"Yes," Megan said, realizing that Aileen was right, "they were heroes. And believe me, I'll remind Mr. Gilchrist of that. But it would help if you were there too."

"No." Aileen shook her head. "Please don't ask me anymore."

"All right," Megan said, accepting that Aileen was not going to come along. "I'll go myself. But I'd like to take Jenny and David."

Aileen paled. "But why!"

"Aileen, I could talk myself blue in the face but it wouldn't have the same effect as seeing little David and Jenny."

Aileen sat up quickly. She grabbed Megan's arms and cried, "Megan, no!"

"But why?"

"Haven't they been through enough already! Don't you see what this could do to them?"

"Yes, it could *help* them," Megan said angrily. "Staying cooped up in this miserable little room isn't doing them any good!"

"Please!" Aileen begged. "Don't take them."

"I don't understand this," Megan said with complete exasperation. "We're fighting for our very existence. What are we supposed to do if the railroad isn't willing to help us? Mend clothes or remain in Omaha and hope we can find work, perhaps as maids to some railroad official. Or could I work in a saloon and . . ."

"Megan, stop it!"

Jenny awoke and began to cry. Megan felt awful. She went over to the child and picked her up, then rocked her until Jenny quieted.

"Give her to me," Aileen said, reaching for her daughter.

Megan gave the child to Aileen, then she went over to the cracked mirror hanging on their board wall. She brushed her hair until her anger subsided, then grabbed a shawl draped over a chair. "I'll be going now."

Belle sat up. "Megan, would it help if I went along with you? Mr. Gilchrist seemed to like me. Maybe I can . . ."

"No," Megan said, "you stay here with Aileen and the children. I doubt that what I have to say to Mr. Gilchrist and his railroad will take long. It's afterward I'm worried about."

"He'll help you if he can," Belle said. "I'm sure that he wants to."

"Of course he does," Megan said. "After all, it isn't his money that we're after."

Belle got up from her pallet and stretched. "I don't think the Union Pacific has any money."

"What makes you say that?"

"I don't know," Belle replied. "Because you can just see how worried Mr. Gilchrist looks."

"The railroad has money," Megan said, "it's just that they don't want to spend any more of it than necessary so they can fill their own pockets with the profits from Congress. I've heard it said that Thomas Durant is as rich as a king and I don't doubt that for a moment. He has this great palace car that is never used except when he comes to town. And each night our friends sleep in the mud."

Megan couldn't mask the resentment she felt. She left the tiny hotel room calling back, "If he was here, I'd give him a piece of my mind!"

From the moment he awoke, Glenn dreaded the day and the idea of facing not only Megan Gallagher, but dozens more only slightly less embittered by their fates. The night before, he'd hunted up General Casement and explained that he'd already given out all the cash.

"Then give 'em credit vouchers," Jack had instructed. "That's what I did when the Union Army couldn't meet its payroll."

"Good idea," Glenn had replied.

Now, as this morning wore on, Glenn signed credit vouchers that might or might not be redeemable by the Union Pacific Railroad. Megan Gallagher wasn't the first in line that morning but Glenn quickly recognized her voice and she was definitely stirring up the people and telling them that it was only fair that they be fully compensated for their losses.

"Mrs. Gallagher," Glenn called, "I'll see you right now."

Megan looked surprised. "I'll wait my turn in line, Mr. Gilchrist. Just like everyone else."

"That won't be necessary."

"Oh, but it will!" Megan smiled. "And besides, I'm curious to know what you're offering today."

Glenn didn't see how he could do anything but take the next family in line. A few minutes later, he heard them tell how they'd lost a horse, their tent, and everything they owned, but no family.

"I'm afraid that I haven't any cash right now," Glenn admitted. "But I'm going to give you this voucher for credit."

"For credit, sir?" the man asked, looking anything but pleased.

"Yes," Glenn replied, hurrying to explain. "It says that the Union Pacific Railroad will award you damages of . . . oh, let's say a hundred dollars for your horse and other belongings."

"It was a good horse! And my wife had real China dishes. There was a rifle and . . ."

"Is a hundred fifty dollars fair?"

The couple looked at each other. The woman nodded and then the man.

"All right then," Glenn told the man as he filled out and handed the voucher to the man. "You can show that to the merchants in Omaha and it should give you credit against groceries and whatever else you need."

"We'd rather have cash, Mr. Gilchrist," the man's wife said.

"I know, but the Union Pacific is fresh out of cash. That's why Dr. Durant rushed off to Washington just a few days before the flood."

The couple had no choice but to take the voucher.

When it was Megan's turn to enter the tent, Glenn steeled himself. He'd fully expected not only to see Megan, but also her widowed sister and the two children.

"Aileen didn't feel up to coming," Megan explained, taking a chair across the table from Glenn. "But she asked me to tell you how much she and the children miss Mr. Fox. I have no idea what will happen to them now."

"Why not return to the East?" Glenn asked. "This is no place for respectable women."

"No," Megan agreed, brushing back her hair and leaning her elbows on the table, "it isn't. But there's nothing left for Aileen or I back east."

"Then you're going to look for work in Omaha?"

Megan shrugged. "I don't know."

"You and your sister could probably find something," Glenn said, realizing he did not sound very hopeful. "But once the rails start moving westward, the population of this riverfront town will dwindle to nothing again. Maybe you'd do better down in St. Louis."

"And maybe the Union Pacific could help us find work."

"I don't think so. It'd be against company policy to hire women. Especially . . ."

Megan's eyebrows raised. "Especially what?"

"Especially young, attractive women, Mrs. Gallagher."

"Oh."

Glenn extracted an envelope from his coat pocket and pushed it across the table. "This is the last of the money and I saved it for you and your sister."

"How much are two husbands worth?" Megan asked quietly.

Glenn didn't like the way Megan phrased the question. "I guess that depends on what kind of men and husbands they were, doesn't it? Anyway, all I can award you is three hundred dollars."

Megan did not reach for the money. Her eyes locked with Glenn's. "I think you know that both men weren't very good husbands, Mr. Gilchrist."

"Take the money," he heard himself tell her.

"No."

Glenn pushed the envelope at her. "Take it, Mrs. Gallagher, because there won't be any more coming."

"This is not right, Mr. Gilchrist."

"Take it!"

"No." Megan stood up. "If I took your money, then I'd be accepting your terms. I can't do that."

"You have no choice. Neither one of us does."

"Oh, but I *do* have a choice," Megan said. "I will refuse this pittance and stir up so much trouble for the Union Pacific that it will have to pay us fairly."

"If we pay you more, we'll have to up what I've already paid everyone else."

"All the more reason for me to leave that envelope on the table," Megan said, turning to leave.

"Wait!"

Megan froze, then slowly turned to look back, her eyes mocking him. "Are you going to tell me you were lying, Mr. Gilchrist, and you have another, fatter envelope in your pocket?"

Glenn stood up. He walked around the table and pulled the flap closed. "No," he said, going back to his chair. "I don't have any more money. In fact, most of what I'm offering is an advance from friends against my future salary."

Megan's eyebrows raised in question. "Do you expect me to believe that?"

"It doesn't matter. What you *must* believe is that there really may never be as good an offer from the Union Pacific Railroad. We're operating on promises and credit. But don't tell anyone I confessed we're almost dead broke."

"In that case," Megan said, "the high and mighty Mr. Durant will have to sell his fancy furnishings out of his palace car. I would not accept your Credit Mobilier stock, you know. Instead, I'd try to ruin its value."

"What can you possibly do to cause this railroad trouble?"

Megan returned to her chair and regarded him thoughtfully. "Mr. Gilchrist, why on earth should I tell you?"

"Because I think you're bluffing," he said, eyes dropping down to the envelope, fingers inching it closer to her.

"I wouldn't bluff away three hundred dollars," Megan said as she continued to ignore the envelope.

Glenn drew back his hands and steepled his fingers. He couldn't help but smile. "I admire the hell out of you, Mrs. Gallagher. You've the nerves of a Mississippi riverboat gambler."

"I *am* a very good poker player."

"Take the money." He was pleading now.

"Mr. Gilchrist, I believe it when you tell me that you really don't have a fatter envelope. And I don't want to get you in trouble, but I'm not bluffing and I won't accept three hundred dollars."

"All right. Have it your way. But I would like to know your intentions."

Megan paused and after a long deliberation, she said, "In a few days, there will be newspapermen swarming into Omaha. Somehow, they'll get across the river and they'll want to write about this tragedy. There already were a few in town, but they're local people and, therefore, of no importance."

Glenn saw the light. "You intend to plead your case to the press."

"Exactly. I didn't graduate from some fancy Ivy League college like you did, Mr. Gilchrist. In fact, I've only three years of schooling, but I'm not stupid."

"No doubt about that."

"And I have every intention of talking to every reporter who will listen. And they *will* listen, Mr. Gilchrist. I'm going to tell them how shamefully the Union Pacific Railroad treats its workers and their families. I'll tell them about how our heroic men went back into that flooding river to save each other and how we risked our lives to keep your damned locomotive and flatcars from being swept downriver. And now the very best the Union Pacific can offer most of us are one-way tickets out of Nebraska and worthless vouchers. Vouchers that will probably get us only about ten cents on the dollar with the Omaha merchants."

Megan leaned back. "Do you think the newspapers of this country might enjoy printing this kind of story, Mr. Gilchrist? And what would your leader, the rich Dr. Durant say?"

Glenn didn't respond. When Durant heard about this, he was going to go berserk.

Megan took a deep breath and continued. "People like to root for the downtrodden and I think this is the kind of injustice that will fire their indignation. Can you imagine what such a story would do to the promotion of Credit Mobilier stock and how much it would turn the United States Congress against this railroad?"

"Yes," Glenn said quietly, "I can."

"So can I." Megan came to her feet. "I'm not running a bluff, Mr. Gilchrist. And I'm not asking for the moon."

"What *are* you asking for?"

"I don't know yet," she confessed. "A fair shake for all the people of this shantytown and enough money so that Aileen and I don't have to live like dogs. We all want to get to California."

"Mr. Durant would probably pay for stagecoach fares to California. And if Miss King also wanted to go, then I could . . ."

"Oh, no," Megan said, "You're not going to get rid of us *that* easy."

"I know you won't believe this," Glenn said, "but I don't even want to 'get rid of you.' "

"Of course you do."

Glenn shook his head. He was about to commit heresy. "No. What you're asking for is only fair. Maybe you do need to stir up a groundswell of indignation through the press, Mrs. Gallagher."

"If I do," Megan said, "it'll come down on Dr. Durant and the other top Union Pacific officials."

"We're already up to our neck in controversy and trouble," Glenn admitted. "This whole idea of a transcontinental railroad has caused nothing but anger and bitterness since it was first proposed almost eight years ago. The South wanted it, the North wanted it, everyone wants it but even more importantly, they want to make sure no one else gets it."

"Then why bother?"

"Good question." Glenn pulled back the money-stuffed envelope. "This country was torn apart by the Civil War. I happen to share the view of many that a transcontinental railroad will bind it back together."

"Never!" Megan declared. "Hatred runs too deep. The devastation is far too great. North and South will *never* trust each other."

"Quite true, but this railroad will forge a new, stronger bond between the East . . . and the West. In time, this bond will thicken and forge the North and South into one great nation."

Megan found herself nodding her head. "I'd never thought of it that way, but you're right."

"President Abraham Lincoln saw it first," Glenn told her. "That's why he wanted a transcontinental. He *knew* that this country would be mutilated and festering for generations after the war. And he *knew* that the healing would have to take place on the American frontier. Where there were no Civil War cemeteries to mourn or blood-drenched battlefields to remind men and women of the terrible price we paid to preserve this nation."

"I didn't even know this railroad was his idea."

"It was. Just three years ago, he summoned General Dodge to Washington to ask him where a transcontinental railroad should begin. General Dodge informed the President that, without question, the eastern terminus of a transcontinental railroad should be Omaha. That greatly troubled Mr. Lincoln."

"Small wonder," Megan said. "Mr. Lincoln must have realized there'd be a great flood."

"No," Glenn said with amusement, "the reason President Lincoln was troubled was that he just happened to own a quarter section of land close by. He was said to have later remarked to Dr. Durant, 'If I fix it there they will say that I have done it to benefit my land. But I will fix it there anyhow.' "

Glenn leaned back in his chair. "You see, both General Dodge and President Lincoln knew that Omaha was the best and the right place to start this railroad line."

Megan was silent. Glenn watched her intently. Finally, he said, "What are you thinking?"

Her eyes were misty. "I saw President Abraham Lincoln once. He was so tall. A homelier man you'd never want to see. He had this long kind face. It was sad. Very sad. I wish he'd lived to see iron rails link this nation."

"So do I. He was my father's idol. My older brothers revered him and died for his ideals. I was young and the last and only son. My father begged me not to join and I gave in to his wishes. I wish I had not."

Glenn ground his teeth together. "All that I can do now is to help realize Lincoln's bold dream. That's really why I'm here, Mrs. Gallagher."

A tear slid down Megan's cheek. "I feel awful about what I said. I don't want to destroy Lincoln's dream."

Without thinking, Glenn reached out and placed his hands in Megan's hands. "It may be corrupt, it may be unfair and even indifferent to justice and suffering. But it cannot be destroyed."

"What shall I do?" Megan asked.

"Tell me what you want," Glenn urged. "Talk to Aileen and then let me know what is fair. I'll wait until Dr. Durant returns and we'll both take a stand for justice."

"He may fire you."

"Then so be it."

"And if he refuses us a just settlement?"

"Then I'll resign and we'll both take this case to the eastern newspapers."

"All right," Megan said. "We'll need some time, though. And I won't go back to Boston. California is my dream."

"Why?"

Megan told him about her Uncle Patrick. "He said it never rains in California and the sun shines almost all year around. He said the soil was as dark as molasses and almost as rich. He said no one willing to work would ever go hungry in life out in California."

Glenn held his peace. He'd also heard the fables about the rich soil and climate of California. He also knew of its lawlessness, and now that the forty-niner gold rush was over, how hungry men roamed the mountains and valleys in packs, scavaging for food and work. Of how they were abandoning California for the Comstock Lode where riches could still be found.

Megan studied him closely. "Don't you believe in California?"

"I don't believe in places, only people. Like my father, my brothers, and Abraham Lincoln. I don't think it matters where people are because those of quality prevail over adversity, weak people always quit or fail, even in the midst of great opportunity."

Megan agreed, but only to a point. "Or they die in war, floods, or famine, Mr. Gilchrist. If you were a strong person, you still might have starved during the Irish potato famine or . . . I'm sorry, but you might have died on some battlefield like your brothers."

"Dying isn't failing," Glenn argued. "At least, I never thought it so. Did President Lincoln fail a year ago because he was felled by an assassin's bullet? I think not."

"I think not either," Megan said as she smoothed her borrowed dress and prepared to leave. "And I think we've both become entirely too philosophical."

Glenn came to his feet. "I don't. I'm not a philosopher, but I do love to talk about things beyond our all-consuming but ordinary day-to-day needs."

"My sister's needs are far greater than mine," Megan said. "You've made me think about this railroad in an altogether new way. I confess, Mr. Gilchrist, that when I walked in this door, I hated the Union Pacific. Now I see it as President Lincoln's dream to heal this nation and I don't want to have a part in its failure."

"You won't," Glenn promised. "Come back as soon as you decide what is right. I'll do my utmost to see that justice for you, your sister, and Miss King is served."

Megan waited until he swept the canvas flap aside. She studied the long line of people waiting for their own "justice" to be served. And then, with a sad shake of her head and not envying the task Glenn faced this day, she walked back to her hotel, lost in her own very complex and troubling thoughts.

What was fair, what was right? And equally as important, what was in keeping with the true spirit of President Lincoln's transcontinental dream?

CHAPTER

9

"You want to tell me what the hell is going on?" Dan Casement asked as Glenn made his way toward Thomas Durant's private railroad car. "Glenn, I've never seen The Doctor as mad as he is this morning."

"I'm afraid his mood isn't going to get any better after he hears what I've got to tell him."

"Which is?"

"Which is that the Union Pacific is going to have to come up with the money to do better for those who lost everything during the flood, including members of their families."

"But I thought you were almost finished handling that?"

Glenn stopped. He towered over Dan and looked down at him. "I've been handing out a bunch of nearly worthless vouchers that are being redeemed by our Omaha merchants for just a fraction of the dollar. People have lost *everything,* Dan, and are getting compensated with pocket change. It isn't right."

When Glenn resumed walking again, the much shorter man had to practically run to keep up with him. "Maybe it isn't right," Dan Casement said, "but it's not *your* fight, Glenn! Let those people get lawyers and—"

"Aw, come on!" Glenn shouted. "Lawyers? They haven't enough money for food!"

"Well, it isn't going to help them if Durant cuts your head off and serves it to 'em on a silver platter. You're going to get fired."

"I don't care," Glenn said as he approached the palace car. "If Mr. Durant won't listen to me, then this railroad is headed for even worse troubles."

Dan stopped. "It was nice working with you," he said as

Glenn knocked on the back door of the railroad car. "I'll probably have to do *both* our jobs now that you're gone."

Despite the tension he felt, Glenn was able to smile. He really liked Dan and they had worked very well together. Glenn didn't want to lose his job; he wanted to save the railroad from a public relations nightmare.

"Don't count me out yet, Dan."

"Come in," Durant's voice commanded from inside the coach.

Glenn stepped inside. Durant as well as several other gentlemen from the East were seated around a conference table. No one stepped forward to offer him a drink, shake his hand, or even give him a smile. They were a very grim, prosperous-looking bunch of well-fed men.

"Have a seat," Durant ordered without granting Glenn the courtesy of introductions.

Glenn took his chair. Glancing around the circle of faces, he was sure that he'd lost his job, just as Dan had predicted. At least he didn't see a chopping block and a silver plate for his head.

"Glenn,'" Durant said, reaching for the letter that Glenn had written two weeks earlier. "You write to tell us that this Gallagher widow is going to, in your words, 'cause the Union Pacific Railroad a public relations nightmare.' "

Durant's dark eyes snapped up from the letter. His long, thin face was stiff with anger. "We've all read your letter and agree that we might have a problem. We also agree you've made one very major mistake."

"And that is?"

"You allowed Mrs. Gallagher to become a problem," Durant said. "You should never have allowed this woman to take the matter this far."

Glenn flushed. "So far, she hasn't done a damn thing, sir."

"She's threatened our reputation!"

Durant lowered his voice. "She's made a very, very serious threat. Will she carry it out?"

"Yes, sir."

Durant's eyes tightened at the corners. "How?"

"Like I said. She will attract the press and—"

"Wait a minute, young man," a big, beefy-looking gentleman with long white hair and muttonchop whiskers interrupted. "Exactly how is Mrs. Gallagher going to do this? It's my understanding that she and her sister are just a couple of poor women who lost their husbands in the flood. And you mention some girl that also lost her parents."

"Her name is Isabelle King. She's known as Belle."

"Listen," the man said, "our company has already issued a statement about the flood admitting that there was a considerable loss of life and property. I believe, as do my colleagues, that this is a dead issue."

"No pun intended," Durant deadpanned. "And Mr. Dillon is correct. We have already explained the tragedy and informed the eastern press that restitution is being made—which, Jack informs me, was entirely your duty."

Glenn bristled. "With what! Worthless vouchers? Mr. Durant, I was giving away empty promises. The vouchers were nearly worthless, just as Mrs. Gallagher predicted they'd be."

"It sounds to me as if you are placing entirely too much faith in whatever Mrs. Gallagher says, young man," another of the company officers said acidly. "Are you forgetting who pays your wages?"

"For the past three weeks, nobody," Glenn said rashly.

"Gentlemen!" Durant pounded the table. "I think we all need to take a drink and calm ourselves."

Glenn felt tighter than a coiled snake. He could feel animosity pressing in at him from all sides. Accusations were written all over their rich, overfed faces.

"To unity," Durant said, raising his glass after they'd been filled by one of the two aides who hovered around the table. No one seconded the toast, but they all drank. Glasses were refilled in silence and then Durant folded Glenn's letter and tapped it thoughtfully with his forefinger. Finally, he looked up and said, "Are you still a loyal employee of this railroad, Mr. Gilchrist?"

"Yes."

"Then how do you recommend we handle this . . . this distraction?"

Glenn had hoped for this question. "I've already tried to find out exactly what Mrs. Gallagher is after, but so far she hasn't given me an answer."

Dillon threw up his hands and exploded like a volcano. "My God, if the woman doesn't even know what *she* thinks is fair, how on earth can we satisfy her demands!"

"I think," Glenn said, "you need to invite her, Mrs. Fox, and poor Miss King to this coach and apologize to them for the tragedies they've suffered."

There was a long silence. Everyone looked to Durant who had never seen fit to apologize for anything. Durant shrugged. "All right, I'll apologize in the name of this railroad. And then?"

"Then we write up a settlement and ask those unfortunate young women to sign it."

"I will see to the precise wording of the contract," a man Glenn supposed was a lawyer said.

"Good," Glenn said. "After that, it's finished."

Durant nodded. "Very well. Invite them."

"For when?"

"For now," Durant said. "We'll wait. We have other business to attend to."

Glenn hesitated. "It might be better to give them a little notice as a courtesy."

"To hell with that!" Dillon stormed. "What's courtesy have to do with anything after someone threatens to destroy your reputation."

"Agreed," the lawyer said.

Durant crushed the letter in his fist and tossed it into a nearby wastebasket. "Get them," he ordered.

Glenn wasted no time in arriving at the hotel where Megan, her sister, and Belle were staying.

"No men allowed upstairs," a stout woman announced, physically blockading the stairs.

"I need to see Mrs. Gallagher, Mrs. Fox, and Miss King," Glenn said. "And I need to see them right now."

The woman was missing all of her teeth and had the red, bulbous nose of a drinker. Her round cheeks were webbed with bright red capillaries. She smelled bad and the lobby was a pigsty. Glenn found it difficult to imagine that Megan would choose to stay in a place like this. Maybe it was the only one that would take boarders on credit or Union Pacific vouchers.

"Here," Glenn said, dragging two bits out of his pockets. "Get them, please."

The woman's ruined face broke into a smile. "So, you're a real gentleman after all!"

"Quickly!" Glenn ordered.

The woman's smile died. She turned and hobbled up the stairs, her great buttocks swinging from banister to wall. Moments later, all three young women appeared at the top of the landing.

"Dr. Durant and his friends want to see you now."

"But . . ."

"There won't be a second chance."

"But we're . . . we're not ready!" Aileen cried.

"Yes we are," Megan called down. "Give us two minutes, Mr. Gilchrist."

The three disappeared and Glenn could hear them arguing and shouting from clear down in the lobby. He paced back and forth with agitation. He was sure that Megan would have the grit to see this confrontation to the end, and so would Belle, but Aileen was the obvious weak link. From the look on her face moments earlier, Glenn doubted if Aileen would even come down.

He was mistaken. It took more than two minutes, but the three soon appeared smoothing their skirts, brushing their hair, hands and faces wet from a quick scrubbing.

"We look awful!" Aileen cried, holding little David Fox in her arms while Megan led a wide-eyed Jenny down the stairs.

"Stop it!" Megan said harshly. "If we look poor and in a bad fix, then so much the better!"

"She's right," Belle said, fastening the top button of her blouse and pinching color into her already rosy cheeks. "We want them to know exactly how bad things have gone for us."

Glenn was surprised to hear this calculating remark from such a young, grief-stricken girl. Belle sounded as strong and determined as Megan. Good. The men she was about to meet were also strong and determined.

"It's going to be fine," Glenn said, helping Aileen toward the door. "Just don't be intimidated by these men. Tell them straight out what happened."

"And then let me tell them what we want," Megan said.

Glenn glanced over at Megan. "So, you've finally decided?"

"We have."

"Want to tell me ahead of time so that I'll know if I need to duck in case The Doctor pulls his derringer?"

It was meant as a joke, but poor Aileen didn't know that. She paled. "He'd do . . ."

"No," Glenn said, quickly realizing his mistake. "I was only kidding."

"He wouldn't . . ."

"Of course not," Glenn said. "He's a medical doctor. Dr. Durant is a tough businessman, but he's not physically violent. At least, I don't think he is."

"He's just a rich man," Belle said, her voice grown-up sounding. "Men with lots of money work hard at keeping it."

Glenn cast a sideways glance at Belle. She seemed very much different than he'd remembered. No longer frightened and lost. Megan must have instilled her with determination. Too bad she had not also been able to put some spine into her trembling sister.

As they approached The Doctor's palace car, Aileen's nerves started to come unraveled. "Can't you please just do this without me," she begged.

"No!" Megan said harshly. "Not this time. Aileen, if you can't do it for us, do it for your children. Now come on!"

Belle took David from her arms and said, "You can do this. You have to, Aileen. Don't let these sonsabitches buffalo you."

Glenn and Megan were both shocked by this rough language. Aileen, however, just nodded her head and followed them inside.

Durant's greeting was quite different from the one that Glenn had received. Now, Durant was all smiles as the introductions were made and the other officers of the railroad stood to extend their greetings.

Chairs were brought for the ladies. Glenn was left to stand. Aileen stared in wide-eyed wonder at the beautiful interior of the coach, Megan stared at Durant, and Belle appeared fascinated by her hands. Glenn held his breath and said a silent prayer this was going to work out right.

Durant turned on his charm like a city street lamp. "Ladies . . . and lovely children," he began, "I want to begin by thanking you for coming here on such short notice."

When Megan continued to stare at him without the hint of a smile and Aileen began to run her fingers over the glass-like mahogany surface of the polished conference table, Durant cleared his throat. "Uh-hem, well then. I also wish to extend the Union Pacific's sincere condolences for the terrible loss of life and property suffered in the recent flood. As we all know, it was an act of God, whose actions we cannot hope to fathom."

Durant took a quick glance heavenward, then continued. "Mr. Gilchrist has informed me of your extraordinary losses and we extend our deepest regrets."

Belle's eyes filled with tears and she made a small, choking sound in her throat. Glenn saw her hands tighten on the arms of her chair as she fought to retain her composure. Durant looked to Glenn who hurried over to Belle's side and put his hand on her shoulder. Belle, bless her heart, bit her lower lip and overcame her powerful emotions.

The railroad officials looked extremely dismayed by the tremendous effort that Belle undertook to spare them her grief. Mr. Dillon dragged his silk, monogrammed handkerchief from his pocket and offered it to the young lady.

"Words cannot express our sadness for the loss of your dear mother and father."

"Thank you, kind sir," Belle sniffled.

Durant dropped his veil of charm. He leaned forward and said, "Ladies, we cannot presume to bring back your loved ones. As God is our judge, we are deeply sorry for their tragic demise, but want to make material amends so that you need not suffer financial hardships."

"How much are we talking about?" Megan asked bluntly.

Durant was clearly taken aback by the directness of the question, but Glenn wasn't. It was, he thought, typical Megan Gallagher.

"We want to be fair," Durant said, "why don't you tell us of your needs?"

Megan looked to her sister, then at Belle. "I lost a husband but my sister lost not only a husband, but her children's father. I think both Miss King and my grieving sister would be satisfied with . . . five thousand dollars—each."

"Mrs. Gallagher!" Durant cried after a moment of stunned silence. "Surely you understand that such a figure is entirely out of the question."

"I don't understand any such thing," Megan said. "It's small compensation to her and those fatherless children. I think the newspapers would agree, don't you?"

Durant yanked out his own handkerchief. He mopped his brow and snapped to an aide. "Ernest, it's stuffy in here. Open a couple of windows."

"Yes, sir!"

Durant looked to his colleagues. "Gentlemen?"

"Pay her," Dillon said. "It's what, five years wages?"

"Ten," the lawyer snapped.

"Pay her," Dillon repeated. "Same for Miss King."

"But . . ."

"I agree," another of the officers said, "we want to make sure this matter is both satisfactory and *confidential,* don't we?"

Durant scowled. "Ten thousand dollars is a lot of satisfaction, gentlemen. But if it's what you . . ."

"Wait a minute," Megan said, "we settle this in one package. I also demand five thousand dollars."

"That's not fair," Dr. Durant said quickly. "Their losses—and I don't wish to sound as if this is an accounting, for heaven's sake—but their losses are greater. Miss King lost *both* her parents and, in your sister's case, not only she but *also* her children suffered losses."

Megan began to draw figure eights with her forefinger. Glenn almost smiled to see Durant and the other officials sweat and squirm as the seconds ticked by and the tension mounted. Finally, Megan looked up and said, "Are you proposing that my losses are half, or would they be a third?"

"Well," Durant said, eyes blinking rapidly, "I'm not sure that's what I meant."

"What did you mean?"

"I . . . Miss Gallagher, fairness dictates that you agree that your losses are the lesser of the parties present. Am I correct?"

Everyone held their breath, including Glenn. Megan said nothing.

"Mrs. Gallagher," Dillon said blurted, "just give us a damned figure."

Megan looked at Belle and her sister. "Are you both satisfied with five thousand?"

Belle managed a brave smile. Aileen dipped her chin and said nothing. Megan heaved a deep sigh. "I want," she began, "three thousand dollars and tickets to California for all of us."

Glenn felt the breath flow out of him as he relaxed. He knew that The Doctor and his colleagues would agree. In a few days, when the next infusion of money came to the Union Pacific, these young women would be paid in drafts and then sent out of Omaha as quickly as possible. He felt proud of Megan and at the same time saddened that she was leaving. He realized that in telling her why he was on the Union Pacific payroll and of his deep belief in Abraham Lincoln's great dream, he'd shared a part of himself with Megan Gallagher. Even more, he'd allowed himself, consciously or subconsciously, to think that she might have shared that same great transcontinental vision.

"Agreed," Durant said after looking at each of his peers and seeing them nod their heads. "But only on the condition that all three of you sign a legally binding contract stating that you will henceforth bear no malice or display no ill will toward this railroad. That this entire settlement and meeting is confidential, forever, and that you can never make any further claims for damages."

"All right," Megan said. "But I also have a condition."

Durant's bushy eyebrows raised. "And what," he said in a guarded voice, "might that be?"

"That you agree to compensate—at full value—every Union Pacific voucher issued to the people of our shantytown."

"Impossible!"

"No," Megan said tightly, "it is not! Mr. Gilchrist has a ledger of names and voucher amounts given. I know of many, many cases where the recipients of those vouchers got practically nothing for their value."

"This is not a matter for negotiation, Mrs. Gallagher," Dillon warned.

Megan came to her feet. "Then we have no contract, no agreement."

"Megan!" Belle cried. "I . . . I need that money!"

"And you will have it and more, I swear it, Belle. We'll find lawyers who will champion our cause. They'll win us all honest settlements and—"

"Mrs. Gallagher!"

It was Durant and he was shaking with pent-up anger. "Mrs. Gallagher," he growled, "in order to prove our fairness, we agree to this final condition."

Glenn wanted to scream. There it was! Megan had won.

Megan read every word of a contract that was shoved before her and, to everyone's surprise, so did little Belle. Aileen was either too excited or upset. There were a few questions clarifying facts, a couple of amendments, and then the contract was signed. Thomas Durant ordered an aide to bring his checkbook and with a great flourish he drafted checks totaling $13,000.

There was no traditional toast after an important signing. The women were quickly ushered outside. Glenn started to leave with them but The Doctor's voice brought him up short. "Mr. Gilchrist, you haven't been excused."

Glenn had to struggle not to tell the man that he didn't need anyone to excuse him. But Lincoln's dream got in the way and made him nod his head and close the door.

"Mr. Gilchrist," Durant began, "if I told you that I was deeply disappointed in the way this entire affair was handled, it would be a grave understatement. How much money did you hand out in the form of vouchers?"

"I can't give you an exact amount without—"

"Then an approximate amount!"

Glenn flushed with anger. "Seven thousand dollars to this point in time. There are still a few yet to deal with."

"Then deal with them promptly!" Durant snapped. "By my calculations, this—this damned flood has cost us in excess of twenty thousand dollars in personal settlements and twice that much in materials lost."

There was a long pregnant silence broken only when Glenn, deeply offended, said, "If you had been here, sir, you'd have seen how heroic an effort was made to keep our losses down to that limit. Why, if that locomotive and those flatcars alone had been lost, it would have represented a loss of nearly a hundred thousand dollars. I don't mean to be cavalier about the Union Pacific's money, Doctor, but I do want to remind you that this railroad should consider itself very, very fortunate to hold its losses well under a hundred thousand dollars."

Durant stared at Glenn in amazement. Finally, he said, "Is that right, Mr. Gilchrist?"

"You know it is, sir."

"Can I tell the United States Congress that piece of good news? I'm sure their reaction would be as unfavorable as my own."

"Thomas," Dillon said sternly, "I think Mr. Gilchrist is simply trying to tell us that it could have been much, much worse. Isn't that right, young man?"

"Exactly."

Durant glared at him and finally said, "I question your allegiance to the Union Pacific, Mr. Gilchrist, but I'm not going to ask for your resignation."

"If it pleases you, then by all means ask for it," Glenn challenged.

"No." Durant turned away. "But I think your talents might be more appropriately used in other capacities."

"Such as?"

"I'll come up with something," Durant promised with a cold smile. "You are excused."

Glenn stormed outside and headed up the muddy streets, oblivious to his surroundings. Someone called his name but he pushed their voice away and kept walking until he found himself beside the river. He snatched up a big rock and hurled it as far as he could over the flowing water.

"You've a good arm," Megan said.

Glenn whirled around and the anger washed out of him. Megan was smiling. She picked up a small rock and threw it into the Missouri. "I can't throw worth beans."

"You don't need to throw," Glenn told her. "Remember when I said you should be a Mississippi riverboat gambler?"

"Yes."

"I was wrong. You should have been a general."

"I can't stand the sound of cannon and I'd fall to pieces on the battlefield."

"I completely disagree," Glenn said, thinking how remarkable she had been in the palace car. "So what are you going to do when you reach California? With all your money, you can buy a business or just retire."

"On three thousand dollars?" Megan chuckled. "I plan to do far better than that, Mr. Gilchrist. Far better. And tell me, did you get fired?"

"No."

"I'm very glad."

"Why?"

"Because you should be one of the ones to build this railroad. Those men in that fancy car need people like you."

Glenn scoffed. "I have a feeling that The Doctor is going to reassign me to cleaning latrines or washing dirty dishes. Something like that."

"And you'd quit?"

Glenn picked up a flat rock and sent it skipping across the water. It bounced seven times, which was a lucky number. "I don't think I would," he decided. "That would mean that

The Doctor drove me off and he'd won. I can't allow that to happen."

"Good." Megan brushed back her hair and sat down on a piece of driftwood. She closed her eyes and turned her face up to the warm spring sun. "I feel the same way."

Glenn had been about to stoop and pluck another flat stone from the mud but now he stopped. "What do you mean?"

"I mean that I'll take the Union Pacific's money, but California can wait awhile longer."

"I still don't understand."

Megan opened her eyes and smiled. "Neither do I, yet. But I will."

Glenn scowled. "Mrs. Gallagher, you'd never be happy in Omaha."

"I know that."

"Well then? You can't . . ."

"Hush, Mr. Gilchrist," Megan said, "haven't you learned yet that you shouldn't tell me what I *can't* do?"

Glenn laughed, the sound echoing across the big, boiling water. "I'm sorry. You're right. But will you do one thing for me?"

"Of course."

"Before you go . . . if you go. Tell me first."

"Why?"

"So I can kiss you good-bye," Glenn blurted, then blushed, for he had not meant to say that. Not meant it at all.

It was Megan's turn to laugh. "In that case, I certainly will!"

Glenn looked deep into the woman's stunning eyes, then he turned and selected another rock and set it to dancing on the water.

CHAPTER

10

Liam O'Connell felt shiny. Shiny as his silver-plated spurs and the string of cheap conchos that decorated his new flat-brimmed hat. With his high-heeled riding boots and Colt six-gun strapped to his narrow waist, Liam knew that he was the envy of his former friends still loading ties and rails. They were so jealous they wouldn't even drink with him anymore. But who cared? Joshua Hood and his crew were the men he'd now ride, hunt, fight, and, yes, even proudly die beside.

On this fine spring afternoon, Liam kept sauntering up and down the boardwalk in front of Jasper's Dry Goods Store where he'd bought his new outfit on credit, just admiring his image in the big plate-glass window. And what a fine picture he made! From his dragging spur rowels to the crown of his new hat, he stood well over six feet tall. His gun, holster, and cartridge belt were hard used but serviceable. Liam was convinced that having worn hardware strapped to his narrow waist kept him from looking like some eastern dime-store dandy. He was especially proud of his new razor-sharp, long-bladed skinning knife, a personal gift from Joshua Hood.

Liam threw his shoulders back and felt big. And grateful. Grateful beyond measure to Joshua Hood who, true to his word, had hired and then vouched credit for him. And glory be to God, they were leaving on a buffalo hunt in just two days! Liam wanted to bust his breeches. Hood promised he'd lend Liam an honest horse and a serviceable rifle, then teach him to handle both.

Whenever Liam met rust eaters with whom he'd slept, whored, and drank, he could not help but feel superior. Where had they been the morning of that terrible flood? Had they risked their lives to save a drowning woman and child? No! They had the very same opportunity to be heroes but failed to grasp the moment. And so they'd forever remain poor rust eaters while he was now a scout and a buffalo hunter. Life was good and it was about to get even better.

If there was any cloud at all casting its shadow over Liam, it was the memory of his drowning brothers-in-law. Sometimes, deep in the still of the night, Liam would see the faces of Keith Gallagher and Hugh Fox swim up from the murky depths of his dreams. Their mouths would be distended with silent shrieks, their hands clawing and reaching out for Liam. He would shrink away, terrified by their horror-filled expressions. And just when he would decide he must reach out and save them, both men would disappear in a swarm of bursting crimson bubbles. At that point, the entire vision would wash scarlet-red. The shrieks he'd heard would become his own and he'd sit bolt upright to clutch his own throat and gag for air as if he were drowning.

After such petrifying episodes, Liam would be bathed in a fear-sweat. His heart would be pounding and he would be out of breath. It took a good long while for him to become calm again and he'd tell himself over and over that everything had worked out for the best. That if Gallagher and Fox had lived, they would have disgraced themselves and ruined both his beloved sisters. And because of their whoring, Liam reminded himself that his brothers-in-law might also have given Megan and Aileen the "French" disease. Whenever Liam thought of this, anger would completely overwhelm guilt.

Once he was calm, Liam would remind himself that if God was really all-seeing, consideration would be made for the girl whom Liam had actually saved. The one whose life had finally earned him respect in Joshua Hood's eyes and the Union Pacific job of his dreams. Liam told himself he was now the equal of any man. He was a hero, saving a good girl and ridding the world of a pair of degenerate and unfaithful sonsabitches unworthy to marry Megan and Aileen.

"Oh, Liam!" Megan called, rushing up to her brother. "I've been looking everywhere for you!"

Liam hooked his thumbs in his cartridge belt. "What do you think?" he asked, one eye on his sister and the other on his storefront reflection.

Megan stepped back to regard her brother and what she saw was truly amazing. Her brother looked wonderful. "Where did you get . . ."

"Right here," he said, tipping his hat toward Jasper's. He pirouetted a full circle. "Joshua Hood looked me up yesterday afternoon and I'm working for him now, Megan. Can you believe it!"

"In a heartbeat," Megan said, grabbing Liam by the arms. "You told me about what he'd promised, but I didn't expect . . ."

"He's a man of his word," Liam boasted. "If Joshua Hood says he'll do a thing, by damned, it's as good as done."

Megan clucked her tongue with admiration but then her eyes widened with concern. "You're wearing a gun, are you going to have to use it out there?"

"I don't know. Maybe. But there's no danger. I'm going to be riding with mountain men and Indian fighters. You should hear the stories they can tell! God, there's not a one of them that hasn't killed a few Indians. Most have taken squaws. They all speak sign language—something I'll have to learn right away."

Liam's eyes shone with a joy Megan had never seen before. He looked almost, well, beatific. "I wish our father could see you now," Megan whispered. "He'd be so proud."

"And you will be too," Liam vowed. "I'm getting a ten-dollar-a-month raise and I'll start helping both you and Aileen."

"You don't need to do that, not after today."

Liam wasn't listening. "Megan, I'm going to be a great scout. I'm going to learn everything I can about Indians and buffalo. Maybe I'll ketch me up a pretty squaw and . . ."

Noting the alarm in his sister's expression, Liam realized who he was talking to and caught himself. "And maybe I'll have her make me a pair of buckskin breeches like Joshua wears."

"I hope you never see an Indian," Megan said. "If killing buffalo is part of your job, well, stick to that. It'd be wrong to kill Indians, Liam. They're people."

"They'll be trying to kill us. There's nothing in the Good Book that says a person can't fight to save his own life."

Megan wanted to change the subject. Later, when Liam wasn't so excited about this new challenge, she'd talk to him about the sanctity of all life. Megan believed that unnecessarily murdering Indians, Negroes, or Mexicans would get you to hell as quick as murdering white people. People were God's children, no matter what their color. No matter even if they believed, as was said of the Sioux, Cheyenne, and other heathen tribes, that the earth, sky, moon, and sun were themselves gods to be worshiped.

"I'm so proud of you," Megan said. "And I have wonderful news. You don't have to worry about Aileen or her children. You don't have to worry about me either."

He frowned. "What do you mean?"

"We've struck a deal with the Union Pacific," Megan said, bursting to tell him her own spectacular news. "Mr. Gilchrist, bless his heart, helped too."

"What *are* you talking about?"

Megan took a deep breath, then she grabbed Liam's hands in her own. "I'm not sure that I can believe this myself, but . . . but look!"

Megan unfolded her $3,000 check and Liam's eyes bugged when he saw the figure. He stared and stared. Megan said, "It's signed by Dr. Durant himself."

"What . . . three thousand dollars!"

"For my husband's life," Megan said, her smile dying. "And for what we lost."

"You didn't have anything in that shanty worth spit!"

"I know," Megan said. "But I did have a husband. Aileen got five thousand dollars and so did poor Miss Isabelle King for losing both her parents."

"Five thousand dollars!"

Megan stepped back. Liam didn't look happy. In fact, he looked extremely upset. "Why yes, what's wrong!"

Liam threw his hands into the air. "That's . . . that's thirteen thousand dollars altogether."

"That's right." Megan didn't understand. Her brother was furious. "What is the matter?"

"It's wrong!" Liam cried. "Your husbands were ornery, drunken, whoring—"

Megan's hand moved of its own accord. She reacted without thought and struck her brother hard across the mouth. He staggered, touched his mouth, and stared at his own blood.

"Apologize!" Megan cried. "Right now!"

"No!" Liam shouted. "Them drowning was the best thing that could of happened to you and Aileen. We could have done fine by ourselves now. You didn't need to skin the Union Pacific out of so much money—it's about to go broke as it is, Megan! If it folds, we're all out of a job. You didn't need that much money!"

"I can't believe what I'm hearing," Megan breathed, reeling backward with shock and confusion. "I thought you'd be over-joyed that Aileen and I wouldn't have to worry about money anymore. That we'd have an opportunity to better ourselves. To make a new life. But you're not. You're . . . you're *jealous*! That's what you are."

"I am not!"

"What else could it be?" Megan demanded. "A minute ago, I congratulated you on your new outfit and good fortune and I was genuinely happy. But when I tell you of *our* good fortune, you can't stand to hear it!"

Liam gulped. He no longer felt shiny. He felt rotten. Old egg rotten.

"It's a sad thing that you've become, Liam! You're a sad, sad excuse for a brother!"

Megan whirled and left her brother standing in front of the dry goods store window. She marched down the street and bit her lower lip to keep from crying. How could her own brother be so small and so petty?

"Hey, Mrs. Gallagher! Hold up there!"

Megan turned to see Joshua Hood trotting along beside, keep-ing pace with her as she marched along the boardwalk. "Mrs. Gallagher, is something wrong?"

"Yes!" She kept walking.

"I saw you and your brother yelling at each other. Is it because I gave him a new job and you're angry that he might get scalped or stomped by a buffalo or something?"

"What business is it of yours, Mr. Hood?"

"Well," the scout said, "I just don't want to be the cause of trouble between a man and his beautiful sister, that's all. Especially seeing as how she's just been widowed."

Megan said nothing. But when she came to an intersec-tion, Hood reined his horse up in front of her, hopped down, and removed his broad-brimmed hat with a flourish. "Mrs. Gallagher, I also wanted to extend my deepest regrets over what happened to your husband. Same for your sister's husband. I didn't know either man, but I'm sure if you married them, they must have been good men."

Megan knew she should have ordered the Indian fighter and hunter to step aside, but then she remembered that he'd already made her acquaintance and he did have lovely manners despite his rough appearance. Soon after her arrival in Omaha, Hood had actually thrown his buffalo coat down in a puddle so that she did not have to get her feet muddy. The gesture had been so extraordinary in a frontier town, that everyone seeing it had stared and Megan had blushed. Unsure of what to do, she'd nearly turned around and fled but Hood had gently taken her arm and escorted her across his coat. It was an act that she would have expected of a Southern gentleman to a Southern belle, but not to a poor Irish girl trapped in a raw river town.

"Mr. Hood," she said, forcing a brittle smile. "I don't wish to be rude, but what happened just now between Liam and me has nothing to do with you."

"I'll watch out for him," Hood promised. "I know he's greener than fresh horse shit, but he'll season. He's got guts."

"I'm sure," Megan said, stepping around the man and hurrying on down the street.

"Mrs. Gallagher," Hood called, leading his horse after her. "I thought you'd be plumb pleased about me taking on your brother. I thought maybe you'd even favor me with a smile and a thank you."

"Thank you, Mr. Hood."

"Did I twist your tail or somethin'?" Hood asked. "I'd like to, but I wouldn't dare, ma'am."

"And Mr. Gilchrist thinks I speak too directly to the point," Megan muttered.

"Huh?"

"Nothing."

"Could I tie up my horse and escort you someplace? This is a rough town. No mud puddles and no buffalo coat to throw down for you this time, ma'am, but I'd do it all over again even if you are mad at me."

"I'm not mad at you," Megan snapped back at him.

"I hope not." Hood dropped his reins when they came to the boardwalk's continuation and just left his sorrel gelding.

Megan looked back. "Are you just going to walk off and leave that animal?"

"Horses aren't dogs, ma'am. He's not likely to follow."

"You can't just leave him to wonder what happened."

"I doubt he's too worried," Hood said. "Not half as worried as I am about why you got your feathers in a ruffle."

"They're not in a ruffle, Mr. Hood!"

"But you got your rump in hump fer some damned reason."

Megan stopped in midstride. "Mr. Hood," she said patiently. "Why don't you retrieve that poor, confused horse and do whatever a good scout is supposed to do."

"I'm fixin' to take your brother and some of the boys out to shoot some buffalo. Want to come along and watch?"

"Absolutely not!"

"Didn't think so. Can we go to dinner or something?"

Megan whirled on the man. She was completely exasperated by his boldness and she no longer regarded him as a gentleman, coat or no coat. That gesture must have been something he'd heard of in a dime-store novel. The kind where ladies were pure of heart and men were all as noble as knights.

"Mr. Hood. I don't think I want to talk to you anymore today."

"What about tomorrow?"

"No."

Hood shrugged. He removed his hat and ran his fingers through his thick wavy hair. "You are the prettiest woman I ever seen in my life, Mrs. Gallagher. It sure makes me feel sorry for your dead husband, him not being able to enjoy what he had, you know."

Megan blew steam from both nostrils. "Really, Mr. Hood, you are *too, too* much!"

She left him there and when she was a half block down the street and thought to glance back, he'd gotten back on his beautiful sorrel horse and ridden away. Megan sighed. She wished she hadn't found Liam and seen, with her own eyes, his sick jealousy. If nothing else, she had always excused her brother's failings by saying he had a good heart. Now, she wasn't sure he even had that. Liam, she was afraid, was rotten to the bone.

But, dear Lord, she loved him. Would always love him and it would break her and her sister's heart if Liam got himself scalped. Liam didn't know enough to know what he didn't know. Megan's only consolation was that Joshua Hood was a fearsome fellow by any standard. He was rougher than a cob and uncouth and unclean. But he looked brave and very strong. Joshua Hood seemed very much like a man who would not get himself killed by Indians.

Megan prayed that Liam stayed close to Hood and quickly learned how to hang on to his scalp.

CHAPTER
11

Joshua Hood checked his cinch, making sure it didn't pinch the sorrel's hide, and then he turned to survey his hunting party. Except for young Liam O'Connell, they were a tough, seasoned bunch, each handpicked for their marksmanship as well as their Indian savvy. Joshua led his sorrel gelding over to Liam who seemed to be having difficulty with his own cinch.

"Some problem here?"

Liam flushed. The other nine men grinned mawkishly and everyone tried not to laugh. Liam trembled with anger and humiliation. "I forgot exactly how you told me to tie this latigo to the cinch ring."

"Here," Joshua said, taking over and demonstrating once more.

"I think I got it this time," Joshua finally said in a low, embarrassed voice. "Sorry I forgot."

"Don't be," Joshua replied, glaring those of his men into subdued silence. "Just remember, sometimes we all forget or don't understand. When that happens, the smart man *asks* someone who does know or remember. That way, he doesn't make stupid mistakes. And mistakes, Liam, are what get men killed out here."

"Yes, sir."

"I'll never fault a man for asking," Joshua said, loud so that all his men could hear. "I will fault him for doing something wrong that puts either himself or the rest of us in danger."

Joshua finished cinching the horse, then dropped the stirrup. "You ride up in the lead with me."

"Why sure, Mr. Hood!"

"Joshua," the man said. "Not Mr. Hood or Josh, but Joshua."

"Yes, sir."

"And not sir, either."

Liam just nodded, then climbed onto his horse, knowing he looked clumsy. He picked up the reins and jerked the horse's mouth. It threw its head and Liam, who'd only been on a horse a few times, cried, "Whoa!"

Joshua grabbed the horse's bit. "Ease up on your reins, Liam. Despite a little age, this horse has got a soft mouth. No need to be jerking him around like that."

"No, sir, I mean Joshua."

"This is a good horse," Joshua said, running his hand across the roan's smooth, muscular neck. "He's not as fast as some of the other horses, 'cause he's probably about fifteen years old, but he's steady and smart. He'll cover for your mistakes, Liam. If you fall off him, he won't run away. He won't bite, kick, or buck. He can be shot off and he's strong enough to trot for a hundred miles and not be winded."

"Yes, sir," Liam said, wishing the horse were fast. "But if we get jumped by the Sioux, I'd sure not be trotting him. And I'd want a fast horse so I wouldn't hold anyone back, either attacking or retreating."

The other men chuckled and even Joshua had to smile. "If we get jumped by Indians, we'll parlay."

"Parlay?"

"Talk. Palaver. In Sioux, or in sign. It don't matter."

"But . . . but what if they want to scalp us?"

"Then we'll talk about that too," Joshua said matter-of-factly. "If they're set in their mind, we'll just shoot 'em and go on about our business of supplying the railroad with buffalo meat."

"Yes, sir," Joshua said, his mind racing. "Unless there's a whole bunch of them and they kill us instead, huh?"

A short, muscular young man who could not have been twenty burst into heinous laughter. He had been the quickest to make fun of Liam and his laughter stung the worst.

Joshua spun on the horseman. "Shut up, Calvin!"

The laughter died in Calvin's throat. He reined his horse off, tossing Liam a smirk that burned to the quick. Of all Joshua's men, Calvin Miller was the only man that Liam detested. Sooner or later, Liam figured he and Miller were going to tangle and Liam was afraid he'd come off the loser. And right now, he had enough problems trying to fit into this group without also getting his face stomped into the dirt. He wished Miller would give him a little slack, but that wasn't in the man's nature. Calvin Miller was like a predator—when he sensed weakness or blood, he went for the kill. Chafing at the bottom of the pecking order in this hard group, young Miller wanted to make sure everyone knew that Liam, and not himself, was now sucking hind tit.

Joshua turned back to Liam. "It happens that men get over-run and scalped sometimes," Joshua admitted. "It's part of the game."

"Game?"

Joshua nodded. "Yeah. What we want—buffalo and a big strip of land for the Union Pacific—belongs to the Indian. He don't really think he owns it, but he knows damn well our railroad don't. More and more, the Indian is going to understand the way we think and realize that he's going to have to fight or die."

"I never thought of it like that," Liam said.

"You need to start looking at things from the Indian's point of view," Joshua offered. "We're still hired by the Union Pacific to kill buffalo and stand off Indians, but sometimes looking at it from your enemy's side of the stream can make it easier."

Liam did not think so, but he kept his silence. What good did it do to look at it from the Indian's perspective? Even Joshua admitted that it changed nothing and it might even make a man a little slower on the trigger and therefore more vulnerable. Liam had an unreasoning fear of Indians. Like everyone else, he'd heard of white men being scalped alive and then castrated and left to flop around on the prairie for Indian target practice.

Liam wished that there were more men in this hunting party or that they were foraying out with a bunch of soldiers to keep them company, but since that was not to be, then he'd hold up his end of things. Or die trying.

"Hood?"

Joshua turned to see Glenn Gilchrist. Glenn had a paper in his hand and gave it to Hood without comment.

"Just tell me what it says," Joshua ordered.

"It says that you are to take along six wagons and freighters and bring them back loaded with a couple tons of buffalo meat."

"Six, huh?"

"That's right."

To Liam's way of thinking, Joshua did not look too happy about this. His suspicions were confirmed when the scout and hunter said, "We were counting on doing some scouting up the Platte. Are we going to have to escort the damned wagons all the way back here?"

"No," Glenn said, "you can deliver the meat to General Casement and his cooks out at the end of the line. They're expecting you because they're running low on meat."

"Six wagons of buffalo meat will be nothing but a pile of flies and rot if this warm weather holds," Joshua said. "Could be we need to jerk it out on the prairie if we kill more than a day's ride from the tracks."

"I'd do as the order commands," Glenn said.

Several of the scouts spat tobacco juice to show their displeasure with taking anyone's orders. Glenn, seeing this, motioned Hood off to one side. When they were alone, Glenn said, "I see that you've outfitted young Liam O'Connell."

"That's right."

"I don't understand that," Glenn said frankly. "He lied to both of us, trying to bluff his way into this job without any qualifications."

"He has qualifications," Joshua said. "He's got guts. That's the number one qualification in my book."

"All right," Glenn admitted, "he's a liar but he's got guts. That's not going to do you much good if or when bullets or arrows start flying out on the plains."

"Sure it will." Joshua scowled. "What's all of this got to do with you?"

"Just trying to understand your reasoning."

"What you do or do not understand isn't important," Joshua said pointedly. "And I think you're trying to meddle again in my business."

Glenn felt his hackles rising. "Taking on a kid who can't shoot or ride a horse and who doesn't understand the first thing about the frontier is a mistake."

"I'll take the responsibility for teaching him what he needs to know." Joshua's eyes narrowed. "I think what's bothering you is that Megan will feel a little beholden to me for helpin' her brother. And feeling that way, she might be grateful and decide I'm a pretty nice fella. Is that it?"

Glenn's fists knotted at his sides. "You got it all wrong."

"Do I?" Hood shook his head. "I don't think so, Mr. Gilchrist. And if the truth be known, I do hope that Mrs. Gallagher will feel obliged to me. I'm going to bring her back some little Indian trinket if I come across something I believe might strike her fancy."

"I think you're using the kid to get to her sister, Hood. Maybe it will work, but I doubt it. She's not going to let anything stop her from getting to California. That's what she really wants. And now she's got the money to do it."

"What does that mean?"

"Ask her brother," Glenn said. "And while you're at it, ask him to read your orders since you obviously don't know how to read."

This time, it was Hood who flushed with anger and whose hands balled at his sides as Glenn turned his back on the man and walked over to Liam who was pretending to suddenly be very interested in the contents of his saddlebags.

"Congratulations on getting what you wanted," Glenn said, placing his hand on the roan's neck. "That young woman whose life you saved wants to meet and thank you."

Liam looked at Glenn. "She does?"

"Yes."

"She going to give me a reward or something?"

"She just wants to say thank you," Glenn said. "Her name is Rachel Foreman. She lost her husband in addition to that baby you sent downriver."

Liam's cheeks reddened. "I didn't want to send it downriver! I didn't have any choice. She'd have drowned if she hadn't turned loose of the thing."

"That's what Rachel says she came to realize a couple of days ago. And she wants to make sure that you don't feel bad about it."

"I don't feel bad about anything."

"I can believe that," Glenn said cryptically.

"You through?"

"I guess. What shall I tell Mrs. Foreman?"

Liam shifted on his horse. He could tell that everyone was listening and he knew what he said now was going to be measured by these tough men. "You tell the Foreman widow she don't owe me anything. Tell her I'm glad I could save her and sorry she lost the baby. Maybe she should get married again and have another. She's real young and I'm betting she's pretty enough to find another man damned quick."

"I'll tell her what you said," Glenn replied, stepping away from the group. He looked over at Joshua Hood and called, "Those six freight wagons are being hitched and they'll be ready to roll by noon."

Hood didn't say anything. He just stared at Glenn with a long thoughtful glare and then he reined his sorrel around and led off toward the freight yard where the wagons were being readied.

The next three days were both a trial and a wonder to Liam. A trial because the saddle galled the insides of his legs raw, causing them to burn like fire. Not wanting to say anything to show his inexperience, he rode in constant agony until the saddle sores were too painful to hide.

"Here," Joshua said, reaching into his saddlebags and pulling out a jar of vile-smelling grease. "I use this buffalo grease for galls, cuts, and mosquito bites. It'll take some of the fire out of those sores. Another thing that will help is to ride your stirrups shorter than you would otherwise. That'll cock your knees out a little from the leather and cut down on the rubbing."

To Liam's great relief, the buffalo grease did wonders to ease his discomfort. Enough so that he could finally enjoy the Nebraska springtime. Now that the heavy winter snows had melted in the drenching rainstorms, the grass was alive and wherever the sun touched the hills there were huge bursts of spring flowers. The colors were magnificent. Purplish crocus competed for attention with a quilt of multicolored primrose. Vibrant orange geraniums swayed to the beat of the wind and danced with black-eyed susans. And down along the streambeds, wild grapes, raspberries, and strawberries blossomed in splendid profusion.

Liam yearned to see buffalo, but they were elusive, Joshua explaining, "The forty-niners and immigrants following the Oregon Trail have pretty much wiped the buffalo out along the Platte River valley. I know where we'll find buffalo a little farther north. If we didn't have to play nursemaid to these damn wagons, we could really do some sight-seeing."

"Maybe after we shoot enough buffalo to fill those six wagons we can head off to do some scouting, huh?"

"Maybe," Joshua said, eyes always roaming restlessly across the rolling green hills.

Joshua's veteran hunters demonstrated their marksmanship whenever they chanced upon a distant herd of antelope. Liam soon discovered that antelope were very wary and did not band closely together like sheep or cows. Small and extremely flighty, they tested even the buffalo hunter's shooting skills.

"Want to try that rifle of yours?" Joshua asked at the end of their second day out.

Liam studied a trio of antelope, judging them to be at least two hundred yards distant. They appeared bug-sized and their heads were up, ears twitching. They looked ready to bolt and run.

"I don't think so," Liam said, sure that he couldn't even come close to bringing down one of the sleek animals.

"You got to try sometime," Joshua said. He looked to his men. "Liam can take the first shot, then back him up pronto."

The hunters nodded and yanked their buffalo rifles up to their shoulders. Liam did the same. Joshua had already instructed Liam how to load and fire, but no man could teach another how to shoot straight. "Maybe I ought to dismount and lay my rifle across the saddle," Liam nervously suggested.

"You step down, they're gone," Joshua said, dragging his own rifle from his saddle boot and raising it to his shoulder. "Take your shot."

Liam turned the roan's head toward the antelope. He picked the closest one, cocked back the hammer of his Sharps .45-caliber buffalo rifle and squeezed the rear trigger that "set" the front trigger. Taking a deep breath, Liam caressed the front "hair" trigger, as Joshua had instructed, then aimed and counted one-thousand-one, one-thousand-two, one-thousand-three, and fired. The big-bored rifle belched smoke and flame and its roar was joined by a half-dozen other rifles an instant later. All three antelope were slammed down like haystacks in a high wind.

Liam lowered his rifle and his eyes widened with wonder. "Did I get him?"

"You sure did," Joshua said with a grin as he reloaded his own rifle and indicated for Liam to do the same. It was the cardinal rule that was to be followed. Reload first no matter what else needed to be done.

Liam felt as if he might bust his buttons he was so proud of his shot. He could hardly wait to examine his kill. In his haste, he spilled a jigger of black powder and dropped one ball to the earth and had to dismount.

"Just take your time," Joshua said patiently as he booted his own rifle. "Those antelope aren't going to run away from anyone."

"That's for damn sure," Calvin Miller said. "I expect, Joshua, it was you who really shot the closest one."

"No," Joshua said evenly. "I aimed for the one on the left. Liam got the near one."

Miller wanted to argue the point but one of the other men nudged his arm in warning and Miller clamped his mouth shut. He gave Liam a contemptuous look as he picked the errant lead ball from the ground and then he rode slowly off toward the three downed antelope.

Joshua waited until Liam was remounted and reloaded. He motioned the others to go on ahead and when they were alone, he said, "Can you fight any better than you can ride?"

"Fight?"

"With your fists."

Liam followed Joshua's eyes, which were fixed on Calvin Miller. "You're asking me if I'd have any chance against Miller?"

"Yeah."

"I don't think so," Liam said, unwilling to again lie to this man. "I've fought before, but I'm nothing special."

"Maybe one of these times we'll ride over a hill and I'll show you a few tricks that might help when Calvin decides to whip you to a nubbin'."

"He looks stronger than me, but if we tangle, he'll at least know he's been in a fight. I won't back down from him."

"If you did, he'd hound you out of this bunch," Joshua said. "Miller is strong and he's hard, but he loses his head and fights out of his mind. A thinking man, even a weaker one, can take him if he is smart and knows what to do."

"Which is?"

Joshua shrugged. "Kick his grapes off. Or if you can't do that, bust him in the throat. Right under the chin."

"I could smash his windpipe and kill him!"

"If he don't do it to you first," Joshua said before he touched spurs to his sorrel and rode after his men.

During the next hour, Liam learned how to gut and skin an antelope. Apparently, when you killed an animal, another one of Joshua Hood's rules was that you had to skin it. That almost made Liam believe he'd rather not shoot a buffalo, which was about four times bigger than an antelope.

But they did find buffalo. The very next day, Joshua angled up a small river choked with budding cottonwood trees. The party pulled the wagons into the trees and then rode up to within a hundred yards of the crown of a flowery hill where they dismounted and let their horses graze. Taking their rifles, Liam followed the hunters up to the top of the hill where they dropped into a bed of mayflowers and stared down into a narrow, winding valley clotted with buffalo.

Liam's heart filled his throat. For a moment, the sight of the great beasts almost brought a shout to his lips. "They're *huge!*" he whispered to no one in particular.

One of the hunters, overhearing him, said, "Yeah but they can't see worth a damn. In less than five minutes, we'll kill enough to have those wagons filled."

Liam dragged his Sharps up close to his side. The buffalo were much bigger and uglier than he'd expected. Great wads of winter hair dangled from their massive bodies. Calves as big as ponies danced and frolicked through the herd. Bulls grazed peaceably while the cows seemed more restless.

"Which one first, Joshua?" one of the men asked.

Hood squinted, drew his hat down tight, then pointed. "That big cow off on the right. See the one with her head up? I think she's the leader."

"If she ain't, you'll be hearing about it."

"If she ain't," Joshua said, "I expect that I had better hear the sound of all your rifles firing."

"How many?"

"Each wagon ought to carry four carcasses," Joshua said. "Couple dozen. Kill no cows with calves."

Liam nervously licked his lips. "How do we know what to shoot?"

"We'll fan out a little," Joshua said. "You stick with me and I'll point out the one you're to hit. Remember, don't aim for the head but shoot for the heart. It's right behind the forelegs. If you miss that, you'll likely get lung and one of us will finish him off later."

Liam nodded. The hunters separated, all of them fading back from the hilltop, then ranging apart some thirty or forty yards. When they were all in position, Joshua motioned them to choose their separate targets.

"What's happening?" Liam whispered, unable to control his excitement.

"Every herd has a leader," Joshua explained. "You might think it would be a bull, but it's usually a cow without calf. If you down her first, the others will be confused. It's like killing a Sioux war chief. For a few seconds, no one is in command and until one of them takes charge, we can drop them at will."

"And they won't run?"

"Sometimes they do, most often not." Joshua winked. "Buffalo are about as smart as a herd of city folks. They'll mill around and try to figure out what is wrong. They won't be able to see us and we're downwind of 'em so they won't be able to smell us."

Liam nodded but he had a hundred questions to ask, all of them swirling around in his head.

Joshua glanced down the line of hunters. "You take that big bull standing by that flat rock."

"The one with the missing horn?"

"Yeah. Aim a little lower than you'd expect. Shootin' downhill can be deceivin' 'til you get used to it."

"Right," Liam said, swallowing noisily, burying his elbows into wildflowers, and raising his heavy buffalo rifle.

"Cock the hammer back," Hood said, even as he cocked his own hammer. "Now draw down fine, take aim at the heart, pull back real easy on your hind trigger."

Liam did it exactly in time with Joshua and their back triggers clicked in unison. "Now," Joshua whispered, "take a deep breath, count, and fire with me."

"I didn't really hit that antelope, did I?" Joshua blurted.

"One-thousand-one . . ."

Joshua's rifle boomed and its smoke washed over the wildflowers. One hundred fifty yards away, the restless cow collapsed in the front end, waved her head at the sky, then rolled over with bloody bubbles filling her nostrils as she sank to the earth. One hundred yards away, Liam's bullet tore a fist-sized hole through the bull's ribs and destroyed the animal's heart. Liam blinked smoke from his eyes and the rifle slipped from his hands as a tremendous volley of rifle fire blanketed the valley, echoing and reverberating back and forth across the confused herd.

Here and there, as if pulled down with invisible wires, buffalo flipped over or took a few racing steps and then somersaulted to thrash upon the bright, sun-drenched grass and sea of wildflowers. Calves bolted through the herd, bawling in terror. Cows and bulls milled and bawled too. Once, Liam had read of how a Boston fire had trapped a crowd in a theater house and how most of the victims had trampled each other to death in their blind panic and confusion. Now, as he watched this great buffalo herd lost in aimless terror, he recalled that account and then he remembered Joshua's comparison with city folks. It was an apt analogy and Liam had no desire to reload and shoot again. Instead, he clutched the stock of his rifle and watched his bull buffalo twitching in death, dark eyes blinking rapidly as if trying to see its own onrushing death.

The shoot ended in less than five minutes. Only two of the dying buffalo had to be shot a second time and one of them was attributed to Calvin Miller.

"Hell," a buckskin-clad hunter joshed, "even the greenhorn got his bull first shot."

"He got lucky," Calvin said, cheeks coloring as he burned Liam with a hateful glance. "Next time he'll miss."

Liam ignored the remark. He felt so good that no one could dash his soaring spirits. Besides, if luck had part of his clean kill, he'd gladly take it.

"Watch, that cow yonder," Joshua said, standing up in full view of the confused herd as he pointed.

Liam did watch. Out of the hundreds of cows, somehow, Joshua had exactly identified the next one to assume leadership. She was smallish but the only one not shaking her head and milling. Suddenly, she whirled, raised her tail, and went racing away. The herd followed her and within a few minutes they were just a brown smear sliding over a distant green hill.

Liam removed his hat and although the air was fresh and cool, he was sweating. He mopped his brow with his sleeve, replaced his hat, and then, following the example of those around him, reloaded his rifle.

"Bring up the wagons!" Joshua shouted to the drivers down in the trees.

Liam looked at his boss. "You going to show me how to skin it?"

"I will," Joshua said. "But only once and when I'm finished with my own kill, you'll be expected to do yours. My contract with the Union Pacific calls for us to keep the hides. They'll bring us a hell of a lot more money than wages."

"What's a hide worth?"

"Depends," Hood said, "on how well you skin it out. Could be worth enough money to put a dent in what you owe me for your horse and rifle."

"Then I'll be real careful," Liam promised, watching the hunters drawing their knives and striding down the flowery hillside to claim their own hides.

Liam waited for Joshua while his heartbeat slowed to normal. He stared at the wide, rolling hills, tasted the lingering smell of black powder, filled his lungs with the perfume of wildflowers. His eyes stung with grateful tears and he wiped them dry.

"Gunsmoke can blind a man," Joshua said, pulling a long, bone-handled knife from its Indian-beaded sheath.

"Yeah," Liam replied, falling into step with the Union Pacific Railroad's chief scout while drawing his own new skinning knife.

CHAPTER
12

"Relax," Dan Casement said as Glenn paced back and forth in his tiny hotel room while constantly checking his watch. "General Dodge isn't going to fire you."

"I'm not so sure about that," Glenn replied. "There's little question in my mind that The Doctor has given him a terrible account of my employment with this railroad. I expect that Durant has held off firing me so that General Dodge can do it and save him the unpleasantness."

Dan was sitting in a chair, feet propped up on the windowsill, his small compact body totally at ease. "For your peace of mind, it might help you to know that my brother and I have both written the general long reports as to what is happening here. Both of us commended your work."

Glenn pulled up short. "You did?"

"Of course."

"What about the flood losses and that personal settlement issue that Durant is so angry about?"

Dan blew a smoke ring and it sailed gently out the second-story window. "The fact that you strongly recommended that the levee be cleared of all Union Pacific equipment and supplies before the flood is well documented. Durant was the one that made the decision not to commit enough men to the job but instead to divert laborers to push the roadbed to Papillion. A roadbed that was poorly constructed and largely washed out during the heavy rains."

"And what about the settlements I made for personal and material damages to the shantytown people?"

"You did what my brother and I recommended and gave them all the cash available and then passed out redeemable vouchers.

117

The settlements were made in good faith; all were fair except those made to Mrs. Gallagher, Mrs. Fox, and Miss King, which seemed rather excessive."

"But you explained the reasons for those large settlements to General Dodge."

"Of course," Dan said. "Rather than be annoyed, he was impressed with Mrs. Gallagher in particular for fighting for her family."

"Good," Glenn said with relief.

"General Dodge especially appreciated that we agreed to honor those vouchers at full value instead of a few cents on the dollar."

"He sounds like a fine man. What's he like?"

Dan Casement thought about that for a moment. "My brother knows Grenville better than I, but I think it would be safe to say that he will earn the Union Pacific immediate legitimacy and respect."

Glenn raised his eyebrows. "Isn't that a bit of an exaggeration?"

"Not really. Grenville is a man who commands respect. Actually, his physical appearance is quite ordinary. Average height and looks. Mid-thirties. He seems nervous, but he's not. He just has a tremendous amount of energy. You'll be struck by how Grenville is always in motion. You'll also notice that he really listens. He's decisive, forceful, but I'm afraid he lacks wit or humor."

"Too bad."

"Yes." Dan puffed on his cigar. "Don't attempt to make jokes with him, Glenn. Be serious and come straight to your point. Don't criticize The Doctor, but state your side of the case succinctly and be forthright. Grenville is a serious man and he expects others to be the same way. If he likes you, you will always be his friend, but if he doesn't . . ."

"A bad enemy, huh?"

"Not like Durant can be," Dan said, "because you will always know what General Dodge thinks. He is utterly lacking in duplicity. He is also very, very brave."

"I understand that he had quite a distinguished military career."

"That's for sure," Dan said. "At the bloody Battle of Pea Ridge, down in Arkansas, Dodge was wounded for the second time when an exploding Confederate shell blew a gaping hole in his side. I know for a fact that he had three horses shot out from under him in that battle alone, and after his terrible wound, he was not expected to live. But he did."

Dan's voice dropped and it was clear his emotions were close to the surface. "General Dodge once confessed to me that the surgeons hauled him over two hundred fifty miles of rough roads in an army ambulance to the nearest Union hospital. When that didn't kill him, they promoted him to the rank of brigadier general."

"Was he making a joke?"

"I don't think so. Two years later he was General Sherman's top officer in the campaign to capture Atlanta. By then he'd been promoted to the rank of major general and was considered by General Ulysses S. Grant to be one of his finest generals. But while preparing to lead a charge, Dodge was struck in the head by a sniper's bullet and this time they were sure that he would die. He was unconscious for nearly three days."

"It's a wonder he's still alive," Glenn said.

"If Grenville's devoted wife hadn't rushed to Atlanta and stayed at his side nursing him day and night for weeks, he would certainly have died. They say that Dodge was a skeleton when they transported him back to his home in Council Bluffs. But if you ask the general what was his worst time, he'll never mention his battle wounds."

"Then what *was* his worst time?"

"Ask him," Dan urged. "It's an answer you'll never forget."

Glenn wasn't sure he wanted to ask. He looked at his watch again. "I might as well head off out now. "I don't want to be late."

"You won't be," Dan said. "It's still half an hour until your appointment."

Glenn picked up his hat. "I know, but I think I'd better leave now anyway."

Dan dropped his feet down from the sill with a thud. He reached for his own hat but not before he pitched his cigar out the window. He started toward the door, then stopped and went back to peer down on the street.

"What is it?" Glenn asked.

"I just wanted to make sure I didn't toss that stogie into a wagon load of hay or supplies. Actually, someone picked it up and is happily smoking it."

Glenn shook his head with amazement. "There are some pretty desperate men out there. The best thing that can happen is for the Union Pacific to start rehiring and putting a full effort into construction."

"And she will," Dan promised. "That's part of what Grenville will want to talk to you about."

"Have you requested that I remain here and work with you?" Glenn asked.

"No," Dan said. "I wanted to, but you wouldn't last a month around The Doctor. You'd probably take a poke at him and wind up being arrested for assault. No, Glenn, much as I'd enjoy working with you, I think it would be best if you worked ahead of the tracks, not behind them. That way, you'll be out of Durant's sight and therefore out of his mind. It's your best bet."

"I agree," Glenn said, "and I hope that General Dodge agrees as well."

"Just don't waste his time with a joke," Dan said. "He won't find it amusing, no matter how funny."

"You speak like one who's learned from hard experience."

"You're right," Dan answered, clapping Glenn on the shoulder. "I told Grenville the one about the lecherous butler and his wealthy socialite madam. The one where he discovers she has a hollow wooden leg. Have you heard that one, Glenn?"

"No, and I'd rather not hear it now, if you don't mind," Glenn muttered, his mind on this crucial first meeting with General Dodge, the Union Pacific Railroad's new Chief Engineer.

Dan chuckled to himself as he followed Glenn downstairs. "It's actually quite hilarious. I'm sure you'll agree, but Grenville didn't. Not even a smile! Anyway, there was this really lecherous butler and he . . ."

"Sit down and tell me about yourself, Mr. Gilchrist," Chief Engineer Dodge said. "I knew one of your brothers."

Glenn blinked. "You did? Which one?"

"John. He was one of the finest young lieutenants we had. I predicted a brilliant future for him before we heard he'd fallen on the battlefield. I understand that your other brother attained the rank of captain before he too died to preserve our Union."

"Yes," Glenn said. "I wanted to join but my father couldn't have stood the loss of all his sons."

"Then you did the right thing."

Glenn nodded, captivated by the spare man who had been given such a heavy responsibility and yet who appeared so relaxed and confident. Dan Casement had been right when he'd said that Grenville Dodge was not an imposing man, but a very direct one. He possessed the most penetrating eyes that Glenn had ever seen and there was an honest and direct openness about him that made you want to share confidences as if you'd known him for years, instead of minutes.

"I suffered a bad head wound at Atlanta," Dodge said. "My mistake for I should have ducked. But I confess that my main contributions to the Union were not on the battlefield but rather in repairing train trestles and tracks destroyed by the South."

"That's not what I heard," Glenn said, recalling his conversation with Dan Casement only minutes ago. "You were critically wounded at least three times on the battlefield."

"Yes," Dodge admitted thoughtfully, "God and my dear wife, Ruth Ann, brought me through."

Glenn *had* to ask. "What was your darkest hour, sir? If you don't mind my asking."

Dodge stared past him, his eyes tightening at the corners with a distant, visible pain. "It wasn't the war casualties that most deeply pierced my heart, Glenn. It was the assassination of President Abraham Lincoln."

"You were at the Ford Theater?"

"No, thank God. But by then I'd come to consider the President as my dearest friend. We had first met in 1859 right across this Missouri River when he arrived in Council Bluffs just to meet and ask me about what I considered the best jumping off point for the transcontinental railroad."

"And you told him it was right here."

"Yes, I did. But I learned almost as much as he did that day."

"You did?"

"Oh, yes," Dodge said emphatically. "Do you know the most important lesson I learned that day from Mr. Lincoln?"

"No, sir."

"I learned to listen."

"To listen?"

"Yes! It sounds so simple and yet so few have learned this vital art. And while Mr. Lincoln was one of the finest storytellers that I've ever heard, he also was one of the most gifted listeners. On that first visit he made to Council Bluffs, we sat on the broad front porch of the Pacific House after dinner one hot August evening and he began by saying, 'Tell me, Mr. Dodge, what do you think of starting our transcontinental railroad right here?' "

Dodge smiled sadly. "He asked that one question and then I talked almost constantly for the next two hours! And all he did was listen. That's all! He completely shelled my woods, Glenn. After two hours of just listening, he knew everything about the best survey routes for a rail line that I had spent years learning! And when I was finished talking, Mr. Lincoln told me that he agreed with my assessment and that someday Council Bluffs and Omaha would become a major hub for future roads and rail lines."

Dodge laced his fingers together. "On the night President Lincoln was assassinated, I was in St. Louis and they awakened me at midnight. It was last April fifteenth and Secretary of State Steward warned me to prepare to counter any potential uprising by Union people against known Southern sympathizers. So I issued a notice in the morning paper that people were to stay at home and that every business was to remain closed."

Dodge sighed. "I needn't have worried. That first day of mourning was one of the saddest that I have ever known. And do you know what?"

"No."

"It was the Southerners who were the most upset about Lincoln's death. They understood what a terrible price his assassination would exact on the shattered, defeated South. On the Reconstruction."

"I see."

"They knew instinctively that Abraham Lincoln would have been as compassionate as he had been resolute during the long, awful years of war. I next received orders to go to Springfield with my command to attend the burial ceremonies. I took my place at the head of the funeral procession and it was, Glenn, the absolute saddest day of my life. The streets of Springfield were lined with thousands and thousands of mourners, most in tears. As we marched down the street, it was as if we were in a corridor of sorrow for you could hear nothing but the sounds of people weeping and sobbing. Children would rush to the funeral coach to kiss it and throw flowers. Negroes would step forward, then collapse to their knees weeping and praying. My men were blinded by their own tears—as I was by mine."

Glenn could see the general's eyes cloud with mist and his own throat ached with hearing this account.

"Thank you for being a good listener," Dodge said, roughly clearing his throat and composing himself. "Now, what is your appraisal of this operation, Mr. Gilchrist?"

"I'm afraid that I'm not qualified to make an appraisal, sir."

"Of course you are." Dodge leaned forward. "General Casement and his brother Dan both speak highly of you. I've heard and dismissed Durant's allegations that you are unfaithful to the Union Pacific or neglectful in moving supplies up to higher ground before the flood."

"Thank you."

"And I also dismiss that you were acting contrary to the Union Pacific's interests regarding the personal and property settlements made to those who suffered from the flood. In fact, I've reviewed a few of those cases and found your settlements to be quite fair, except in three overly generous cases that were explained to me."

"Yes, sir."

"That Mrs. Gallagher must be quite a woman."

"She is."

"Too bad she's not a man. Anyone who can run that kind of a bluff would make an excellent order buyer."

"It wasn't a bluff, sir."

"Oh? If that's the case, it's all the more to her credit. I regret the expense but admire the woman's spunk. But back to what we were saying. Mr. Gilchrist, I don't have time for men who refuse to give me honest and open opinions."

Glenn squirmed a little in his chair. He had hoped to avoid stating his views, but Dodge had left him no choice.

"All right, until the Casement brothers arrived a few months ago, this whole operation was a shambles. There was no one in charge of engineering, construction, or procurement. Each official operated independently and so the right hand never knew what the left was doing. In many cases, tons of duplicate supplies were ordered. Once shipped up the Mississippi and Missouri rivers, the freighting costs were so enormous that returning them to their manufacturers was out of the question. We'd have orders given one day and rescinded the next. Working on the Union Pacific Railroad was chaos."

"Precisely," Dodge said after a few moments of studied silence. "No chain of command. No coordination. No direction. No control. No plan and no goals!"

"Yes, sir."

Dodge relaxed. "Jack Casement wants you out front surveying and helping build bridges. How does this square with you, Mr. Gilchrist?"

"I'll go where I can serve best."

"Realizing that there is great danger out there from attack by the Indians?"

"Yes, sir."

"Have you ever built bridges?"

"No, sir," Glenn said. "But I designed a few in college."

"In college." Dodge nodded. His expression neither betrayed amusement nor gave any hint that he was in the least bit impressed. "Are you a good surveyor?"

"I am, sir."

"You've actually surveyed?"

"When I was hired, I spent several months under Mr. Reed and others. I believe I have a good feel for it."

"All right, then," Dodge said. "We'll find out. I can't make you chief surveyor because you lack experience, but I want you to become the assistant to our chief surveyor, Mr. Benjamin Goss. He's worked for me in the army and there are none finer. He'll teach you how to survey the right way. And he'll teach you a lot more about how to stay alive in Indian country."

"Very good, sir," Glenn said, feeling his pulse quicken.

"But I want you to do much more than just assist Ben in surveying," Dodge said. "I want you to be my liaison. My eyes and ears. I've done some of the survey work up into the Black Hill country. But I still need constant feedback from way out in front of the track laying. In addition to gathering valuable information and surveying data, you'll also report to me personally—and frequently. I hope that you are an expert horseman, Mr. Gilchrist."

Glenn nodded. "I've always owned and loved horses. I consider myself quite a good rider, sir."

"How are you with written reports? I'll need them for The Doctor and for Congress. Especially the latter. You *must* be able to write concisely and yet with color. I'll plagiarize your reports shamelessly, Mr. Gilchrist."

"My father was a poet, among other things. I edited my college newspaper."

"Excellent!" Dodge beamed. He rose and extended his hand. "I have a good feeling about you, Glenn. I think you are going to be invaluable to me. A trusted source that I will come to rely most heavily upon."

"You can count on me," Glenn said, knowing how trivial this sounded and yet determined to back it up with his deeds.

"I'm sure that I can." Dodge opened the door for Glenn. "I want you to remain here in Omaha another few weeks or so to help Dan Casement get things in order. Then we'll start pushing the tracks westward and I'll send you far up in advance of the track laying."

"Yes, sir!"

Glenn knew he was being excused. He started outside but Dodge's words stopped him. "Mr. Gilchrist, I do have one very important reservation about our new relationship."

"Sir?"

"I won't try to tell you otherwise, you are being reassigned into a very dangerous and important job. I am quite concerned about you being the last son. I'm sure that your father . . ."

"He's dead, sir."

"I'm . . . sorry."

"Me too, sir. I'll be awaiting your orders to leave Omaha and you can give them with a clear conscience that if something happened to me, I have no family to mourn my passing."

"I'll commission you the fastest horse I can find in Omaha," Dodge said with a quick but amused smile.

"Yes, sir!" Glenn grinned, thinking that Dodge, for all the sternness of his demeanor and reputation, did have at least a token sense of humor.

In the days that followed, Glenn saw how Dodge's arrival had galvanized the Union Pacific into action. Coincidentally, Congress unloosened its purse strings and provided a fresh infusion of funds. Overnight, a thousand desperate men were placed on the payroll and paddlewheel steamers churned up the formerly ice-clogged Missouri bringing fresh supplies and all manner of men and women eager to feed off the largest payroll in the country.

As expected, the number of tent saloons, eateries, and hostels mushroomed. Already overcrowded, Omaha's established businesses were strained beyond capacity. Merchants gouged the new arrivals and gorged off the expanded Union Pacific payroll. Prices shot up and lawlessness and drunkenness preceded nightly shootings. Omaha lost any semblance of respectability. General Dodge pleaded with the United States Army to send soldiers to police the streets and maintain order, but the Army was having its own problems with the Indians and refused to intervene in what it considered Omaha's temporary municipal pestilence.

Glenn worked from dawn to dusk helping Dan Casement and an army of supply clerks order and route vital supplies to the front of the construction line where Jack Casement was forming a track-laying operation that was reputed to be a marvel of efficiency.

"Hello," Megan called late one afternoon, catching Glenn in the middle of ordering a load of spikes to the front of the track.

"Hello," Glenn said with genuine pleasure. "New dress?"

Megan pirouetted for him and every man in Glenn's shipping crew grinned and forgot their work. "Yes. Do you like it?"

It was a yellow dress with lacy white collar and cuffs. Megan was wearing white shoes with a matching white purse and stylish hat. The contrast in her appearance to her poor former rags and worn shoes was startling. Now, Megan was a radiant vision of loveliness.

"You're beautiful."

Megan's cheeks colored. "Have you a few minutes to spare?"

"Of course," he said, shouting a few orders to be carried out in his absence. He offered his arm and Megan accepted it as they walked out of hearing of the others.

"Lovely day, isn't it," Megan said happily.

"It is," he agreed, unable to take his eyes off of her. "What brings you around after so long?"

"I have some news that I wanted to share with you," Megan said. "I thought, since you were so helpful in our settlement, you should know how we've spent a big part of it."

"Of course I'd like to know."

"Aileen bought a bakery," Megan said. "It's the one just up the street."

"Congratulations!"

"It's doing over two hundred dollars of business a week," Megan said proudly. "And I've bought a restaurant."

"You did?"

"Yes. It's not permanent. It's a very large tent with a hardwood floor. There are tables and chairs enough to seat a hundred men at a time. We've all the dinnerware and silverware we need in addition to the stove and cooking utensils. There are these huge copper cooking pots, big enough to bathe in but they're for soup."

"I had no idea that you or your sister were interested in that sort of thing," Glenn said, trying to sound pleased and excited.

He must have failed because Megan said, "You don't sound very happy."

"I'm happy for both of you if it works," Glenn said. "It's just that my guess is that a bakery and a diner are very tough businesses to run."

"We'll learn," Megan vowed. "If I like the business, I'll have a permanent restaurant built. I've already got a choice building site picked out."

"Megan," Glenn said, choosing his words carefully, "are you aware that Omaha is going to shrink down to nothing when the Union Pacific drives west?"

"Yes, of course! But that won't be for another three or four months. And given the huge profits we stand to make until then, Aileen and I figure that we . . ."

"Megan," Glenn said, "we're pulling out in a matter of *weeks*."

Megan paled. "How do you know this!"

"General Dodge himself told me so," Glenn replied.

"Durant was heard by a friend of mine to say that we'd be here at least four more months!"

"Not true," Glenn said. "I'm sorry. Omaha will be like a ghost town by mid-June."

"A ghost town?"

Megan looked so shocked and upset that Glenn quickly amended his statement. "Actually, Omaha will retain a small work force. You see, we'll continue to use our new roundhouse for all major repairs. The levee will be repaired and remain the shipping point for most of the supplies brought upriver. I'd say we'll keep at least several hundred workers in Omaha year around. Many have families."

"Several hundred?"

"Yes. Megan, I'm . . ."

"Oh, dear God!" Megan breathed, reaching out to steady herself against Glenn. "We're ruined!"

Glenn led Megan over to a spool of wire and sat her down. "Listen," he said gently, "I'm sure that the bakery and your tent diner will continue to earn you a good living."

Megan looked up at him. "I went over the figures. In three months, we'd have broken even. In six months doubled our investment. But now you're telling me this boom is about to end?"

"I'm afraid so."

"What are we to do?"

Glenn knelt beside Megan. "How much, exactly, of your settlement did you spend?"

"About half. Belle's money is still in the bank."

"Half." Glenn tried to hide his disappointment. "Well, maybe there is someone that you can both sell out to."

Megan shook her head. "I'd have to tell them the truth! Not like Durant who . . . who had us set up!"

Glenn had little doubt that The Doctor actually had conspired to deceive Megan and Aileen out of revenge and spite. "Listen, I've got to get back to work. How about I come by tonight and take you and your sister out to dinner?"

Megan dipped her chin in agreement. "I'll show you my new business."

Glenn wasn't very excited about the prospect of eating in a tent diner that was the source of Megan's being swindled out of half of her settlement. But perhaps something could be salvaged if they put their minds to the task.

"Very good," he said. "Six o'clock?"

"Yes," she replied, eyes vacant with shock.

As Glenn watched Megan leave, he saw a young woman who'd just had all the joy knocked out of her. Glenn was sick about that and yet, he knew that the more time that Megan and

Aileen had to shore up their losses, the better off they'd be. And perhaps a buyer could be found. If not, the O'Connell sisters were in for an extremely hard time of it when the railroad plunged westward and largely deserted poor Omaha.

CHAPTER
13

Megan was sitting in the lobby when Glenn arrived. At his appearance, she jumped to her feet and hurried to meet him. "Thanks for coming on time."

"Where's Aileen?"

"She's upstairs with the children. I tried to get her to come down, but she was so upset that she wasn't up to dinner."

"I understand," Glenn said, leading Megan toward the door. "And now we're going to eat in the tent you bought?"

"Yes. If that's all right."

"Sure. Who's doing the cooking?"

"Me, starting tomorrow when I take legal possession of the business."

Glenn held the door open for Megan and they went outside. It was windy and cool and he was wearing a jacket. Megan had no such protection so Glenn removed his jacket and gave it to her. "Your dress is pretty but not very well suited for cold weather."

"I know. I had intended to buy a coat of some kind," Megan said. "Nothing really fancy, but nice. Then, after learning about the Union Pacific's plans to leave Omaha in the next few weeks, I completely forgot."

"Damn Durant!" Glenn stormed. "I get angry just thinking about how he set you and Aileen up with a false rumor."

"It was stupid of me not to have gotten more facts," Megan said. "I should have at least asked you. But we were so excited about the settlement and then the opportunity to buy the bakery and diner that we jumped at the chance to be in business for ourselves. Now, it seems we've made terrible mistakes."

130

As they walked up the main street of Omaha, they had to thread their way through a boisterous crowd. "Yesterday was payday," Glenn explained, glancing over the bat-winged doors of a saloon. "So businesses are going to prosper for the next few days."

"And we'll prosper as well," Megan said. "As long as there are customers to serve, I mean to give them good hearty meals at fair prices."

"I'm sure you'll do well," Glenn said. "Have you ever cooked for big groups of men?"

"No, but I'll learn. I know how to cook what the Irishmen love. Corned beef and cabbage, lots of potatoes, beef, and mutton. It's not exactly French cuisine, you know."

"No," Glenn said with a smile, "I suppose not. What about your sister?"

"She'll do just fine. Aileen is a wonderful pastry cook. Her apple and cherry pies are prize winners."

"I'm sure that they'll be in great demand," Glenn told her.

"There it is," Megan said, hurrying toward a large tent flanked by other tents lining the west end of the street.

But when they went inside, the huge tent was filled to over-flowing with loud and drunken customers. Dishes and eating utensils littered the tables and men with bottles of whiskey were drinking out of coffee cups. Even by Omaha's wild standards, this was a riotous party.

"I don't understand this at all," Megan said with alarm. "What's going on!"

Before Glenn could venture a guess, Megan dashed across the room to vanish behind a six-foot wooden partition into what Glenn was sure was the kitchen. Glenn rushed after her not seeing either Bill Donovan or the foot that the freighter swung into his path. Glenn tripped and spilled heavily to the floor. He twisted around just in time to see Donovan's boot flying toward his face. Glenn tried to move his head but wasn't fast enough. The boot caught him in the side of the face and it went numb.

"I've been waiting for this too long," Donovan hissed. He reached down and dragged Glenn up, measured him, and punched him in the right eye.

Glenn crashed back down to the floor. He knew he had no chance against Donovan unless he somehow cleared his senses. Squirming under the table, he tried to escape but Donovan grabbed his feet and began dragging him back into the aisle.

Glenn kicked out at the man, felt his legs break free, and scooted back under the table. Donovan bellowed with laughter and yelled, "Come on out of there, Mr. Gilchrist!"

Glenn slithered under a second table as Donovan began to grab and overturn tables. Dishes spilled across the floor and shattered as men roared with delight. Glenn prayed for a few moments to clear his head before Donovan hauled him erect and again smashed his face.

"Damn you, stand up and fight!" Donovan bellowed, kicking Glenn in the ribs.

Glenn tried to get up but Donovan kicked him again and he momentarily lost consciousness. He felt himself being dragged erect. He tasted Donovan's whiskey breath and peered helplessly into a pair of cold, merciless eyes. Donovan drew back his fist and snarled, "When I'm through with you, *Mister* Gilchrist, even your own whore mother won't be able to recognize you."

Glenn kneed the man in the groin. Donovan grimaced but there was not enough power in Glenn to really hurt the man. "You're dead," the Irishman grated.

And if it wasn't for Megan with a big frying pan in her fist, Glenn would have been dead. One instant he was just praying for a quick, merciful ending, the next he saw Donovan's eyes cross and then roll up in his skull as the heavy iron frying pan gonged against his skull.

Donovan dropped and Glenn joined him on the floor. Fighting to stay conscious, Glenn heard Megan yelling and scolding the unruly crowd, telling them to get out of her tent diner. Glenn heard two more gongs and cries of pain. Very quickly, there was a stampede for the door but not before men threw over the last remaining tables and ground the shattered remnants of plates, saucers, and cups under their heels and dragged the unconscious Donovan out by his heels.

"Are you all right!" Megan cried, dropping to her knees.

"No," he groaned, trying to clear his vision. "I feel like I've been run over by horses."

"You don't look so good, either," Megan said. "I'll get a dishrag and some cold water. Your face is really swelling."

Glenn gingerly touched his eye. "Ouch!"

"It's going to be a real shiner," Megan called as she hurried back to the kitchen.

When she returned, she cradled his head in her lap and applied the cold compress but it was too late. His right eye was already swollen shut. With his good left eye, however, Glenn could see the tears streaming down her cheeks.

"I'm going to live," he said, touched by her concern for his pain. "I'll be all right."

"I'm not crying over you—it's my dishes! They're nearly all ruined. Cups. Saucers. Everything lost!"

He rolled his head to his left. Megan was right. The place was destroyed. "I'm sorry," he told her. "I wasn't much help."

"Did you buy that derringer I told you to get?"

"No."

"See then! Donovan would have beat your face in if I hadn't blasted him with that big frying pan."

"Yeah. Thanks."

A tear landed between Glenn's eyes. "What am I going to do now," Megan sniffled. "I'm finished."

"Maybe you and Aileen just weren't meant to be in the food business," Glenn said, unable to think of anything better to say.

Megan's reaction was not what he expected. "Oh, yeah!" she cried, dropping his head on the tent's board floor. "I'll be damned if I'll just walk away from my investment!"

Glenn looked up at Megan whose hands were on her hips and who was glaring at the destruction all around. "The owner, damn his soul, invited all his friends for a party," Megan explained. "They went through half the food stock that I was supposed to get with the deal."

"Then sue him for breach of contract," Glenn whispered, trying to crawl erect.

"I can't! The fool told me he's already spent most of the money!"

Glenn abandoned the idea of trying to stand up. Instead, he sat cross-legged and pressed the cold compress to his eye. He watched Megan stomp back and forth, grabbing tables and righting them, crushing broken cups and dishes under her feet and crying all at the same time.

"Megan," he said when she flopped down beside him, buried her face in her hands, and wept bitterly, "I'm so sorry."

"Me too," she cried. "Me too!"

"We'll think of something," he promised, reaching out and pulling her head to rest on his shoulder. When she just kept crying, Glenn said, "If you're still hungry, we can go someplace else and I'll buy you dinner."

"I want a drink," she sniffled. "I want three or four drinks!"

"I've a bottle up in my room and . . ."

She recoiled as if bitten. "Oh, no you don't! You may think I'm down and helpless but you're wrong. I'm not falling for that line again."

"You mean you did once?"

Megan pulled a silk handkerchief out of her dress. She blew her nose rather lustily. "Once," she admitted. "Mr. Gallagher caught me in a weak moment. And I did feel sorry for him at the same time. It was a terrible set of circumstances that led me to agree to marry him, God rest his poor drunken soul."

"I see," Glenn said, not seeing at all. "Can you help me up?"

"I can." Megan was strong and she hoisted him to his feet without any difficulty. She righted a table and he leaned heavily against it.

"Your poor face," Megan said with a grimace. "It's going to be purple and swollen as a grape."

"Next time, I'll take your advice and pack a derringer. After this beating, I'd not hesitate to shoot Donovan on sight."

"Now you're talking," Megan clipped. "A man like that needs a bullet in the belly. Either cure him of his meanness, or kill him."

As bad as he felt, Glenn had to smile but that made him wince with pain. "Ouch!"

"You *are* a mess, poor thing," Megan said, touching his cheek. "And you came to take me out to dinner and cheer me up, now look what you get for your good intentions."

"I'll survive. I doubt that Donovan is feeling a whole lot better. I heard that big iron skillet gong when it whacked his skull."

"His skull is so thick it dented the skillet," Megan said with a look of satisfaction. "Do you know of a place where we can go and have a quiet bite to eat and a few stiff belts of decent Irish whiskey?"

"I do."

"But not your hotel room."

"No."

She offered Glenn her arm. "Saints help me," she clucked, leading him unsteadily toward the door. "I don't know what in the world I'm going to do with this place now."

"Clean up this mess and open for business just as planned," Glenn said, reeling to a halt by the tent's opening before Megan cinched it up tight. "Feed your customers on tin plates with tin cups. They won't break. In three or four weeks, I think you can make a good profit because Omaha is crawling with men and money. After that, sell out."

"Or follow the railroad west."

Glenn blinked. "You can't be serious."

"Oh, but I am!"

"But *we* feed our crews for free on the line!"

"But you won't have the kind of food that I'll be servin'."

Glenn didn't feel up to arguing the point. Maybe Megan was right. Perhaps a good tent diner could turn a profit going from one hell-on-wheels town to the next. But a bakery? Highly doubtful.

"Wouldn't you like the McConnell women and dear Belle to follow you across the West?" Megan asked as she tied the flap shut and they started back up the street.

Glenn's skull was pounding. Everyone he passed stared at his lopsided face and Glenn knew that he must be a piteous sight. His ribs hurt so badly he walked a little bent over and he offered a silent prayer that none were cracked or broken. Damn that Bill Donovan! The next time they met things would be different—he hoped. Right now, they were one victory apiece. Glenn wasn't sure he had one more fight in him against the bigger, stronger man but he was determined to find out first chance.

Donovan would pay or Glenn meant to die trying.

It took some doing, but Megan managed to use Glenn's suggestion and find a hundred tin cups and plates to replace her shattered dishes. Inside of two days, she had the tent reopened for business with a very short list of rules. No one was allowed inside the tent packing a gun. Guns were to be deposited at the old cash register that had come with the business. Everyone who expected to eat had to be wearing a shirt and shoes and no chewing tobacco was allowed in Megan's Place. After they ate, customers were welcome to smoke, but not spit. There was no menu, the specialty of the day was all that was offered and it was six bits and that included two refills of coffee. No whiskey, beer, or liquor of any kind was allowed. If a fight broke out, no matter who started it, the combatants were ejected and never allowed back inside.

Megan's rules were strict by Omaha's standards and there were more than a few belligerent customers who refused to obey them. In each case, Megan asked them to leave and if they refused, other loyal customers came to her aid and the rules were physically enforced. Contrary to some who predicted the rules would kill Megan's business, they actually increased it. The harder element who liked to get drunk and raise hell stayed out of the tent but those who wanted a peaceful and satisfying meal were more than happy to oblige such civilized rules of conduct. Another reason for Megan's success was her food.

"This is the best corned beef and cabbage in Omaha," men would say over and over. "And the coffee is fresh and strong."

In addition to her own simple but excellent cooking, Megan never missed a chance to promote Aileen's bakery goods. "Do you like the rolls? If you do, there's more where they came from just up the street in my sister's new bakery. A slice of pie is two bits extra and you'll want seconds. My sister bakes all the pies and there are none better."

Few men would dispute the quality of Megan's fare or her sister's pies and pastries. Word quickly spread among the rough men that Megan's Place was the best food in town for the money and that her sister's bakery goods were almost as good as their dear mothers'. Overnight, both the O'Connell sisters' establishments were booming successes.

Megan hired three plain and middle-aged Irish women to help her with the cooking. She hired younger, single women to do the serving and Belle often filled in when she wasn't busy at Aileen's bakery. Another woman who proved to be very popular with the male customers was Rachel Foreman, the girl Liam had saved from drowning but who had lost her infant son.

Rachel and Belle were equally ambitious and seemed to enjoy vying for tips among the customers. Both were short, saucy, and voluptuous but while Belle was dark and pretty, Rachel was fair and cute with a spattering of freckles across her nose and rather large pale blue eyes. And despite both having suffered great tragedy in the Missouri flood, the girls had a lot of charm and sparkle. Men tipped them well and even though Belle's U.P. settlement made her a wealthy girl by Irish working standards, she hustled just as hard as Rachel for both praise and tips.

"They're looking for husbands," one of the Irish cooks said with disapproval as she watched the pair work the crowd of men, causing them to laugh and make a big fuss over the two girls. "And that's shamefully obvious."

"There's no harm being done," Megan said. "Besides, Belle isn't looking to get married, she's still only fifteen."

"Ha! She's eighteen or my name isn't Winnie McCoy!"

"Eighteen? No," Megan said, watching Belle hurry among the tables, refilling coffee cups, pausing to smile or giggle with some lonesome railroad worker. "She lost her parents during the flood and has no family."

"She never knew her parents."

Megan's head snapped back. "What are you talking about?"

"I knew the King family in St. Louis. There was a passel of them lived there and most were always into some kind of mischief. Town drove 'em out finally, they was such trouble. That girl was raised an orphan by her aunt and uncle. Megan, worse trash you never seen."

"Winnie, I think you must have the wrong King family," Megan said. "Belle is originally from West Virginia, later from Chattanooga, Tennessee."

Winnie shrugged. She was a square-set woman, probably in her mid to late forties with thick forearms and gray-streaked hair. "You can think what you want, but I saw that girl once when her aunt was arrested for stealing a cow. The family was always looking to cheat someone out of something."

"You *must* be mistaken."

"Belle's uncle was a tall, one-armed man with a big scar on his cheek."

"I wouldn't know," Megan said.

"And her aunt was a fat woman with one droopy eyelid and a big mole on the tip of her nose. She had a high kind of whiny voice. Her name was Esther."

"I never met either one of Belle's parents."

"Of course you didn't because Belle never had any. The people she lived with were her aunt and uncle. They raised her wild as an alley cat."

Megan shook her head. "Belle is a fine girl and I'm sure that you've confused her with someone else."

Winnie clamped her mouth shut and Megan suddenly wanted some fresh air. "We're running low on corned beef and I've got to have more rolls from the bakery. I'll be right back."

Megan hurried out the back of the tent. Aileen's Bakery was only a few doors up the street and Megan was in the habit of making a dash back and forth several times each evening. Tonight, Aileen was busy cutting gingerbread cookies while one of her assistants handled a steady flow of customers at the front counter. Aileen's two children were over in a corner, sound asleep on a makeshift bed of empty flour sacks.

"It's really busy tonight," Megan said, grabbing a tray of hot dinner rolls. "I'll probably need two more trays and as many pies as you can give me."

"Got seven in the oven," Aileen said, perspiring and working quickly over the cookies. "But after that, I'm closing shop."

"By then, it will be at least eleven o'clock and I'll be ready to close too," Megan said.

She stopped at the back door and looked back at her sister. Aileen actually appeared happy. These days she was far too tired to dwell on the loss of her husband or their uncertain future once the Union Pacific began to empty Omaha. Aileen had always loved to bake and now she was making a real profit from her talent. That made Megan feel good.

"Aileen?"

She looked up from the cookies with eyebrows arched in question.

"Did you ever meet Belle's mother and father?"

Aileen's brow furrowed with concentration. "Yes, I vaguely remember that her father was a one-armed man. Her mother was a heavy woman. There was something about her that . . . yes, she had one droopy eyelid and a big mole on her nose. It was so large that you really had to work not to stare at it, poor woman. Why do you ask?"

"No reason in particular," Megan called as she left with the trays of hot dinner rolls.

But the next day, Megan could not get Winnie McCoy's remarks out of her mind and so she left her diner and went hunting for Glenn. She found him in the new roundhouse ordering locomotive replacement parts.

"You always surprise me the way you appear so unexpectedly," Glenn said. "And give me a wonderful excuse to take my mind off my work."

"Could I ask you a question?"

"Sure."

"Didn't you tell me that a woman brought Belle to you and explained that she was only fourteen and had lost her parents in the flood?"

"Of course. That's why the Union Pacific paid her five thousand dollars." Glenn raised his hands palms up. "What an odd question."

"What did the woman look like?"

"The one who brought Belle to us?"

"Yes."

"As I recall, she was quite heavy and rather a sad sort. She had a droopy eyelid and a very unsightly mole right here." Glenn touched the tip of his nose. "Why?"

Megan quickly looked away. "I . . . I was just wondering."

"Is something wrong?"

"No," Megan said, brightening. "Just curious."

"I asked the woman to stay here at least until we found Belle a foster home or someone who could take her in, but she refused. Said her husband insisted they leave Omaha the very next day."

"Where were they going?"

"St. Louis."

Megan ran her hand absently across her eyes and took a deep breath.

"Are you all right?" Glenn took her arm. "You look a little, I dunno, dazed, I guess. Are you working too hard?"

Megan took a deep breath. "Yes, I am."

"I'd like to take you out for dinner."

"You know that I appreciate the offer, but as long as the Union Pacific crews are in Omaha, I'm going to make hay while the sun shines."

"I understand."

"Any word on when you'll be leaving?" Megan asked.

"Not yet, but I'm ready for a change."

"I'll worry about you way out there beyond protection from the Indians."

"I'll be fine," Glenn said with more bravado than he felt. "And speaking of Indians and scouts, I heard that Joshua Hood and his boys just returned to Omaha. Liam is fine. I saw him riding up the street with them and he looks like he's been riding a horse and shouldering a buffalo rifle since the cradle."

A cloud passed before Megan's eyes. "I'm glad," she said stiffly.

Glenn took her hands in his own. "Listen," he said, "I'm not one to meddle, but . . ."

"Then please don't."

"But," Glenn continued, "Liam will grow up and probably turn out just fine. So whatever he did to cause you such pain, I hope you can forgive him. I know that he reveres you, Megan."

She laughed, but not well.

This troubled Glenn. He leaned forward and kissed Megan on the forehead. "He reveres you and so do I."

"Ahh!" she cried, mustering up the pretense of dismay and pushing him aside. "You're full of the blarney, Mr. Gilchrist! And I've got to get back to my tent and kitchen."

"I'll come by tonight for a meal, light on the cabbage but heavy on the corned beef and rolls."

"And the pie and coffee," Megan said.

Glenn chuckled and Megan let the man go back to his work. The moment she turned away from the handsome young engineer, her thoughts became dark and troubled. Who was Belle King, really? And had she actually lost her parents in the flood or had it all been a clever ruse to swindle $5,000 in the form of a railroad settlement for parents who had never really existed?

Megan shivered with dread. She was afraid that cute, but strong-willed Belle was not the tragic and heartbroken girl that everyone had originally supposed. In fact, she might well be as old as Megan herself and, in addition to being a very good actress, was an accomplished liar and cheat. If so, Megan wanted no part of the girl. As for the $5,000 that Belle had won from the Union Pacific, if Megan's suspicions were confirmed, restitution would have to be made and then Belle King might very well face criminal charges. Durant, stung by their $13,000 in settlements, would show Belle no mercy. He'd do his very best to have her imprisoned.

Megan had intended to go back to her diner and start the preparations for the evening meal. Now, however, she headed up the street toward the fancy ladies boarding house where Belle had moved after getting her hands on that big chunk of Union Pacific money.

CHAPTER
14

"Who is it?"

"It's Megan," she said in the hallway.

Belle opened her boarding house room door and smiled. "What a surprise! Did I do something wrong last night before I left the diner? I saw Winnie scowling at me and knew that she was mad at me again."

"Can we talk?"

Belle was dressed in a pink silken wrapper. She looked very young, soft, and kittenish. Brushing back her thick, dark mane of hair, Belle motioned Megan inside. "Come in."

The room was bright and cheery with lace curtains and a quilted bedspread. There were framed paintings on the walls and even a profusion of wildflowers in a vase with a note, probably from one of Megan's admiring customers. The furniture was elegant and French Provincial. Megan wondered what such a divine room like this would cost, probably four or five times what she, Aileen, and the children were paying.

"Would you like to sit down?" Belle asked. "I was just about to ring for coffee. Or would you rather have fresh tea?"

"Coffee will be fine."

Belle went to the bell rope and gave it two quick tugs. Downstairs, there was the sound of a buzzer and Megan supposed that the coffee would be brought up in a few moments.

Belle took a brush to her thick dark hair. "I am definitely not a morning person," she said, studying Megan closely. "I like to sleep until noon. It's a luxury that I've never been able to afford."

"With that five-thousand-dollar settlement, you could sleep in for years and never lift a finger."

Belle stopped brushing. "That's true, but then I'd be broke and right back where I started."

"Were your parents poor?"

"Very," Belle said. "We never had any money."

"What do you intend to do with your five thousand," Megan asked. "If you don't mind telling me."

"Like you and Aileen, I'm looking to invest it in a business of some kind."

"Such as?"

"I don't know. Is this why you came to talk? Do you need a partner?"

"Oh, no," Megan said quickly. "Nothing like that at all."

"Then what?"

Megan heard a soft knock at the door and waited while a tray with an urn of coffee, cups, sugar, and cream was brought into the room.

"Sugar or cream?" Belle asked.

"No thank you," Megan said, trying desperately to think of some delicate way to broach a very touchy and unpleasant subject. If Winnie was wrong, if there was some mistake, then Megan knew she would feel terrible for suspecting that this girl had duped the Union Pacific and everyone else including herself.

"I, ah . . . I was talking to Mrs. McCoy and she said something about you that has caused me concern," Megan began, taking her coffee with a nod of appreciation.

"That woman didn't like me from the moment we met," Belle said, adding two teaspoons of sugar and pouting thick cream into her own coffee. "I've tried to be friendly with her, Megan. You know how hard I work at keeping the customers happy."

"You are very popular, and so is Rachel. You're both part of the reason why we are doing so much business every noon and night."

"Thanks," Belle said. "I can't help it if Mrs. McCoy has taken such a strong dislike to me. I try to stay out of her way, but that isn't always possible."

"Of course not," Megan heard herself say, "we all have to work together." Megan caught herself thinking that this girl looked too young to drink coffee, or anything other than water, juice, or milk. "But the thing that concerns me is that Mrs. McCoy says that she knew you in St. Louis."

Belle raised her brows. "I never saw the woman in my life before I came to work for you."

"She described your aunt perfectly."

"My aunt?" Belle set her cup and saucer down so hard that coffee spilled. "What are you talking about, Megan? I don't have an aunt! At least, not in Omaha."

Megan lost her taste for coffee or anything else. "Mrs. McCoy described your aunt as the same person who brought you to Mr. Gilchrist after the flood."

Belle had taken a seat but now she stood. "Would you *please* stop playing word games and come to the point! I'm getting very upset with you."

Megan also came to her feet. "I'm afraid that I have no choice but to believe Mrs. McCoy when she says you were always an orphan."

"What!"

"That you had no parents and concocted this whole story up to swindle money from the Union Pacific Railroad."

Belle slapped her hands over her ears and cried, "I don't believe I'm hearing this!"

"And that you aren't a poor fourteen- or fifteen-year-old girl, but instead a very clever young actress who has used me and my sister and Mr. Gilchrist to hoodwink the Union Pacific Railroad out of five thousand dollars."

"Get out of here!"

Megan stood her ground. "I want the truth. If you won't give it to me, I'll be forced to go to the Union Pacific and tell them what I do know. I'm sure that inquiries will be sent to St. Louis and an investigation will follow. Mr. Durant isn't going to let five thousand dollars go without a fight."

Belle's dark eyes widened with outrage. "*You* have the nerve to accuse *me* of fraud? You whose husband was a womanizer and a drunkard. You who had thrown him out of your bed and were about to end your marriage?"

"I wasn't!"

"You were too!" Belle raised a finger and shook it in Megan's face. "Your husband was a millstone around your neck and so was Aileen's husband."

"Aileen loved Hugh!"

"That's right," Belle said, "she did love him and more's the pity for being such a weak fool."

Megan reached back and slapped Belle so hard the girl's head rocked sideways. Belle screeched like a cat and threw herself forward. Megan twisted and grabbed the smaller woman, then tripped her to the floor. They struggled. Belle was strong but Megan was even stronger and managed to get astraddle the girl and pin her hands to the carpet.

"Stop it! Megan, let me up and I'll scratch your eyes out!"

Megan held the girl tight, listening to her curse and wail in anger and frustration. When Belle finally stopped struggling, Megan said, "It was all a trick, wasn't it?"

"No!"

"Yes!"

"If you tell them, I swear I'll get people to testify that you hated your husband. That you'd thrown him out of your shanty and that neither he nor Aileen's husband was worth a damn! If I lose my money, so will you!"

Megan's heart was pounding and her mind raced. She couldn't believe what she was hearing. This was no girl. This was a hellcat of a woman. "How old are you, really?"

"Twenty!" Belle struggled. "Get off me!"

Megan wasn't sure that she dared to set this tiger free. As outraged as Belle was, if she had a gun, the girl might actually try to shoot her.

"If I let you up, will you tell me the truth?"

"Why should I? I don't owe you anything!"

Megan had no choice but to let Belle up anyway but she did grab the empty coffee urn in case Belle leapt for her throat or a hidden gun.

Belle's wrapper was twisted open and there was little doubt that she was a grown woman. Belle straightened herself and glared at Megan with clenched fists. "Get out of my room."

"Tell me the truth or I'm going to the Union Pacific right now and I promise you that they will get to the truth."

Belle took an advancing step but Megan held her ground. She realized they were both breathing hard. This whole scene seemed unreal but it *was* real and it wasn't very pretty.

Belle whirled and stomped over to a beautiful French dresser. She opened a drawer and Megan almost jumped for the door, certain that she was about to be shot. But instead, Belle removed a bottle of imported liquor, then uncorked and drank it straight. Wiping her lips on her dressing gown's sleeve, her eyes were pitying when she regarded Megan.

"All right," Belle said. "That old bag, Winnie McCoy, did know me in St. Louis and the woman that brought me to Mr. Gilchrist really was my aunt. So what!"

"So you didn't lose your parents in the flood, did you?"

"I lost them to Indians a long, long time ago when we were homesteading near the Kansas border. I hardly remember them. All I know is that they and my brothers were both murdered while I was staying at Aunt Cleo's. After that, I was shifted like baggage among relatives in St. Louis. None of them wanted me. I was just an extra mouth to feed. When I was fourteen, my uncle started bringing men home to use me and he'd collect the money for drink. I had a miscarriage at sixteen and almost died. I can't ever have children."

Megan sat down heavily. She clenched her hands in her lap and stared at them while Belle vented her pain and anger.

"I was a full-time whore the next year and I was stabbed in a saloon when I was nineteen." Belle's voice shook with fury. "Do you want to hear the rest, or are you beginning to understand why I don't give a damn about anything but survival?"

Megan looked up. "I'm sorry," she said, realizing how inadequate the words must sound.

"Don't be! The last thing I want is pity! Yours, Gilchrist's, or the Union Pacific Railroad's! I just want money. My uncle finally drank himself to death last month. Aunt Cleo and I had to have a new start. But she was too old and too heavy to get work and I swore I wouldn't ever allow myself to be used again. So we starved. We were out of food and hope when that ice broke and the river flooded. Like everyone else down on that river bottom land, we lost what little we had in this world. Only they at least had a chance to get jobs. Cleo and I had no chance at all."

"And so," Megan said, "in desperation, you and Aunt Cleo hatched up this ruse you played on Mr. Gilchrist, taking advantage of his sense of justice. Putting him at odds with his own employer."

"He's a college-educated man, he can take care of himself. Megan, we had everything to gain and nothing to lose. The most we expected was twenty or thirty dollars. Enough to buy food and a ticket back to St. Louis. But we got lucky. Very, very lucky! For the first time in my life, something good happened and suddenly, Cleo and I had more money than we'd ever dreamed."

"Where did she go?"

"Across the river to Council Bluffs. We split the five thousand dollars fifty-fifty. They'll have to kill both of us to get that money back. For Cleo and me, it's our only chance."

Megan came to her feet. She opened her mouth to speak, then closed it and shook her head.

"What are you going to do now?" Belle demanded. "Are you going to let your conscience ruin the only hope any of us women have? Do you know what we all face without money? If you don't know, then think! We're young and you and I can find husbands, maybe even sober, hard-working ones. And we'll be expected to be, oh, so grateful for anything we can get. But what about your sister with two small children? She'll find it much harder. And there is no hope for my Aunt Cleo. She'd starve in some gutter and no one except me would lift a finger to save her."

Megan was almost overcome with despair. "What you say might be true, but, Belle, I just don't think I can live with the knowledge this whole thing has been a . . . a clever trick."

"Then give your own damned money back to them because your husbands weren't worth the cost of a pine box! If you want to ease your conscience, then *you* make restitution because you are as guilty of telling a lie as I am."

Megan wanted to protest but could not. There was just too much truth in this girl's words.

Belle moved closer and the heat went out of her voice. "Listen to me, Megan. Us women got to stick together. With our settlements, we've finally got a chance at freedom and we *must* seize it by the throat and hang on to it for our very lives. And if you can't live with the guilt, then make a lot of money and repay the railroad later."

Megan realized that she was beginning to nod her head in agreement. It was shocking but so was the story she'd just heard. She'd had rough times, but her life had been a breeze compared to that of Belle King. And Belle was right, the money was their only chance and it could someday be repaid. Besides, The Doctor would want more than repayment, he'd want revenge.

"So what are you going to do, Megan?"

Megan looked at Belle and said, "I'll pay the railroad back if we make good."

Belle clapped her hands together. "Now you're talking! And maybe I'll do the same."

"No you won't. And furthermore, I don't want anything more to do with you, Belle. You've deceived me and everyone else and I don't trust you."

"Fine," Belle said, deflating with pain. "I don't need you, your sister, or anyone else. I've got friends and I've got plans to follow the rails west. By the time they reach California, I'll be almost as rich as Durant."

Megan started for the door.

"Hey!" Belle called.

Megan turned and Belle said, "You're not so saintly white yourself, you know. I've seen the way you eye Glenn Gilchrist because you think he has family money."

"Shut up!"

Belle laughed. "It's true. But if Durant were younger, I'll bet we'd both be making a play to get him into bed."

"You're disgusting!"

"Am I? Well, I know this much—this is a man's world and the only way a woman can get ahead is in a man's bed. The trick is not to get pregnant and I've already told you that's not going to be a problem for me. But you had better be thinking about it."

"You make me ill," Megan said, throwing the door open.

"One more thing," Belle said, following her into the hallway. "If you really love your sister and those two children, send them back east wherever they came from."

"What do you care?"

"I care," Belle said. "Aileen has a true heart but she's fragile and weak. This is no place for her kind on the frontier."

Megan wheeled around and left. The moment she got outside, she stepped into a side alley, leaned up against the boarding house wall, and closed her eyes. How could she have been so naive to have been tricked so completely by that conniving wench?

No matter, she and everyone else had been fooled and that was all that counted. Megan took a deep breath to compose herself and then she stepped back onto the sidewalk and headed for her diner. There was a lot of work to do and since Belle was not coming in tonight or any other night, she would have to work extra hard.

When Megan arrived at the diner, Liam was standing in wait. Only it didn't seem possible it really was her brother. He looked completely different. His clothes were bloodstained and matted with grease and buffalo hair. He had the beginnings of a full beard and he looked taller and quite fierce.

"Liam?"

He dredged up a wary smile. "Do you still hate me, Sis?"

Something broke in Megan. Perhaps it was pent-up emotions from having just confronted Belle, or maybe it was just the strain she'd been under since buying her diner. Whatever it was, she burst into tears and ran forward to throw her arms around Liam, hair, bloodstains be damned.

"What's the matter?" he asked, holding her tight. "Is something wrong, besides me, I mean?"

Megan couldn't answer that. She just held Liam and cried until there were no more tears in her and then she sniffled, found her own handkerchief, and blew her nose.

"Come on inside and tell me all about your hunting trip," she said, untying the tent flap.

Liam followed her inside. "You own this?"

"Yes."

"You don't sound very excited." Liam looked closely at her. "What's wrong?"

"We'll talk about it later," Megan said. "Tell me all about your hunting trip. I want to hear some good, exciting news."

Liam grinned. "It was everything that I dreamed it'd be and more. You should have seen the way we killed buffalo! I liked to die from saddle sores on the way out but Joshua gave me some buffalo grease to salve the insides of my legs. On the way back, I didn't hurt at all and I wasn't bouncing nearly so high in the saddle."

"Good!" Megan said. "I can hardly wait to see your new horse."

"He's a dandy old fella and strong. We get along real well. In fact, I'm getting along with all of them except this one fella about my age named Calvin Miller. Joshua says I'll have to fight him before long and he's going to teach me how to whip Miller good."

"I see."

"I never been so happy, Megan."

"I'm glad."

"And . . ."

Liam was interrupted by the appearance of Rachel Foreman arriving for work. They stared at each other and then Rachel's hand flew to her mouth. "You're the one!"

Liam shrugged. "I'm sorry about your baby."

Rachel's eyes filled with tears and they brimmed over and went sliding down her freckled cheeks.

"Oh, God," Liam groaned. "She's cryin' too! What's the matter with you women today?"

Megan dried her own tears. "I don't know," she said, "maybe it's something in the air or that's catching among us females."

"I never heard of that," Liam said, not realizing that his sister was only teasing.

Rachel sleeved her cheeks dry. She stuck out her hand and curtsied. "Mr. O'Connell, I owe you my life. I can't thank you enough for pulling me out of that icy water."

"It wasn't such a big thing."

"Oh, yes it was!" Rachel stepped forward and gazed up into Liam's eyes. "I don't know how I'm ever going to thank you enough."

Liam's grin was slow and bold. "I guess we can think of something," he said, eyes dropping to Rachel's bosom.

"Liam!" Megan cried. "What is the matter with you?"

"Not a damned thing," he said, placing his hand on Rachel's shoulder and drinking her in with his hot hunter's eyes.

CHAPTER
▬▬▬ **15** ▬▬▬

Joshua Hood dismounted and tied his fine sorrel gelding to The Doctor's palace car recently purchased from the United States Government. Called the Lincoln Car because it had been made especially for President Abraham Lincoln in 1864, Joshua recalled that sheets of boiler iron had been placed between the inner and outer walls of the palatial car to protect Lincoln from attack while traveling. If that were true, it was a damn shame that Lincoln had not been in this car instead of going to the Ford Theater the night of his assassination.

Joshua was wearing a clean shirt under his buckskin jacket. He'd removed his big-rowled spurs so not to rake the coach's polished wood floor. He'd greased his boots, washed his face and neck, then bought a bright red bandanna to put around his throat. Removing his hat, Joshua slicked back his long hair with his fingers, then knocked on the door.

One of Durant's aides ushered Joshua inside. The interior of the Lincoln Car was dim but Joshua could see that it ran heavily to black walnut; the furniture was upholstered in dark green velvet. Joshua had heard that the car was fancy, but this was finer than anything he'd ever visited, and that included New Orleans's most opulent saloons and gambling parlors.

"Mr. Hood, would you like a cigar and a glass of brandy?" Durant asked.

"That'd be okay by me," Joshua said, nodding to Durant, then to General Dodge.

A cigar was brought to him on a wooden plate with a little cutting knife to nip off the tip. Joshua ignored the fancy silver knife and bit the tip off the cigar, then spat it onto the tray. He did accept a light from the aide and the brandy was so smooth it went down like peppermint candy.

"Mr. Hood," Durant said, "tell us about your expedition up the Loup River. I understand that you stayed completely away from our construction line along the Platte."

"Yes, sir," Joshua said, "I did. No chance of runnin' across any buffalo thataway."

"But you did jump a herd along the Loup River."

"Not the Loup," Joshua said. "Just a tributary. There's a valley where I've always found buffalo this time of year. They were there again. It was pretty easy shooting, Mr. Durant."

"What about the herds farther west?" Dodge asked pointedly. "We expect to be moving at the rate of better than a mile a day. Are you going to be able to keep us supplied with fresh buffalo meat and venison?"

"Most of the time," Joshua said. "But I'd keep a large herd of cattle moving with us for when the buffalo move farther south."

"And the Indians," Durant said. "How do you think we should handle them?"

"I mean to see if we can strike a peace," Joshua said. "Better for them and better for us."

"You won't make a peace," Dodge flatly predicted. "The Sioux and the Cheyenne will fight us every mile of the way. The Arapaho are a little more inclined to accept the inevitable and act as scouts. I want you to make contact with them and let them know that the Union Pacific will treat them as friends if they remain peaceful."

"Anything else?"

"Yes," Dodge said, "escort Mr. Gilchrist up to our forward surveying party so that he can make notes and observations. Then bring him safely back to me with a full report on everything you see."

Durant's jaw muscles corded. "I tell you, Grenville, that young engineer is not to be trusted."

"I think he is," Dodge argued. "Anyway, we'll give him a chance to prove his abilities."

"Or inabilities," Durant snapped, clearly annoyed.

Dodge was not listening but instead was studying Joshua. "I understand that you have lived with the Cheyenne and Arapaho."

"Only with the Arapaho but I know a few Cheyenne."

"As you can tell," Dodge said, "I'm extremely pessimistic about the Indians. But I'll ask you anyway—can we buy this railroad a safe construction passage across their hunting grounds?"

Joshua hooked a finger through his bandanna, loosening it to give himself more air. "I can try, General, but you know the situation about as well as I do. Ten, twenty years ago before the forty-niner gold rush and all the traffic along the Oregon Trail, these Indians could be snookered. They believed our promises or at least could be bought. That just isn't the case anymore."

"Your job," Durant said, "is to try to buy or convince them that it is in everyone's best interest not to fight."

"Yes, sir, I understand that, even if it ain't necessarily true."

Dodge motioned for a cigar. As silence grew, Dodge carefully demonstrated how to use the little silver knife and when he had his cigar prepared and lit, he scowled. "Mr. Hood," he began, "I know you are a decent man of courage and resourcefulness. That's why we hired you as chief scout. We also realize you are sympathetic with the Indians. This is acceptable, even commendable. However, progress must never be denied and the Union Pacific Railroad represents progress."

"Yes, sir."

"Now we're prepared to help the Indians and . . ."

"How, General?"

"We'll respect their hunting grounds," Dodge said. "You'll hunt only enough meat to feed our crews. No slaughter for sport or for just the taking of hides. The Army will feed the Indians in the winter if the buffalo herds break up or drift south and refuse to cross the tracks."

"That's fine," Joshua said, "but as you both know, the Plains Indians are nomads. They follow the herds. You find buffalo, you generally find Indians. It's that simple."

"Nothing is 'that simple,' " Durant corrected. "What is important here is that we buy ourselves a peace, at least until we can spike the rails down and cross these high plains. After that, we're all quite sure that the Indian problem will soon resolve itself in our favor."

Joshua could not help but feel a kernel of anger form in the base of his gut. He understood exactly what Durant was saying. Once the transcontinental railroad was completed, more and more people would ride the rails out to settle in Nebraska,

Wyoming, and other points along the tracks. Towns would spring up and the Indians would be forced onto reservations. Their way of life would die in the name of progress.

As if reading his mind, Dodge said, "I don't wish to debate the issue with you, Mr. Hood, but there really are no friendly Indians. Washington doesn't seem to understand how easy it is for the Indians to slip into a small stage station or survey party camp and kill whites while driving off their stock. They ambush soldiers, cut the telegraph lines, and then vanish before they can be punished."

"They're tough and move fast," Joshua agreed. "I respect them as enemies."

"Make sure," Durant said, "that they *remain* your enemies, because they most certainly are this railroad's enemies."

"Yes, sir."

General Dodge puffed thoughtfully. "You have to understand, Mr. Hood, that unless we can set aside large reservations for these Indians where they can be free from the immigrants and out of progress's way, it will be impossible to make any permanent peace with them until they are thoroughly whipped."

"I'm afraid that they'll have to be exterminated," Joshua said. "I don't believe they will ever live on reservations."

"You're wrong, sir." Dodge leaned back in his chair, puffing rapidly. "I don't think they need be eradicated from the face of the earth, but for at least the next generation, they'll be forced to live on the reservations our government creates. After that, it is my firm hope and belief that they will give up their old way of acting and thinking and amalgamate into our white society."

"They'll what?"

"Amalgamate," Dodge repeated. "You know, intermix."

"You mean intermarry?"

"That too, to some extent. Mr. Hood, I'm sure that you are not well educated in the course of world history, but if you were, you'd see that this is just a case of civilization running its natural course. Strong peoples have always conquered weaker ones and integrated them into their own society. It's the natural order of things. It's happened throughout recorded history and it's happening right here in the American West."

Joshua did not wish to argue against far better educated men, but he didn't believe this "amalgamation" business. Hell, the whites and the Negroes down in the South hadn't done much in the way of "amalgamating." Joshua was pretty sure that Negroes had been enslaved on plantations since the mid-1600s. He knew this because he'd talked to many of them down in Texas and Louisiana and they could count back many generations of slaves. And even though they'd been freed after the Civil War, Negroes still lived apart from the whites and Joshua thought they always would.

"Mr. Hood," Dodge was saying, "we can't change the natural bent of civil strife and history. Not even the President of these United States can. Nations and peoples evolve. They grow strong, they defeat weaker opponents and then eventually become lax and are themselves conquered."

Dodge paused for a sip of brandy, cleared his throat, and went on. "If you are honest, you know that the Indians have done that among themselves for untold centuries. The Sioux, for example, were driven westward or they'd have been destroyed. They in turn defeated whatever people were here before them and so it goes among all of humanity."

"Yes, sir," Joshua said. "So who do you think is gonna whip our butts and take us over someday?"

Durant and the general exchanged amused glances and Durant said, "That is not our concern, Mr. Hood. I think it's safe to say that this nation has a long, bright future ahead now that we have defeated the South and its pernicious philosophy of separatism. But to exist, we must be progressive."

"And that means this railroad."

"Exactly," the vice president of the Union Pacific stated.

Joshua tossed down his brandy. This conversation greatly troubled him. He was sure of only one thing and that was that the Sioux and Cheyenne would not readily accept Dodge's grand historical view of amalgamation of races and civilizations. The Indians that Joshua knew would rather die than be tethered to some damned government trading post and boxed in by the arbitrary boundaries of a white man's reservation.

"I'd like you to deliver Mr. Gilchrist to the front survey team and then reconnoiter for a week or two. After that, bring him back down the line to us."

"You'll still be in Omaha?"

"Maybe," Durant said.

"I hope not," Dodge said. "We've about gotten the roadbed to Papillion repaired and then will really slam the iron down.

We're in a race with the Central Pacific and it's a race I mean to win."

"With Jack Casement and Sam Reed driving the rails," Dodge said, "we'll show Congress that we mean business."

"Yes, sir," Joshua said, coming to his feet.

"Don't lose that thick mane of hair," Dodge warned. "And don't let Mr. Gilchrist lose his either."

Joshua nodded and shook both men's hands, then he jammed the cigar between his teeth and went outside. He untied his sorrel and swung into the saddle. He wasn't too damned pleased about playing nursemaid to Glenn Gilchrist but orders were orders. At least he would be leaving Omaha in the next day or two. But first, as long as he was washed and wearing a clean shirt, he guessed he would go court Megan. Hell, maybe he'd get lucky and she really would be overcome with gratitude that he'd hired her brother as a scout and hunter. Maybe, but Joshua very much doubted it.

"Afternoon, Mrs. Gallagher," Joshua said, removing his hat and stepping around the partition to see her working in the kitchen. "I hear that you cook the best food in Omaha."

Megan beamed. "For the price, I'd say that was a fair statement. Hello, Mr. Hood. I've been meaning to look you up and tell you how grateful I am for your taking Liam under your wing. He's like a new man."

"He's going to be just fine," Joshua said. "He's real green, but we all were at one time or another. The kid has guts and spirit. He's smart, willin' to learn, and he takes orders from me."

"I can't imagine anyone *not* taking orders from you," Megan said, standing before a huge tub of wet potatoes she was peeling for the evening meal.

"Can I help you with them?"

"Peeling potatoes?" Megan asked with surprise.

"Sure! I've peeled a few thousand in my time. Carrots too. Lot easier than skinnin' a buffalo, ma'am," he said, unsheathing his skinning knife and coming over to pluck a potato out of the tub.

"All right," Megan said. "I can use the help, that's for sure, but I'd think it a little demeaning for the Union Pacific's chief scout."

"Nothin' wrong with honest labor of any kind," Joshua said with a wink, " 'cept that it usually don't pay very good."

Megan laughed. "You look very honest, Mr. Hood."

"Joshua. I don't know any Mr. Hood, ma'am."

"And I don't know any ma'am. Just Megan."

"Fair enough." Joshua smiled. "I got a little present for you, Megan."

She stopped peeling and smiling. "I . . . I don't think that would be proper, Joshua."

"Why not," he said, dropping an unfinished potato into the big tub and dragging a silver and turquoise pendant and chain from his buckskin jacket. The pendant was shaped like a bear's claw and the turquoise was small and definitely heart-shaped. It was exquisite.

"This wasn't made by the Sioux or the Cheyenne. Most likely, it was traded through Santa Fe and found its way north. Probably made by the Zuni or the Navajo. Anyway, I thought it'd look right shiny on you."

"The heart-shaped turquoise surrounded by the bear's claw. Is it symbolic?"

"You mean, does it mean something?"

"Yes."

He chuckled. "Everything means something, Megan. Sometimes we love most the things we hate."

"I don't understand."

"Neither do I," Joshua said. "I'd like to think that the bear claw represents the bear's strength and willingness to die for what it loves."

"I like that interpretation better," she said, admiring the pendant. Without her bidding, Megan's hand moved out, palm up. When Joshua's hand touched hers, she felt a spark and pulled her hand back so quickly the pendant and chain dropped into the tub of peeled potatoes.

"Oh, dammit!" she cried, retrieving it quickly. "I'm sorry."

"Here, give it to me and then turn around and I'll fasten it around your neck."

Megan started to argue that it still wasn't proper but he was turning her around and reaching over her head. When he leaned close and his hands brushed lightly across her hair, Megan felt a shock wave ripple through her body. She caught a glimpse of his strong brown hands and felt his warm breath on her neck. For reasons she didn't even want to think about, Joshua Hood rattled her senses.

After what seemed like forever, he said in a low, husky voice, "There you go, Megan."

She turned around and he was staring at the pendant, or her bosom or both. Megan felt her cheeks warm and hoped that she wasn't acting like some ninny and blushing for all the world to see.

"It's beautiful," she said. "But the only way that I'll allow myself to keep it is if I repay you with a gift."

"A dinner would be fine. And then maybe we could go for a walk out in the prairie moonlight."

She looked away. "I don't think so."

"Why not?"

"Because," she said, "I'm a widow and trying very hard to become a respected businesswoman."

"So?"

"It would be bad for business and improper."

Joshua scowled. "I'm leaving tomorrow morning to take Mr. Gilchrist up to the head survey party. I just thought that we might get better acquainted before I left. I *will* take care of your kid brother as if he were my own, but if I stepped in front of him to shield him from a Sioux arrow, I'd like to die remembering the taste of your sweet lips."

Megan laughed. "Mr. Hood, you are *shameless!*"

"I am for a fact," he admitted. "Does that mean no kiss?"

She shook her head and started to tell him that, yes, that was exactly what it meant. But she was too slow and before she knew it, Joshua had her in his powerful arms and was kissing her mouth, taking her breath away and leaving her weak in the knees.

"Mr. Hood!" she cried, pulling free. "You're no gentleman!"

"Nope, I am not," he conceded with a big, self-satisfied grin as he licked his lips like a lion after a good feed. "Pretty gal, I'd never make that claim."

"I don't want to be alone with you unless you grab a potato and start peeling this instant."

"You got a soft body, Megan," he said, reaching into the tub and fishing out a potato. "I been thinking about you some and now I'll be thinking about you even more."

"You can think all you want, but it won't do you any good. I've only been widowed less than two months and all I can think about is making this business work."

"I hear it's working fine."

"Yes, but when the main body of construction workers leaves Omaha, what am I to do?"

"Fold up this damned tent and follow us west."

Megan stopped peeling. "Just like that?" she asked, snapping her fingers.

"Yep."

"You act as if it were so easy."

"Nothin' is easy that's good. Gettin' you to bed sure isn't going to be easy but . . ."

Megan hurled her potato at him. It struck Joshua in the forehead and ricocheted over the partition into the dining area. A moment later, someone lobbed it back and yelled, "Ain't cooked enough yet, dammit!"

Joshua chuckled. Megan put her hands on her hips and glared at him until she felt ridiculous. Then she said, "You're a brute, Mr. Hood."

"Joshua."

"Mr. Hood until you start minding your mouth and your manners."

"Sorry."

They peeled in silence for nearly a quarter of an hour and then Megan finally said, "I won't give you what you desire, Mr. Hood. But I'm not going to lie to you and plead that I'm a grieving widow, 'cause I'm not."

"Appreciate an honest woman."

"Honesty is telling you that I want no man for a good long while. At least until we reach California and I have a chance to mark out a future for myself, my sister, and her two children."

"Megan, that won't be for years and years. Maybe never. I don't think you know what this railroad is up against. I've never been to California, but to get there we have to cross a lot of Indian and desert country. Either one or both of us might get used up or killed before then. Why waste pleasurin' time?"

"Peel!"

Joshua peeled but he also kept one eye on Megan while making sure that he didn't slice his own thumb clean off at the joint. And watching Megan made the peeling almost entertaining because, several times, he caught her sneaking a glance over at him. Unless he was a bigger fool than he looked, Joshua felt that he saw a sparkle of interest in Megan's sky-blue eyes.

If so, it had to be because of him and him alone 'cause it certainly wasn't because she enjoyed peeling these damned slimy potatoes.

CHAPTER
16

Glenn was delighted with the horse that had been chosen for him to ride west following the railroad's expected track along the Platte River. The tall gelding's name was Sundancer and he was a palomino, a slim, athletic-looking horse more golden than white with a long flaxen mane and tail.

"Do you like him?" General Dodge asked.

Glenn ran his hands over the gelding's heavily muscled neck and shoulders. "Who wouldn't like such a fine mount? Nice saddle too."

He'd expected a McClelland saddle but this was a three-quarter or "Montana" rig with single cinch and ox-bow stirrups.

"Mr. Hood was the one that actually picked out the saddle," Dodge admitted.

Glenn glanced over at Joshua. "Thanks."

"Don't mention it."

Dodge tipped his hat back. "As you can see, Mr. Hood prefers a modified rim-fire rigging, the kind that they use down in the Texas brush country. That big saddle horn is good for roping cattle but I doubt that it's of much value up here in buffalo country."

Joshua patted his own big saddle horn and his callused hands ran over his rawhide reata. "I guess you should have been here to see us the day me and the boys were ropin' and pullin' folks out of that icy ole Missouri River, General. At times like that, McClelland saddles ain't worth spit."

"I can't argue with you on that," Dodge conceded, "but for long-distance riding, I'll take the McClelland any day over those heavy western rigs."

Dodge turned back to Glenn. "If you want a lighter McClelland, then we can get one when you return. But in the meantime, I want you to take a good long look at the Platte River trestle we're just starting to build. Also, when you reach the head survey party, give this letter to Chief Surveyor Ben Goss and tell him to answer and give you a reply to my questions."

"Yes, sir."

"Glenn, I'd like you back here in no more than three weeks. That means that you won't have a lot of time to do much survey work, but I promise that there will be plenty of that before we reach the Laramie Mountains. Right now, the Indians are as much on our minds as the survey route itself and so I've asked Mr. Hood to see if he and his men can make contract with the Arapaho and maybe even the Cheyenne. Hopefully, they can buy us some peace."

"Maybe it would help if I went with him so that I could answer any questions that—"

"No," Joshua said flatly. "It'll be dicey enough if I visit the Cheyenne without having to worry about a dude."

Glenn felt hot anger fire his blood. He started to say something but General Dodge spoke first. "Mr. Hood," Dodge said, "I think Mr. Gilchrist might be an excellent intermediary for the Union Pacific management. Being an engineer, he's very familiar with our preliminary survey maps and I believe he has a fine grasp of the engineering problems the Union Pacific will face. He'll know how long the construction will take from one point to another and those might be very important questions to the Indian."

"I'd rather not take him," Joshua insisted, jaw clenched with stubbornness. "With all these last-minute supplies we're supposed to deliver to Mr. Goss, three weeks isn't going to give us much time to parlay with the red man."

"Then take a month if you need it," Dodge said. "But not one day longer."

"Yes, sir," Joshua said. He addressed his men. "We'll be leaving in one hour. Everyone be ready!"

Most of the scouts and hunters made a beeline straight for the nearest saloon. Glenn, however, stayed with his new horse and began to go over every piece of his gear. He had an old Navy Colt but no rifle and he'd opted to take a canteen even though their trail would follow the spring-swollen Platte River. His bedroll was important and he lashed it down behind his cantle and made sure that it was covered with an oilskin in case they were drenched by a rain squall.

"One hour," Joshua said, leaving his horse ground-tied, and he went to visit Megan's Place.

Glenn watched the scout until the man disappeared into the big tent, then he continued going over his gear, item by item. When he was satisfied, he also headed for the dining tent. Megan would be there preparing for the noonday meal and he wanted to make sure that she remembered him more than she remembered Joshua.

Liam and his friends were on their way to the saloon too but Rachel intercepted Liam. She was breathless and quite pretty but there was a deep concern in her pale blue eyes. "I heard you were about to leave."

Liam waited until his snickering friends walked past before answering. "That's right. We're leaving in an hour."

"And you weren't even going to tell me!"

"You don't need to raise your voice, Rachel."

"Why not!" she cried. "You said you loved me and now you don't even have the decency to say good-bye!"

Liam could see that Rachel was going to start crying and probably ranting so he took her arm and hustled her off down the boardwalk. She did begin to cry and Liam wished she'd stop because people were giving him hard looks.

"I do love you," he said, desperate to make her stop crying. "But I just thought it would be easier this way. My sister would have told you I was gone. I hate good-byes."

She jerked free of his arm and whirled on him, scrubbing tears away with a forearm. "Well, I hate disappearances! How about that!"

"Listen, you don't own me, Rachel. I saved *your* life, not the other way around and don't you forget it."

"I haven't forgotten anything. Especially not how you kissed me and I let you touch me last night."

"We didn't even do it. If you loved me, we would have."

"Stop it!" Rachel cried.

"Well? We would have."

Rachel wiped more tears from her eyes. "Where are you going with them?"

"Clear out to the head of the line," Liam said. "To the surveyors and then on to find Indians."

Rachel paled. "Indians?"

"That's right. The Arapaho and maybe even the Cheyenne."

"But they've been attacking the whites! I just heard . . ."

Liam put his hand over her lips. "Joshua Hood isn't taking us out to get scalped. I think we'll be fine, Rachel."

"Oh, Jesus," she whispered, throwing her arms around his neck, "I'm so worried!"

Liam held her tight. It occurred to him that they had walked to the edge of town and that the river was just a few hundred yards away where there was grass and trees and privacy. "Come along, darlin'," he urged.

Rachel sniffled and hugged him as they walked to the river. When they were out of sight and all alone, Liam pulled her down on the grass. "Do you love me?"

"I'd give my life to save you," she told him, "same as you already did for me."

Liam kissed her and eased her down against the damp earth of the Missouri riverbank. His hands began to unbutton her dress. She hardly resisted except to whisper, "Liam, no, please."

"Even Mr. Hood can't swear we won't get scalped," Liam said shamelessly. "We might never have this moment again, Rachel."

She looked up into his eyes as he continued to undress her. "I remember us hanging on to that railroad tie as we were being swept down the river. I thought sure we were both dead but you never gave up. You have an iron will, Liam. You're stronger than me. I can't deny you."

Liam fumbled at his own buttons. His heart was pounding with desire. "Then don't try, darlin'," he breathed. "I reckon we only got about forty-five minutes, so let's just stop talkin' and try to make the most of every damn one of 'em."

Rachel closed her eyes and freely gave him her love. He was only the second man she had ever had and far wilder than her late husband. Liam was insatiable and Rachel was filled with pride to offer herself to such a strong, passionate man.

"Honey," she whispered after a long time, "we've got to go. I heard someone calling your name."

He raised his head. His face was streaked with perspiration and his eyes were glazed with pleasure. "Are you sure? The blood is beatin' in my ears so loud I can't hear anything except it and the river."

"I'm sure. I wish I hadn't heard them calling, but I did."

Liam rolled off of her. He jumped up and yanked his pants back around his waist, then buckled on his gun belt and grabbed his hat.

"I'm sorry to leave you this way," he said. "But it'd be best if they don't see us both comin' up lookin' all bothered."

"I know," she whispered. "Just kiss me good-bye and tell me you'll think of me and that you love me."

He glanced over his shoulder, clearly anxious to leave.

"Liam, please!"

He studied her nakedness and grinned. Then he knelt on the damp riverbank and kissed her long and sweet. "I'll miss and think about you, Rachel. I can't wait to get back and do this again."

He started to rise but she grabbed his shirt and pulled him back to his knees. "Tell me you love me and that we'll be married."

"Married!" Liam pulled free and climbed unsteadily to his feet. "I never said nothing about getting married!"

"You mean you *don't* want to marry me?"

"Well, I never said that either." Now Liam thought he did hear his name being called. "Darlin', I *got* to run now. We can talk about all this the next time."

Rachel grabbed her dress and covered herself. "If you don't at least tell me you love me, there won't *ever* be a next time."

"All right, all right! I do love you. Now good-bye!"

He whirled and raced off through the trees. Rachel fell back on the riverbank and tears ran down her cheeks. She didn't know if she was crying because Liam had said he loved her, or because he was leaving, or because he had no intention of marrying her.

Maybe she was crying for all three reasons.

A short time earlier, Joshua had folded his arms and leaned back against the partition as he watched Megan work. "So you won't give me a good-bye kiss, huh?"

"No chance."

"I see that you're at least wearing my pendant."

Megan's eyes dropped to her chest. "I am. It's beautiful."

"Glad you like it."

Megan was cutting cabbage. "Will you please watch out for Liam? He's so excited I'm afraid that he might make some mistake out there and either get hurt or killed."

"I'll keep him in sight at all times, Megan. Aren't you even a little worried about me?"

Megan brought a heavy chopping cleaver down hard, splitting a head of cabbage right down the middle. Both halves rolled away. Megan looked up with amusement. "Does that tell you anything, Mr. Hood?"

"Hell," he muttered, "I guess it does. I just hate to go off with a broken heart."

"You'll survive."

"Sure he will," Glenn said, coming up behind Joshua and stepping into the kitchen. He removed his hat. "I knew that you'd want me to stop and say good-bye."

Megan looked from Glenn to Joshua and back to Glenn. "I want you both to be careful out there and I'll miss each of you while you're gone, even if you are both a bit pesky."

"Pesky!" Joshua cried, looking offended. "Mr. Gilchrist, can you believe your ears?"

"I'm afraid that I do," Glenn said, playing along in fun. "It's a sad day considering this woman has the two handsomest men in the whole Territory of Nebraska, and the best she can do is call them pesky."

"It's a sad thing for certain," Joshua said, looking very solemn.

Megan opened her oven. "I've some of Aileen's dinner rolls warmed up from last night. Also some roast and potatoes. We're not ready for dinner yet, but I would hate to see the two handsomest men in Nebraska ride off without a good meal under their belts."

"What a woman!" Joshua exclaimed.

"She is a wonder all right," Glenn agreed.

Megan laughed and quickly filled two huge plates. "You gentlemen can eat out in front or sit in here and pester me while I get this cabbage cut and cooked."

Joshua inhaled a dinner roll. "I'll stay in here and visit. I think Glenn would rather go out and sit at a table."

"Not a chance," Glenn said, taking his own plate.

"Well then," Megan said, going back to her work, "we can just talk like old friends while I work and you both eat."

"Suits me right down to the ground," Joshua said.

"Me too," Glenn mumbled around a mouthful of roast beef.

When they were finished and almost an hour had passed, Glenn strolled over to Megan and kissed her cheek. "Good-bye, my dear."

"Good-bye," she said, no longer smiling. "Be careful."

Joshua took his cue and kissed Megan on the other cheek. "I'll be plenty careful too, my dear."

"You leave first," Glenn said, motioning toward the door.

"No," Joshua said, "*You* first."

"Both of you get on out of here," Megan chided. "We've all got jobs to do."

Glenn and Joshua went out together. They walked down the street to where the horses were waiting. Everyone was ready to ride except Liam who was missing.

"Where's O'Connell?" Joshua snapped, no longer jovial.

"He ain't come back yet," Calvin Miller answered. "Maybe he got scared and decided to stay in Omaha."

"Not likely," Joshua said. "Start calling him out. He'll come running."

Miller wasn't too pleased about calling but he had no choice. And after a few minutes, Liam suddenly emerged from down by the river, running toward them for all he was worth.

"Where the hell you been!" Joshua angrily demanded.

"I . . . I was takin' a leak."

"The hell you were!" Calvin Miller scoffed. "I saw you go off with Missus Rachel Foreman, that widow girl that works at Megan's Place. You got fresh grass stains on your knees from porkin' her down by the river! And her husband ain't hardly cold in the grave!"

Something snapped in Liam. He spurred his horse straight into Miller's horse and threw himself at his constant tormentor. Liam's rage and humiliation gave him unnatural strength. He bashed Miller in the face and they toppled to the ground. Miller landed on the bottom and the breath was slammed out of his lungs. He lay stunned and sucking for air like a fish out of water while Liam's knuckles rained like hailstones on Miller's face, turning it bloody. Vile curses and spit poured from Liam's mouth. Beneath him, Calvin Miller began to bellow with pain and terror. He could not get his breath and there was blood in his mouth, his nostrils, and even clouding his eyes.

Powerful hands tore Liam off the beaten man and shoved him up against a horse. "Liam! It's over!" Joshua shouted in his face. "The fight is over!"

Liam began to shake. He looked down and saw what he'd done to Calvin's face. It was unrecognizable. Liam held his fists up and saw that they were covered with blood. He began to shake like a reed in the wind.

"Get on your horse," Joshua ordered. "Now!"

"But what about . . ."

"Your horse!"

Joshua shoved Liam around and almost threw him up into the saddle. He turned to kneel beside Calvin Miller. "You got what you been askin' for, Calvin. You can stay here . . . or come. Your choice so long as you remember just one thing."

Calvin stared up at him through swelling, fearful eyes.

"The thing is, Calvin, this trouble is finished between you and Liam. No more bad blood. No revenge, no second chance. It's just done."

Joshua waited a moment. "Do you understand what I'm telling you, boy?"

Miller nodded.

"Then what'll it be. Stay here or come along and no hard feelings 'cause you got what you deserved. Which is it?"

Miller rolled over on one of his haunches. He spat blood into the dirt and then he wiped his face with his sleeve. "I'll catch up," he breathed, trying to hide his face from the others.

"If you try to get even or anything, I'll kill you myself. You understand me?" Joshua warned.

"Yes!"

"Good." Joshua walked over to his sorrel. "Let's ride!"

Glenn mounted. His eyes kept jumping from Miller to Liam as if he'd never seen either one before. For certain he'd never seen such a terrible beating.

As if reading his thoughts, Joshua reined close and said, "Get used to blood and pain, Mr. Gilchrist. Where we're going, you're bound to see a whole lot more."

Glenn didn't reply. He touched his heels to Sundancer and followed the silent buckskinners west.

CHAPTER
17

Glenn had not been prepared for the aloof way he was treated by Joshua and his scouts. They were a dirty, rugged breed and Glenn supposed they just took a natural dislike to anyone who didn't wear greasy buckskins and whose fingernails weren't clotted with dirt. The three freighters who were driving the supply wagons up the line weren't a bit friendly either. Of the entire group, Liam O'Connell was the only one who would offer Glenn so much as a glance or a friendly word.

To hell with them, Glenn thought, for he was perfectly happy with his own company and the exciting prospects that lay in wait. The country was sprouting green and the sky was clear and cloudless. A great arc of squawking Canadian snow geese floated past overhead, their necks were dark fingers pointing them north. Papillion had already been abandoned as the rails moved westward so that first night out, they camped at what had been the site of Elkhorn. The grass was grazed down to the dirt and there was litter everywhere, making it plain that this town had not lasted more than a few weeks before the rails had lured its citizens on down the line.

"Sonsabitches leave a mess, don't they?" Joshua said to no one in particular as they made camp.

Glenn heard coyotes howl that first night out on the prairie and he smelled the wind blowing the scent of wildflowers across the plains. They arose before dawn and continued westward, Joshua constantly urging the supply wagons to keep up his pace.

The second night they reached Columbus, a tent city already in decline where supplies had been forwarded and where men worked to repair the washed-out tracks. The devastating effects of the recent flooding were very apparent. Miles and miles of track showed signs of having just been underfilled where entire sections of the roadbed had been washed away. The damage was especially bad at either end of the long bridge that spanned the normally gentle Loup River.

Jack Casement hailed them from before his tent. "Gentlemen! I hope you've brought whiskey and cigars!"

Glenn laughed. "Afraid not," he said, riding up beside Joshua while the other men dismounted. "We've been ordered by General Dodge to go to the forward survey party with these provisions."

"Damn," Casement swore, not sounding all that disappointed. "Dismount and we'll put you boys up for the night anyway. In the morning, I'll show you how this railroad intends to lay track faster than anyone has ever dreamed."

"What's the hurry?" Joshua remarked. "The Central Pacific is bogged down in the Sierras and will likely still be there when you reach 'em."

"Don't count on that," Casement warned. "I just happen to know a little about their construction boss. His name is Harvey Strobridge and he's a hard-driving man. If he can't whip those Sierras in a fair amount of time, I'm sure that he's going to dismantle an entire train and have it sledded over Donner Pass, then reassembled on the eastern slope so he can lay track right on down the Truckee River into Reno."

Glenn had not heard this prediction before. "Could he actually do such a thing?"

"Desperate men take desperate measures," Casement said. "Of course he could and he will if that's what it takes to gain some momentum. The stakes are too high to get trapped in those high California mountains for two or three years while we gobble up the land and money Congress has awarded a transcontinental railroad line."

Joshua loosened his cinch. "Mr. Casement, I hear you had a little race with Spotted Tail, a Sioux chief."

Casement grinned. "That's right. One afternoon, he and about a dozen of his warriors showed up and we all grabbed our rifles. But it became clear that their intentions were peaceful. So we let them come on down to take a closer look at the Iron Horse, as they call it. They were extremely curious."

"I'll bet," Joshua said, tight-lipped. "Then what happened?"

"Well, they could talk a little English so one thing led to

another and the first thing I knew, those Indians were showing off how they could shoot their bows and arrows."

"I'd have given anything to see that," Glenn said.

"They are incredibly accurate. After the shooting, they demonstrated their horsemanship and that led to some of the men challenging Spotted Tail and his braves to a race—their horses against our Iron Horse."

Glenn chuckled. "Not much of a match, I'd guess."

"Oh, it was at first," Casement said. "The Indian ponies are swift and they easily outdistanced our locomotive for the first quarter mile. We had talked Spotted Tail into climbing into the locomotive's cab so that he could cheer his braves on to victory, a mile up the line. But after a quarter mile, those ponies started to slow up while our locomotive was just gathering steam. It passed the Indians and swallowed them up in a cloud of smoke. Chief Spotted Tail turned away, madder than anything, and you should have heard our boys yell!"

Joshua wasn't smiling. In fact, his eyes were wintery. "And then what happened?"

"Not much," Casement said. "Spotted Tail and his Sioux left us soon after that. They weren't bragging anymore and seemed pretty upset."

The muscles in Joshua's cheeks corded with anger. "Did it occur to you, General, that Spotted Tail might have been playacting?"

"What is that supposed to mean?" Casement asked, his own grin fading.

"I mean that now the Sioux understand that the Iron Horse is powerful and can't be outrun over any distance. My guess is that when Spotted Tail turned away in defeat, he turned his mind onto how the engineer was operating the throttle and the brake of that locomotive."

"No!"

"Yes," Joshua said, "so now he understands how to operate a locomotive. General, I don't mean to be hard, but I think you might have won the race, but lost the battle."

Casement rubbed his jaw. "Do you really think it was all a trick?"

"No," Joshua said, "the Sioux are extremely proud of their hunting skills and the speed of their ponies. They probably thought they could win the race. But when it became obvious that they could not, my hunch is that they learned a lot of valuable information about the Iron Horse to use against us in the future."

Casement sighed. "I guess you might have something there, Mr. Hood. Maybe Spotted Horse outfoxed me."

Hood didn't say anything more on the subject, but it was clear that he thought so too. He changed the subject by asking, "How are you doing for fresh meat?"

"Not so good," Casement admitted, still looking very troubled over the realization that he had been outwitted by Spotted Tail. "We saw a few antelope on the hills and I gave a couple of those sharp-shooting Southern Rebs permission to go hunting. But two or three antelope split among nearly three hundred famished laborers barely flavors a stew. We could use some buffalo meat. The men are already sick and tired of a steady diet of beans, potatoes, and beef."

Joshua looked off to the north. "We'll find you some buffalo tomorrow, I expect. Skin 'em out and bring in the carcasses for your butcher. Stake the hides out on the prairie and pick 'em up on the return."

"Fair enough," Casement said. "I'd go with you except that I'm afraid my men might desert the work crews and return to Omaha."

"Why?" Glenn asked.

"No pay."

Glenn shrugged. "What could they spend it on out here anyway?"

Casement's eyes twinkled. "You'll be surprised to see that not all of these tents belong to the Union Pacific Railroad. In fact, if you take a second glance up the track at the north end of Columbus, you'll see that a fair number of 'em are tent saloons and gambling parlors."

"And you allow that?"

"Can't stop it. I tried," Casement said. "But these Irish would have thrown down their pikes, shovels, and sledgehammers and gone back to Omaha. So I let the riffraff come along. Thing of it is, without money, there's not much mischief to get into anyway."

"You should be getting more pay very soon," Glenn told the construction chief. "Dodge said he was expecting it any day now."

"That's the best news I've heard in a while. There's been a lot of grumbling around here lately."

"There's also been a lot of work," Glenn said. "I can see what kind of a mess the track and roadbed were in when you arrived."

"It wasn't graded and packed solidly enough," Casement complained with a scowl. "Furthermore, some of those soft cottonwood rails have already split and had to be dug up and replaced. From now on, we're using more hard and burnetized wood. Tomorrow morning while your friends hunt buffalo, we can take a ride up to the end of the line and I'll show you the kind of operation I've put together."

"General, the word reaching Omaha is that your work crew is a model of efficiency."

Casement grinned. "As an engineer, I think you'll appreciate what we are up against and the progress we're making. No offense to you, Mr. Hood."

"None taken," Joshua said. "Glenn, I'll take care of your horse. Why don't you and the general talk construction while me and my boys talk buffalo hunt."

"Fine."

As Hood led the horses away, Casement said, "He's a hell of a man, that one. I've commanded soldiers and once in a while I used to come across an enlisted man who looked and carried himself like Mr. Hood. Not often, but just often enough to discover that they are rare. They're tough, resourceful, and they fear almost nothing except failure or the dishonor of being branded a coward."

"I don't think such men are all that rare. Both my brothers chose death before dishonor and so did thousands of other soldiers."

"That's true," the former general said, "but I was referring to the quality of leadership. Hood is the kind of man who will lead the charge, so to speak. Unfortunately, most of that kind were the first to die in battle, your brothers included."

Glenn was anxious to change the subject. "How far ahead is the track right now?"

"About six miles up the line. Columbus is starting to move west. Next little tent town is Silver Creek and it's right along the Platte. We'll move up to it tomorrow and by tomorrow night, Columbus will be nothing but a bald patch of prairie."

"You can sure see where these hell-on-wheels rail camps have come and gone."

"Is that really what they're calling them?"

"Yes."

"It's a fair description," Casement admitted. "Columbus was bad, Silver Creek won't be any better. The morning after a payday, I'm lucky if we've got half the crew ready and able to work. Men get drunk, fight and hurt each other. They are rolled and robbed; they get worked up over the whores and that makes them act crazy in the head. I tell you, Glenn, laying track is only half the bother; Sam Reed and I consider that keeping the men happy and on the job is the *real* challenge."

"At least there is no shortage of new recruits pouring into Omaha," Glenn said as they went to the general's tent where he poured them both a glass of whiskey.

"Compared to the troubles that they're having getting workers on the Central Pacific, we are lucky," Casement admitted. He propped his feet up on his bed. "Tell me all about General Dodge and how he's getting along with The Doctor. Have they strangled one another yet?"

"No," Glenn said with a chuckle. "But your brother and I are pretty sure that those two won't be speaking to each other by the time summer is over."

"I agree." Casement raised his glass. "To the Union Pacific!"

"The Union Pacific," Glenn said, matching the toast.

The evening passed very quickly and pleasantly for Glenn. Dinner was brought to the general's tent and they talked late into the night about the engineering difficulties that the Union Pacific was expected to face in the weeks and months ahead. Glenn learned that Casement and Reed fully intended to go all the way to North Platte, over 250 miles from Omaha, before they halted operations for the winter. At North Platte, where the river forked, a wooden trestle 244 feet in length was already under construction.

"We'd like to have it finished by the year's end so that we don't have to lay any more track across river ice," Casement said with a wink.

"That would be a relief."

"Tell me the truth, were you *that* sure that last winter's Missouri River ice would support an entire supply train?"

"No."

"Then why did you do it?"

"Three guesses, and the first two don't count."

"The Doctor."

"Exactly."

Casement sighed. "I guess the good news is that the farther we go, the less we'll also see Durant."

"I'm sure that's true. He'll be up to his eyeballs with politics and trying to keep the railroad from going broke."

"That's important work," Casement said, "but I'd ten times rather build than spend all my time trying to buttonhole congressmen for money."

"Me too."

Glenn was given a cot that night in a large tent reserved for Union Pacific officials and guests. It was simple and comfortable. A little after midnight, thunder growled out on the prairie but it was soft and distant. It lulled him to sleep and Glenn did not awaken until he heard the clanging of a bell announcing to everyone on shift that breakfast was being served.

Dressing quickly, Glenn stumbled outside and followed sleepy-eyed men to a huge canvas dining hall about four times the size of the one that Megan had bought back in Omaha. Breakfast was simple fare, but there was all a man could eat and the coffee was strong and hot.

What little conversation there was centered around the usual complaints that occupy the minds of hard-working men. Money, women, work, and weather. Since the spring weather was ideal, the women were expensive, and the pay was late again, Glenn sensed a lot of discontent among the laborers.

One large, red-bearded fellow was particularly vocal. "The wages are good, sure. Laborers get two-fifty a day, spikers three dollars, and ironmen three-fifty, but the damned foremen get a hundred twenty-five dollars a month for doing nothing but standing around shouting orders like a bunch of hyenas!"

"Ah, Michael," another Irishman said, "you're just mad because you ain't a 'hyena' yourself anymore. If you hadn't gotten drunk and pissed all over the side of General Jack's tent, you'd still be makin' that big money with your hands doing nothin' but holdin' up your pockets."

Michael blushed. "Yeah," he admitted, "I guess I did sort of deserve a demotion. But mark my words, they'll make me a foreman again and I'll raise billy hell with you boys!"

"Aw shut up and finish your breakfast and get the move on!" a foreman yelled as he moved down the aisle, banging an empty tin cup with a fork signaling everyone to finish up and move out for work.

Glenn remained at the table drinking coffee a few minutes longer. Then he went looking for Jack Casement. He could see that Columbus was quickly being dismantled. Everywhere he looked, tents were coming down and being packed onto wagons in preparation for a relocation at Silver Creek. Glenn saw all sorts of unsavory types of gamblers, shills, whores, and con artists. They reminded him of birds of prey following a flock of pigeons and he supposed that they made most of their killings at night.

"There you are!" Casement shouted from horseback. "Your palomino is saddled. Have you had breakfast yet?"

"I have."

"Then let's ride for Silver Creek, Mr. Gilchrist. There's a lot to be seen before this day is over."

Glenn collected his reins from one of the many stock tenders overseeing the Union Pacific's herd of cattle and remuda of mules and workhorses. The tender was very young.

"How old are you?" Glenn asked the peach-faced kid.

"Fourteen, sir!"

"And where do you hail from?"

"Philadelphia."

"Long way from home."

"This is my home now."

Glenn nodded because it was true. He didn't know how many men were already employed out on the line but it might be nearly one thousand counting the wagon drivers, graders, trestle builders, rust eaters, and surveyors. And in this cool early morning air, Glenn could fairly taste the excitement and the energy of this great effort to bind east to west.

As they began to ride up the line through Columbus, Casement was hailed by dozens of men, civilians as well as Union Pacific employees. Most just wanted to wish the small but dynamic leader a good day, others had so many questions that Glenn marveled at Casement's knowledge of detail.

"Ike Norman!" Casement shouted at a man in a black frocked coat who was orchestrating the loading of a tent full of gambling tables and roulette wheels. "Mr. Norman, I demand a word with you."

The sharp tone of Jack Casement's voice left no doubt that he did not consider Ike Norman to be a friend. The saloon and gambling parlor owner scowled, muttered something to one of his helpers, and then straightened his coat and starched white shirt before sauntering forward. Norman was a dissipated-looking fellow in his early thirties. Large and just starting to go to fat, he was still quite handsome and obviously prosperous. Glenn recognized a good fit of clothing and expensive fabric but for those who did not, Norman sported a heavy gold watch and chain as well as a diamond stickpin.

"What do you want, Jack?"

Casement's cheeks colored at Norman's insulting familiarity. "Last night another one of my rust eaters was robbed and then beaten after leaving your gambling hall and saloon."

"So what am I supposed to do about that?" Norman asked, sarcasm heavy in his voice. "If a man gets robbed, do you want me to set up a charity?"

In answer, Casement dismounted and advanced on the big man. The U.P. construction chief looked to Glenn like a bantam rooster about to attack an eagle. Ike Norman was about six inches taller and a good seventy-five pounds heavier and there was still enough hump in the man's thick shoulders to tell Glenn that not all of the saloon owner had yet gone entirely soft. However, Jack Casement always wore a pearl-handled Colt on his hip and was reported to be damned quick and accurate with that fancy pistol.

"You listen to me, Ike," Casement warned, hand shading his gun. "If my men keep getting cheated, beaten, or rolled because of you, I swear that you won't be in business much longer!"

Norman wasn't packing a holstered six-gun although he probably had a derringer hidden somewhere. He rested his hands on his hips. "Jack," he snapped, "I run an honest business and I resent the insinuation that I do otherwise."

"I don't give a damn *what* you resent! Just because we haven't been able to prove you're behind the troubles my men are having doesn't mean that I won't take action to have you, your tent, and your thugs run out of Nebraska."

"I've got my rights."

"You've just been warned for the last time," Casement said.

"The next time that I hear of anyone being cheated or hurt in your place, you are out of business!"

Ike Norman wanted to take a swing at the much smaller man and it even seemed to Glenn that Casement was daring him to try. But finally, Norman spun on his heel and stomped off to work, shouting at his men to hurry up and load the wagons.

When Casement remounted, Glenn could see that the former Union general was steaming. They rode out of town following the tracks and a stream of wagons moving toward Silver Creek.

"That sonofabitch is pushing me to my limits," Casement said after nearly a quarter of an hour of silence. "There are at least half a dozen vultures like him with their crooked roulette wheels and dishonest dealers. I can't stop them from plying their trade because neither the Army nor the railroad wants to be bothered. But Norman doesn't clean up his operation soon, I'm going to be forced to do it for him."

"That bad, huh?"

"He's slick. You'll never catch Norman actually dealing marked cards or robbing anyone because he always hires the dirty work out. But he's the one behind it. I've been told that he extorts money from other businessmen and if they don't pay, he sends his henchmen to see that they can't walk."

"He orders their legs to be broken?

"Or worse."

Glenn twisted around in his saddle for a second look at Ike Norman. The big man was watching him too. Glenn turned back around and they continued riding up the line. He could not help but think about Megan and how she would have to be involved with such men as Norman if she and her sister insisted upon following the rails west. Would Norman try to force her to pay him a protection or license fee? If he did, Megan was bull-headed enough that she would most certainly refuse and then what? Would Norman order her legs to be broken?

"I hope you do get rid of him and his kind," Glenn said.

Casement's grin was wintery. "I saw plenty of his scummy kind during the war. They'd never join the army but hang around on paydays and cheat my soldiers out of their pay. Back then, we'd round them up and throw them on wagons or else force them into our ranks and put them in the first line of every battle charge. Even so, they were always present. Men like Ike Norman are vermin, pure and simple."

They rode on in silence until just before noon when Glenn saw the rear of the supply train and the mushrooming tent city of Silver Creek. His concern about Megan was temporarily replaced by curiosity and anticipation. He observed what looked like dozens of supply wagons being loaded from flatcars and as they rode closer, Glenn began to get his first inkling of just what kind of an incredible track-laying enterprise Casement and Sam Reed had devised to reach North Platte before year's end.

Suddenly, a horse and rider came flying out of Silver Creek as if the hounds of hell were on their heels. The rider was whipping his horse unmercifully.

"That damned fool!" Casement shouted. "He'll kill that animal within five miles at that pace."

Glenn agreed. "Let's stop him," he said, urging his palomino forward to intercept the rider.

Together, he and Casement managed to block the rider's path. The general yelled, "Hold up there, damn you!"

Recognizing Casement, the man reined in his horse. "Mr. Casement!"

"What's wrong now, Jimmie?"

"The grading crew up by Lone Tree was attacked just before dawn last night. Six men were killed and three others wounded. Two of the dead were caught out of camp. They were both scalped and gutted. I'm going for a doctor!"

"Send a telegram to Omaha instead."

"The line has been cut again, General!"

Casement's eyes jumped over toward the telegraph line, then back at Jimmie. "All right then," he said. "But pace that horse or you won't even get to Columbus. There's a doctor packing up his things there, tell my aide to give him a company horse and an escort forward to Silver Creek right now."

"Yes, sir!"

The man galloped on. Casement glanced sideways at Glenn and his face was pale with anger. "That's the third attack we've had in the last two weeks. The Sioux hit and run. Our forward crews haven't a chance and it's already getting hard to find men willing to volunteer to work out front."

"What about the surveyors?"

"I don't know," Casement admitted, just before he forced his mount into a gallop. "We haven't heard from our chief surveyor, Ben Goss, and his crew in over a week."

Glenn put his heels to Sundancer's flanks. Almost instantly, he regretted not purchasing a rifle. Against attacking Indians, it was now grimly apparent that he was going to need some long-range killing protection if he was going to keep his own scalp from being lifted.

CHAPTER

18

Silver Creek was in chaos. The gambling halls and saloons were closed and hundreds of men were milling about when Glenn and Jack Casement arrived. Everyone was shouting and arguing, some were hot to go after the Sioux, others wanted to quit work and rush headlong back to Omaha before they too were attacked and scalped.

"Silence!" Casement bellowed from the top of his horse.

When the army of laborers kept up their clamor, the chief of construction yanked out his pearl-handled Colt and fired it into the air. *Now* he had their rapt attention.

"All right," Casement yelled, holstering his gun and raising his arms. "Everyone settle down!"

"There are still men under fire up at Lone Tree!" a man shouted.

This announcement caused another storm of controversy forcing Casement to again fire his weapon. "I'll take forty riflemen and we'll go to Lone Tree right now. Who wants to volunteer?"

Five hundred men stepped forward and there was another huge argument until Jack Casement shouted, "Starting with men whose last names begin with A and who can shoot straight and are Civil War veterans. Step forward!"

A handful detached from the crowd. "Now men whose last names begin with B!"

By the time that D was reached, Casement had at least forty volunteers and he ordered them to get their rifles, three days' worth of provisions, and the best horses available from the Union Pacific's remuda.

"I want to see the wounded," Casement said, "take me to them now."

"There's only one here," a foreman said, motioning Casement to follow him, "the others either couldn't make it out because they were hurt too bad, or else they elected to stay."

"How bad off is this man?"

"He's dying," the foreman said, leading Casement and Glenn into his tent. "Caught two arrows in the back as he was riding for help. One of them slipped under his ribs and was buried in his kidney. Even a surgeon couldn't save him now."

"And the other arrow?"

"It was stuck in his back up near the shoulder. He didn't even know it was there he was so scared."

"Poor bastard," Casement said as they entered the tent.

The dying man was very pale and when Glenn first saw him, he thought sure they were already too late. Casement removed his hat and Glenn did the same. The construction chief sat down beside the wounded man. "Can you hear me? This is Jack Casement. I need to ask you a few questions."

The dying man's eyelids raised very slowly because of a thick film jelling them shut. The man was in his thirties, thin with a handlebar mustache and bad teeth. His breathing was rapid and shallow. He couldn't focus and his eyes darted frantically about the tent's canvas ceiling.

"What's your name?" Casement asked in a gentle voice. "We'll want to notify your family."

"Ellis Johnson."

"Where you from, Ellis?"

The man closed his eyes to whisper. "Springfield, Illinois."

"Are you married?"

Ellis shook his head.

"Do your parents live in Springfield?"

"Dead. All of 'em dead now, sir."

"What happened to you and the grading crew up at Lone Tree?"

Ellis tried to open his eyes but now they seemed glued. Casement snatched a rag from a bedside basin. He tenderly sponged the man's eyes clear and gazed into them. "What happened at Lone Tree?"

Ellis gasped loudly and his hands fluttered at his sides. Glenn thought sure the man was about to take his very last breath. Instead, he gripped Casement's forearm and shook it powerfully.

"We was restin' down in a draw. They came over the top on us. Right down in among us. They was like devils screamin' and shootin' arrows. I saw men die hard. Saw others run down as they tried to escape to the river. I ran too but I was faster than them and I got me on a horse. I kin ride, sir. I kin ride better'n any damned Indian!"

"I believe you, Ellis. You rode away to get help. Is that it?"

"Yes, sir! I didn't have a gun on me. Couldn't fight a lick. Just die in the gully. So I came runnin'. Only I picked me a slow horse, Mr. Casement. He was so gawd-awful slow!"

Tears began to course down Ellis Johnson's hollow cheeks. "I felt the earth shakin' and when I looked back, there was an Indian right on my tail. He started shootin' arrows. He missed onc't, then he got me twice."

"What happened? Why didn't he finish and scalp you?"

"He musta runned out of arrows," Ellis said as his lips drew back from his rotten teeth into a crooked smile. "That's what I think, sir. He had me but he runned out of goddamn arrows and he lost my scalp!"

The foreman leaned over and whispered to Casement, "The rump of his horse had three arrows sticking out of it. Horse is in bad shape too."

"Can the poor beast be saved?"

"I think so. I imagine someone dug the arrows out of its haunches."

Casement leaned closer to the dying man as he removed a pad of paper and pencil from his shirt pocket. Glenn saw him jot down the grader's name and the words SPRINGFIELD, NO FAMILY on the notepad, then jam it back into his pocket.

"You did just fine, Ellis. We're going after those Indians right now."

"Will you put a bullet in one for me, sir?"

"If we catch them. Ellis, how many Indians attacked you at Lone Tree camp?"

"Seemed like hundreds."

"We'll do our best to get them," Casement promised. He patted the man on the shoulder, then left the tent with Glenn in tow. When they were outside, Casement snapped, "Let's get the volunteers and ride."

"Do you think there really were hundreds?"

"No. Probably a dozen at the most. Men always tend to

overestimate the enemy's strength and numbers when they are losing a battle."

"But . . ."

"Besides," Casement said, coming to his horse and stepping into the saddle, "bows and arrows are of damn little use against guns and rifles, eh, Mr. Gilchrist?"

"Yes, sir," Glenn said, wishing again that he'd had the forethought to buy a rifle.

As they galloped west toward Lone Tree over forty strong, Glenn's mind churned with a curious mix of dread and anticipation. Dread when he considered what would happen to them if there really were hundreds of Indians just up the line, anticipation when he looked to both sides of him and realized that he was riding next to a general surrounded by tough, vengeance-minded Civil War veterans. His own hand kept touching the butt of his Colt pistol as they followed the newly graded roadbed still waiting for its iron necklace.

Unlike most of the men surrounding him, Glenn had never killed a man before. He had not tasted battle although its ravages were indelibly pressed on his mind and memory. He had walked the northern battlefields, seen the carnage and destruction, and mourned the loss of his own brothers. In a way, he had suffered even more than the real war veterans because of his own guilt at not joining their ranks because of his father's adamant insistence. He'd studied the newspapers' battlefield accounts until he'd memorized the most intimate and gory details. He'd suffered the Union defeats and gloried in the Union victories.

"General, Lone Tree is just beyond that rise," a man called.

Casement drew rein. The rise of land was about a half mile away. Casement said, "We'll split into halves and come in from both sides. Mr. Baker?"

"Yes, sir!"

"You were a sergeant in the army, right?"

"Yes, sir!"

"Take half the men and circle off to the left. When I raise my arm, we'll sweep over the hill with arms ready to fire. Maybe we'll catch them murdering Sioux at Lone Tree. If we do, we'll take no prisoners. Is that understood?"

"Yes, sir!"

Glenn elected to remain with Casement. While all the other

men were checking their rifles, Glenn inspected and reholstered his pistol.

"Let's go," Casement said.

Glenn prodded Sundancer up beside the general and they moved into an easy canter that quickly brought them around to the left of the rise of land. Drawing his horse up, Casement looked back, then raised his hand in signal. When he brought it down, they all spurred over the rise and headlong into what had once been a Union Pacific grading crew camp nestled along the Platte River. But now there was nothing but ashes and death.

Glenn's eyes swept across the panorama of smoking canvas tents and the already bloating corpses of men, a pair of mules, and a small dog all pincushioned with arrows. Casement dismounted. Glenn and the other men did the same and no one said a word. Glenn counted eight dead men. Nothing had survived the Sioux attack; nothing moved in this death camp.

"Every fourth man hold the horses. The rest of you fan out up and down the river and search for survivors. Keep your weapons ready to use," Casement ordered.

Glenn's heart was drumming in his chest as he joined the hunt for any survivors. He did not hold out much hope that anyone other than Ellis Johnson might have escaped, but several minutes later one of the men called out to the search party.

"Over here!"

In seconds, they were all crowding around a pair of frightened laborers who'd jumped into the Platte River and hidden under a massive claw of dripping tree roots. Quaking with fear, the laborers had not dared come out and they were blue with cold. Casement ordered that dry clothes be found for the pair. When they were warmed and calmed down, their stories matched that of Ellis Johnson.

"We should go after the Sioux, General," Baker urged. "Their tracks lead north and they can't be more than a few hours ahead of us. If we ride hard, we could still overtake them."

But Casement shook his head. "General Dodge left me pretty clear instructions on this," he said to the men. "We're to patrol the line and fight to defend ourselves but not to pursue the Indians."

"But why?"

"Because this is Indian land and the farther we venture out from the tracks, the more it is to his advantage," Casement said.

"My job is to lay track at all costs. If there is to be any Indian hunting, then it will either be done by the United States Army or by Joshua Hood and his boys."

"But, sir!"

"You heard me," Casement said. "I want four volunteers to take these two men back to Silver Creek. The rest of us will proceed on up the Platte until we find Mr. Goss and his advanced survey crew."

"And if they've also been wiped out by the bloody savages?" a man demanded.

"Then we'll bury them," Casement said in a calm voice. "Bury them and return to Silver Creek and continue advancing the rails west. Is that fully understood?"

Under Casement's stern eye, those who objected were forced to dip their chins in reluctant agreement.

"Dear God, they were devils!" one of the rescued men wailed. "We could hear the Sioux shrieking like witches and over their cries, we could hear the screams of our friends dying!"

"That's enough," Casement commanded.

"You never heard such screams!" the laborer shouted, eyes round and rolling crazily about. "They must have been a'cuttin' their—"

"I said, enough!"

The man started to babble on but the sergeant grabbed and propelled him toward a horse. "You can ride this horse double on the way back to Silver Creek. Get them out of here and have them seen by the doctor as soon as possible."

"Form a burial detail," Casement ordered. "I want the names of the dead and then I want them buried within the hour."

The volunteers were eager to bury the dead. They quickly dug graves in the soft, damp soil along the Platte and after a few words were spoken over each of the fallen, they were hastily covered over.

"Let's mount up and ride," Casement said, looking to the west. "Even I don't know exactly how far ahead Ben Goss and his surveyors are right now."

"Could be a hell of a long ways," Glenn opinioned.

"That's right," Casement said. "But then again, they might have decided things were getting a little too hot out here and that it would be smart for them to get out while they still had their scalps attached."

"I hope so," Glenn said.

That night they made a cold camp and when they started out early the next morning, the mood of the volunteers changed from murderous anger to a palpable apprehension. The river was full with spring runoff and a flat, overcast Nebraska sky reached into eternity. Glenn made the remark to Casement that he was certain they could have seen anything moving for a hundred miles in all directions.

"These Great Plains are deceptive that way," the construction chief told him. "The skyline looks as flat and clean as a billiard table, but it's not. What you can't see are shelves, ridges, and draws where thousands of Indians or buffalo can hide. You think you can see every square foot of ground for a mile in all directions but there is probably at least one low spot just a few hundred yards away where the Sioux could be lying in wait to attack. And this doesn't even consider how many could be hiding in those stands of cottonwood and tall brush that choke the riverbanks."

"I see," Glenn said.

"No," Casement contradicted with a tolerant grin, "you *don't* see, and neither do I. That's why you can never assume that you're alone out here on the plains."

Glenn was still thinking about that when they actually did cross over a slight shelf of land and then beheld the fork of the Platte River. It was then that they also saw a small tent city of Union Pacific workers.

"That's our North Platte trestle," Casement said, using his telescope, "and unless my eyes are going, Ben Goss and his party of surveyors are encamped with the trestle builders."

At this news, everyone visibly relaxed and it even seemed as if the sun broke through the somber layer of clouds that had put a chill on the plains.

Glenn was as happy as anyone to meet Ben Goss, the Union Pacific's chief surveyor. The men at North Platte were delighted to see old friends and it was a fine reunion. After introductions had been made all around, Casement, Goss, and Glenn retired to the surveyor's tent where a bottle of brandy appeared.

"To health," Goss said, raising his glass in toast.

"To long life," Glenn said, raising his own glass.

They drank to that and when they got down to the business of discussing the railroad, Glenn sat back and listened.

"So," Goss said, "General Dodge has made you my assistant, huh?"

Glenn nodded. He had already formed a good opinion of the surveyor. Goss was in his early forties, medium height, and slightly underweight. He had Dodge's nervous energy and directness. And when he looked Glenn straight in the eye and said, "We'll be working here for a while yet, but by midsummer, we'll be moving west, Indians permitting. Are you sure this is the life for you?"

"Quite sure."

"Good. I understand that Dodge has asked that you return to him with full details of our surveying work."

"That's right. But afterward, I'm supposed to return."

"Splendid," Goss said, sounding as if he really meant it. "I could use an assistant and if, as Jack tells me, you're to be the liaison between the front line and the main line, then I hope the general has given you a good horse."

"He has."

"I think we'll get along fine," Goss said. "Tomorrow, we'll go over the construction plans for this big trestle. I'm sure that you'll find the work an engineering challenge."

"From what I've seen, it's nothing like I read about in any college textbook."

Both Goss and Casement managed a smile that, considering recent events, seemed quite remarkable.

"Sir!"

They all looked to the tent opening. "What is it?" Casement asked.

"There are horsemen on the horizon coming fast."

Glenn was nearest the door and he didn't ask to be excused. Along with the rest of the camp, they grabbed their weapons and took cover. But then they relaxed.

"It's that goddamn Hood and his rowdy buffalo hunters," someone growled. "Look at 'em ridin' along as if they was in Central Park on ponies."

Glenn stood up and grinned. He didn't care a whole hell of a lot for Joshua Hood, but there was something about the man that made you glad he was on your side.

CHAPTER

19

Joshua dismounted and handed his reins to Liam. "Hobble 'em with the rest and keep an eye out for Indians."

"Sure," Liam said, watching Glenn Gilchrist, General Casement, and a man he didn't know coming to meet them. "We going to kill a few more buffalo for these folks?"

"I reckon," Joshua said quietly. "If we don't have to attack the Sioux first."

Joshua nodded to Glenn and the surveyor, then shook hands with General Casement. He wasted no time coming directly to the point. "We saw the Lone Tree camp and the graves. I guess it went hard for them boys."

"You could say that. Where have you been, Mr. Hood?" Casement asked, not in a demanding way, but clearly not pleased about Hood's critical absence.

"We had to ride about seventy miles up the Loup River to find a good stand of buffalo. When I'm forced to drag along meat wagons, it does slow things down."

"Any idea which band of Sioux might be responsible for that murderous attack on Lone Tree camp?"

"Nope. It could have been a small hunting party or it could even have been a war party under one of the principal chiefs. The thing you have to remember is that the Indians lack our military chain of command. The Indians are a far more independent sort."

"Which is why they're doomed to defeat," Casement said. "Did you follow their tracks north?"

"Just long enough to make sure that they weren't doubling back to strike again."

Casement turned around with a scowl on his face. "As you can see, Mr. Hood, we've about ninety men here and about half

188

that many horses. As you can also see, we're building a damned trestle across this river and it's going to take a hell of a lot of timber. Some of it we can cut from the trees along this river, but some will have to be freighted up from Silver Creek. What this camp needs is meat and protection."

"We'll go hunting tomorrow," Hood said. "We'll ride south and see if we can get 'em quicker than we did up on the Loup."

"What about the Sioux?"

"What about them, General? You askin' me and my boys to track the ones that killed our men at Lone Tree and kill 'em?"

"Could you?"

"Not very damned likely, General. Tracks showed me that there were probably about seventy. It'd be a bad fight for us and one we'd probably lose. More and more of the Indians are getting their hands on guns and rifles."

"I'm painfully aware of that fact, though it doesn't appear to be the case during the attack at Lone Tree camp. I just hate the idea of giving up on those murderers."

"We could all go with him," Glenn impulsively suggested.

"Yes," Casement said, "but that would be counter to Dodge's orders and we'd be leaving this camp vulnerable to attack."

"What do we do then?"

Casement looked to Joshua Hood. "You're the Indian expert. What do you suggest?"

"I'll hunt this week and decide about the Indians next week," Hood decided out loud. "They aren't going to leave their own traditional hunting grounds."

"What about the Arapaho?" Casement asked. "Any chance of enlisting them against the Sioux?"

"Maybe. But they're still at least two hundred miles to the west."

Casement expelled a deep sigh. "I just wish the United States Army could have seen Lone Tree camp. When General Dodge hears about this latest attack, he's going to want to take offensive action. As for myself, I have to return to oversee the laying of track. I'll be leaving with most of the volunteers tomorrow at dawn. I'll ask General Dodge if he wants to form a company of men and go after the Sioux."

"He wouldn't find 'em," Joshua said. "Least not the same bunch that hit Lone Tree."

"Maybe not," Casement said, "but it would put the whole damned Sioux nation on notice that such attacks won't be tolerated."

"It would cause more harm than good," Joshua said.

Casement was upset and it showed when he said, "Provision this camp with meat and do a lot of scouting. I don't want to hear of any more surprise attacks."

"Yes, sir." Hood turned and left them to rejoin his hunters.

"What do you think about him?" Ben Goss asked Casement.

"I think he respects the Indian too damn much for his own good. But I am equally sure that when it comes to a showdown or a hard fight, Joshua Hood and his men will be on the winning side. What's your opinion of the man, Glenn?"

Glenn watched the tall hunter join his unkempt buckskin brigade. "I agree," he finally said. "There will be no more surprise attacks as long as those men are on guard out here."

The next week passed very quickly at North Platte. The trestle was just starting to be built and Glenn spent long hours with Chief Surveyor Goss as they reviewed and then reworked plans for the long and complex North Platte trestle. In addition to structural calculations and springtime flooding considerations, they worked out a detailed list of building materials that would be needed to complete the huge project before the arrival of the tracks near the approach of winter.

"General Dodge, Durant, and the other top officials of the railroad see North Platte as a major supply and building point on the line," Goss said. "The way I understand it, these major bases will be situated all along the Platte and then continue west."

"Have they picked the next one?"

"I think it will be at Julesburg. But backing up a little, my impression is that there's to be one not far from Fort Kearney. That way, we hope to force the United States Army to defend it from Indian attack."

"Makes sense," Glenn replied. "Except for a few soldiers and supply details that arrived in Omaha, we've seen damned little of the Army."

"I think they'll have to take more responsibility for our protection," Goss said. "At least for protecting the main track-laying crews. But out here in a survey party . . . well, we don't stray very far from our rifles and all the men are outfitted with Colt revolvers."

"I've noticed," Glenn said. "How many are in your survey party?"

"Fourteen, including myself. It's not a very glamorous life, you know. I hope you aren't disappointed."

"Of course not," Glenn told the man.

"Sometimes a cavalry patrol will arrive from Fort Kearney. When they do, they usually bring their own game. Maybe an antelope but quite often wild turkeys that are so tame they can practically be shot at will when they are found."

"I haven't had the pleasure of eating any yet."

"You will. That and buffalo." Goss smiled. "During the last great thunderstorm we had, an immense sea of buffalo came racing past our camp. Because of the lightning and the thunder, we were nearly scared out of our wits!"

"Did they come close?"

Goss's eyes widened. "Closer than we wanted, I'll tell you! When we realized that the thunder was not only from the sky but coming from the sound of their hooves, we ran out of our tents and fired our weapons. That didn't do a thing to turn them."

"So what did you do?"

"We waved blankets and that seemed to divert them or else they would have flattened our camp. Even so, many of my men jumped into the Platte though the water was freezing cold."

Glenn took a deep breath. "It's an adventure out here, isn't it?"

"Oh, yes," Goss said emphatically. "For those of us used to the hell of war, the silence of these plains is a balm to the soul. Most days and nights the only sound you hear is the soft moaning of the wind. And given the Indians, that's enough."

Glenn frowned. "I know that you were a Confederate officer. Apparently, our Union officers don't hold that against you."

"Not at all. General Dodge, for example, shared Abraham Lincoln's dream of full reconciliation. It's my hunch that he actually prefers to hire Confederates in order to balance the scales."

"I see."

"Our past," Goss continued, "whether it was in the North or the South, means absolutely nothing out here. Some of my surveyors and engineers probably fought each other on some distant battlefield. They don't discuss the Civil War. They discuss this wide-open land and the dreams they share of helping to build cities and towns upon its rich soil. Most seem to believe that our nation's future is here in the West."

"Do you share that belief?"

"No," Goss said, "I think that there has already been entirely too much talk of America's regionalism. Of the differences between the North and the South or the East and the West. I like to think of it as just one nation, but I do believe that the real excitement for young, dynamic men such as yourself is to be found out west."

"I agree," Glenn said. "This land is so big it intimidates you."

"It did me too," Goss admitted. "At least at first. I came from South Carolina. I'd never seen open spaces like these in all my life. I felt . . . exposed."

"Yes! Exactly."

"As if God and all of man were watching me. I felt like an ant crawling across a green tablecloth. I'd look up at the sky like a rodent expecting a hawk to swoop down and scoop me up with its sharp talons. I felt small and weak in the shadow of the sky."

Goss chuckled. "I probably sound a little ridiculous. But I felt all those things."

"So did I. In the forests, you can hide but out here on the plains . . . well, there is no place to hide."

"True," Goss agreed, "but then after a while, I turned my thinking around and saw all this openness differently. I convinced myself that—if I couldn't hide—the Indians couldn't hide either. Therefore, they might see me, but at least they couldn't surprise me up close as they might have in an eastern forest."

Goss threw up his hands to indicate how ridiculous all this was and they both laughed. Even so, Glenn was relieved to hear another man from the East express what he had also felt when first exposed to the vast, open plains of Nebraska.

Joshua and his hunters were gone five days but they returned with plenty of buffalo meat to feed the crews. Some of the meat was jerked and some smoked. Before Glenn realized it, the time had come to return to Silver Creek and report to General Dodge.

"Mr. Gilchrist?"

Glenn turned to see Liam. "How are you getting along?" he asked the young man.

"I'm doin' real fine now," Liam said. "Never had it so good."

Indeed, young O'Connell had changed much since Glenn had first seen him in Omaha. Liam was flourishing out on the plains despite the hard riding and dangerous work with the scouts and hunters. His eyes were no longer perpetually bloodshot from whiskey and they regarded you steadily instead of sliding away like they'd done the first time that Glenn had met the young man. He still felt that Liam was a liar and untrustworthy, but at least he was in excellent physical shape and appeared to have matured under Joshua Hood's watch.

"Mr. Gilchrist, I understand that you are going back to Omaha."

"I'm going to find and report to General Dodge. If he's in Silver Creek, that's as far down the line as I'll ride."

"Oh."

Glenn waited, sensing confusion in the younger man. "Is there something you wanted me to do?"

"Yeah," Liam said, dragging out a couple of pieces of paper. "I wrote letters to Rachel Foreman and to my sisters. I was hoping you might deliver 'em."

"I will if I get to Omaha. If not, I can put them in envelopes they have in the office car and forward them there."

Liam brightened. "Would you do that? It'd mean something to me—and to them."

"Sure."

Liam scuffed the toe of his boot. Glenn knew the young man was working up to another request. "Something else I can do for you?"

"Oh, no, sir! You just tell my sisters that I'm fine. When they hear about the Indians' killing those men at Lone Tree, I know they'll be real upset. You tell 'em that I'll be fine under Mr. Hood and not to worry none."

"I will."

"And . . . and tell Megan that I hope she decides to follow these rails west and bring Rachel along too."

Glenn smiled. "I'll pass that along. Is that all?"

Liam turned his face away a little. "Just one thing. I hope you don't cross Mr. Hood."

Glenn's smile slipped. "Did he say I'd 'crossed him'?"

"Not in so many words," Liam admitted. "But I can tell he's mad that you are going back to see Megan and he can't. It wouldn't do to cross him, Mr. Gilchrist. You've been fair to me all along and I'd not like to see you hurt . . . or worse."

"Thanks," Glenn said. "But it appears that we are both interested in your sister."

"Megan is pretty special. Aileen too," he quickly added.

"Yes, they are."

Liam handed his letters over. They were smudged and folded into very small squares. "Thanks, Mr. Gilchrist," he said, stabbing his dirty hand out.

Glenn shook the younger man's hand. "Don't mention it," he said before Liam turned away.

That same morning that Glenn had taken Liam's letters, Joshua had spent working grease into the buffalo hides to soften them. Now, as Glenn prepared to leave at daybreak, the Union Pacific's head scout approached Glenn with his hands caked with hair and grease. Wiping them on his stiff buckskins, Joshua said, "I hear you're about to leave for Omaha."

"Wrong. I'm going to the head of the track. That's where I'll find both Generals Casement and Dodge."

"If you get to Omaha, stay away from Megan. I mean to make her mine."

"What you 'mean' to do matters nothing to me," Glenn told the chief scout in a hard, flat voice. "And I'm sure that Megan will make up her own mind about what kind of a man she likes."

"I *know* what kind she likes and you don't fit the bill, Mr. Gilchrist."

"We'll see."

Joshua stepped closer to Glenn and their eyes locked. "There'll come a time."

"I'm sure of it," Glenn said to the man before he turned and walked away.

He hadn't thought too much about Megan lately, but Joshua reminded him that he needed to see her soon. Glenn was sure that Megan wasn't going to remain in Omaha after the big Union Pacific crews left town—but damned if he was going to share that insight with Joshua Hood.

• • •

Glenn reined Sundancer up to watch as a U.P. grading crew of about seventy grunting, sweating laborers worked to grade a roadbed in advance of the tracks. Using horses and mules to pull scrapers, the foremen kept his men hard at work. Hand dumpcarts were quickly piled high with rocks and excess fill dirt was transferred up and down the line. The day was warm and most of the men were shirtless. And though it was still early summer, the grading crew were as uniformly brown as hickory nuts and the strenuous work had stripped them down to rippling muscle.

It was a pleasure to watch the grading crew move steadily west. Occasionally, they chanced upon a big rock that required heavy digging with Ames shovels or pikes, but mostly they advanced the roadbed as efficiently as a military work detail might sweep and swab a barracks' hallway. In the quarter hour that Glenn sat watching from atop Sundancer, the roadbed was advanced several hundred feet and the men worked so hard that they did not pay him any attention.

Even more impressive was the sight that greeted him early that same afternoon when Glenn witnessed a sight that he doubted he would ever forget. It was a ballet of muscle and iron. A symphony of ringing hammers, dashing horses, and grunting, sweating rust eaters. The ballet was a marvel as it presented itself. First, lightweight carts, each drawn by a horse, were loaded with railroad ties and then raced forward where crews would rip the ties off the wagons and slam them down, then jump forward to await the momentary arrival of the next wagon.

In the meantime, horses on the opposite side of the track would drag lightweight rail carts up the line loaded with sixteen rails plus the exact required number of spikes, bolts, and fishplate couplings. The bed of each of these carts was equipped with rollers so that five men could sweep each rail off the cart in an instant, stagger forward, and drop it exactly into place. An instant later, two "gauge men" would insure that the rails were exactly four feet eight-and-one-half inches apart. Almost before the gauge men had lifted their measures, spikers would begin swinging their hammers. The operation was so precisely timed that the hammer blows rang in perfect unison. As soon as all sixteen rails and their couplings were removed from the lead rail cart, it was unhitched and shoved off the tracks making room for its heavily laden replacement. Thirty seconds to a rail for each gang, four rails placed and spiked every working minute.

Glenn marveled at the concentration and organization that Casement had created. The spikers were especially impressive. They neither missed nor varied from their tempo of three strokes to a spike, ten spikes to a rail, four hundred rails to the mile.

Young men, old men. Black, brown, and white men. All heaving and sweating and driving forward at the rate of more than a mile a day to chain the Nebraska prairie. To lay down a glistening ribbon of rail that mocked the red man and the blue sky. That proclaimed that civilization could never be denied and that progress would claim its inevitable victory.

Casement spotted Glenn and motioned him over. "Well, what do you think?"

"It's amazing," Glenn said.

"It's a *military* exercise," Casement explained. "That's why I wanted as many ex-soldiers as we could find to be employed on my work crews. These men understand the importance of teamwork and accepting authority. They may not like it, but they do accept it."

Glenn nodded with agreement. He would have guessed that there were over five hundred men and each of them was working at high speed like the moving parts of a racing locomotive. Not one person save the foremen was standing around and even they were spotting and solving problems before they could interrupt progress. In their own rough, coarse, and profane way, each man on the line was transformed into something truly magnificent as the imperfect parts of Casement's grand track-laying machine laid the rails west.

Even Casement could not hide his satisfaction as his restless eyes constantly darted back and forth. "This will get even faster as the men gain experience," he predicted.

"That's hard to believe."

"Believe it. Right now we are laying between one and two miles a day, depending on how many minor hitches we encounter. Before we are through, I'm betting we will lay as much as five miles of track between sunup and sundown."

"Five miles? In *one day?*"

"Yes."

Glenn didn't think it was humanly possible. In fact, he didn't see how these men could work any faster without collapsing. To his eye, there wasn't a heartbeat of delay anywhere.

"You wait and see if I'm not right," Casement said. "I'm paying them a flat daily rate but we'll add incentives and bonuses when we really turn the heat up."

"Yes, sir," Glenn said dubiously.

Casement chuckled. "I can see you don't believe me. That's all right. I'll remind you of this conversation when we lay that five miles of track either in the Wyoming or the Utah Territories."

"A mile a day is pretty darned impressive to me, General."

"It is to most everyone," Casement said. "Even General Dodge was smiling before he returned to Omaha."

Glenn frowned. "I was hoping I'd find him here and be able to give him my report and then quickly return to North Platte."

"I'm afraid not. Dodge is mopping up operations in Omaha. He's making sure that everything is in place there to keep us supplied with our needs. The men can't lay track if we haven't rails, spikes, fishplates, and ties."

Glenn nodded with understanding. He could see that the rails had already bisected and passed Silver Creek. Following his eyes, Casement said, "Won't be long before the town will be packing up and leapfrogging us up to Lone Tree."

At the mention of that name, Glenn felt a pang of sadness. "I rode through there this morning and the graves were trampled so you can't even tell where we buried the men."

"That's because we reinterred them in Omaha," Casement said. "And I don't suppose that Joshua Hood and his men made any effort to track down those murdering Sioux?"

"No, sir. They were hunting buffalo and scouting to make sure that the men at North Platte weren't going to be scalped."

"That should be the Army's job," Casement said. "I don't want to be critical but what the hell is the Second Cavalry stationed at Forts Kearney, McPherson, and Sedgwick doing these days? They sure aren't helping us any."

"No, sir," Glenn said, unwilling to vent his own anger and frustration to an ex-general about the indifference of the United States Army toward the Union Pacific and its problems with the Indians.

"Well," Casement said, "get yourself some food and put up for the night. Tomorrow you had better ride on to Omaha and report to General Dodge. I'm sure that he's eager to hear your

report on the progress we are making between here and North
Platte."

"Yes, sir."

"Come by this evening and give *me* a report too," Casement
said. "In repayment, I've some excellent cigars and brandy."

"Very good, sir."

"Are you sure that you weren't a soldier?"

"No, sir. Why?"

"You just have an officer's bearing," Casement said. He
winked and added, "And you may take that as a high com-
pliment."

"Yes, sir."

As Glenn rode on past the track-laying operation, he had even
more reason to admire Casement's organizational skills. The rust
eaters were supported by a series of specially designed eighty-
five-foot-long platform cars all pushed by what was called the
"work train." The forward car nearest the point of track laying
was piled high with rails and the immediate supplies needed for
each day's work along with a blacksmith shop for emergency
repairs. Next came three immense sleeping boxcars outfitted
with triple tiers of bunks. Amazingly, each of these mammoth
sleeping cars could bed over a hundred men although most
construction laborers abandoned the cars and chose to sleep
outdoors, weather permitting. After the sleeping cars came the
dining car that Glenn had seen in Omaha with its tin plates nailed
to a single table running the entire length of the car. Following
the dining car was a car partitioned into a kitchen, storeroom,
and engineer's office. After that came more cars with all manner
of supplies fresh off the levee in Omaha.

Whenever Omaha crossed his mind, Glenn thought of Megan
O'Connell instead of General Dodge. He didn't feel very guilty
about that. After all, he knew exactly what he would tell the
general, but he hadn't a clue about what he would say to Megan
and what might happen between them.

One thing he could predict, with General Dodge about to
remove the last remnants of the construction crews from Omaha,
Megan and Aileen were probably starting to feel the economic
pinch. As good as their meals and pastries might be, businesses
in Omaha would be dying and the O'Connell sisters would be
faced with some very painful and difficult decisions.

CHAPTER
20

Megan closed her tent after dinner and walked over to the Union Pacific's main departure station. Leaning against the weather-worn wood, she observed a ten-car-long supply train packed with construction workers chug out of Omaha. A grinning rust eater spotted her and began to yell her name and wave. It was an effort for Megan to return the man's farewell.

When the train bled into a speck on the flat Nebraska horizon, Megan walked back into town, feeling aimless and depressed. This noon, she had served only eight customers and the supper meal always attracted an ever smaller number that wasn't enough to keep her in business.

Aileen's pastry business was doing a little better because many of the U.P. officials had their families in this town and those people did enjoy Aileen's scrumptious desserts of cookies, cakes, and pies. Indeed, after school, there was always a line of hungry children with their pennies, nickels, and dimes waiting to be served. But even for Aileen business had trickled away to a bare subsistence living.

The good news for Megan was that by being frugal during the first few months after she'd opened, she had managed to save enough money to recoup her initial U.P. settlement. However, no longer did she consider buying a city lot and building her own restaurant. The business in downtown Omaha just wasn't there and wouldn't be for a good many years to come. Once the transcontinental line was completed, Omaha's city fathers were certain that the town would boom again but until that time . . . well, Megan had far more ambitious plans.

"Afternoon, Mrs. Gallagher," a tall man in a dark suit called as he came across the street to join her. "I saw you down at the station. Kind of sad, isn't it?"

"Afternoon," Megan said, looking up at Thomas Maxwell whose bank was also suffering from the U.P. exodus. "It is sad, but it's also exciting to think of what a transcontinental railroad will do to bind together this country."

"Bind? I doubt that. All it will do is carry fools off to California and other parts of the wild West," Maxwell proclaimed. "I see nothing exciting or profitable in that."

"That's because you'll never leave Omaha," Megan replied, annoyed by his reaction.

"And you will?"

"Definitely."

Maxwell sighed. He was an irksome bachelor who had been interested in Megan since her husband's drowning in the flooded Missouri River. The interest was definitely not mutual. Maxwell was stiff, formal, and entirely without humor. He acted like he was seventy-five and was so set in his opinions that he almost threw Megan into fits of frothing exasperation. The man had money and his bank would survive Omaha's impending downturn, but Megan would bet that he would bemoan his losses for the rest of his dreary, complaining life.

"Mrs. Gallagher, I really think you should restructure your plans. We once talked about your buying a very choice business lot that my bank just happens to own. We could offer you extremely attractive terms."

"I fed exactly eight people for the noonday meal," Megan said. "Nine including myself. That is hardly enough to pay off a bank loan."

"Smart money is patient money," Maxwell lectured as he wagged his bony forefinger.

"Smart money is big enough to be patient," Megan corrected. "I have no intentions of going broke waiting for Omaha to blossom again."

Maxwell puckered his bloodless lips. "Your sister does not share that view."

"Aileen is content to wait. I am not."

"How unfortunate," Maxwell clucked as if he'd just been told of a death in the family. "And as for your 'going broke,' that need not be a concern, pretty Megan. I could . . . ah, make you a very attractive offer."

Megan glanced sideways at the man, her eyebrows raised in

question. Yes, this proper fool really was suggesting what she thought he was suggesting. Megan decided, after putting up with him so many times, she was finally going to pin him to the wall. "Are you making some kind of illicit proposal, Mr. Maxwell?" she demanded.

His eyes widened with alarm and he retreated a half step under Megan's glare. "I—I don't know what you mean. Honest!"

"I think you do," Megan said. "But it doesn't matter. One way or the other, I'm leaving Omaha."

"You disappoint me greatly. The West is no place for a woman alone. You might even get scalped by a Sioux."

"I doubt that."

"Or worse," Maxwell added.

Megan pushed past the banker and continued up the street.

When she arrived at Aileen's Bakery, her sister was as busy as usual baking in her kitchen. There were six pies steaming although three others from the day before remained on the front counter still unsold. "Hi!" Aileen said, reaching for one of her own delicious oatmeal cookies and offering it to Megan. "Would you like one?"

"No thanks. If I worked here, I'd weigh two hundred pounds."

Aileen giggled. "I've put on enough weight so that my dresses are too tight."

"You look better than you have in years," Megan said, meaning it. "And happier."

"I am feeling well and perhaps it's even a blessing that business has slowed down for a while."

"Maybe for quite a while," Megan cautioned.

"That's all right," Aileen said. "Did I tell you that I found a wonderful house for us all to rent! It's perfect, Megan. You'll have your own room, and so will I and the children. Between our two businesses, I doubt we'll hardly ever have to cook. Now that so many people are leaving Omaha, the rents are falling like stones and we can get this lovely house for only ten dollars a month."

"That is cheap," Megan said, trying to sound enthusiastic. "But I've told you that I'm leaving Omaha. For some reason, you just don't seem to want to accept that."

"It's because you'd be crazy to go west," Aileen said. "Listen, I know things are very slow, but everyone says that they will improve. We've still got the big Union Pacific roundhouse and all those repair shops. The railroad has reinforced the levee and they've built those new warehouses to store supplies ferried upriver. Omaha will rebound in a few months."

"I don't think so," Megan told her sister, "but I like your optimism. And I'm glad that you think you can keep the bakery."

"Megan!" Aileen shoved the cookie into her mouth and chewed it rapidly. Swallowing, she said, "I can't make it here without you. You *must* stay. David and Jenny wouldn't know what to do if you went west."

"They've already made new friends and they seem very happy," Megan said, knowing that she would dearly miss her sister's two sweet children.

Aileen cocked her head a little to one side. "Please don't leave," she said. "We're alone now."

"You're not alone," Megan reminded. "You've got your children."

"And you!"

Megan could see that she wasn't getting across. She went over and took Aileen's flour-dusted hand in her own. "Aileen," she said, "I *have* to go."

"But why?"

"I . . . I just do," Megan said. "You know how I've always dreamed of California."

"Then let's go together. But not until the transcontinental can take us there. Just wait until then, Megan."

"I can't," she said. "It might be another two or three years until the railroad is completed. That's too much of my life to be stuck in a town that holds few good memories."

"Things are a lot different for us now," Aileen argued. "Since we went into business for ourselves, things have been good, haven't they?"

"Not bad," Megan conceded.

"I like Omaha," Aileen said. "I love the children rushing in after school to buy sweets and I thoroughly enjoy visiting with the wives that come for pastries. I think they like me."

"Of course they do."

Aileen took a deep breath. "Megan, I know you're not going to like what I'm going to tell you, but I've decided to join the Presbyterian Church."

Megan's jaw dropped. "We were raised Catholics!"

"I know," Aileen said, looking away quickly. "But I like the

Presbyterian minister better than Omaha's gruff old Catholic priest."

"That's no reason to dump your faith!"

"And you've no right or reason to leave me and the children and go west!"

Megan took a back step and collected herself. "Let's calm down. I don't want to fight with you, Aileen. Not when I'm planning on leaving soon."

Aileen's eyes filled with tears. "It seems like just when things start to get better and I find a little happiness, something goes wrong."

Megan came over and hugged her sister. "Listen," she whispered, "we each have to do what we must. And we know that if either one of us is down, the other will help. Isn't that right?"

Aileen sniffled. "Yes."

"I'll help you," Megan promised. "I know you were counting on me to split the rent on this new house that you've got your heart set upon. And I'll still do it."

"That wouldn't be fair if you're going away."

"I'll need someplace to leave belongings that I can't risk losing out on the line. So I'm still going to need that bedroom."

Aileen pulled back. "Are you sure?"

"Quite."

"Oh, Megan! Won't you change your mind?"

"No. Please don't ask me again, and in return, I promise I'll never again bring up the subject of your faith."

"All right," Aileen said, stepping back. She smiled bravely. "How about a cup of coffee and a slice of yesterday's cherry pie to seal the deal?"

"I'd love that," Megan said, deeply relieved that her sister was taking this so well but troubled by the fact that she was tossing her church aside for no other reason than she did not care for the local priest.

The next day, Megan began to take definite steps to follow the Union Pacific rails west. She knew there was no hope of selling her business and so her only real alternative was to transport it westward. She went to the U.P. offices and asked for Dan Casement, remembering how highly he was regarded by Glenn.

"Mrs. Gallagher?" Casement asked.

"Miss O'Connell," she said, deciding right then and there to drop her late husband's name. "May I have a few minutes of your time, sir?"

Dan Casement beamed. He was a handsome little man and his smile encouraged Megan and hardened her resolve. The railroad official extended his hand to her. "Come into my office."

Casement's office was just a stone's throw from the now almost vacant levee. It was stacked from floor to ceiling with books and catalogues of every description. The desk, however, was very neat. Megan recalled that Glenn had considered this man to be an organizational genius and an expert in logistics.

"Have you heard from Mr. Gilchrist lately?" Megan inquired, after she was offered a seat.

"As a matter of fact, we expect him to return to Omaha any day now. General Dodge gave him one month to reconnoiter and then report back."

"Then the general is still in Omaha?"

"He's leaving tomorrow."

"Will you go too?"

"No," Casement said, sounding genuinely disappointed. "I'll be staying in beautiful Omaha at least through this year and probably until the entire line is finished."

"You don't sound too pleased."

"I'm not," Casement admitted. "My brother is having all the fun out there on the Great Plains. I hope to find my own replacement and join him before this railroad is completed. But of course, I'll stay here if this is where I'm most needed. And you?"

"I have to leave," Megan said. "And that is why I've come to speak to you."

"Oh?"

"I was wondering if this railroad would transport my huge dining tent and supplies to the head of the line."

Casement just stared at her until Megan grew nervous.

"Is there something wrong? I mean, I would pay your employer. Isn't transporting things what a railroad does to make money?"

He laughed. It was a nice laugh, though. "Miss O'Connell, you are either very forgetful or very naive. I think it must be the latter."

"Why?"

"Have you forgotten that you skinned The Doctor and this railroad out of a very hefty settlement this spring?"

"It was a fair settlement!"

Casement's smile evaporated. "I won't argue that point. Nonetheless, it was still a gall to our vice president who would be less than well disposed to assist you in any way."

Megan came to her feet. "I see. Well then, I guess we have nothing more to discuss."

"Please, sit down," Casement said. "I think there is a good deal that we can discuss."

"Such as?"

"Such as why you want to follow the rails west."

"My reasons, sir, are not your concern."

Dan steepled his fingers. For such a small man, he had large, capable hands. "I'd like to think that you want to go west because of Mr. Gilchrist?"

"So, among other things, you're a matchmaker, eh?"

He blushed. "I like Glenn very much and I think he feels the same way about you."

It was Megan's turn to color a little. "Mr. Casement," she said, "if the Union Pacific definitely won't help me, then what have we to talk about?"

"Oh, a great deal! You see, Miss O'Connell, I know the freighters. I could get a reliable one to dismantle your tent, pack your restaurant supplies, and haul everything west to the railhead—at a price that you'd never be able to bargain for on your own. Does that suggest we might have something further to talk about over dinner tonight?"

"It does," Megan said. "As long as it's understood that this is strictly a business dinner."

"Of course! Like I said, Glenn is a very good friend."

"Then you really must be an incurable matchmaker," Megan said, coming to her feet.

They arranged a time and place and Megan left. She felt better about this already. All that remained was to see if Dan Casement could deliver as promised and then figure out if she could pay the price to follow the rails west.

That evening over a scrumptious dinner of veal and fresh creamed corn, whipped potatoes, and French wine, Dan said, "Megan, I have found a wagoner that I trust and who will take down your tent and haul it and everything that was under canvas west to Lone Tree for just fifty dollars."

"That's an excellent price!"

"It is," Dan agreed. "Frankly, it's a better deal than he'd offer the Union Pacific for a similar load. But he owes me a few favors and he will also have room to haul some badly needed supplies to the head of the line so he'll still make a tidy profit."

"What is his name?"

"Walt Guthrie. He's a nice old codger. His horses are slower than oxen but he's dependable and competent. I trust him completely."

"I appreciate this very much."

"I hope you can say that next month or next year." Dan sipped his wine. "Have you *really* thought about what you are about to do?"

"Of course."

"Then how do you think you can possibly make any money when everyone on the line will be eating *free* company food?"

"I've . . . well, I've done fine up to now."

"That's because half the people you fed weren't on our payroll and those that were had ready cash and very few places to spend it. Megan, I'm in charge of purchasing supplies and I can tell you that everything you serve is going to cost you double on the line—right from the start—because of the freighting charges."

"Double?" Megan drained her wineglass.

"Yes, and that's just the beginning. The farther you go west, the higher your food costs. That means that while you might still eke out a profit charging, say, four bits for dinner at Lone Tree, by the time the tracks reach North Platte, you'll have to raise your prices to six bits."

"That's awful."

"And the prices will rise dramatically as the line moves into the Wyoming Territory. By Cheyenne, an egg will cost you the price of a meal here in Omaha. Bacon, beef—all of it will skyrocket. Before very long you will be forced out of business because of the Union Pacific's own free dining car."

Megan wanted to argue. She wanted to shout a protest. But she couldn't. "I . . . I guess I've really been shortsighted," she managed to whisper, shaking her head and feeling like a fool.

"Listen," he said, reaching across the table and patting her on the shoulder, "there's always more than one way to skin a cat."

"What do you mean?"

"I mean if you *really* want to follow Glenn Gilchrist and this railroad west—and make a profit doing it—then you need to turn that tent diner into a saloon and gambling hall."

"What!"

"I'm serious," Dan said. "There's a lot of money to be made in gambling. That's why there are so many tent saloons and gambling halls already following our tracks."

"Then you certainly don't need another."

"Oh, but we do need one more," he countered. "One that is *honest.*"

Dan couldn't hide the excitement in his voice. "I may be asking you to leap into a den of lions, but I sincerely believe that you could make a lot of money and run an honest establishment. You could be rich by the time we reached California and you'd also be doing your customers a tremendous favor by not rigging the roulette wheels and not hiring crooked dealers. Your whiskey and beer wouldn't be concocted in some damned slimy water trough or cause our workers to go blind the morning after a drunken payday. And you'd offer our people a place to drink and gamble without fear of being cheated. What do you say?"

Megan stared at Dan Casement and inhaled his enthusiasm with great gulps. "I . . . I don't know! Could I do it?"

He laughed. "I don't know either. Could you?"

"Not without experienced help. I don't know the first thing about saloons and gambling."

"I could probably help you find someone who knows as much about drinking and gambling as old Walt does about driving a team of slow horses."

"It's a hard, dangerous business. Or so I'm told."

"It can be. But if you hire honest people, treat your customers fairly, and don't allow firearms in your tent, then you'd find it tolerable. And a hundred times more profitable than selling meals."

"Why?"

"Because a barrel of whiskey is cheap to transport and will earn you more than a whole wagonload of foodstuffs that you'd also need to cook and serve. And because a few poker, monte, and roulette tables can be found secondhand and also transported at minor expense."

"And the bar?"

Dan shrugged. "To start, a few boards resting across empty whiskey kegs. You already have the glasses."

"I have tin coffee cups."

"Trade them if you wish. If not, they'll suffice. Believe me, the two-fisted drinking men you'll serve out on the line are not going to object to tin cups. All they care about is if you're pouring a decent brand of whiskey at a fair price."

"I can do that."

"Then what about it, Megan? You can't compete with free railroad food. What about good whiskey and fair gambling? Do it right and you'll be a very wealthy woman by the time we reach the Sierra Nevada Mountains."

"I'll try!" she vowed, banging her fist down on the table.

They both laughed with nervous excitement. He said, "You've got a lot of work to do in a very short time and maybe Glenn will show up and take a few days off to help you. I can't help much during my office hours, but we can meet here for dinner and plan each day out until you are ready to roll."

"I don't know how I can ever repay you."

"Marry my friend Glenn Gilchrist and name your first boy after me," Dan suggested with an impish grin.

Megan's cheeks warmed and she lowered her eyes a moment while another bottle of wine was ordered to celebrate her new adventure.

CHAPTER

21

Glenn was astounded to see how empty Omaha had become during his brief absence. The main street, once clogged with horse and foot traffic, now seemed empty and lifeless. Glenn was dusty and weary but he rode Sundancer straight up to the main Union Pacific offices and dismounted.

Two young men in starched white collars were smoking cigarettes outside the offices and Glenn said, "Can one of you tell me where I can find General Dodge?"

"He's inside. And who would you be?"

"Glenn Gilchrist, assistant chief of surveying. I've a report for the general from the end of the line at North Platte."

One of the young men dropped his cigarette. "General Dodge will be glad to see you. We all heard about the massacre at Lone Tree. Goddamn Indians! I hope the general forms a company and we all ride out and annihilate them bloody Sioux."

Glenn didn't have a comment. The man was younger than himself and much greener. He looked like he was fresh out of some Ivy League college and reminded Glenn of himself only a year earlier. Glenn loosened his cinch, removed his saddlebags, and used them to bat the dust off of his clothes. Ignoring their open curiosity, Glenn pushed inside the U.P. offices and located General Dodge working at his desk.

"Good afternoon," Glenn called.

Dodge looked up and smiled. "Glenn! You're just the young man I was hoping to see."

"I am?"

"You are," Dodge said, motioning Glenn into his private office. "Close the door behind you, then sit down and bring me up-to-date on what is happening up the line. I'm heading out that way myself tomorrow and I'd like to at least appear to be informed."

Glenn closed the door and told the general all about the Indian trouble at Lone Tree. Dodge, true to his word, proved himself an excellent listener. He didn't once interrupt until Glenn completed his full report almost an hour later.

"And your assessment of the Indian situation?"

Glenn knew better than to equivocate. "I think Joshua Hood feels that chasing after the Sioux would be a mistake. Even if any were found, they'd most likely be the wrong ones."

"But you say that Hood doesn't believe the Lone Tree attackers are from one particular band."

"No," Glenn responded, and then reiterated Joshua's comment regarding how the Indians did not have a military chain of command like the United States Army.

"It sounds to me," Dodge mused, "as if Hood is saying that no particular chief of the Sioux is in control."

"That's the way I read it."

"Damn," Dodge muttered, "that does make it a lot more difficult to try to negotiate a peace, doesn't it?"

"I recall you once telling me that you didn't expect to make peace with the Indians."

"I don't," Dodge admitted. "But I keep wanting to prove myself wrong. What did you think of Ben Goss?"

"I liked him."

"He's not only a gentleman, but also a great engineer and surveyor," Dodge said. "You'll learn a great deal from that man."

"I'm sure of that."

"May I see that list of trestle construction materials and supplies you and Ben prepared?"

Glenn gave Dodge the list. Dodge took his time examining the list. Twice, he asked Glenn questions and then made small notations. Finally satisfied, he looked up at Glenn and said, "Deliver this to Dan Casement. He'll be able to handle it faster than anyone else I know., The man is indispensable."

"Is his office still down beside the old levee?"

"Yes. He wants to be sent out to the end of the line to join his brother, but I need him right here in Omaha."

"Makes sense."

Dodge leaned back in his office chair and laced his fingers behind his head. "Yes, it does make sense but I can't blame Dan for wanting to go west where the real action takes place. I feel that way myself. I understand that Jack has that construction crew working like a well-oiled machine."

"He does. I couldn't believe that track could be laid so fast. And Mr. Casement vows to hit five miles a day by the time that he reaches the Utah Territory."

Dodge chuckled. "Well, his contract calls for a maximum of three miles a day just so that he doesn't forget that quality work is just as important as production records. The last thing we want is to have to replace the entire line in a year or two because we slammed it down too damned fast."

"Yes, sir," Glenn said, standing to leave.

"Glenn, you look a little peaked and you've lost a few pounds you didn't need to lose. What's the matter, wasn't the food out on the line very good?"

"It was fine, sir. It's just that I've covered a lot of hard and fast miles since leaving the trestle construction gang at North Platte."

"You still like your horse?"

"I wouldn't trade Sundancer for love or money."

"And that hybrid Tex-Mex saddle?"

"It attracts attention but I've come to like it fine. Better in fact than a McClelland."

"Good," Dodge said. "But you do look worn down. I'd like you to help Dan fill that North Platte trestle list and then take a week off. Report back up the line and we'll see where you can best serve next."

"Yes, sir."

Glenn started to leave but Dodge stopped him when he called, "I hear there is bad blood between you and Joshua Hood."

Glenn turned. "Bad blood?"

"Yes. Over Mrs. Gallagher."

Glenn shifted uncomfortably.

"Never mind," Dodge said. "Your face tells the whole story. And it's none of my business except that I don't want to lose either one of you and I suspect that you'll have to work together. By that, I mean that you'll need Mr. Hood to escort you up and down the line if this Indian thing worsens."

"Yes, sir."

"And, Glenn, you don't want to fight a man like Hood."

"I don't want to fight *any* man," Glenn said. "But I won't be bullied or prodded and I'll stand my ground."

Dodge pulled a cigar out of his pocket, bit the tip off, and spat it into a trash can. "I admire that attitude. It's the same kind that I admired in your brother, Lieutenant John Gilchrist. But it also got him killed."

"Would you have preferred my brother to have stayed back out of harm's way?"

"No," Dodge said without hesitation. "But we're not fighting the Civil War all over again. Then I had a policy of shooting any soldier who killed his comrade in arms."

"Better tell that to Joshua Hood," Glenn said before he tipped his hat and excused himself.

Glenn turned his horse, saddle blanket, and bridle over to the care of the foreman of the Union Pacific remuda and then he wasted no time in finding Dan Casement. It was a happy reunion.

Dan took one glance at Glenn and exclaimed, "You've lost weight!"

"So I've heard."

"What's the matter? Aren't they feeding you well enough out there in the rail camps?"

"I've been saving myself for Megan's Place and some of Aileen's cherry pie."

"Sit down," Dan said, "we've got a lot to talk about."

"Can't it wait? I'd like to check into a room, get a bath, shave, and clean up. Tomorrow, I'll tell you all about North Platte, Lone Tree, Silver Creek, and the other rail camps and towns."

"I want to talk to you about Megan."

Glenn's eyes tightened with sudden concern. "Is she all right?"

"Yes. Sit down and relax. Would you like a cigar and a sip of brandy?"

"All right."

Glenn waited impatiently for both and when their cigars were lit, Dan said, "Megan is fine but her business is finished here in Omaha."

"I suspected she wouldn't be able to make it once Omaha practically became a village again. What about Aileen's Bakery?"

"Aileen is doing a little better thanks to the ladies and the children. But Megan has decided to pack her tent up and follow the rails."

"She about said as much, so this doesn't come as any big surprise."

"Well then," Dan said, "how about this for a surprise—instead of the dining hall like she had here in Omaha, Megan is going to open a saloon and gambling hall."

"What!"

Dan chuckled. "If you could see the look on your face! Marvelous! Better than I'd dared hope."

"Quit grinnin' and make sense."

"All right. I explained to Megan that her food costs would skyrocket because of transportation costs and drive her out of business. There was just no way she could make a go of it against the free Union Pacific dining cars."

"They're *not* free. The men are charged twenty dollars a month."

"That's true, but it's always deducted from their wages. If meals were not deducted, our laborers would either gamble their wages away or quickly squander their money on whores or bad whiskey and we'd have to feed them anyway. That's why it's a mandatory deduction. A cost built in to the wage rate."

"All right," Glenn said, conceding the point. "So Megan can't compete."

"That's right. But she can make a very, very good return on her money by opening a saloon—with good whiskey and an honest gambling hall—both starting out in her big tent."

Glenn wasn't convinced at first, but the longer he listened to Dan, the more sense it made. Finally, Glenn said, "I don't think that Megan can do it by herself."

"She agrees. That's why we've got to help her to find a manager. An *honest* manager."

"Can one be found?"

"I would think so," Dan said. "If he were paid well enough and watched close enough."

"But you don't have anyone in particular in mind."

"No," Dan conceded. "But I've already put the word out and so has Megan."

"I can't wait to see her."

"We're having a 'business' dinner tonight," Dan said. "And you're the surprise guest."

Glenn tossed his brandy down and stood up. "Give me the time and the place and I'll be there."

"Good. Megan is going to need a lot of help in the next week or two. I can't do much but I'm hoping that Dodge will give you a little time off and—"

"He already has," Glenn said. "My orders are to help you fill the North Platte materials list, then take a short vacation. And there is no way I'd rather spend it than being around Megan."

"Perfect!" Dan grabbed and pumped Glenn's hand. "And by the way, how is young Liam? Megan has told me quite a lot about him."

"Liam is fine. In fact, he seems to be in his natural element among the buckskinners. He gave me two letters and one of them is for Megan."

"She thinks the world of her brother, you know."

"I know." Glenn looked closely at Dan. "Just as long as she hasn't also started to 'think the world' of you too!"

Dan exploded with laughter. He was a man who enjoyed being teased about everything except his stature. *That* touchy subject could provoke him into fisticuffs quicker than you could snap your fingers.

That night when Glenn saw Megan sitting at the dining table with Dan, chatting happily away about the exciting plans that they were making, Glenn knew that he was in love with the young widow. For several moments, with customers passing by and some staring at him curiously, Glenn lost himself in Megan's beauty. No doubt about it, she was worth fighting Joshua Hood for, even if it might well cost him his life.

"Sir?" the waiter said. "Is there something wrong?"

"Not a thing in the world," Glenn told the man before he gathered his composure and then went over to greet Megan.

When she saw him dressed in a new suit, shaved, and barbered, Megan jumped up from her chair and threw her arms around his neck. "What a wonderful surprise!"

Glenn hugged her tightly. "You're beautiful. Will you marry me?"

She laughed, stepped back, and said, "Will you help me open an honest saloon and gambling hall in Lone Tree or whatever is the newest rail town?"

"It might be a place called Grand Island," he told her. "But wherever it is, I'll see that you are delivered safe and intact."

"Thank you, Glenn."

He gazed into her eyes and heard himself say, "Think nothing of it, Megan darling."

After dinner, Dan excused himself and left the couple. Glenn removed Liam's letters and slid them across the table. "This is for you and the other one is for Rachel Foreman."

Megan just stared at the two smudged and tightly folded letters until Glenn said, "Aren't you going to open yours?"

"All right."

She unfolded the letter, spread it out on the tablecloth, and Glenn could see that it was very short. Megan read it in a glance and when she looked up, she appeared both relieved and happy. "It seems that my brother is finally starting to grow up a little. I think working for Joshua, while I worry about the danger, is the best thing that ever happened to him."

"He looks and acts happy."

Megan folded the letter and slipped it along with the one for Rachel into her purse. "I'll show Liam's letter to Aileen in the morning. Rachel will be thrilled when she receives hers."

"Is she in love with Liam?"

"I'm afraid so."

"Why do you say 'afraid'?"

"Because I know Liam. He's maturing, but he's not ready for love or responsibility. Furthermore, he's very selfish and I'm almost certain he will use Rachel and then discard her with a broken heart. The last thing poor Rachel needs after already losing her baby and husband is to be taken advantage of by my brother."

"I see," Glenn said, wanting to tell Megan that he would never exploit her even if she was weak, which she definitely was not.

"Rachel hasn't said anything, but if she insists on being near Liam and following the rails, I'll ask her to work and live with me in the rail camps."

"How soon do you want to leave Omaha?"

"Yesterday."

"Realistically."

Megan raised her wineglass and Glenn refilled it. "Realistically," Megan said, "I'd guess that I can leave in about one week."

"Then so can I."

She arched her brows. "Does that mean that you want to escort me up the line?"

"Indeed I do."

She raised her glass and Glenn matched her toast. "Glenn, would you like to be my business partner?"

He had started to drink but now he set his glass down. "Are you crazy? I don't know anything about saloons or gambling halls and I care about them even less."

"That's what I thought," Megan said, "but I wanted to make the offer anyway."

"I'd like to make you an offer," he said, feeling the wine and the woman's beauty stirring his passion.

But Megan shook her head. "It's only fair to tell you what I told Joshua—that I'm not going to get involved with any man. At least not until the rails join and I'm basking in the warm California sun."

"Why?"

"I was married five years," Megan said. "And except for about the first five weeks, they were hell."

"I don't mean to attack someone who is no longer alive to defend himself, but I never understood why you married Keith Gallagher."

"The man you saw was a far cry from the boy I fell in love with and married. And I'm an altogether different woman. I was just a desperate little girl five years ago. Starry-eyed. Searching frantically in all directions for a way out of Boston and the poverty I'd seen destroy my parents.

"Keith was handsome, fun when he was sober, and he had the gift of spinning story tales. He charmed me. I thought he was real, but he was illusion and when I revealed this to him, that illusion shattered like a cheap mirror."

"Then that explains it."

"I don't know if it does or not," Megan said. "I can't tell you how often I've wondered, if I'd been a little more diplomatic, a little kinder, if I could have given him the confidence to be the man he yearned to become."

Glenn toyed with the stem of his wineglass, quite at a loss as to what to say. But then, Megan's hand stilled his own and she said, "Glenn, by the time the rails meet in the West, we'll all know each other very, very well. There will be no more illusions. And the work will be done and I intend to be an independently wealthy woman. That's when we can talk about offers and commitments."

"But not a moment sooner?"

"I'm sorry, but no."

He took a deep breath and let it out slowly. "As long as Joshua also keeps your California commitment in mind, I guess I can live with it."

"Joshua is like most men—he wants what he wants and he wants it right now. I suspect he may well find that he is incapable of patience or that I am not a prize worth waiting for."

"I disagree."

Megan looked deeply into Glenn's eyes. "We are about to undertake this wonderful, exciting adventure. Let's not spoil or dilute it. All right?"

Glenn had no choice but to nod his head. He knew that Megan was right, but his desire for her was so great he was not at all sure if he would have any more success at waiting than his rival. Only time, he sadly supposed, would tell.

It took Glenn three busy days to help Dan get the North Platte materials list filled but his mind was on Megan and not his work. Finally, Dan said, "Listen, why don't you just go help her and I'll muddle along here somehow."

"You'll be better off with me out of your hair."

"In your state of mind, that's probably true," Dan admitted.

Glenn hurried to Megan and learned that she had traded her large supply of dishes, pots, pans, and eating utensils to a steamboat captain for ten barrels of good rye whiskey along with two empty barrels and three oak planks to serve as her bar.

"Nice work," Glenn said.

"He skinned me," Megan answered. "He's going to ferry my kitchen goods down to St. Louis where he'll make a killing. But I'm not going to let him have them until I taste the whiskey."

"Excellent idea. What about the gaming tables?"

"There are several gambling parlors right here in Omaha that didn't have the money to go west and I've contracted to buy their tables and cards—if they aren't marked. Can you recognize a marked from an unmarked deck of cards?"

"No," Glenn admitted. "I'm not much of a gambler."

"Walt Guthrie says he can tell and will inspect each deck."

"I haven't met him yet."

"Then you're in for a treat."

Glenn smiled. "What is that supposed to mean?"

"It means he's quite a character. Look, here he comes now."

Glenn turned to see a bandy-legged little man with a thick barrel chest and arms that seemed much too elongated for his trunk. He sort of rolled across the tent's wooden floor. "Afternoon, Miss O'Connell!" he called. "You get that whiskey yet?"

"No but I'd like you to go over to the Blue Babe Gambling Hall where a Mr. Drake will let you inspect the cards and the tables. If everything looks good, come back and tell me what you think they are worth."

"I'll do it!" Guthrie said cheerfully. "Are you Mr. Gilchrist?"

"I am."

The old wagoner stuck out his horny paw and his grip was like a vise. "Glad to meet you! Real damned pleasure. Megan has told me about you and so has Dan!"

"All good, I hope."

The little bantam cackled. "No, sir! All bad!" He burst into loud guffaws.

Glenn couldn't help but like the man. When he'd disappeared, Glenn said, "Is Walt always so cheerful?"

"He has been since I've known him. He's my little diamond in the rough."

"Well," Glenn said, "let's just hope that he can tell an honest from a dishonest deck of cards or roulette wheel. Otherwise, the sterling reputation that you're planning to build is just going to disappear in smoke."

Megan started to say something but a shadow caught the corner of her eye and she turned to the doorway. "Belle?"

Belle stood poised at the tent's entrance, looking very apprehensive. "Megan, can we talk when you have some free time?"

"Miss Isabelle King!" Glenn called. "By all means, come on in! Do you remember me? I'm the one that you were brought to after the flood."

"I remember you," Belle said, shooting a glance at Megan whose lips were pressed together in tight disapproval. "And I know you helped get that wonderful settlement."

"You lost your parents. No amount of money can compensate you for such tragedy."

"No, sir, but—"

"What do you want?" Megan interrupted.

Glenn looked at Megan with surprise. "What's wrong?"

"Nothing," Megan said icily. "I just want to know what Belle is after now."

Glenn didn't understand why Megan had suddenly become so abrupt. He supposed she and Belle had had a minor disagreement, one he hoped could be easily mended.

"Megan, I want to join you and go up the line," Belle announced. "And I want to ride along with you. Work at your new saloon and gambling hall."

"I don't need your help."

"Rachel wants to go too," Belle said, ignoring Megan's curt rejection. "We worked hard for you when you opened your diner and helped make it a success. I think we can do the same in your new saloon and gambling hall."

When Megan just stared at the girl, Glenn said, "Megan? Don't you think they would be a tremendous help? I'm sure that . . ."

"Glenn, would you please let me make up my own mind about this?" Megan snapped.

Hurt, he nodded. "I think I'll take a walk and come back after you two have had a chance to settle whatever it is that has come between you."

When Glenn left, Belle marched forward and said, "You needn't have bruised his feelings. Mr. Gilchrist is a gentleman. Anyone can see that. He's not like the kind of men we've both known."

"Get out of here."

Belle held her ground. "Megan, you need me and I need you?"

"I'll hire Rachel, but I don't want anything to do with you."

Belle took a back step. Her eyes blazed. "So you're still playing the suffering saint! Have you really forgotten that your husband's drowning was the best thing that ever happened to you?"

"Shut up!"

But Belle couldn't shut up. She was yelling now, totally out of control. Megan reared back and slapped her.

Belle's eyes burned with hatred. "I'm going west and if there is anything I can do to destroy you, Megan Gallagher, you can bet I'll do it!"

"Others have tried," Megan said, trembling with rage.

Belle threw back her head and laughed. It was a terrible sound and Megan felt a shiver of dread a moment before the vicious little charlatan stormed out of her tent.

CHAPTER
22

Walt Guthrie's pair of dilapidated old freight wagons were almost loaded and ready to roll by ten o'clock that morning under a humid and cloudless day. Sundancer was tethered to the back of the second wagon where Glenn's saddle and few belongings were safely stowed. Omaha's business district was almost deserted and the town's streets were ankle deep in mud thanks to a week of heavy spring rains. The mud was drying fast leaving the street etched by wagon wheels.

Sweating and heaving Glenn and the old wagoner muscled the last of the gambling tables onto the back of the wagon. Taking a deep breath and mopping his brow, Glenn turned to see Megan looking off toward her sister's bakery.

"Why don't you visit with Aileen a few minutes before we go?" Glenn suggested. "I'd say we ought to be ready to pull out in about a half hour."

"I just wish Aileen and her children were coming."

"She isn't ready," Glenn said. "Maybe she'll change her mind later."

"If she does, it will be because Aileen's Bakery fails."

"Go on," Glenn urged. "We can finish loading and then I'll come get you just before we pull out."

"All right," Megan said, heading up the street.

Rachel came over to stand beside Glenn. "It's breaking her heart to leave Aileen."

"Yes," Glenn said. "But I don't think Aileen is strong enough for the Union Pacific's hell-on-wheels camps."

"Pretty bad, huh?"

"It'll be rough," Glenn admitted. "I'm glad that you and Megan will be living and working together. You'll also have a lot of friends watching out for you."

"And a few enemies too," Walt said, coming over to join them.

Glenn looked sharply. "What is that supposed to mean?"

"It means that Megan is going to have to worry about a whole lot more than just corralin' a bunch of hell-raisin' drunks come payday. She's goin' to have to worry about men like Ike Norman. You don't think that kind of varmint is goin' to let her take away their customers, do you?"

"I hadn't thought about that. I doubt that Megan has either."

"Who is Ike Norman?" Rachel asked with concern.

Walt spat in the dirt. "Ike's an ex-gunslick and a cold-blooded sidewinder that'll do about anything necessary to eliminate honest competition."

"If he tries to hurt or even intimidate Megan," Glenn vowed, "I'll see that he's tarred, feathered, and run off the line, if not hanged from a telegraph pole."

"Might not be easy to prove the man is guilty of any wrong," Walt said. "Him and his kind are as crafty as badgers. You aren't likely to ever catch 'em actually breakin' the law, threatening, or killin' anybody. No, sir! But they'll do the hiring."

Rachel looked to Glenn who said with more assurance than he felt, "When we get to the end of the line, I'll have a talk with Ike."

"If you do," Walt said, "you'd best have your hand buried in your pocket and a derringer fillin' your hand."

"Thanks for the warning," Glenn said, watching Megan disappear into the bakery.

"Aileen?" Megan called.

Aileen looked up and her eyes were red from crying. Little Jenny came running to throw her arms around Megan and sob. "Please don't go, Auntie."

Megan's heart almost broke. She knelt and said, "Don't you worry, I'll send for you soon. Before long, we'll all live in California someday where the sun shines the whole year and it never snows. We'll buy a big Spanish hacienda and raise oranges, peaches, and lots of delicious things to eat."

Jenny looked up and sniffled. "Auntie Megan, please stay with us."

"I can't," Megan said, lifting the girl into her arms. "But I promise that I'll send for you. Hopefully soon."

Aileen came over and took Jenny, then gave her a cookie and sent her out back to play. When she turned to Megan, she said, "Jenny will really miss her auntie. Little Dave is too young to understand why we are separating."

"It's for the best," Megan said. "If I stayed here, I'd go broke or else have to marry the likes of Mr. Maxwell."

"At least you'd never want for anything," Aileen said. "Mr. Maxwell owns a bank."

"Yes, but he's as tight-fisted and musty as an attic," Megan said. "He makes me feel old."

"At least you'd be living respectably. Who knows what might happen to you out on the Great Plains? I'm so afraid that you might get hurt or murdered."

"Nonsense," Megan argued. "I've got Rachel and Glenn to help."

"But Glenn will often be up ahead of the tracks surveying."

"Yes, but there are others. Walt Guthrie will be around the railhead hauling rails or supplies. And there is always Joshua Hood."

Aileen snorted. "Joshua Hood? Why he's one of the ones that I'd be *most* worried about if I were you. He's a wild man and you told me he was very bold."

"Oh, he is," Megan conceded, "but he has a code that would never allow him to hurt or compromise me."

"How can you be so sure?"

"Because the first time we met, he threw down his coat just so I wouldn't have to step in a mud puddle. A man that would do that has to possess a strong sense of chivalry not often seen outside of Dixie."

"He looks like a renegade to me," Aileen said, clearly not impressed.

Megan knew that she had to leave. She hugged her sister and whispered, "Aileen, if things go sour for you in Omaha, just get on the train and come up the line to stay with me. If you are ever dead broke or in trouble, telegraph and I'll wire money back to you the same day."

Aileen nodded her head. "The same goes both ways," she said. "You face all the danger."

"I'll do fine." Megan gently pushed her sister out to arm's length. "It will help me a lot to know that you are going to be all right here in Omaha while I try to make enough money so that neither one of us will ever have to worry about finances again."

"I'll be all right," Aileen said. "Thanks to you, I can afford our new house and my business is holding steady."

"Good!" Megan forced a smile. "Bye."

"Bye," Aileen whispered.

When Megan climbed into the second wagon that Glenn had agreed to drive up the tracks for Walt, she was dabbing at tears.

"Dammit," Glenn said in a low voice as he pulled her to his side and gave her a hug. "I wish that I could do or say something that would make this easier on you, Megan."

"There's nothing to be done for it," Megan said, glancing back over her shoulder as they pulled down the main street of Omaha and headed up the well-worn road that followed the rails west. Megan laced her fingers together and sat rigid on the wagon seat. When Glenn looked over at her with troubled eyes, she said, "It's just that sometimes, we have to do things that are hard. Aileen and I have been strong for each other since our parents died. We practically raised Liam together and when Aileen married, *I* was the one that thought the world would end. For weeks after her marriage, I felt so lonely that I cried myself to sleep at night. But finally, it got better. It will this time too."

"I felt the same way when my brothers died," Glenn confessed. "Even more when I lost my father. But it finally does get better."

"I just worry about Aileen," Megan said. "She's strong in some ways, but weak in others. And she does have the children to worry about."

"She'll be all right," Glenn said reassuringly, "I asked Dan Casement to keep a close eye on her. He said he'd be glad to. When I introduced them yesterday, I could see that they liked each other."

"Anyone would like Dan," Megan said. "He's such a happy man."

"He is a whirlwind," Glenn said, "Just like his brother. You can say what you want about The Doctor, but when he picked General Dodge as chief engineer of the Union Pacific and contracted the Casement brothers to lay track, he showed a lot of intelligence."

"I still don't like him," Megan said. "What was the name of the abandoned camp just up ahead?"

"Papillion," Glenn told her. "It was the first real tent city. At one time, Papillion boasted almost a thousand laborers."

Megan shook her head. There was only a single gray tent now, but she could see where the prairie was bald and churned up with lots of debris littering the otherwise green landscape. Two slovenly looking men were sitting on a bench in front of the tent. As the wagons approached, the pair called inside and another man came out to join them. When he saw the wagons, he hitched up his britches and checked his gun.

Walt Guthrie hauled on his lines and motioned for Glenn to drive up beside him. Walt reached down at his feet and dragged up a double-barreled shotgun. He checked its loads and said, "These three jaspers are big trouble. I've seen them before."

"Then let's just circle Papillion," Glenn suggested. "We sure don't need gunplay around the women."

"Can't. The prairie is too wet. We either stay on the road or we risk getting bogged down with these heavy wagons. That happens, we've got big problems."

"So what are you suggesting?" Glenn asked.

"You're packing a Colt, keep it handy."

"I've got a derringer," Megan said, patting her purse.

"Well I don't!" Rachel cried.

"Then get in back," Walt commanded, his voice turning hard-edged. "Act like you're lookin' for somethin'. Then duck if there's trouble."

Glenn stared at Papillion. "Walt, are you sure that you aren't overreacting?"

"Never hurt to be too cautious," the older man said. "Besides, I've a grudge with that big bastard who just snapped his suspenders. I'm willin' to let bygones be bygones, but I ain't sure he's going to be so charitable."

"What happened between you?" Megan asked.

"Woman trouble," Walt said, laying his shotgun across his lap and giving his horses a sharp whack with the lines. It caused his team to jump forward and Rachel to spill over into the back of the wagon. "Just stay down, since you already are," Walt ordered.

"*He* had woman trouble?" Megan asked, reaching into her

purse and extracting her derringer and slipping it into the folds of her skirt.

"That's what he said," Glenn answered. "I don't like this at all. I think you should get into the back of the wagon same as Rachel."

"Not on your life," Megan said. "Besides, Walt is always exaggerating things. I'm not too worried."

Glenn managed a smile, but he *was* worried. The heavily armed men were approaching and they didn't look one bit friendly. Glenn looked over at Walt and the little bantam rooster had shifted his double-barreled shotgun's muzzle to point at the advancing men.

"Megan, climb in back and stay down!" Glenn ordered, reading the murderous expressions on the three men and seeing how their hands were poised over their six-guns as they tromped through the drying road mud.

"I can't . . ."

Glenn lashed his arm out and swept Megan off her bench seat. He heard her angry protest as she toppled into the bed of the wagon. "Stay down and don't argue with me!"

The man with the suspenders halted and lifted his hand. "That's far enough!"

Walt didn't pull up his team and Glenn followed the older man's lead. Walt shouted, "Out of my way, Cutler!"

"Pull that wagon up, damn you!"

But Walt didn't pull up. Instead, he grabbed his shotgun and pointed it at the three men. Cutler stabbed for his own weapon but didn't clear his holster as the shotgun's blast ripped him out of the mud and slammed him over backward. Walt shifted his shotgun a fraction of an inch and it belched flame as he cut a second man down. But now he was out of shotgun shells as the last man had his pistol clear of leather. Even as Glenn drew, he knew he was going to be too late. He saw the third highwayman's gun buck in his fist. He heard Walt grunt and saw him clutch his shoulder and rock forward, hat tumbling off his head.

Glenn's six-gun banged in his fist. His first shot was wide, his second shot closer but still off target. Beside him, Megan's derringer barked and the last gunman slapped his left arm even as he pulled his trigger and also missed.

"Shoot him again!" Megan cried.

Glenn raised his pistol, took aim, and squeezed off a third

shot just as the wounded man also fired. Their shots blended and Glenn swore he felt a bullet's hot breath singe his cheek. The man did a little jig in the mud and Glenn shot him again. This time, the highwayman's chin dropped and he stared at a rose that blossomed across the front of his shirt.

Glenn thumbed back the hammer of his gun and was amazed that his hand was steady. He waited, fascinated by this last act of a deadly drama being played out for reasons he did not even begin to understand.

The fatally wounded gunman tried to raise his pistol but couldn't. He fired anyway and a harmless bullet geysered mud at his feet. Then, the man broke at the knees and collapsed, face buried in the mud.

"Walt!" Megan cried, leaping out of the wagon and jumping up onto the old man's lead wagon. "Walt!"

Glenn holstered his Colt, wrapped his lines around his brake, and leapt from his wagon. He was up beside the wounded wagoner in an instant. One glance told him that Walt was not mortally wounded. There was a lot of blood and the wagoner was pale, but he wasn't going to die if they could get the bleeding stopped and a doctor to remove the slug.

"Goddammit," Walt grunted with his head bowed in pain, "I don't know why they can't make a three-barreled shotgun. Are they all dead?"

"Yes," Glenn said as Megan pressed a piece of burlap sacking hard against the wound. "What the hell was that all about!"

"It's a long story," Walt said. "You suppose we could get this shoulder patched and *then* we talk?"

"Sure," Glenn said, realizing that now his hands were starting to tremble.

"We need to get the bleeding stopped and find a doctor," Megan said.

"The railroad only has two doctors on the payroll for things like crushed fingers and other work injuries. I think one is still back in Omaha."

"We're not going back!" Walt shouted. "Dammit, we're on our way west!"

"You're crazy as a loon," Rachel said, handing Megan a clean piece of bandaging. "You could have gotten us all killed, Mr. Guthrie."

"Well, I didn't start it!"

"You opened up on them first."

"Had to! Otherwise they'd have killed the lot of us, taken these wagons, and headed south."

"All right, all right," Glenn said. "We'll drive up the line until we find a doctor. But it's going to be hard on you, Walt. This shoulder is going to feel worse by the mile."

"We got ten barrels of whiskey for chrissakes! Show mercy. Open one!"

"Open one," Megan ordered.

Glenn didn't argue. He had never killed a man before and while in the actual act of doing it, he'd been steady, now he was shaking. He needed a good stiff drink and he needed it right now.

He found two of Megan's tin cups and as soon as he'd tapped one of the whiskey barrels, he filled both cups to the brim. Glenn hurried back to Walt and helped the older man straighten up and drink.

"Ahhh!" Walt gasped. "That's damned good whiskey. More!"

"Here," Glenn said, taking a long pull on his cup and then passing it on to Walt who downed that cup too.

"More," Megan said.

Glenn relayed three more rounds of whiskey up to the wounded man and all of them partook healthy medicinal doses. In a very short while, Walt wore a lopsided grin and his wound had stopped bleeding. "We'd better stop drinking and start up the line while we still can see straight," Glenn said, wiping his hand across his eyes.

"I'll drive this wagon," Megan offered.

"I'll lead off," Glenn told her.

Rachel pointed toward the three dead men. "What about them?"

"I guess we'd better put them into the back of the second wagon and report their deaths to the authorities."

"Who, exactly, are the authorities?"

"General Dodge," Glenn said without hesitation. "But he's not going to be very happy about this."

Walt Guthrie overheard Glenn and barked. "Hell, Dodge will *thank* us! That sonofabitch with the suspenders was already run out of the construction camps because he was such a hardcase. His friends were just as bad. General Dodge would give us a medal if we was soldiers in his Union Army."

"I hope he feels that way," Glenn said. He drove his wagon over to the bodies and since neither Rachel nor Megan offered to help, he had to drag each corpse across the mud and then hoist it into the back of his wagon. It was grim, messy work and Glenn was covered with mud and blood by the time he was finished.

Taking a fresh shirt from his bag, he hiked down to the Platte and washed, then changed his shirt. On his return to the wagons, he ducked into the tent and rummaged around. He was elated to discover a brand-new Henry .44-caliber, fifteen-shot repeating rifle. Other than that, there were several bottles of cloudy, rotgut whiskey but not much of anything else except three buffalo robes that the trio had used to keep warm at night. Unfortunately they were crawling with lice so Glenn left the robes and the whiskey for someone desperate.

"Let's get out of here!" he called, hopping onto the wagon and driving it fast up the road.

Behind him, Glenn heard the sound of singing and he twisted around to see that Megan, Rachel, and old Walt had refilled their glasses and were singing, of all crazy things, "Dixie."

> I wish I was in the land of cotton,
> Old times there are not forgotten
> Look away! Look away!
> Look away! Dixie Land.
>
> In Dixie Land where I was born in,
> Early on one frosty mornin'
> Look away! Look away!
> Look away! Dixie Land.
>
> Then I wish I was in Dixie,
> Hooray! Hooray!
> In Dixie Land I'll take my stand
> To live and die in Dixie;
> Away, away,
> Away down south in Dixie;
> Away, away,
> Away down south in Dixie.
>
> There's buck-wheat cakes and Injun batter,
> Makes you fat or a little fatter,

Look away! Look away!
Look away! Dixie Land.

Glenn shook his head with amazement and grinned. His hand caressed his new Henry rifle and he vowed to do a lot more practice shooting now that he was really heading into the wild West. One thing sure, he couldn't afford to miss twice before hitting what he aimed for—not and survive, he couldn't.

CHAPTER
23

They drove the wagons all night and were lucky to find a doctor in Elkhorn who removed the slug from Walter Guthrie's shoulder, then pronounced him fit enough for continued travel. After that, every fifteen or twenty miles they passed the remnants of earlier rail camps. North Bend. Columbus. Jackson. Silver Creek. All had known boom, then sudden bust as the rails were forged ever westward. There were ashes and scores of busted bottles and empty tin cans in these abandoned camps but not a stick of lumber. Because of the high price of wood, every foot of lumber not burned for fuel was dismantled and reused in construction up the line.

At least twice each day, locomotives rumbled past coming and going from Omaha. The returning trains were pulling empty flatcars to be reloaded; the westbound trains were all laboring to deliver massive tonnages of rails and ties, food and supplies for the great Union Pacific army of track layers that Glenn expected to overtake at Grand Island. Glenn remembered Dan Casement telling him that Grand Island was to be the first engine-changing point on the line. Here, a second ten-stall roundhouse was going to be constructed that would almost rival the one built last winter in Omaha.

To Glenn's further amazement, Dan had also told him that a total of thirty-five locomotives were to be pressed into service on the U.P. line, seventeen of which had already been delivered and were in operation.

This figure had astounded Glenn. During this past spring alone, almost a dozen new locomotives had arrived in Omaha by steamer and had been assembled at the huge roundhouse. They were all of the 4-4-0 type, most of them having sixty-inch drivers and sixteen-by-twenty-four-inch cylinders. However, several were secondhand locomotives that had served during the Civil War, four being ten-wheelers built in Cincinnati and two others built by Norris and Rogers. When Glenn had arrived the previous year, there had only been four locomotives. He could not imagine exactly how so many new locomotives were to be utilized, but he knew that breakdowns were commonplace and that at least a third of the locomotives were always in Omaha's huge repair shops.

"I can't get over how quickly Walt is healing," Megan said early one evening as they camped near the recently abandoned rail town of Lone Tree. "He's remarkably strong considering the bullet wound he suffered."

"He is that," Glenn agreed with a smile. "And the whiskey sure eased his pain."

"I know," Megan said. "I've had to ration it to him since that first day out."

Megan and Glenn strolled down to the Platte and stood beside the water. The days had remained warm and the spring flowers were starting to wither and the grass was bending and sunburning yellow at the tips. They turned to hear a locomotive's lonesome call and watched as it came puffing westward into sight, stack belching wood smoke. When the engineer saw them, he blasted his whistle in greeting, leaned out his cab window, and waved.

Megan and Glenn returned the greeting and then turned back to watch the lazy Platte. Along the riverbank, all the larger cottonwoods had been chopped down and used to fuel the locomotives. Their stumps poked skyward like amputated fingers and served to remind Glenn that the railroad's progress stood to ruin both the land and its ancient, natural way of life. He could see there had once been beaver in this river, but now they were gone, either shot, trapped, or finally starved into extinction by voracious crews of U.P. woodcutters feeding the Iron Horses.

"A penny for your thoughts?" Megan asked.

"I was thinking about all the thousands of trees that the Union Pacific will chop down before it leaves this river. I didn't realize until just a while back that this line follows a river partly so that the Union Pacific will have firewood out on these plains."

"Any chance of them using coal instead?"

"It's too expensive to ship in from the mines of Pennsylvania and West Virginia. Durant and the others are hoping to discover coal deposits in the Black Hills, but there's no guarantee."

"I never realized until just now how much change this railroad will bring to these silent, immense plains," Megan said. "And I have been waiting and hoping to see buffalo, but so far, nothing."

"I'm sure that Joshua Hood and his men have shot what few might have survived the guns of the emigrants who preceded this railroad along the path of the old Mormon and Oregon Trails."

"How disappointing. All last winter, I kept up my spirits by thinking about how we'd see exciting things like buffalo thundering past our tent cities and Indians howling just beyond the range of our rifles. Now it seems all that there is to see are the ruined places where we have built our raw little rail towns and then rooted them up again."

"You'll see buffalo and Indians before we are done," Glenn promised. "Maybe a lot more of the latter than you want."

Megan inhaled deeply of the river's dank earthy scent and also of a million square miles of prairie grass and flowers. "I told my sister that I wanted to be wealthy by the time we reached California, but I also yearn to see the West and absorb its excitement and color."

"It's a beautiful country."

"Yes," Megan agreed. "So beautiful that I feel sorry for the Indians. I find it impossible to blame them for fighting to keep these rails from taming their lands. I know that Joshua feels the same way."

Glenn thought of the bloated carcasses of the scalped white men he'd helped to bury at Lone Tree and said nothing. Later, he and Megan walked hand in hand back to their wagons and helped Rachel make the evening meal. That night, like all the others, they listened to Walt Guthrie regale them with tales of the great American West.

"I met Jim Bridger back in the year of '47," he boasted. "Bridger and me was breaking trail through the Laramie Mountains when we was jumped by a band of Cheyenne Indians. They took us to their village and we was hopin' they'd turn out friendly, but they had other plans. When we got the notion they was going to fricassee us for supper, we gnawed our rawhide bindings loose and sprinted for the closest Indian ponies. They couldn't shoot arrows at us fer fear of hittin' their ponies."

Rachel leaned closer over the campfire. "So what happened then? Did you outrun them back to some army fort?"

"No missy, we did not. Our ponies turned out to be slower than cold molasses but just as we was about to be overtaken, Jim and I whipped them into a ragin' river. 'Bout the width of the Platte, but it was boilin' white as it poured out of them high mountains."

"Oh?" Glenn asked, knowing that there were no huge rivers in the Laramie Mountains. "And what river was that, Walt?"

The old man scowled and thought a moment. "Don't recollect," he finally said. "The Injuns probably had their own name for 'er, but we just called it the Big White Water. Jim and me swam the Cheyenne ponies until they drown, then we jumped off when they turned upside down and lit out swimmin' like fish. Made it across and when we looked back, there was sixteen Cheyenne warriors drowned and them with sense enough to stay on dry ground was madder than teased snakes. I tell you, that was a close call!"

Glenn looked to Megan and winked. He was quite sure that Walt had never been west of Grand Island because Dan Casement had told him that the old man had spend all his life skinning mules in Georgia before the Civil War.

"Yes, missy, me and old Jim Bridger and Kit Carson had ourselves quite a time in them early years. Back then a good stack of beaver pelts would buy a man a couple horses, a grinnin' squaw, and all the supplies he needed to last out another Rocky Mountain winter."

Rachel's eyes widened. "But you never . . . well, you know."

"What?"

Rachel glanced at Megan for help. Megan said, "She wants to know if you actually took yourself a squaw."

"Well hell yes! I probably bought a half dozen. Back in those days, you bought and sold 'em same as you might dogs or horses."

"Mr. Guthrie!" Rachel cried with outrage. "Indian women are *people,* same as the rest of us."

He grinned. "Well, their menfolks didn't think of them as such. And they were sure comfortin' to a man during those long, cold mountain winters."

"I think," Megan said, seeing the look of deepening shock on Rachel's face, "that you have said about enough for one evening, Mr. Guthrie."

"Don't you even want to hear about the time that I fought a grizzly bear with nothin' in my hands except a bullwhip?"

"Not tonight."

"Damn," the wagoner complained. "That's one of my better stories. Jim Bowie was with me when it happened at a rendezvous back in the year of 1841."

"Jim Bowie died at the Alamo in 1836," Glenn said.

Walt Guthrie's eyes narrowed with suspicion. "You sure?"

"Yes."

"Then it must have been in '26 that we fought that bear."

"Jim Bowie was never west of Texas or north of Oklahoma."

Guthrie snorted with outrage. "The hell you say! We was in Utah, by damned, but we was workin' for the United States Government at the time. You see, there was a Mormon uprisin' and they sent us up the Colorader River to see if we could invade the land of Zion. But I'll tell you that one tomorrow night."

Guthrie laid out on his blankets, gazed up the stars for about two minutes, and then began to snore.

"You shouldn't have teased him like that," Megan said, her voice carrying a hint of reproach.

"I know, but he shouldn't have upset Rachel."

"Did he really buy squaws like he would horses?" Rachel asked.

"I doubt it," Glenn said. "All I know for sure is that Dodge actually has hired Jim Bridger to do some survey work for him farther west. So, if we see that famous mountain man and Walt is present, we can have some fun."

"That might not be such a good idea."

Glenn stared into the campfire for a moment and then he said, "You might have something there, Megan. You just might."

When they finally overtook the track layers late one afternoon, Jack Casement and his track-laying machine had pushed a quarter mile past Grand Island. At the outskirts of that bustling tent city, Glenn saw a sign that read:

WELCOME TO GRAND ISLAND
154 RAIL MILES → OMAHA!
CALIFORNIA! ← 1,399 RAIL MILES

Glenn chuckled. "I wonder how they can come up with such an exact mileage to California."

"I don't know, but the size of this rail town astonishes me," Megan said, her eyes flashing as she drank in the swirling hub of activity.

Grand Island was bustling. Walt Guthrie, now recovered enough to drive the lead wagon again, drove into the settlement and hauled up short as Megan drank in the excitement and color. There were about twenty hastily erected wooden structures lining what passed for a main street. Two of the buildings were hotels, three were whorehouses, and four were saloons. The remaining wooden structures were the usual collection of businesses, the largest having a crude banner stretched across its front proclaiming it sold goods at Omaha prices.

Construction had halted for the night and the track-laying crews were eating dinner and converging on the town looking for a little fun and relaxation. Prostitutes were everywhere in evidence and advertised their bodies with a brazenness that would have put a New Orleans back street to shame. Gamblers with fancy embroidered silk vests leered at Megan and Rachel under half-hooded eyes. A fistfight was raging inside a tent and a crowd of already inebriated laborers were trying to drag the brawlers into the street.

An old Indian with long, braided pigtails shuffled to some inner beat around an upturned stovepipe hat at which amused track layers alternately spat tobacco juice or flipped pennies. Close by, the dancer's squaw worked on a pair of beaded moccasins while a little white dog yipped and cried as it struggled to free itself from a leather thong that bound it to the squaw's ankle. At the end of the street a knot of men were trying to stir up a second fistfight between a pair of staggering whores.

"This is like I envision Sodom or Gomorrah," Megan said, watching a man follow a fat lady through the thickets along the river.

"We must have arrived on payday," Glenn said. "Normally, these camps are not quite this wild. Where would you like to set up your tent?"

"I don't know," Megan said, looking overwhelmed by her surroundings.

Glenn looked closely at Megan, then to Rachel who seemed

petrified by the debauchery that swirled around them. "Are you both sure that you want to go through with this? We can still turn around and drive back to Omaha."

Megan straightened on the wagon seat, visibly collecting her resolve. "Not a chance. We're staying."

When they reached the last tents on the main street, Megan indicated where she wanted to unload and erect her tent. Glenn set the brake on his wagon and hopped down. A few curious men detached themselves from the general revelry and one, recognizing Megan, shouted, "Mrs. Gallagher! Did you come to feed us good meals at square prices like back in Omaha?"

He was grinning broadly and his cheerful greeting visibly lifted Megan's spirits. "No, Peter, we're going to open a saloon and gambling hall. Honest games and honest whiskey."

"You brought some good whiskey?"

"Ten barrels," Megan said. She glanced at Walt and amended that slightly by adding, "Well, almost ten barrels."

"Hot damn!" Peter shouted. He cupped his hands to his mouth and bellowed, "Good whiskey at good prices, boys! And pretty wimmen to pour!"

"But . . . but I don't even know what to charge!" Megan cried as a horde of men came hurrying toward him.

"Charge 'em a dollar a tin cup!" Walt bellowed. "They'll pay. It's better than two bits a watered-down shot!"

"Then a dollar it is," Megan said.

There was some grumbling but when Pete paid and took a big gulp, he smiled so broadly that everyone knew Megan's whiskey was worth the asking price. Very quickly, Glenn and Walt had planks laid across the empty barrels and were pouring whiskey as fast as they could manage.

The Union Pacific laborers flocked out of the tents and ramshackle saloons, and for the next two hours it was a struggle to keep track of the money that came pouring into Megan's coffers. By the time that Megan had finally declared her open-air saloon closed, they had gone through two full barrels. Her decision to close shop was not well received by the men but she promised to reopen her business under canvas at quitting time the next day and pour until ten o'clock if that was what the men wanted.

"I should have bought fifty barrels of whiskey," Megan lamented after the last of the crowd had departed. She reached into her pockets stuffed with greenbacks and raised a handful of money to the moonlight. "I made more profit in a few hours tonight than I did all of last week in Omaha!"

"I suppose I had better check in with my boss," Glenn said, thinking that it was time to leave. "Jack and Mr. Dodge will expect a report."

"It'll wait until tomorrow, won't it?" Megan asked. "Why don't we put the tent up tonight and all sleep in late. We've had a hard trip."

"Are you up to it?"

"I am," Megan said. "Rachel?"

"Where else could we sleep except in the wagons?"

"Nowhere else," Walt said. "This town is bustin' at the seams. And it being payday, ain't no respectable wimmen safe outside."

"Then let's do it," Glenn said.

The tent took less than an hour to erect. Afraid that vandals might return in the night and steal the rest of her precious whiskey, Megan insisted that everything be unloaded and stowed under the tent. It was nearly midnight when they finished and Glenn was bone-weary.

"Walt, I'll help you unhitch your teams, water and grain them along with Sundancer," he said.

Walt's arm was still in a sling and although the old freighter was cheerful and uncomplaining, Glenn knew that Walt's shoulder throbbed painfully after a long day on the road.

"Much obliged, I . . ." Walt's words died in his mouth and snarled. "Don't look now, but we got us a skunk by the name of Ike Norman comin' to pay us a night visit."

Glenn turned to see Norman and remembered him from when Jack Casement had confronted the corrupt gambler in Columbus a few months earlier.

"Good evening," Norman called, removing his expensive bowler. "Can I ask who intends to be the proprietor of this humble establishment?"

"You can ask," Walt said, "but that don't mean that you'll get an answer. Ike, why don't you crawl into whatever hole you came out of and leave us alone."

Norman's grin curdled like spoiled cream. "Old man, you smell of sweat, piss, and dirt. Get out of my sight before I put that other shoulder out of commission."

Walt made a strangling sound and might actually have attacked the big gambler except that Glenn blocked his path. "Walt, let me handle this."

Norman measured Glenn. "You look familiar. Have we met before?"

"Not formally," Glenn said. "I was with General Jack Casement a few months ago when he warned you not to beat and rob any more of his men or he'd drive you off this rail line."

Norman paled. "Oh, yes, I recall that scurrilous accusation. Well, as you can see, I am still in operation. Still prospering."

"So it would appear," Glenn said coldly.

"You own this tent?"

"No," Megan said, stepping forward. "I do."

Norman dismissed Glenn and again smiled. He removed his hat and said, "Allow me to introduce myself. I am Ike Norman and I own the Empire Saloon and Gambling Hall. It's a *wooden* structure."

"So what?" Megan bristled.

Norman's eyes raked Megan. "So I heard about your excellent quality of whiskey and I thought it would be pleasant to share a cup with you."

"I'm sorry, Mr. Norman, but Megan's Place is closed."

" 'Megan's Place'? How quaint." Norman pirouetted completely around. "I don't see much here, Mrs. Gallagher."

"Miss O'Connell," Megan corrected. "And if you look closer, you'll see that there are a number of poker, faro, roulette, and other tables and wheels that I'll have in operation by tomorrow after the railroad crew finishes its shift."

Norman's eyebrows raised. "Then I'm to understand that you actually intend to open a full-scale saloon and gambling hall."

"That's right."

"How unfortunate," Norman said, looking pained and at the same time sympathetic. "Because you see, we're already in an oversupply. There's really no room for any more saloons or gambling halls. Anyone in Grand Island will tell you that."

"I'll have to find out for myself, Mr. Norman."

"You'll go broke."

Megan looked him right in the eye. "We'll see."

Norman pursed his lips. "I can tell that you are a very determined woman, Miss O'Connell, so I tell you what I will do. Name a fair price and I'll save you from financial ruin."

"I'm not selling out. Not to you, or anyone else."

Ike Norman pretended not to hear her. He strolled across Megan's wooden floor over to the dismantled tables and the boxes of cups and cards. Turning back, he said, "How about, let's say, a thousand dollars for everything."

"No."

"How much then?"

"It's *not* for sale, Mr. Norman."

"Everything is for sale," he corrected as he came sauntering back to face Megan. "All that is required is to discover the correct price. Now I'm asking you yours."

"Get out," Glenn said. "We have nothing to sell you at any price."

Norman had been about to reach for a cigar, but now he scowled at Glenn. "Who, exactly, are you?"

"I work for General Dodge," Glenn said. "My title is assistant chief surveyor."

"Oh. Well, sir, I most strongly suggest you get out and survey whatever it is you are supposed to survey and let me do business with this lovely woman."

"Go," Glenn said, his eyes locking with those of the heavier man. "While you still can."

Norman's hands dropped to his sides and Glenn's heart missed a beat as the gambler gently brushed back his frock coat to reveal the butt of his six-gun. Glenn wasn't wearing his gun, he'd removed it when he'd started to unload Megan's tent and supplies. Now, he regretted its absence.

But Megan pushed between them. "Mr. Norman, get out of this tent and *never* come back!"

"You are making a very big mistake."

"We'll see."

Norman turned back to Glenn. "I won't forget this," he said ominously. "Bet on it."

Glenn was shaking with fury and he started to tell Norman that he'd be packing his six-gun the next time they met but the gambler was already leaving.

Megan took Glenn's hands. "It'll be all right," she said. "He's just bluffing. Trying to scare me out."

But Walt shook his head. "He'll bluff, but not about this, Megan. That man hasn't even started to pressure you to sell out or fold this tent and go away. You haven't seen the last of Ike. Not by a long shot."

Megan leaned against Glenn. "And I'm afraid that you haven't seen the last of him, either."

"I can take care of myself."

"Can you?" Walt asked. "How good are you with that shooter you forgot to strap back on tonight?"

"I can hit what I aim for."

Walt shook his head. "That ain't near good enough. Ike is a quick-shot artist and a marksman. He's killed three men that I know of and one was a professional gunfighter."

Glenn's mouth went dry. "We'll be all right," he pledged, knowing how hollow rang the sound of his words.

CHAPTER
24

Megan decided not to unpack and set up her gambling tables until she hired a professional gambler to manage that part of her business. It just made sense. If she was to become known as an *honest* operator, Megan realized she had to understand the finer points of the gambling and that wasn't something that she could learn in just a few weeks or even months. Megan was quite sure that finding a good person to manage the gambling part of her operation was going to be crucial to her long-term success.

Unfortunately, she didn't have enough whiskey to even operate her saloon very long. As soon as Megan's last few remaining barrels were empty, she'd be out of business. Walt urged her to charge even more for a cup of rye whiskey but Megan had set her price and would not punish her thirsty customers for their loyalty.

"Walt, can I hire you to drive back to Omaha and buy me a full load of *good* whiskey and beer if any can be found?"

"I can try, but I'll be gone for the best part of two weeks," Walt said. "It's better than three hundred miles round-trip."

"Two weeks," Megan lamented. "I'll be out of whiskey in less than two days!"

"I know, but my horses are old and slow and . . ."

Megan was totally preoccupied with her predicament. "If only I could get . . . yes!"

"What?" Walt asked, seeing Megan's eyes widen. "What are you schemin' to do now?"

"It's a long shot," Megan said, "isn't there a public telegraph office here?"

"Sure. But the Union Pacific is about the only ones that use it back and forth to Omaha."

"Well, I'm going to use it right now," Megan said. She looked over to Rachel who was straightening up in preparation for the evening trade. "Keep your eye on things while I'm gone."

"What are you going to do?" Rachel called.

"Play a long shot," Megan called back to the young woman.

Megan grabbed her purse that held the previous night's saloon receipts. Carrying so much money made her extremely nervous. She'd insisted that Glenn deposit her cash in the Union Pacific's bank car under his own name. He'd done it fearing that carrying large amounts of cash put Megan's life in grave jeopardy.

When they reached the telegraph office, Megan scribbled out a small message that read:

FROM: MEGAN O'CONNELL. GRAND ISLAND, NEB.
TO: DAN CASEMENT. OMAHA, NEB.
PLEASE FIND AND SHIP C.O.D. 50 BARRELS OF
GOOD RYE WHISKEY AND 25 BARRELS OF PRE-
MIUM BEER TO MEGAN'S PLACE AT GRAND
ISLAND. STOP. WILL PAY SHIPPING CHARGES
AND 10% FINDERS FEE ON RECEIPT. STOP. THANK
YOU FOR MY SURVIVAL, DAN! STOP.

The telegraph operator looked up from his desk, pencil still poised in his fist. He read the telegraph out loud, a slight grin playing at the corners of his mouth. "Good whiskey and premium beer, Miss O'Connell?"

"If it isn't good, I won't serve it at Megan's Place. And, sir?"

"Yes?"

"I'd appreciate it if you would keep this message confidential."

"Of course! I wasn't born yesterday, Miss O'Connell. I know Mr. Casement and I know enough about your own history to realize what would happen if top Union Pacific management got wind of it."

"Thank you," Megan said with relief. "It's a long shot, but if it works, you've got a free cup of whiskey coming."

"Very good, miss! I'll send a preliminary message asking Mr. Casement to come to the telegraph office in Omaha. When he does, I'll forward this telegram. That will eliminate a courier and insure this message remains confidential."

"You're a gem," Megan said. "Two cups on the house!"

"I like doing business with you, Miss O'Connell. Anything else?"

"Just add a little prayer it works."

"Be fifty cents, miss."

Megan paid. If her message produced results, if Dan was able to help . . . well, it was a shot in the dark and Megan reminded herself again not to put too much hope into the desperate scheme.

After they'd left the telegraph office, Walt drawled, "I'll be the most surprised man in Grand Island if any liquor shows up on the Union Pacific."

"Don't count us out yet. Dan Casement is a genius when it comes to keeping the railroad supplied. I don't see why he can't also keep me supplied."

"With whiskey and beer?" Walt chuckled. "Liquor is a lot different from railroad ties, Megan."

"I know that. I also realize that if The Doctor thought Dan was even considering my plea for help, he would have a fit of apoplexy. I've asked a great deal of Dan's friendship, but I think he might just take the risk."

"Why?"

Megan paused a moment. "Because I promised Dan that I'd honor him with the name of my first son."

"But you ain't even married yet!"

"I know," Megan said, starting back to her tent.

Walt chuckled. "If Mr. Casement can find and send that beer and whiskey without being caught, it'll be something worth celebrating."

"But not bragging about," Megan warned. "I'm sure that we don't want to get a good samaritan fired, do we?"

"No," Walt readily agreed, licking his lips in anticipation. "I reckon that we sure don't! Might be that he'd do it again and again."

"Might be," Megan said, though privately, she didn't really expect Dan to be able to help her keep a tent saloon stocked with liquor.

"But if he won't," Walt said as they trudged back to Megan's tent, "I'm sure you could buy whiskey from someone else. You'd probably have to pay about what it's being sold for in the saloons here in Grand Island, but at least you'd stay open for business."

"I won't sell bathtub hooch or rain-barrel rotgut for any price," Megan firmly asserted. "I've heard all the stories about it blinding good men. I'll either sell good, safe liquor or none at all."

"Suit yourself," Walt grumbled, "but if you ask me, even bad liquor is better than no liquor."

On the way back to her tent saloon, Megan's thoughts were completely preoccupied with the possibility of what might happen in Omaha when Dan received the telegram. So preoccupied, in fact, that when she entered her big tent she had to blink a few times before she believed the carnage.

"Dear Lord!" she breathed. "What happened!"

"We've been hit," Walt swore.

And indeed, they had been "hit." Someone had smashed her two expensive roulette wheels on the floor and busted off their bases. Two felt-covered gaming tables were slashed and the last of her precious whiskey was leaking between the floorboards into the dirt.

"Rachel!" Megan cried, finally spotting the girl lying on the floor half-covered by an overturned table. "Rachel!"

Rachel was conscious, but just barely. Her scalp was bleeding and there was a nasty purple bruise on her swelling jaw. Megan dropped to her knees and lifted the girl's head to her lap. "Rachel, are you all right?"

Her eyelids fluttered. Rachel started with fright and clung to Megan, her whole body trembling.

"It's all right," Megan said, hugging the girl tightly. "Whoever did this is gone."

Tears brimmed and overflowed down Rachel's cheeks. "I didn't even see anyone! One minute I was cleaning cups and getting them lined up on the bar, the next thing I know I'm stretched out on the floor."

Walt stomped over and knelt beside the girl. "You didn't see anyone?"

"No," Rachel said in a small voice. Her head rolled to one side and her eyes widened with dismay when she saw the destruction. "Oh, Megan, I'm so sorry!"

"Not as sorry as I am," Megan said in a hard voice. "I'll bet anything that we can thank Ike Norman or one of his men for this nasty little visit!"

"That's for sure," Walt said in a voice strangled with fury. "You want me to go over there and shoot him?"

"No!" Megan lowered her voice. "That's just the kind of thing he'd be expecting. You said yourself that Norman doesn't do his own dirty work. He'd have someone shoot you before you got through his door."

"We can't just let him get away with this!"

"We have no choice," Megan said. "I'm just going to have to find someone to help me take care of things around the clock."

"Easier said than done."

"I've been offering one hundred dollars a month and board for someone to manage my gambling hall," Megan said. "But so far, no one worth considering has come forward. Starting right now, I'll offer twice that salary."

"If word gets out that Ike Norman is out to close you down," Walt cautioned, "I'm not sure that even two hundred dollars is going to get you an honest gambling man with guts enough to stand up to Norman."

Megan took a deep breath. "Then I'll keep raising the ante until I *do* find the right man."

"If I was twenty years younger, I'd take the job," Walt fumed with bitterness.

"I know that," Megan said, helping Rachel to her feet. "Walt, I can't go into those saloons, but I want you to do it for me with the exception of the Empire and make sure that everyone knows that Megan's Place is looking for an honest man with enough courage and skill to operate what is left of my tables."

Walt nodded. He went over to the roulette wheels and righted them. He inspected their broken bases and said, "I can fix these in a jiffy, Megan."

"Good! Then find me a man big and gutsy enough to run them honestly."

"I'll try," Walt said without sounding very hopeful. "How about giving your new man a percentage of the gambling profits?"

"Uh-uh. I don't want to give anyone incentives to hike my profits. If we run our games well and honestly, we'll prosper enough without creating undue temptation."

"All right," Walt said, "but do you really think I ought to leave you two women here alone?"

Megan reached into her purse and dragged out her derringer. "We'll be just fine."

"Just don't shoot me by mistake when I come back after visitin' the gambling halls and spreading the word," Walt said, heading outside.

"And while you're at it," Megan called. "Tell everyone what happened so they'll know why we ran out of whiskey and what kind of thugs and cutthroats we're up against."

"I'll do that," Walt said in a hard voice. "I'll let 'em know and you can bet that there's going to be some damned angry men when they learn about Rachel gettin' slugged. Damned mad!"

Megan agreed. She and Rachel had only been in this hell-on-wheels town a few days but they'd already earned both respect and liking from their customers. Good whiskey at a fair price served with a thank you and a smile. Even the hardest of track layers appreciated a fair shake. Only very soon, Megan couldn't even help her customers to wet their thirsts. Not until she found a man knowledgeable and willing to stand up to Ike Norman and his cutthroats and until she managed to get herself another shipment of decent liquor.

Glenn was preparing to return to work at the North Platte trestle but he was admittedly lingering in Grand Island until he was sure that Megan was going to be all right. She'd come to him the day after her tent had been ransacked and poor Rachel had been left bleeding and unconscious.

Damn that Ike Norman! Like Megan, Glenn would have bet his life that Ike was the man responsible for the underhanded attack and destruction of the roulette wheels and gambling tables. But there was no way to prove the man guilty and so he would go unpunished.

Even now, as Glenn marched past Norman's thriving Empire Saloon and Gambling Hall, it was an effort not to rush inside and confront the slick gambler. Fortunately, Glenn's good sense prevailed and he continued on, his thoughts dark with revenge.

Suddenly, he heard a loud commotion inside the Empire and stopped to turn around just in time to see a knot of men crash through the door into the street, kicking, punching, and gouging. It took Glenn only an instant to see that one of the men was

being swarmed over by three others. But even though heavily
outnumbered, the lone man was giving a very good account of
himself. He was short, but powerfully built and had been well
dressed. His starched collar had been ripped from his thick neck
and his suit coat was torn half off his stocky body. At first, the
lone man held his ground against his taller opponents. He stayed
close inside and his powerful arms blurred pistonlike as his fists
ricocheted off the faces and bodies of his startled attackers. But
finally, he was tripped down and overwhelmed.

Glenn raced forward and grabbed one of the three bullies. He
tore him off the fallen man, ducked a roundhouse punch, and
reciprocated with a vicious uppercut to the belly.

"Uggh!" the man grunted, folding to his knees and wheezing
for breath.

Glenn looped his arm around the neck of another of the
attackers and dragged him up to his feet. The man was strong
and he broke Glenn's choke hold and spun around.

"You should have stayed out of this, mister!" the man swore,
winging a boot at Glenn's groin. Glenn managed to turn and
deflected his opponent's boot off the side of his hip. The kick
hurt like blazes and infuriated him enough to yell, "Come on!"

The man lowered his head and charged, spewing a mouthful
of curses. Glenn jumped aside and stuck out his leg, tripping
his attacker. Before the man could pick himself out of the dirt,
Glenn stepped in and chopped downward with a right hand that
flatted his opponent. "Get up!"

The man struggled to his feet. He looked past Glenn to the
Empire where Ike Norman suddenly appeared and bellowed,
"Whip him, damn you!"

The man lowered his head and charged Glenn again. This
time he anticipated Glenn dodging sideways and managed to
wrap his arms around Glenn's waist. They went down fighting.
Glenn took several wild punches to the face before he broke free
and struggled back to his feet. He waited until his opponent had
struggled to his knees and then he attacked, battering the dazed
fellow with both fists until the man covered his bloodied face.

"Enough!"

Glenn lowered his fists. His breath came in fiery gasps,
his knuckles were scalped and bleeding, his face was numb
and swelling. He felt hurt but elated and that sensation was
heightened even more when he turned and saw the stocky man

propel his cringing opponent toward the Empire Saloon.

"Damn you, Ike! Take your goons back and if you sic them on me again, I'll kill them and then I'll come gunning for you!"

Norman grabbed his staggering, whipped man by his collar and hurled him inside. He looked insane with anger. "Scudder, you're finished in Grand Island or any other town on this line. I'll make sure that you never turn a card or spin a wheel again!"

Scudder took a threatening step forward but halted when Norman slapped back his frocked coat, fingers splayed over the butt of his gun.

"You know I'm not packing a six-gun," Scudder said, pulling up short.

"You're packing a derringer."

"That's no match."

"Tough!" Norman said. His eyes flicked to Glenn. "Unless Mr. Gilchrist wants to take your place? He's packing a six-gun."

Glenn's blood turned to cold water. He knew that Ike Norman could easily outdraw and gun him down.

Scudder stepped in front of Glenn and said, "Ike, if you shoot either one of us, you'll hang. So call in your damned whipped dogs and leave that gun in your holster."

Slowly, Ike Norman pulled his hand away from his six-gun. Glenn stepped up beside Scudder and watched as Norman pivoted on his boot heel and charged back inside the Empire Saloon to rage at his employees.

Scudder reached into his pocket for a silk handkerchief that he used to wipe off blood that dripped from his crooked, oft-busted fighter's nose. He was not quite as heavyset as Glenn had first thought but Glenn well remembered Scudder's power and the speed of his fists.

"I think I was losing that one," Scudder said. "My name is Lewis Blackburn Scudder and I owe you a drink."

Glenn stuck out his hand and Scudder crushed it. Glenn winced and said, "You don't owe me anything. Three against one were odds that needed balancing."

"Well, I didn't see anyone else jumping in to help and you whipped two out of the three," Scudder said, massaging his square, heavy-boned jaw. "I'd be obliged to return the favor and at least buy you a drink."

"All right," Glenn said, "but some other time. I've got to meet someone."

"Mind if I walk along?"

"Of course not. What happened between you and Ike Norman?"

"I was his floor manager," Scudder explained. "I didn't like his rigged games. Ike is already a wealthy man and I warned him about cheating. Of course, a greedy man can't get enough and we had a bad falling out."

"So I gathered. What are you going to do now?"

"Looks like I either go back to dealing monte and poker in New Orleans, or else I become a rust eater."

"Which will it be?"

"I don't know. I'm not good at monotonous physical work. Guess I'll probably head for New Orleans."

Glenn stopped dead in his tracks. He turned and studied Lewis Scudder. "Maybe you should meet a lady friend of mine."

"Miss O'Connell?"

"How'd you guess?" Glenn asked with surprise.

"Everyone knows that she needs someone to run her gambling hall."

"You interested?"

"Not if it means ending up in a pine box," Scudder said. "But on the other hand, I just hate the idea of allowing *any* man to run me off. Sure, I'll talk to Miss O'Connell. I've seen her on the street and she's a real beauty."

"And a real lady," Glenn quickly added. "I got a feeling, Lewis Blackburn Scudder, that you and Miss O'Connell could do very well together."

"Nothing would suit me better than to hurt Ike Norman where he lives—his pocketbook."

"Good!"

When Megan saw their battered but happy faces a few minutes later, she was shocked. But within five minutes, Megan and Scudder were shaking hands and the hiring was done.

"Let's celebrate!" Megan exclaimed.

The tin cups were brought out and filled with the last dregs of Megan's whiskey barrels.

"To prosperity!" Megan said, raising her cup.

"To prosperity," Scudder repeated with his lopsided grin as he sniffled through his crooked nose.

Now that Megan had her man, Glenn figured he could afford to hurry westward again and see what he could do to help the chief surveyor, Ben Goss, construct the North Platte trestle.

The next afternoon, Megan found Glenn saddling Sundancer. She threw her arms around his neck and gave him a big kiss.

"Ouch!" he said, for the inside of his lip was torn up in the previous day's fistfight.

"Guess what!"

"Scudder made you a pot of money at cards and roulette last night."

"Yes! But even more important, Dan Casement sent us whiskey and beer! It arrived on this morning's first supply train."

"He did! How?"

Megan pulled Glenn closer to Sundancer so that their words could not possibly be overheard by one of the Union Pacific stock tenders. "Dan sent the whiskey and beer in crates that usually hold bolts and other hardware."

"And nothing even leaked?"

"No! The whiskey and kegs of beer fit inside the hardware crates. And they were all packed and then nailed shut. It was brilliant!"

Glenn grinned until his lacerated lip made him wince. "I knew Dan would come through for you, Megan."

"Well, he sure did. As of today, I'm back in the saloon and gambling business and we are going to make a small fortune."

Before Glenn could nod his head in agreement, Megan dug a handful of money out of her purse. "Would you please bank this cash for me? I'm scared to death to keep so much cash around."

"Sure," Glenn said. "You keep this up and I'll withdraw all your funds and run off a wealthy man."

She looked up into his eyes. "No you won't."

"Why not?"

"Because you want to marry me," Megan told him. "And because, when we finally reach California and this railroad is finished, I'll probably want to marry you too."

Glenn felt his heart fill to bursting. Hands stuffed with Megan's greenbacks, he drew her close and kissed her mouth. She melted like warm butter in his arms. She made the blood pound in his temples and his knees turn to rubber.

Megan pulled back. "Must you leave?"

"I'm working for the Union Pacific, remember?"

"Why don't you quit and come to work for me?"

That made Glenn chuckle. "Megan, you're forgetting that I'm an engineer, not a gambler or saloon operator. I want to do what I was trained to do—survey, design, and build."

"But I just heard that the Indians have attacked the line again and I'm scared to death for you."

Glenn stiffened. "Where'd they attack?"

"Someplace called Wood River. I guess that it's less than forty miles up the line. They say that Joshua and his men are on their way there to meet General Dodge. I'm afraid that our Indian troubles are just beginning. And with you and Liam both out there . . ."

Glenn crushed Megan to his body. "It's going to be fine," he told her. "You just take care of yourself and Rachel."

"And you take care of yourself and tell Liam that I wish he were a rust eater. At least then I'd know that he was safe."

Glenn held Megan close for a few minutes, then he finished his preparations and mounted Sundancer. He waved good-bye to a very worried-looking Megan and set out at a high lope for Wood River.

CHAPTER
25

The Nebraska stars were a vast seabed of glistening pearls and the moon a luminous half melon. To Glenn's left, the Platte River was a broad silver ribbon cast haphazardly across a table of emerald-green. Out in the hills, antelope grazed without fear for the last of the prairie wolves had long ago been exterminated and the lowly coyote threatened only the weak and the lame.

Mile after mile Glenn galloped along the preliminary Union Pacific's roadbed. The roadbed was a wound waiting to be sutured with stitches of wood and iron. Glenn rode through the night, rifle cradled across his lap, eyes piercing the moonlit plains in search of Sioux. About three o'clock in the morning, a convoy of wagons loomed out of the semidarkness.

"Hello there!" he hailed the lead wagon's driver.

The man hauled up on his lines and spat a stream of tobacco. Under the shadow of a drooping hat, the driver's face was masked in darkness. "What are you doin' out here by your lonesome? This country is crawlin' with Indians just waitin' to jump a white man."

"I know," Glenn said. "But I've got to report to General Dodge and I understand he and General Casement are in Wood River where there's been another Indian attack."

"That's right. The bastards killed and scalped six men returning to Grand Island."

"What's going to happen?"

"Damned if we know," the man said, spitting again. "But if a vote was to be taken, me and the rest of the boys would hunt them Sioux down like varmints. It seems like the damned United States Army can't get the lead out of its ass and do what they're paid to do. My guess is that General Dodge is going to start

253

pulling some strings in Washington, D.C., and get them army boys in their saddles. Dodge is pretty upset. He's been over to Fort Kearney and they tell me he raised billy-bob-hell with the Army."

"I'll bet," Glenn said. "Have you heard anything about Joshua Hood and his scouts?"

"Hood is fixin' to take his boys out of Wood River tomorrow at first light and track them Sioux to the end of the earth."

"How much farther is it to Wood River?"

"Only about six, seven miles."

"Thanks," Glenn said, reining Sundancer around the wagon and kicking him into a gallop.

"You best save that horse in case you get jumped!" a teamster shouted as Glenn galloped past the wagons.

Sundancer was still fresh and after the gelding had run for a mile, Glenn pulled him down to a steady, mile-eating trot. In less than thirty minutes, he saw the welcome twinkle of Union Pacific campfires and knew that he was almost to Wood River.

Glenn found Dodge, Casement, and Joshua in the command tent going over last-minute instructions.

"Gilchrist!" Dodge exclaimed, looking as if he'd aged ten years. "Good to see you. What brings you here at this ungodly hour?"

"General, I'd like to ride along with Joshua and his men."

Joshua's reaction was swift and decisive. "No!"

There was a long silence, then Dodge said, "Why not? Glenn's job is to keep me informed and to write reports on whatever he thinks will be of interest. And I think that what you find is going to be damned important."

"General," Joshua said, "I won't refuse to take Glenn, but he's not outfitted and he's not skilled. He'd be a liability."

"I disagree!" Glenn said, passionately defending himself. "I can grain my horse and he'll be able to keep up—you know that, General."

Dodge nodded. "Sundancer will keep up, all right."

Encouraged, Glenn said, "Furthermore, I've got a new Henry repeating rifle in case we have to fight."

Joshua was not in the least bit swayed by Glenn's argument. "Gilchrist is a greenhorn and he'll be in our way!"

Dodge scowled. "Mr. Hood, I'd like Glenn to ride along with you. If it's any consolation, it'll be him and not you that will be responsible for writing up the reports on this dangerous expedition."

Glenn knew that Joshua was unable to read or write. Maybe Dodge knew it too. Either way, Joshua shot Glenn a hard look and snapped, "We'll be leaving at sunup!"

"I'll be ready," Glenn said, watching the man storm out of the tent.

"He sure doesn't like you, does he?" Casement said.

"That's not important."

"Why'd you really volunteer?" Dodge asked.

"I promised Megan O'Connell that I'd watch out for her brother," Glenn confessed. "And . . . well, I never fought in the war and I—I need to put my own life at risk."

Glenn shifted uncomfortably before the two decorated Union generals. "It's hard to explain, but that's the way I feel."

"I understand and nothing more need be said on the subject," Dodge said, taking a nod from Casement. "We both wish you good luck and good hunting. And, Glenn?"

"Yes?"

"I ought to warn you that Mr. Hood is quite upset about the way this Indian thing has unfolded. I know that he has sent word to Chief Red Cloud of the Sioux on one or two occasions, hoping to work out some kind of a peaceful solution."

"But failed."

"Utterly," Dodge said. "After all, we are about to destroy their nomadic life-style and tame this land, aren't we?"

"I suppose that's true."

"Of course it is. After this railroad is completed, at least a few of our rail towns will survive. Others will take root soon after this line is up and running. Within a very few years, this entire midwestern corridor of civilization will fill in with farmers, merchants, and ranchers. There will soon be no place for the red man or his buffalo."

"I find that sad, General."

"In one respect, your sympathy is admirable. In another, it is shortsighted and misguided. Civilization and progress. One culture absorbing another. That's the way it will always be."

"So I've heard," Glenn said.

Glenn shook hands with both Dodge and Casement and then he hurried outside in the predawn to grain Sundancer and to requisition what he'd need for this Indian hunt that made him both quake with fear and tingle with excitement.

"Mr. Gilchrist?"

Glenn turned to see Liam standing in the early morning light. He was holding the reins to his own horse and there was a six-gun strapped around his waist. Liam had grown a full beard and Glenn would not even have recognized Megan's younger brother except for his voice.

"Liam."

"Mr. Gilchrist, are you sure you ought to come along? This could get sort of dicey, you know."

"I've a good Henry repeating rifle."

"I can see that, sir, but can you *use* it?"

"I can and I will."

"Did you give my letters to Rachel and my sisters?"

"I did." Glenn tightened his cinch. Sundancer was finishing his bait of grain and Glenn just hoped the animal would not be too worn out to keep pace with Hood and his hunters.

"And their reaction?"

Glenn turned to study Liam. "I witnessed no reaction. I simply gave both letters to Megan and she passed them on. Did you know that someone in Grand Island tried to destroy Megan's Place?"

Liam tried but failed to hide his shock. "No, sir, I did not! What happened?"

"They knocked Rachel unconscious and broke up Megan's roulette tables. They emptied her whiskey barrels and cut her poker and faro tables."

"Who did it? Tell me and I'll settle the account."

"There are no suspects," Glenn said. "It could be almost anyone, but we think it might have been Ike Norman or someone like him who stands to lose business if Megan prospers."

"I'll have a talk with Ike," Liam graveled. "I'll make sure he don't bother Rachel or Megan again."

"Talk to your sister first," Glenn suggested. "And other than being dazed and frightened, Rachel will be fine."

"Oh, yeah? What's to keep it from happening again? Only worse?"

"Megan hired a very tough gambler named Lewis Scudder. She's also got a freighter named Walt Guthrie who hovers around both women like a mother hen. I wouldn't have left Megan or Rachel if I wasn't sure that they were going to be well protected."

"All right," Liam finally said, "but when we get back—if we get back—I'm going to pay Ike a visit."

"It's your life," Glenn said, "but—"

"Mount up!" Hood commanded. "Let's ride!"

A moment later they were galloping out of Wood River heading northwest. Glenn stayed at the rear of Hood's motley collection of Indian fighters, scouts, and former mountain men. He tried to conserve Sundancer's strength by riding easy and avoiding the jostling of the other horses.

Liam rode in the lead with Joshua.

They traveled all morning at a fast clip. The sun warmed the land, made the prairie grass bob and steam and the flowers sweat with early morning dew. It was almost noon when they came upon the South Loup River and dismounted to hobble the horses and let them graze.

Glenn was bone-weary but excited. He could feel the tautness among Hood's scouts. While they stretched out to rest, Joshua Hood, Liam, and two other scouts rode out to a line of distant hills where they could gain a commanding view of the rolling plains.

They returned about two o'clock and everyone crowded around Joshua who knelt beside the Loup and used a stick to draw a battle plan in the wet dirt. "The Sioux band that killed our boys over at Wood River are about forty strong and they're traveling almost due north."

"Are you sure it's the same bunch?" a scout asked.

"It's got to be them because they stole a half dozen shod Union Pacific horses and their tracks stand out plain as iron-rimmed wagon tracks. They don't seem to be in much of a hurry, either. My hunch is that they don't expect a chase and that we ought to overtake them long before they reach the Missouri River."

"How far is that?" Glenn asked.

Everyone glared at him.

"Just asking."

"Three days' hard ride. Maybe a hundred and fifty miles," someone muttered. "What the hell difference does that make?"

"None at all," Glenn said, curbing an angry response.

"All right," Joshua said. "Now I want to make General Dodge's orders clear to everyone. We're to overtake the Sioux and punish them so as to discourage any further attacks."

"Fat chance that'll work," a big, particularly dirty scout scoffed. "Don't the general know that both the Sioux and Cheyenne live to hunt buffalo and steal horses?"

"Dodge is hoping we can capture their war chief and a few of the others. My hunch is that he'd like to use them as hostages and then trade them back to the Sioux in return for a promise not to attack our survey and trestle-building camps anymore."

"Ain't going to work!"

"I know that," Hood said, showing unusual patience. "But those are my orders. Once they fail, we can handle the Indians our own way."

"Which is?" Glenn asked.

Joshua's eyes flashed anger that quickly passed. His expression turned as bleak as the plains' winter. "We'll have to kill a bunch of Cheyenne and Sioux, I guess. But the real answer to peace is getting our damned United States Government to give the Indians a piece of this country so big that the Sioux or their brothers the Cheyenne can still ride and hunt buffalo."

Glenn removed a notebook and a pencil. "You don't mind if I quote you on this, do you, Joshua?"

"Go to hell," came the hard reply, "and you can quote me on *that,* Mr. Gilchrist."

Glenn scribbled notes, feeling the stern disapproval of his companions as they dispersed to take a short rest. To hell with it, Glenn thought. I'll do my job, let's see if these men can do theirs.

Three days later, Glenn witnessed a sea of buffalo like a dark stain spilling across the Nebraska grasslands. He had no idea how many thousands of the beasts were in that herd, but it was enough to feed entire East Coast cities for months. And when Glenn remarked at their great numbers, one of the scouts growled, "Hell, this is nothin'! Buffalo hereabouts used to be thicker than maggots on old meat."

After that, Glenn kept his excitement and thoughts to himself as they closed in on the unsuspecting Sioux who had attacked and murdered six men at Wood River. Each night they made a cold camp and there was always a guard posted but Glenn was ignored when he offered to take his turn. During the day, Hood and his men said little but as the distance between themselves and the Sioux narrowed, Glenn could feel the tension rising.

His mind whirled with questions and possible scenarios of what would happen when they overtook the Sioux war party. Most of the outcomes that Glenn envisioned were frightening. Forty Sioux against their thirteen? Glenn knew that Joshua was counting on the advantage of surprise and superior firepower over the Indians. But he also had to be aware that a fair number of the renegade Indians were armed with rifles. Mostly old "trade rifles" that included everything from Kentucky flintlocks to muskets and whatever other weapons that the Indian could steal or trade.

There were reports that a few Indians even had Sharps and Colt revolvers and that Civil War rifles were not uncommon. The fact that the Indians had great difficulty obtaining a reliable supply of lead, black powder, and percussion caps was hardly reassuring.

That evening under the blaze of prairie starlight, Joshua motioned his men to gather around and said, "We can overtake this band tomorrow morning but I want to hit them front and back."

"That means we're going to divide our numbers," young Calvin Miller objected. "You think that's wise?"

"I do or I wouldn't suggest it," Joshua said. "If we can catch 'em comin' and goin', there's a good chance the band will splinter off with their stolen horses leaving others to fight."

Joshua surveyed his fighting force of buckskinners. "I'm riding out at midnight. I'd like at least four men."

Liam was the first to offer and Calvin Miller, not to be outdone, was a quick second. Two other men volunteered before Glenn could say, "I'd like to ride ahead with you."

"You serious?"

"I am."

Joshua rubbed his chin and a slow smile spread across his face. "All right, then come on along. But when the fightin' starts, you'd better have that Henry rifle in your hands instead of a pencil and pad. You understand?"

Glenn smarted at the snickers. "I understand."

"Fair enough." Joshua turned to one of his best scouts. "Hiram, you and the others keep closing the gap and stay out of sight until you hear our gunshots."

"Goin' to go hard on you, Joshua, if we ain't close when you five jump them forty."

"Then *be* close," Joshua said with a wink.

Everyone laughed, except Glenn.

He could not help but notice that Joshua was living life to the fullest now that the fighting was to begin. He seemed almost giddy with the prospect of killing or being killed. Joshua's eyes seemed to burn in the starlight. His step and manner, usually indolent and relaxed, were now charged with energy and anticipation. Glenn didn't understand. How could a man love the prospect of battle and death? How could he fail to see that he was mortal and that it might be his *own* life that came to a sudden and violent conclusion?

Glenn wanted to tell Joshua that being excited by the possibility of dying in battle was the fantasy of a sick mind.

"One other thing," Joshua added before he disbanded his followers. "If these Sioux break and run, we don't chase and kill 'em all. If we kill six, that's enough. An eye for an eye, a tooth for a tooth."

"Amen," several of the hunters solemnly intoned.

Joshua looked to Glenn. "Get some rest, greenhorn."

Glenn started to say something about the kind of a man that loved death, but instead, he clamped his mouth shut and walked over to his saddle and blankets. He stretched out on the ground, and in the pale starlight he scribbled the following letter in his notepad:

Dear Megan: Tonight we attempt to reach a frontal position before the Sioux who scalped the men at Wood River and took the Union Pacific horses. I'll fight beside Liam and Joshua tomorrow and I'll try to do my part. There has been no talk of "palavering" on this hunt. I guess that Joshua knows that it is too late for talk now that the killing has begun. I don't like Joshua Hood, but I believe in him and don't think he wants to die any more than Liam or me. But if it is God's will, and if someone should find this note on whatever is left of my person, I want you to know that I loved you very much. I hope you get to California rich and marry a good man and name your SECOND son after me. Your friend to the end.

Love, Glenn Gilchrist.

Glenn read and reread his brief letter. He wished he could write beautiful and poetic words, but he was far more comfortable with equations and the terms of engineering rather than romantic endearments. The letter was short, but sweet. It summed up Glenn's thoughts and would have to suffice. Hopefully, they would survive tomorrow and this brief letter would never need be read by another person unless he chose to show it to Megan someday after they were married and perhaps old and rich with memories.

Glenn turned to another page in his tablet and began to write a brief account of Joshua's plan for General Dodge while it was still all very fresh in his mind. He avoided inserting his own judgments but stuck to the facts and to Joshua's reasons for dividing their small force. He ended by writing:

Joshua Hood exudes great confidence and has instructed us all that no more than six Indians be killed if this battle becomes a rout. I think this is an admirable sentiment but that WE are the only ones that are likely to be routed and set into a full, headlong flight to save our foolish lives.

Satisfied, Glenn jammed his writing tablet into his pocket and then he closed his eyes and tried to calm his near frenzied mind. Why had he volunteered to go with Joshua Hood and flank the Sioux? My God, they'd be *between* himself and the Union Pacific lines over a hundred miles to the south! Was Sundancer fresh enough to outrun the Indian ponies? His horse was certainly fast enough to outrun any grass-fed pony. But could it best those tough little Indian ponies over a hundred-mile retreat?

Don't think retreat, Glenn warned himself sternly. Think victory. Fight as if there was no possibility of retreat. And no matter how bad things might seem, don't panic. You've got as fine a weapon as any man in this group. Maybe you can't shoot half as well as most, but you can be effective if you remain steady and calm . . . and deadly.

Yes, Glenn thought over the hammering sound of his heart. If you must—*be* deadly—or you will be dead.

"Mount up," Joshua said, coming up to tower over Glenn. "Unless you've had time to decide you'd rather ride south instead of north."

Glenn pushed himself up into a sitting position and stared up at Joshua. "If you mean run, it hasn't crossed my mind."

"I'll bet."

Glenn came to his feet. Standing, he was taller than Joshua and he was close enough to feel the man's intense dislike. "You're hoping I don't make it, aren't you?"

"Either that, or that you run so I can tell General Dodge how his fair-haired boy gentleman performed in battle."

Glenn's fists balled at his sides. "The general will tell you that Gilchrist men don't run. That my brothers were the first to charge and die for the Union. I'm going to disappoint you, Joshua, because I won't run either."

"We'll see. There's something about facing a screaming Indian attack that is unlike anything even your brothers had to face."

"I doubt it," Glenn said. "I heard the chilling stories of wild Rebel infantry charges and battle cries."

Joshua started to say something but changed his mind. "Mount up and let's see what kind of mettle you're really made of, Harvard boy."

At that instant, it struck Glenn why Joshua had hated him from the start. It was Megan and jealousy, but it was also because they had come from different worlds. Joshua resented Glenn for having an education. For being from a privileged class. It was that simple, that apparent, now that it had spilled out with the derogatory term "Harvard boy."

Glenn turned away feeling his own dislike for Joshua fade to nothingness. Life wasn't fair and had the Union Pacific's chief scout and hunter been born rich or even of the upper class with its inherent opportunities, Joshua would have been a man to be reckoned with in the halls of Congress or in commerce. He would have been a leader of entrepreneurs, a bold capitalist out to make his mark in politics or industry. As it was, Joshua's only possible stage for achievement was on this wild American frontier. Joshua Hood had previously distinguished himself in the Civil War but due to his lack of education and background, he had never been considered a gentleman, an officer, a military leader.

Ah, but out here on the Great Plains, in these times where violent death and even torture lurked just over the next rolling hilltop, a leader had only to be willing to fight to a gallant death to become a legend among the red or white plains warriors.

To have his story told and retold across a thousand campfires and under a million points of starlight. And for these wild buckskinners, Glenn realized that alone was worth even the most horrible of deaths.

CHAPTER
26

Morning found Glenn and the four Union Pacific scouts hurrying to flank the marauding Sioux. Not a word had passed among any of them and the night had seemed interminable. Just after sunrise, Joshua and Liam had dismounted and climbed to a low rise of ground. When they'd returned to the horses, Liam had looked very pale but Glenn supposed that might have been because of the weak dawn light.

But now the sun was off the horizon and, if anything, Joshua was pushing them harder to the north, taking advantage of every foot of low land. Glenn's nerves jangled from lack of sleep and tension. His gut felt tighter than piano wire and his hand kept brushing the butt of his Colt exactly as an anxious child might smooth a comforter. Over and over Glenn railed at himself for not yet taking time to practice with his weapons. Over and over he told himself that even if he survived this battle, there remained looming confrontations with Ike Norman and Joshua.

But Glenn knew that self-recrimination would do nothing to help him now. Very soon, probably within the hour, he would follow Joshua over a rise of land and come face-to-face with a large war party of Sioux Indians, many armed with pistols or rifles. It didn't take a great deal of imagination to guess that the Sioux would attack without hesitation. When they did, Glenn hadn't a clue how he and his four companions were supposed to survive until the rest of Joshua's scouts came to their rescue. He wanted to ask Joshua Hood how it all was to be accomplished.

Glenn shivered though the air was still and balmy. Suddenly, Joshua raised his hand and signaled for everyone to dismount. Handing his reins to Calvin Miller, he motioned at Liam to follow him up a dry wash where they would have their first close view of the advancing Sioux warriors.

Glenn mopped sweat from his face with his sleeve. He pulled his Henry rifle out of his scabbard and its breech was warm to the touch. He ran his fingers over the fine wooden stock and took several deep, steadying breaths, wishing he was somewhere—anywhere—else.

"That goddamn Liam is always suckin' up to Mr. Hood!" Calvin Miller hissed.

"Shut up!" one of the other scouts commanded in a low voice as his hand slapped at the Bowie knife sheathed at his side. "Shut up or I'll gut you, Calvin!"

Miller licked his lips. He stared at Liam and Joshua as they crawled the last few feet until they could just see out of the wash. Watching Miller, Glenn thought that he had never observed such pure hatred. He had witnessed the vicious fistfight between the two young rivals and still found it difficult to believe that Liam had been able to whip the stronger appearing Calvin Miller. Glenn had also noticed the way the two avoided each other. But this was the first time he had read the true depth of Calvin Miller's hatred and jealousy toward Liam.

When Joshua and Liam returned to their horses, Joshua whispered, "The Sioux are about a mile south and coming directly toward us. We'll give them a quarter hour and then we'll lead our horses out of this wash and open fire."

"Open fire?" Glenn heard himself ask.

"That's right." Joshua yanked his rifle out of his scabbard. "We're the marksmen and we've got the better weapons. If they keep coming, we can always spring onto our horses and outrun 'em. Circle around and join the others. But I doubt that will be necessary."

"Why?"

"Because by then," Joshua said as if it were terribly obvious, "Hiram and the others will cut them down from behind."

Joshua finished checking his weapons and then he leaned against his horse, yawned, and said, "Any questions?"

Glenn knew that he *ought* to have a million questions but he couldn't voice a single one. Joshua's plan was painfully simple. They would play to their own advantage with superior marksmanship and firepower and hope that they could knock down the fierce initial Sioux charge. If they did, then they would themselves attack when Hiram and his men collided with the Sioux from behind.

The next quarter hour felt like a quarter century. Glenn checked and rechecked his weapons, cinch, and even his stirrup leathers. He knew that the others were watching him but he didn't care because keeping his hands busy helped occupy his mind. When Glenn was sure that his weapons and his gear were in perfect working order, he retrieved his notepad but his mind was a blank so he returned it to his pocket.

Joshua looked at him and said, "Remember to shoot low. When a man is nervous, there's a tendency to shoot too high and fast. If you can't hit the warrior, at least you'll drop his pony and give the rest of us a little more time."

Glenn nodded although the idea of shooting horses was an outrage.

"One other thing," Joshua added, loud enough for all to hear, "nobody quits shooting and jumps for their horses until I give the word. If we all stand together, we'll either break the attack or at least leave it so ragged that it won't amount to much. But if even one man breaks our ranks . . . I'll kill him. Understood, Gilchrist?"

"You don't need to talk to me about breaking."

"Good." Joshua pulled his hat down low over his eyes. "Let's pay these Indians back for Wood River," he drawled as he led his horse up the gentle slope of the dry washbed.

Glenn took a deep breath and followed. Any second now, he was going to be in the fight of his life.

When they came up to level ground, the Sioux were scattered loosely around their remuda. Glenn's mouth went dry with fear, and at the same instant, he felt a sense of wonder. Other than a few pathetic "civilized" Indians that he'd seen in the Union Pacific camps and occasionally panhandling in Omaha, these were the first real Plains Indians he had witnessed and they were quite magnificent. They rode in saddles that were hardly more than pads with leather-thonged stirrups, and although these Indians did not wear headdresses or war paint, they were adorned with decorative beadwork and feathers. Their hair was long, braided, and shiny and they had lean, muscular brown bodies and prominent cheekbones. But the most striking thing to Glenn was the immediate and overpowering sense he had that these Sioux *belonged* here. That they were a basic part of their world of sky and grass.

Like their proud masters, the Indian ponies were also decorated with paint and feathers. There were a disproportionate number of paints, sorrels, roans, and buckskins with few bays; all were spirited, small, and compact. The feathers woven into their tails and manes made them dance on wind.

When the Sioux saw Joshua and his men, they did not shout or grow excited. In fact, they did nothing but rein their ponies up short and stare as if the five whites were evil spirits, ethereal objects to be examined and then exterminated. After a full minute, Joshua did a curious thing—he raised his hand in greeting. One of the Indians trotted to the fore on a fine Appaloosa stallion and was quickly joined by several other warriors. The leader lifted a rifle and shook it overhead. These were not spirits, but the hated white invaders. And when Joshua displayed no response, the Sioux war chief butted his rifle to his shoulder and took aim.

Glenn's head whipped to Joshua who did not move a muscle. Time froze until Liam threw his rifle to his shoulder and Glenn clearly heard Joshua whisper, "Wing him in the leg!"

Two rifles crashed as one to shatter the vast prairie stillness. Glenn heard a ball zing past Joshua's head an instant before the Sioux war chief grabbed his thigh and spilled to the ground. After that, everything happened too fast for Glenn to absorb. The Indians flowed into a battle line and charged. Glenn heard a rifle boom next to him and watched as a Sioux was plucked from the back of his horse. He was engulfed in a volley of smoke and belching flame as his four companions unleashed a withering fire into the Sioux ranks. Glenn took aim and fired. He levered his Henry and fired again, low this time. An onrushing painted pony squealed and somersaulted in death.

Glenn was too scared to think as the Sioux bore down on him and his companions. He *felt* rather than saw someone close beside him drop and he heard Calvin Miller bellow something unintelligible. Glenn fired again and again and his mind seized on the crazy idea that if only he shot fast enough, perhaps his gunsmoke would envelope and hide him from the Sioux.

"Mount up!" Joshua yelled. "Let's ride!"

Glenn needed no urging. Sundancer was going crazy, jerking him around, making it impossible to fire with any accuracy.

Glenn's left hand slapped his big saddle horn and Sundancer whirled away from the fierce Sioux onslaught catapulting Glenn into his saddle with his Henry still smoking in his fist.

Just ahead, Joshua was bleeding from a head wound but spurring hard to the south. One of the scouts was gone and Liam was riding like a demon as Sundancer passed him. They began to loop around to the south, praying that they would quickly rendezvous with the other Union Pacific scouts.

Suddenly, Liam's horse broke stride and Glenn heard the young Irishman's cry as his mount softly nosed into the prairie. Liam was hurled from his saddle. He hit the grass, skidded a good ten yards on his back, and came up running. Glenn fought to rein Sundancer around but the big horse had a full head of momentum and wanted no part of the pursuing Indians. Unwilling to abandon Liam to a horrible death, Glenn sawed on his reins, gradually forcing Sundancer into a turn. Joshua was already riding hard for Liam. The head scout hurled his rifle aside, leaned out from his saddle, and extended his arm. Liam made a desperate grab and was propelled skyward. Somehow, Liam ended up riding double behind Joshua as the horse swapped ends and came racing south again. Glenn jammed his rifle into his saddle scabbard and tore his six-gun from his holster, firing wildly at the howling pack determined to lift his scalp. He was certain that both Joshua and Liam were dead men.

"Get rid of him!" Miller bellowed. "Mr. Hood, you'll never make it ridin' double!"

Miller was right. Glenn pulled Sundancer up and fired twice, hitting nothing. He was no pistol shot on a jumping horse. But his dismay was replaced by shock when Miller fired at Liam's back! Miller's first shot was wide and there was no way that it could have been distinguished from the Indians' fusillade of arrows and bullets. But Miller's second shot, fired as he closed in on the pair riding double, struck Liam in the hip and caused him to lurch sideways. Joshua reached back and grabbed Liam's belt, holding him in place behind his saddle.

Glenn gave Sundancer its head and the swift gelding closed on Miller. Glenn raised his six-gun just as Miller was about to fire at Liam again and he shot the crazed scout through the back of the skull. Miller lifted in his stirrups, then pitched out of his saddle, one boot hanging up. Glenn saw Miller's body bounce under his horse's belly and he heard bones crack as Miller's leg was ripped from his trunk by his bucking horse.

Glenn forgot about Miller and rode for his life. Sundancer quickly overhauled Joshua Hood's overburdened mount and Glenn's basic survival instincts ordered him to let Sundancer carry him beyond the hunting wolves hard on his heels. And maybe if Joshua had ordered Glenn to hold up, he *would* have abandoned the pair. But Joshua said nothing. Joshua couldn't release Liam who was tilting precariously and the head scout wouldn't let go of his reins. In fact, Joshua was helpless as the screeching pack of Sioux closed in from behind.

Glenn twisted around in his saddle and emptied his Colt but hit nothing. He holstered the pistol and tied his reins together before pulling them taut over his saddle horn, slowing Sundancer. He yanked his Henry repeating rifle from its scabbard, levered in a fresh round even as he was engulfed in a hail of arrows thicker than a covey of flushed quail. Hitting anything seemed impossible but Glenn recalled Joshua's advice and forced himself to aim low for the lead Sioux ponies. He was surprised when his first slug killed a racing pony and sent its rider spinning to earth.

Glenn levered another round into the Henry and shot a second horse. The line of Sioux wavered, then split into an inverted wedge. Glenn fired, missed. Fired and hit a thin warrior in the belly. The Indian wailed and grabbed for his pony's mane, arrows spilling from his quiver. The Sioux chorus became frenzied as they began to flank their quarry.

"Go!" Joshua bellowed. "Run for it. Save yourself!"

An arrow buried itself into the flesh of Sundancer's mane. The gelding began to whip its head back and forth as it broke stride. Glenn whacked his horse with his rifle, just like the Indians. Sundancer forgot about the arrow in the top of its neck and regained his stride. Glenn shot another pony and then he saw Hiram and the Union Pacific scouts lift up from a draw like earth spirits and unleash a devastating volley of rifle fire into onrushing Sioux horsemen.

This time, the warriors broke and scattered. The sound of their hideous screams changed pitch and Glenn could not fail but note the despair in their voices over the soaring number of riderless ponies. A moment later Glenn and Joshua Hood were bursting through Hiram's line of scrimmage. They toppled from their horses and clawed back to their thin but determined battle line that now harvested the Sioux like a sharp sickle severing wheat.

No more than a dozen Indians breached the line and before they could dismount and attack on foot, every last one of them were shot in their tracks. Joshua, his head streaming with blood, called a halt to the slaughter and the ragged few surviving warriors quickly collected their dead and wounded and forced their ponies north again, howling like birthing bitches.

"Gather the horses that can be saved and shoot the ones that can't," Joshua ordered as he wrapped a bandanna around his head to stanch the bleeding. "Any of these warriors alive?" he asked, going over to ones who'd breached their line only to be shot at near point-blank range.

"Three of 'em are still breathin'," Hiram said. "Do you want me to finish 'em off?"

"Hell no!" Joshua snapped, going to examine each of the fallen warriors. Finished, he said, "These two will live to be swapped for a truce. This other one is dying."

Glenn hurried over to Liam who was writhing on the grass in agony with his pants soaked with blood.

"Let me see," Glenn said, unbuckling Liam's pants and pulling them down a few inches so that he could examine the wound.

"Oh, damn it hurts!" Liam moaned. "Sweet Jesus, I feel like my leg is on fire!"

"You took a bullet in the hip," Glenn said, tearing his shirt out of his own pants and then ripping off some bandaging. "The good part is that the ball passed through the hip but the bad part is that there's certain to be bone splinters needing to be removed."

"Can you do it?" Liam grunted.

"No," Glenn said. "We're going to have to get you to a surgeon."

Liam grabbed Glenn's forearm. "Nobody's taking off my leg, you hear me!"

"Easy. You'll keep the leg, unless the wound turns gangrenous."

Tears welled up in Liam's eyes. "I killed at least three of them bastard Indians! I swear I wish I'd have gut-shot 'em all for doin' this to me."

"It wasn't an Indian that shot you," Glenn said. "It was Calvin Miller. He went crazy and I guess figured it was his chance to get rid of you without anyone knowing. But I happened to be right behind him. When I saw him shoot you and then lift his gun to fire again, I knew that I had to kill him or you were a dead man."

"*You* shot Calvin?" Liam asked, amazement overriding pain.

"I did," Glenn said quietly. "I killed him before he could finish you."

Liam brushed his tears away and rolled his head to look up at Joshua. "Did you hear that, Mr. Hood?"

"I heard. Thanks, Gilchrist. Thanks for not running away and leaving us."

"What happened?" Glenn demanded. "What took Hiram and the others so long?"

"Good question." Joshua called the big man over. "Hiram, what in blazes happened to you boys?"

Hiram toed the earth with his moccasined feet. "We would have come quicker, but two of the Indians stayed back with the remuda and when they saw us comin', they ran the whole damned bunch of 'em smack into our charge. A couple of our boys went down and were almost kilt. We had to pull up and help 'em, then sort things out a little before we could come along."

"You were almost too damn late," Joshua said without heat as he knelt beside Liam and rolled his waistband down a few inches to study the nasty wound.

"Mr. Hood? I'll still be able to ride and scout for you, won't I?"

"For simple certain," Joshua said without a moment's hesitation. "Right now, we're going to bury the dead, then rig a travois for you and the others too shot up to ride. Best thing we can do is to find a surgeon and get this hip of yours taken care of pronto."

"Yes, sir," Liam breathed.

Joshua came to his feet. "You did real good, Liam. You winged that Injun chief like I said but then someone killed him deader than a stone."

"You wanted him pretty bad, huh?"

"Yeah," Joshua admitted, "I did. But I guess we got a pair to take back to Grand Island or wherever the hell we can find General Dodge."

"That's good," Liam whispered, his face the color of marble stone. "Maybe we can swap 'em for some peace."

Joshua looked up at the dead and the dying—both Sioux and white. "I'm afraid that things have gone too damn far now for that. That's why you're going to need to get well and keep shootin' straight."

"Yes, sir."

Glenn stepped aside and would have walked away but Joshua's hand fell on his shoulder and as he passed, the Union Pacific's chief scout said, "You did your brothers proud, Glenn. Real damned proud."

"Thanks," Glenn said quietly as he went to examine Sundancer's arrow wound.

CHAPTER
27

Megan O'Connell was losing money every night at her gambling tables but her saloon was doing a landslide business. Twice more Dan had supplied her with beer and whiskey as the Union Pacific surged westward. Jack Casement's track-laying machine was well oiled now and the rust eaters were routinely slamming down better than a mile of track a day. Megan barely had time to set up shop in Wood River when the tracks swept past them. Everyone was saying that the next hell-on-wheels town would be Kearney, on the north side of the Platte River and almost within shooting distance of Fort Kearney.

"At least if our next rail camp is attacked," Rachel said, "the Army can actually *see* the Indians! Maybe then they'll start protecting the work crews."

"Don't bet on it," Megan said, counting her previous night's profits in the saloon while at the same time fretting over her more than offsetting gambling hall losses. "Rachel?"

"Yes?"

"Why can't we stop losing money?"

"You said you wanted an honest game."

"But not a *losing* one," Megan said. "Do you think that Mr. Scudder is a competent gambler . . . or what?"

"I don't know. How much money are you losing a night?"

"Quite a lot," Megan admitted. "Maybe fifty or sixty dollars."

Rachel sighed. "And you're making up that loss with the saloon's profits?"

"Not anymore."

"Have you talked to Mr. Scudder again?"

"Not since we've been in Wood River. But I'm going to have

to say something to him this afternoon."

"I'd be firm if I were you. That's a lot of money to lose each week."

"I know."

Megan did approach Scudder that afternoon during a lull in business. Lewis Scudder was relaxing outside Megan's big tent, smoking a cigar and reading an Omaha newspaper newly arrived on the morning train.

"Mr. Scudder?"

He looked up and smiled, lowering his paper. "Yes, Miss O'Connell?"

Megan had pulled another chair out and now she planted it in front of the gambler and sat down. "I wanted to talk to you again about our losses."

Scudder looked pained. "Before you say a word, I want you to know that I'm also upset over the three new gamblers we've hired. I'm going to tell them to win—or else."

"Isn't it true that the house has the odds in its favor?"

"Not always."

Megan's eyebrows raised in question. Scudder hurled his cigar into the street. "In faro, for instance, much depends on the luck of the draw. Same can be said about poker. And since we aren't marking or shaving the cards or tinkering with the roulette wheels . . . well, Miss O'Connell, that's why it's called a game of chance."

"I can't believe that you and our so-called gamblers can't at least break even against these rough Irish workmen."

"Most all of those 'rough Irish workmen' as you call them have been playing cards since they were toddlers. They might be unwashed and uneducated, but they aren't stupid and some of them are professional-level gamblers."

"If that's the case, then why do they choose to lay track? Why wouldn't they all take up the gambling profession for the quick, easy money?"

"Because gamblers have to have nerves of steel and fingertips as soft as silk. They have to be sober and closemouthed. They can't brag or bluster. They get challenged and sometimes shot to death when they win and those that start out honest usually wind up crooked or broke. The thing of it is, miss, if your opponent is double dealing or marking cards, you'd better find your own edge or you're out of business."

"Well, unless we do better," Megan said firmly, "I'm out of the gambling business and you're out of a job. I just can't afford to keep losing money."

"I swear we'll turn it around. And look at it this way," Scudder explained. "Gambling keeps the men drinking your beer and whiskey. Without gambling, a saloon business will die. That's a well-known fact."

"I agree. But instead of making a very good living out here, I'm steadily going broke after paying salaries and other expenses."

"It'll get better," Scudder promised. "Starting real soon. Don't worry, we'll turn it around."

"Thanks," Megan said, going back into her tent.

"What did he say?" Rachel whispered.

"He said they'd turn it around."

"Soon, I hope."

"So do I," Megan answered.

But during the next week right up until they were about to leave Wood River for the next rail town of Kearney, Lewis Scudder and the other three gamblers under Megan's tent *didn't* turn things around on the gambling tables. There were two nights when they almost broke even, but on the night after payday, they lost almost two hundred dollars, far more than Megan could offset with her saloon profits.

"Tomorrow we pull stakes for Kearney," Scudder announced. "Before we open up there, I'll have some better men on the gambling tables and we'll start showing a nightly profit."

"I hope so," Megan said, "because I can't take but a few more weeks of these losses. I haven't even got enough money to send for our next shipment of liquor."

"Who are you buying it from?"

"I have a good friend in Omaha," Megan said, keeping the secret that only Rachel, Glenn, and Walt shared at this end of the track.

That evening, Megan asked Walt Guthrie to sit in on a few of the games.

"I'm just an average gambler," he protested. "I wouldn't know a shaved card from a shaved head."

"Please," Megan said, desperate. "Rachel and I are going six ways to sundown working behind the bar. We can't sit in even if it were acceptable."

"All right," Walt said. "But I warn you that I'll probably lose your money."

"Just try and figure out what is going wrong," Megan pleaded, giving the man twenty dollars. "I've *got* to find out."

"My guess is that Scudder is a lousy gambler. That's why Ike Norman fired him."

"That's not the story I heard from Mr. Gilchrist."

Walt just shrugged. "Let me poke around this evening. I'll stay sober and keep a clear eye on your gamblers, Megan."

"Thank you!" Megan gave her old friend a hug of gratitude. "I don't know what I'd do without you, Walt."

In reply, he grinned and held up her money. "Who knows," he said, "maybe tonight I'll even get lucky enough to win."

"Go ahead," she told him, with more than a hint of irony in her voice, "everyone else who comes into Megan's Place to gamble wins. Why shouldn't you?"

That evening they were so busy pouring and serving drinks that Megan barely had time to observe her old friend across the crowded expanse of her tent. Megan saw Walt play poker against Scudder for nearly an hour and then drift to the other tables and play with each of her hired gamblers. And despite Walt's protestations that he was a poor gambler, Megan was confident that her dear old friend would give her some answers in the morning over their ritual of coffee. If not, Megan knew that she was going to have to close her gambling hall although she entirely agreed with Scudder about how men liked to drink and gamble. Ike Norman knew that too and there was no doubt that he would exploit Megan's loss of gambling to drive her into financial ruin.

The next morning Megan arose early and there was hot coffee steaming for Walt Guthrie. But Walt didn't show up as promised and by noon Megan was concerned.

Megan's worst fears were realized when a Union Pacific official entered her tent, caught her eye, and came over to say, "Less than an hour ago, Walt Guthrie was found shot to death."

Megan's legs buckled and she would have fallen if the official had not grabbed and helped her to a chair. Hot, salty tears spilled down her cheeks. She looked up and blurted, "Didn't anyone see anything, or even hear gunfire?"

"We were moving the work train up and down the track last night. They found Walt's body stuffed under a tarp."

Megan covered her face and squeezed the tears from her eyes.
"Was he robbed?"

"Yes. His pants pockets were pulled inside out and emptied."

"Who could have done such a thing!"

The official sighed. "Miss O'Connell, I'm not proud to say this, but there are men on our crew who would slit your throat for a glass of green beer. I'm told that Mr. Guthrie won some money here last night."

"I don't know," Megan said. "But he was gambling."

The official was in his forties, tired-looking with satchels of sagging flesh under his eyes. "I knew Walt. Liked him a lot. My name is Jeff Dugan and I'm the one who contracts for independent wagon drivers."

He stuck out his hand but when Megan ignored it, he continued, "Walt was slow but dependable and I kept him busy. He was a man that I could always count on."

"He was a loyal friend."

"Did he have any children? Any family that ought to be notified?"

"No."

"We'll sell his horses and wagons, then use part of the proceeds to make sure that Walt gets a fine burial in Omaha. There's an orphanage across the river in Council Bluffs run by the sisters of—"

"That will be fine," Megan interrupted, sick at heart and wanting to be alone with her grief and her guilt.

"I'm real sorry about this," Dugan said. "Walt was rough on the outside, marshmallow soft on the inside. He'd do anything for a friend and I know we'll all miss him dearly."

The official said something else Megan didn't comprehend because she was thinking about how it was her fault Walt Guthrie was dead. If she hadn't asked him to gamble, he wouldn't have been murdered.

The rest of the afternoon Megan felt as if she were sleepwalking and when Rachel and Scudder heard the news, they were almost as upset. Megan wanted to close her place and wrap herself in sad memories of Walt Guthrie. But it was payday and very soon when the Union Pacific whistle blew and the work ended, her customers were going to flock into her tent howling for whiskey and beer. It didn't seem right that people should be celebrating only hours after Walt had been murdered, but that was the reality of this lawless construction line.

"Megan!"

She looked up and blinked with surprise to see Glenn and Joshua burst into her tent. Megan flew into their arms and hugged them both with all her might.

"I can't begin to tell you how much I need to see your smiling faces," Megan blurted, afraid that she was going to start crying. "Walt Guthrie was murdered last night after leaving here and I'm about to lose both my mind and this business."

"It's going to be all right," Glenn told her. "We heard about Walt. I'm afraid that we've got some more bad news for you."

Megan paled. "Liam?"

"Yes," Joshua said. "He was shot in the hip by one of my own men. But he's going to be fine. We just got back from the surgeon and he says your brother ought to heal as good as new."

"Not quite," Glenn corrected in a gentle voice. "Liam is always going to walk with a limp and there might be some lingering pain. It's too early to know if he'll be able to ride a horse again."

"Sure he will!" Joshua snapped. "The kid is as hard as rails."

Glenn ignored the scout. Joshua was just trying to spare Megan any more pain. "Liam must rest three or four months until the hip knits back together. Only then can the Union Pacific doctors tell how much permanent damage he's suffered."

"I'll take care of him," Megan promised. "And there's Rachel. She's in love with him."

"He's lucky to have two beautiful women to care for his needs," Joshua said. "But he's not going to be happy recuperating in the rail towns. Liam is already swearing he'll be fit to hunt and scout for me in a few weeks."

"Nonsense!" Megan protested. "If I have to, I'll chain him to a bed."

"The doctor will help you," Glenn said. "Now, what's this about your business failing?"

"It's the gambling part that is taking me down. I've been losing more at faro, poker, and roulette than I've been making at the bar."

"I don't understand that," Joshua said. "Who did you hire to run things?"

Megan looked to Glenn, who said, "Joshua, I never told you but I jumped into a fight between Ike Norman's thugs and an honest gambler who was tossed out of Ike's saloon. Lewis is a hell of a man and I thought he'd be perfect working Megan's tables."

"What's his last name?"

"Scudder."

Joshua's jaw dropped and then snapped shut like a bear trap. "I know that rattlesnake. And as we rode into town, out of the corner of my eye I caught a glimpse of him entering the Rails End Hotel with Ike Norman."

"You can't be serious!" Glenn exclaimed.

"The hell I ain't! I know Scudder. He gut-shot one of my boys last winter over a game of cards. He carries a derringer up one sleeve and aces up the other. You've both been suckered."

"But the fight! It was three against one and—"

"Hell," Joshua scoffed. "It was a *setup!* Glenn, they knew you were coming, and if you'd have walked on without interfering, they'd have ducked back into Ike's place for a drink and come up with another hoax. You and Megan are both far too trusting."

"Damn!" Glenn swore.

"Let's go get him," Joshua said, spinning on his heel to leave.

"Wait a minute!" Glenn shouted.

"You wait," Joshua called back. "Scudder shot one of my friends and now he's robbed Megan damn near into the poor house. It was Ike Norman's way of breaking her, don't you see that?"

"Yes, but *I'm* the one that introduced him to her."

Joshua stopped and looked back. "You want to kill him?"

"I . . ."

"Hell no you don't! So I'll do it myself," Joshua said, turning to stride away.

"Glenn, help him!" Megan cried as the scout marched up the street.

By the time that he caught up with Joshua, the chief scout and hunter was almost to the Rails End Hotel. Glenn knew this was a time for reason or they both might end up in pine boxes. "You can't just go in shooting."

"I won't."

As they barged into the clapboard hotel, Glenn swore. "I've

heard that Scudder is awfully good with a gun."

"Like I told you before, he keeps a spring-loaded derringer up his sleeve and mighty sudden. That's how the sonofabitch got my friend."

"Well, can't we at least *talk* about this!"

"Talking time is over," Joshua said, marching across the lobby, knocking boarders out of his path. The desk clerk looked up, read Joshua's eyes, and growled, "You'd better go back wherever you came from, mister. We don't want any trouble here."

"Don't matter what you want," Joshua said, advancing on the clerk. "Where's Ike Norman and Lewis Scudder?"

"How the hell should I know?"

Joshua took a handful of the desk clerk's shirtfront. He hauled out his six-gun and poked it into one of the clerk's nostrils. "I'll ask just once more while you've got a nose and a skull to attach the damned thing to. Where are they?"

The clerk's eyes crossed to the gun barrel and when Joshua cocked back his hammer, the man screamed, "In room four just up the hall!"

Joshua shoved the clerk away and when they found the room, it didn't even have a lock. Joshua threw open the door and there they were—Scudder and Norman—tighter than ticks on a hound as they huddled over whiskey, cigars, and a pile of Megan's money.

"Get up, Scudder!" Joshua ordered, holstering his Army Colt. "Stand up and go for your gun."

Scudder's eyes flicked sideways to Ike Norman who said, "Now wait just a damn minute here! What's going on?"

"It's obvious enough, ain't it! Your man has been stealing from Megan O'Connell while he's working for you on the sly! That is Miss O'Connell's money."

"Prove it!"

"I don't have to," Joshua said. "It's easier just to kill you both."

Norman raised his hands and managed to smile. "I'm unarmed."

"So am I," Scudder echoed.

"The hell you are. Stand up and draw, both of you!"

But the pair didn't move and Glenn said, "Joshua, you can't just gun them down."

"Watch me!"

"But—"

A two-shot derringer appeared from Scudder's sleeve as if by magic. He fired, missed, and tried to fire again but Joshua's six-gun bucked smoke and lead. The shots were so closely spaced they sounded to Glenn like thunder rolling through a deep canyon. Scudder slapped at his fancy vest and red roses appeared. He stared at his shirt, eyes widening with amazement. Then he looked up at Joshua and his lips moved but there was no sound and he keeled over, dead before he struck the floor.

"Now you," Joshua said, turning his smoking gun on Norman.

The man's grin soured and his complexion turned fish-belly white. He jerked his hands even higher. "You kill me, you'll hang!"

He looked to Glenn. "He *will* hang, Mr. Gilchrist!"

"Don't," Glenn ordered the Union Pacific's chief scout. "It would be murder."

"It'd be a good deed! I'd be doing every man-jack on this line a big damned favor!"

"Please," Glenn said. "I don't want to have to testify that you gunned down a helpless man in cold blood. I don't want to see you hang . . . and neither would Megan."

The gun began to tremble in Joshua's fist as the scout waged war with himself. At last, his gun barrel inched downward and Joshua went over and scooped up Megan's cash. "I'm payin' her back and, Ike, one damned fine day I'm paying you back too!"

And then Joshua whirled and charged out the door leaving Glenn and Ike Norman alone. Norman lowered his hands and ever so slowly, a smile reappeared on his face. "Do you also have something to say to me, Gilchrist?"

"Only that if Joshua Hood is ever ambushed in one of these hell-on-wheels towns, I'll shoot you on sight."

"Thanks for the warning," Ike said with an air of boredom before coming to his feet. He straightened his shirtfront, selected an expensive cigar, and nipped its tip off with his perfect white teeth. He spat the tip down on Scudder's riddled body and regarded Glenn with near contempt. "There *will* come a day— so enjoy those precious few you have left, Mr. Gilchrist."

Glenn blocked the door. There was something he had to ask. "Lewis Scudder really was working for you, wasn't he?"

Ike chuckled as he lit his cigar and regarded the dead gambler at his feet. "Sure. And in another two weeks, we'd have bled the handsome bitch dry."

Glenn's clenched fist streaked upward from the point of his right knee. It was a wicked uppercut carrying every ounce of Glenn's strength and it caught Ike Norman flush on the jaw. The saloon owner staggered. His eyes turned glassy as his knees started to buckle. Glenn delivered a left cross from out in the hallway and Ike dropped as if he were pole-axed.

Glenn rubbed his stinging knuckles and said, "*Now* I'll enjoy my days pushing Union Pacific rails west."

Glenn left Ike unconscious beside the dead gambler. He expected to find Joshua consoling Megan and that meant that there was no time to waste. Like Ike Norman and Lewis Scudder, Joshua Hood was just not a man to be trusted—at least not in respect to their lovely Miss Megan O'Connell.

AUTHOR'S NOTE

RAILS WEST begins this exciting series with an actual historical event. In the spring of 1866, the last Union Pacific supply train did cross the thawing ice of the Missouri River and almost plunge to a watery grave. Later that spring, breaking ice did sweep downriver and wipe out an entire Union Pacific levee claiming both lives and property.

Great care has been taken to insure historical accuracy in *Rails West!* The author owes particular thanks to Union Pacific's research consultant, Mr. George Cockle of Omaha, Nebraska. Another individual owed special recognition is Lonnie Beesley of Denver, Colorado, a lifelong railroad buff whose expertise on railroad mechanics and operations was invaluable. And finally, I wish to credit the wonderful national park staff at the Golden Spike National Historic Site located where the Union and Central Pacific rails joined on May 10, 1869, at Promontory Point, Utah. To observe the working replicas of the famous steam locomotives, "Jupiter" and "119," was an unforgettable experience and one available to everyone who visits this historic site and museum.

As the Union Pacific slammed down its own rails, the effort became a ballet of steel and muscle backed by grit and determination. It was the West's greatest race as characters very much like Glenn Gilchrist, Megan Gallagher, Joshua Hood, and Ike Norman fought to emerge victorious. In succeeding novels, *Rails West!* will capture the essence of their struggles as the Iron Horses thundered across the Great Plains, the searing deserts, and the lonely, lofty western mountain ranges.

SPECIAL PREVIEW!

If you enjoyed *RAILS WEST!*, here's
an exciting look at the second
book in the *RAILS WEST!* series,

NEBRASKA CROSSING

. . . continuing the stirring epic of the courageous
men and women who built the Union Pacific
Railroad across the plains—to make America
one nation from shore to shore.

*Turn the page for an excerpt from
this bold new series by Franklin Carter.
Available in October 1993 from Jove Books . . . .*

Indians! Real Indians. Wild Indians. Laddy Sullivan's eyes went wide, and he began to tremble. With excitement more than fear but, aye, there was fear there too. Never mind what was said about a truce having been arranged with the savages. These were the first true, fierce, wild and free Indians Laddy Sullivan—it was really Laechmon Shay Sullivan, but that was a case of the name being larger than the lad and who needed that— ever saw, and he was as fascinated now as a wee hen peering into a snake's narrow eyes. Danger or no, the fascination of it was hypnotic. And immobilizing. Laddy was frozen where he stood, unable to move or to pull his eyes away. Indians! Real ones. Sweet Jesus, Mary and Joseph!

It was difficult to see from so great a distance, but he did not believe the Indians were painted. Did they not paint themselves, then, as he'd been told? They were armed, though. They weren't so terrible far off that he couldn't see that. The Indians rode small, pot-bellied ponies, and they carried lances and bows held casually in their hands or laid light and balanced across their laps on the ponies' . . . the ponies' . . . it took him a moment to call the unfamiliar word to mind . . . the ponies' withers, that was it, withers. Laddy was but three months off the boat, and there was much he had yet to learn. The subject of wild Indians was but one of many in which his education proved lacking.

"D'you see 'em, Barney, do ye?" he whispered.

"I see 'em, boy," Barney said in a tight, grim voice. "I see the sons o' red bitches."

"Should we be runnin' now?" Laddy asked with a bit of a catch in his throat. For in truth there was no place they might run to for safety. Barney was stickman and Laddy his helper,

287

and the two of them were out a good three hundred yards ahead of the nearest other pair in the advance survey party. There were eighteen men in this crew and a thousand more behind them. But the remaining sixteen of this particular crew were too far off to count on for help. And the thousand and more others that made up the grading and support and construction gangs of the grand Union Pacific Rail Road? Why, they were a hundred miles or more back. Much help they would be if these wild Indians proved hostile. Laddy's throat was dry and scratchy, and there was a blockage that kept him from being able to swallow.

The Indians moved toward them in plain sight. A quarter mile away or more still. But too close. Much too close. They rode loose and easy atop their stocky ponies, weapons carried low, the bunch of them—there must have been a dozen warriors . . . no, fifteen; Laddy counted and there were definitely fifteen of them coming slow and steady across the dry, wildflower-studded grass—strung out in no particular formation that Laddy could detect.

"Whatever you do, kid, don't run. Don't set them off."

Barney's advice seemed silly in the extreme, but Laddy accepted it. He more or less had to. He was sure if he tried to run he would find himself unable to, was sure his muscles would refuse his commands whatever he might will himself to do, and it seemed preferable at the moment to stand and do nothing than to try to move and not be capable of doing it.

He could hear hoofbeats even though the Indians were still quite distant, and that surprised him. Then he realized the horse he could hear was behind him. And it was no Indian who rode it, for Laddy could hear the creak of leather and tink of chain that said it was an American horse with all the loud accoutrements that implied. Indians, he'd been told, rode their ponies with only a pad and perhaps a rawhide thong for equippage. In another few minutes he should be able to see for himself the truth of that claim. If he should live so long. Sweat beaded cold and greasy on his forehead, and there was a taste of bile at the back of his tongue.

"It looks like we'll have company for lunch." A voice came from the direction of the saddle sounds. Immediately Laddy felt better for he recognized the voice. It was Assistant Chief Surveyor Mr. Glenn Gilchrist who'd ridden out to join them here and to stand beside them to meet the wild Indians.

Mr. Gilchrist's presence released Laddy from the frozen thrall fear had imposed on him, and he was again able to move. And to breathe. He turned and gratefully looked up at this tall boss with a highborn gentleman's fine manners but with eyes that were kind and gentle. It was Mr. Gilchrist who'd given Laddy this job, ignoring the liabilities of youth and inexperience and trusting Laddy to give an honest day's work in exchange for an honest day's pay. Laddy was only seventeen and small for his age, his people on the wee side to start with and his particular growth not helped by the failure of the potato crop back home. No other had been willing to take on a lad who was so undeniably slight of stature and lacking of experience. But Mr. Gilchrist had. Mr. Gilchrist believed in him. Laddy felt a particular affinity, therefore, to Mr. Gilchrist. A particular sort of trust. He stood now with considerably less fear as Mr. Gilchrist reined his handsome yellow horse to a halt and watched the approach of the Indians.

"Is it a fight we'll be havin', Mr. Gilchrist, sir?" Laddy asked.

"Not at all," the fine gentleman assured him. "We are under a truce with the Sioux now, remember? They are welcome in our camp. We'll feed them and talk a little while, and then they'll go on about their hunting or whatever business it is they have here. We've nothing to fear from them nor they from us."

Laddy shivered. "It isn't them bein' scared of us that I'm thinkin' about, sir. Killin' is their business. That's what I was told. Killin' railroaders 'specially."

"We've lost men to Indian attacks in the past, Laddy, that's true enough. Entirely too many. That's why Mr. Hood and General Dodge met with the Sioux leaders. They parted friends. The Sioux will no longer make war on our people. And we in our turn will make them welcome in our camps." Mr. Gilchrist smiled. "The general feels it is much better to feed the Indians than to fight them. I agree. A few barrels of food are more easily replaced than the lives of good men."

"Are wild savages t' be trusted, Mr. Gilchrist, sir?"

"Mr. Hood says their word is good. I suppose he should know. He used to live with one of the tribes. It wasn't the Sioux he lived with, but he knows them. And he knows the sign language all the Plains tribes use. He says we can take these people at their word. Their fear is that they can't trust us. That is what we have to prove here today. Mind you make them welcome."

"Yes, sir. But you'll forgive me if I'm hopin' Mr. Hood knows what he's saying." Laddy knew who Mr. Hood was. That would be Mr. Joshua Hood, a leather- and buckskin-clad frontiersman who appeared as wild as any Indian and who was in charge of the railroad's scouts and meat hunters. All the lads on the line idolized Mr. Hood and his scouts as dashing, devil-may-care dandies. Dash in, aye, and twist the devil's tail. But when it came to solid, sensible judgment then even a lad like Laddy would know that it was Mr. Gilchrist's word to be sworn to and not that of the more volatile Mr. Hood. And it was Mr. Hood who said these wild Indians were to be trusted.

Laddy gave Mr. Gilchrist a close look and was reassured to see that the gentleman was leaving his fine, brass framed rifle in its leather keeper, nor was he paying any mind to the revolver that rested at his waist. Mr. Gilchrist was trusting implicitly the word of Mr. Hood. And that even though there was talk among some of the lads that Mr. Gilchrist and Mr. Hood were rivals for the affections of a certain lady.

Laddy'd seen that certain lady and had to concede that she would be spoil well worth the contest. She'd come to Laddy's attention because she was the sister of the strapping American Irishman who among Mr. Joshua Hood's scouts was Laddy's particular idol, Liam O'Connell, late of Boston and now of the great and open plains of vast Nebraska. Liam had been wounded in a fight with Indians—a battle undertaken before Mr. Hood's treaty mission in the company of Union Pacific Chief Engineer Grenville Dodge—and it was to his sister's care that he was taken. It was when Laddy came round to give Liam a word of comfort that he first saw Liam's sister Megan O'Connell. And no wonder a gentleman as fine as Mr. Gilchrist or a frontiersman as passionate as Mr. Hood would wish to court her. Megan was tall for a woman, with flaming red hair and a bold carriage about her. She had beauty, wit and courage. A man—or a boy—could see that quick enough. If things had been just the least bit different, why, Laddy himself might have. . . .Ah, but things were only as they were. There was no point to deluding himself about that, Laddy acknowledged now. Better to think about wild Indians than the charms of Megan O'Connell. Laddy was more apt to be accepted as a man grown by standing firm in the face of these Indians than by making a fool of himself chasing after Liam's big sister Megan.

"They look friendly enough," Barney said.

"Aye," Laddy agreed. "I'm seein' no paint. That's good, ain't it?"

"They're just coming in to have a free lunch," Mr. Gilchrist assured his crewmen, "like Mr. Hood and the general promised they could. Can you see those skin containers slung behind them?"

"Aye."

"They carry their fighting duds in there. Mr. Hood asked one to open his bag and show me. He had stoppered horn vials of paint and a hat made of skin and feathers and ermine tails, and he had a breastplate made of small bones and porcupine quills strung on sinew and some sort of talisman thing in a pouch that he handled with special care and wouldn't talk about. Mr. Hood said that could be something as simple as a twist of grass but whatever it was it was very special, very magical to the bearer, probably something suggested to him in a trance or a vision. Anyway, if those men were planning to attack us, their war bags would be empty now and they would be wearing their paint."

"That's good t' know. I be thanking you."

"You're welcome, Laddy."

The Indians were closer now. The leaders of the group were less than a hundred yards away, still riding forward at a slow and steady gait. Their bows, Laddy could see now, were unstrung. He found that particularly interesting because he hadn't known bows could be unstrung once they were made and did not understand why anyone would want to unstring them. He asked Mr. Gilchrist.

"The strings wear out rather quickly. They last longer . . . the bows do too . . . if they aren't under tension all the time."

"I should've figured that out, shouldn't I? I mean, it makes sense. I should've seen it."

Mr. Gilchrist smiled. "Then I should have seen it for myself too, but I didn't. Just like you, Laddy, I had to ask. That's how we all have to learn things. There's no shame in not knowing something, only in not bothering to learn."

Laddy grinned and was feeling quite comfortable now, in spite of everything, as he stood so close to Mr. Gilchrist while they waited for the Sioux warriors to reach them.

The Sioux were a sight. Lord, they were. They rode tall and proud, heads high and shoulders square, bending to no man. They were dark of body, dark of hair, dark of eye. Most of them wore little more than breech cloths, with perhaps a few ornaments woven into their braids or some necklaces and armbands or other such adornments on their bodies.

Laddy would have expected them all to be as lean as wolfhounds, but they were not. Several of the men were quite roly-poly, and many of the rest were fairly flabby, their bellies bouncing with the movement of the ponies.

They were close enough now that Laddy could begin to observe them fairly well, one of them picking his nose while another chattered—nervously? It almost looked like it; could wild Indians be nervous about meeting white men? How odd to think that—and a third raised himself off his pony's back so he could scratch himself before settling back onto the grass-filled cloth pad that he was using for a saddle.

Now that they were coming closer, these wild Sioux warriors seemed . . . human. Less threatening, certainly, than Laddy would have believed possible.

Laddy turned his head to see if the others in the survey party were preparing for the arrival of their guests.

The road they were staking for the graders to prepare and the tie layers to build was out on the open grass. To the south less than half a mile was the barely visible dark foliage that marked the brushy, sporadically tree-lined course of the Platte River. Where the stakes were now being placed the road would curve slightly to avoid a line of low ridges and turkey-foot coulees that broke up the flat prairie toward the north. The land here was not nearly so flat and table smooth as it appeared to be, and no one knew that better than the surveyors whose job it was to maintain a nearly constant grade as the railroad right of way slowly, inexorably climbed ever higher as it moved westward.

Laddy gave the terrain a brief glance and then looked overhead to the bright, buttermilk sky. A hawk wheeled and soared far above the earth and closer, to the north, a pair of squawking thrushes burst into the air.

He looked back at the Sioux. The leader of the band was not more than sixty yards distant now. For some reason he had drawn rein and was peering with some alarm to his left, into the coulee where the thrushes rose a moment earlier. The warrior stiffened and wheeled, his jaw falling open and his head tipping back.

"What . . . ?"

Laddy never had time to finish his question.

There was a crash of noise from the mouth of the coulee, not thunder, more like a long rattle of dry sticks breaking.

Pale wisps lifted into the air, soft and white like tendrils of morning mist drifting over the River Shannon. But it couldn't be mist. This was mid-day and the country terribly dry.

There was the crackle of sudden sound and then the leader of the Sioux swayed back, righted himself for an instant and then toppled face forward to earth. The Indian hit the ground head first and made no move to catch himself or lessen the impact of his fall. Laddy took a step forward, thinking to see if the Indian was all right.

"What the . . . !"

"Get down, Mr. Gilchrist, take cover," Barney, an army veteran with a dozen fierce battles behind him, bellowed in quick reaction.

"But what . . . ?"

Another volley of fire burst from the mouth of the coulee, and four more Sioux were dropped from their ponies.

Before the survivors had time to gather their wits, a solid phalanx of blue-clad troopers on blood bay horses burst into view, and a bugle's brittle call danced on the dust-filled air.

Laddy stared in horror as the soldiers charged through the stunned Sioux, revolvers barking, gunsmoke swirling, sharp cries punctuating the ugly speech of the guns.

He saw one Indian shake his head and turn to face an oncoming soldier. The Indian's mouth worked as he said something Laddy was much too far away to hear, and he lifted a medallion from where it was suspended against his bare chest, turning it so the soldier could see. Or perhaps in the belief that the thing, whatever it was, would shield him from harm. Laddy would never know the Indian's intent. The soldier leveled his revolver and shot the Indian in the chest, his bullet striking roughly the same spot where the medallion recently lay. The Indian fell, and his pony scampered wildly away.

Another Sioux spun to meet the charge of the soldiers' revolvers with a lance point. Bullets from at least three different guns thudded into his body, and he disappeared in the hoof-churned dust beneath the soldiers' horses.

The few remaining Indians broke and ran with no chance to offer resistance. The formation of soldiers scattered as well into myriad small chases and smaller combats.

Laddy saw two troopers ride close behind a fat Indian and take turns shooting into his back until the Sioux finally dropped.

A young warrior—could he even be considered a warrior? Laddy was not sure; the Indian looked no older than fourteen if that—clung tight to the side of his frightened, rearing pony while all the others either died or raced away for safety, leaving this one youth behind, unable for the moment to control his mount.

Most of the soldiers charged past him, and for a moment Laddy thought the boy might escape.

Then a handful of stragglers coming out of the coulee saw him and spurred their horses at him.

The boy was cut off from his own kind, and there was nothing in any direction to offer hope. Except perhaps in one. He sawed at his pony's mouth and slammed his fist between the animal's ears to force its feet back to earth, then whirled toward Laddy and Barney and Mr. Gilchrist and the rest of the survey crew. This was where safety had been promised, and this was where he ran.

Shouting soldiers, steel and brass gleaming in the sunlight, raced after the copper-skinned boy.

They rode close behind the youngster, revolvers cocked and leveled.

"No, damn it, don't," Mr. Gilchrist shouted.

"Jesus, Mary an' Joseph," Laddy mumbled, intending it to be a prayer.

The boy was close enough now that Laddy could see the terror in his eyes. And the hope as he hauled back on his rein to slide his pony to a halt only a few paces in front of Laddy.

"Quick," Laddy shouted. "Over here."

Two of the soldiers reined away at the last instant. A third stopped, so close his horse's shoulder collided with the flank of the Indian boy's pony, jostling the boy and nearly unseating him.

"Here," Laddy repeated. "Quickly."

The Sioux boy's mouth opened.

The soldier behind him extended his fist, a cocked revolver in it, and gestured with the muzzle of the gun as if to prod the Sioux in the back of the head. But instead of poking him with the gun the trooper fired. A sheet of flame spread round the boy's head in a curious, halo-like effect, and the front of his face twisted and took on a new and ugly shape as a crimson spray briefly filled the air between him and Laddy.

The boy was flung down, rag limp and lifeless, virtually at Laddy's feet, and the whooping, grinning soldier spun away to search for other prey.

Laddy was stunned. And sickened. Wisps of smoke rose from the back of the dead boy's head and the stink of singed and burning hair filled Laddy's nostrils.

It was too much. Simply too much. His vision blurred and darkened. He was on his knees, throwing up into the grass. He dimly knew that. Could taste the acid and feel the sharpness of it on his teeth. He could hear Mr. Gilchrist's voice reaching him through the mists of his tenuous hold on consciousness but could not understand what Mr. Gilchrist was trying to say to him.

Then the mists closed in and claimed him, and he could neither hear nor feel any more.

It was . . . simply . . . too, too much.

J.R. ROBERTS

THE
GUNSMITH